pages of a mystery."
—*Library Journal* (Starred Review)

Praise for the Jade del Cameron Mysteries

Treasure of the Golden Cheetah

"Cinematic in its descriptions of Africa, compelling in plot—this is a true whodunit—and skilled in characterization, *Treasure of the Golden Cheetah* is the best so far of an outstanding series. And Arruda's cliff-hanging ending will have readers yearning for the quick appearance of Jade's next adventure." —*Richmond Times-Dispatch*

"Jade, a fearless, well-developed main character who is at home with a gun, is the main attraction here, though the vivid detals of 1920s Africa add to the appeal." —*Booklist*

"Suzanne Arruda brings the flavor and flair of the golden era of silent movies and colonial Africa into each scene and chapter. This book is certainly a page-turner. It would be handy knowing some of the back story of this enchanting series, but *Treasure of the Golden Cheetah* also stands alone as one heck of an exciting tale." —*The Wichita Falls Times Record News*

"What an adventure! Jade is one strong, savvy woman, and her cheetah sidekick, Biscuit, makes a striking companion. If you like excitement, romance, and exotic locales, this book will spirit you away."
—Sandi Ault, Mary Higgins Clark Award–winning author of the Wild series

The Leopard's Prey

"Great characters, careful plotting, and an unusually beautiful depiction of Africa." —*Library Journal*

continued . . .

Turn to the back for an excerpt from Suzanne Arruda's new Jade del Cameron hardcover, *The Crocodile's Last Embrace.*

"A lively mystery adventure with a strong sense of both its historical period and its exotic locale." —*Kirkus Reviews*

"Melds [Isak] Dinesen's evocation of a bygone Africa with [Agatha] Christie's ability to fashion a sharp whodunit. . . . Arruda writes with flair, creates an intriguing puzzle, and plays fair with clues. But the main attraction of this series is Jade herself—sometimes reckless, never feckless. And yes, there's a dangerous leopard in the mix, but neither a killer cat nor a human killer can prevent the plucky Jade from saving her man and providing absorbing entertainment." —*Richmond Times-Dispatch*

Stalking Ivory

"Suzanne Arruda is fast creating her own unique and popular niche in mystery fiction. With deep research and rich imagination, she gives us Africa, in the 1920s, and a bold new heroine in Jade del Cameron. This is a series that deserves a long life." —Nancy Pickard, author of *Confession*

"The resilient Jade will charm readers as she asserts her independence in rugged Africa." —*Publishers Weekly*

"British East Africa is the seductive setting of this sequel to the author's exuberant debut, *Mark of the Lion*. . . . Like its predecessor, this book is deliberately over the top, and great fun to read." —*The Denver Post*

"Another top-notch mystery. . . . Fans of Ernest Hemingway and Agatha Christie alike will find this second tale of Jade's exploits a ripping good yarn."
—*Richmond Times-Dispatch*

Mark of the Lion

"Jade del Cameron . . . brings new meaning to the word gutsy. Vividly portraying the long-ago age of shooting safaris and British stiff-upper-lip attitudes, this novel is filled with appealing characters." —*The Dallas Morning News*

"From the extraordinary opening sentence in the shell-torn trenches of France in the Great War to the green hills of British colonial East Africa, *Mark of the Lion* sweeps the reader along with an irresistible narrative and literary drive. If you're looking for a fresh new mystery series, a vivid historical setting, and an especially appealing heroine, look no further. One of the most memorable mystery adventure stories I've read in a long time."

—*New York Times* bestselling author Douglas Preston

"This debut novel delivers on its unabashedly romantic premise and for good measure throws in a genuine mystery. . . . It's storytelling in the grand manner, old-fashioned entertainment with a larger-than-life heroine far ahead of her time."

—*The Denver Post*

"*Mark of the Lion* is historical mystery at its best with a dynamic amateur sleuth and well-drawn supporting cast of quirky characters. First-time author Suzanne Arruda hits the reader with a gripping opening and builds tension, twists, and turns from there . . . a compelling premiere performance. . . . I hope Arruda's working on her second book!"

—*New York Times* bestselling author Karen Harper

"There's something for everyone in this new series debut—mystery, history, adventure, travel, even a bit of romance." —*Library Journal* (Starred Review)

"Arruda manufactures an intriguing backdrop for the debut of her new series, delivering both a heady sense of East Africa's cultural and geographical landscape during the early 1900s and an outspoken heroine, who proves herself gratifyingly ahead of her times in numerous ways." —*Booklist*

"Arruda's debut is an enjoyable romp through a colorful place and period in which the heroine has a Douglas-Fairbanks-in-a-split-skirt charm."

—*Kirkus Reviews*

"An exciting, well-paced debut. . . . Arruda's [Africa] feels more like a travel writer's—awesome beauty that is unknowable and untouchable. But it's a place worth visiting. And Jade is a character worth getting to know."

—*The Philadelphia Inquirer*

Other Books in the
Jade del Cameron Series

Mark of the Lion

Stalking Ivory

The Serpent's Daughter

The Leopard's Prey

TREASURE OF THE GOLDEN CHEETAH

A JADE DEL CAMERON MYSTERY

SUZANNE ARRUDA

AN OBSIDIAN MYSTERY

OBSIDIAN
Published by New American Library, a division of
Penguin Group (USA) Inc., 375 Hudson Street,
New York, New York 10014, USA
Penguin Group (Canada), 90 Eglinton Avenue East, Suite 700, Toronto,
Ontario M4P 2Y3, Canada (a division of Pearson Penguin Canada Inc.)
Penguin Books Ltd., 80 Strand, London WC2R 0RL, England
Penguin Ireland, 25 St. Stephen's Green, Dublin 2,
Ireland (a division of Penguin Books Ltd.)
Penguin Group (Australia), 250 Camberwell Road, Camberwell, Victoria 3124,
Australia (a division of Pearson Australia Group Pty. Ltd.)
Penguin Books India Pvt. Ltd., 11 Community Centre, Panchsheel Park,
New Delhi - 110 017, India
Penguin Group (NZ), 67 Apollo Drive, Rosedale, North Shore 0632,
New Zealand (a division of Pearson New Zealand Ltd.)
Penguin Books (South Africa) (Pty.) Ltd., 24 Sturdee Avenue,
Rosebank, Johannesburg 2196, South Africa
Penguin Books Ltd., Registered Offices:
80 Strand, London WC2R 0RL, England

Published by Obsidian, an imprint of New American Library, a division of Penguin Group (USA) Inc. Previously published in an Obsidian hardcover edition.

First Obsidian Trade Paperback Printing, June 2010
10 9 8 7 6 5 4 3 2 1

New American Library Trade Paperback ISBN: 978-0-451-22943-4

The Library of Congress has catalogued the hardcover edition of this title as follows:

Arruda, Suzanne Middendorf, 1954–
Treasure of the golden cheetah: a Jade del Cameron mystery/Suzanne Arruda.
p. cm.
ISBN 978-0-451-22789-8
1. Del Cameron, Jade (Fictitious character)—Fiction. 2. Americans—Kenya—Fiction. I. Title.
PS3601.R74T74 2009
813'6—dc22 2009015675

Set in Busorama Display
Designed by Elke Sigal

Printed in the United States of America

This book is dedicated to my new daughter, Emily.

Welcome to our family.

ACKNOWLEDGMENTS

MY THANKS TO the Pittsburg State University Axe Library Interlibrary Loan staff for their tireless efforts to help me run down the railroad manuals, especially the 1919 *Handbook of Railways in Africa Vol. I*; The National Wild Turkey Federation's Women in the Outdoors for their fun, adventure-oriented programs; Dr. John Daley, history department chair, Pittsburg State University, and Jim Williamson, roving editor of *Gun Week*, for assistance with rifles and blanks; Dr. David Middendorf for some ideas on delaying trains; Mr. Pat Cedeno, vice president of Growth Initiatives for WATCO Companies, and to the WATCO Locomotive Group, for advice on sun kinks in the rail lines; Mr. David Mars of Vintage Air Tours and his 1929 Curtiss-Wright Travel Air for the open-cockpit experience; author Terry (Tessa) McDermid for her help as my writing buddy; my publicist, Megan Swartz, for all her hard work; my agent, Susan Gleason, and my editor, Ellen Edwards, for their continued belief in and efforts on behalf of the series; all my family—"The Dad," James, Michael, Dave, Nancy, Cynthia, and Emily—for helping me shamelessly promote the books. I especially wish to thank Joe, the greatest husband and Webmaster a writer could ever want, for all his help and support; and Wooly Bear for continuing to keep her hairballs off the keyboard.

Any mistakes are my own, despite the best efforts of my excellent instructors.

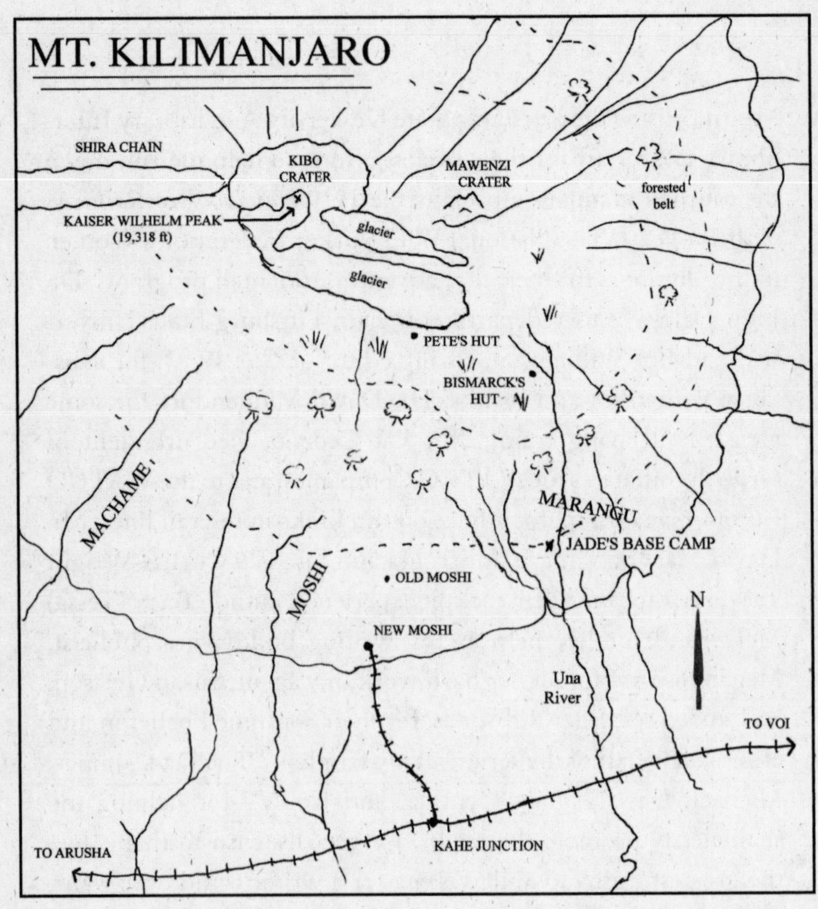
MT. KILIMANJARO
SHIRA CHAIN
KIBO CRATER
KAISER WILHELM PEAK (19,318 ft)
MAWENZI CRATER
glacier
glacier
forested belt
PETE'S HUT
BISMARCK'S HUT
MACHAME
MARANGU
JADE'S BASE CAMP
MOSHI
OLD MOSHI
NEW MOSHI
N
Una River
TO VOI
TO ARUSHA
KAHE JUNCTION

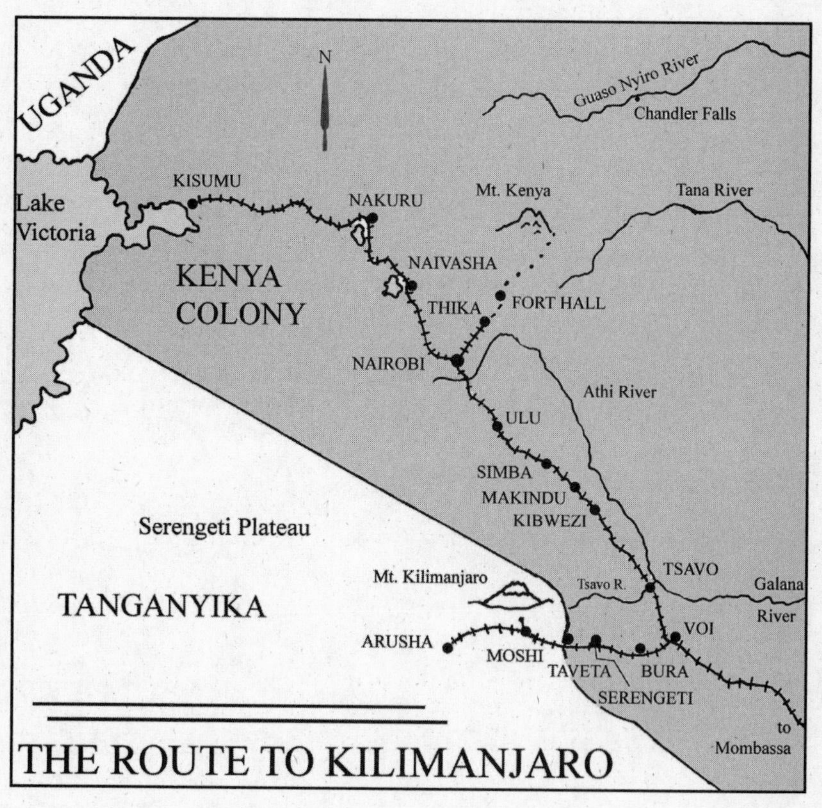
UGANDA
N
Guaso Nyiro River
Chandler Falls
KISUMU
Lake
Victoria
NAKURU
Mt. Kenya
Tana River
NAIVASHA
KENYA
COLONY
THIKA
FORT HALL
NAIROBI
Athi River
ULU
SIMBA
MAKINDU
KIBWEZI
Serengeti Plateau
Mt. Kilimanjaro
TSAVO
Tsavo R.
Galana
River
TANGANYIKA
ARUSHA
MOSHI
VOI
TAVETA
BURA
SERENGETI
to
Mombassa
THE ROUTE TO KILIMANJARO

TREASURE OF THE GOLDEN CHEETAH

CHAPTER 1

KENYA COLONY, *Mid-September 1920*

The frontiers of Africa have been pushed back. What was once inaccessible has become commonplace. The newest site falling prey to such familiarity is the seat of God, Kilimanjaro.

—The Traveler

THE WOMAN ASTRIDE THE POPPY RED INDIAN POWER PLUS MOTORcycle would have been considered beautiful in many cultures. Her appeal went beyond her lithe, well-muscled figure, her short hair rippling in black waves around an olive complexion, or her eyes the color of brilliant moss.

No, her real beauty lay in her strength of character, in her easy grace and confidence, and it echoed in her soft contralto laugh. To Sam Featherstone, Jade del Cameron was simply the most gorgeous creature on earth, and that included the powerful male cheetah that stood beside her. Even from six hundred feet up in the air he could spot her beauty, though most of it was presently hidden under the broad brim of a battered, brown felt hat.

Sam leaned a little farther out of the front cockpit and signaled Jade by pointing north. His friend and fellow pilot, Lord Avery Dunbury, sat behind him at the controls so that Sam could man the movie camera. Communication between cockpits wasn't practical because of the noise from wind and the biplane's OX-5 engine singing its purring hymn to the sky. Sam glanced over his shoulder at Avery and nodded. Avery gave him a thumbs-up, and they climbed to eight hundred feet, banking north.

The Curtiss JN-4, or "Jenny," responded smoothly, testimony to the loving care Sam gave it, or perhaps to the brightly painted symbols on its wings and the beads on the spars and wires, gifts of the Maasai who'd once guarded it. Sam spied the herd first, a mixture of eland, greater kudu, and Thomson's gazelles. He readied his camera and signaled with a swirling hand gesture to Avery.

They circled around the animals, keeping enough distance from them to avoid spooking the herd. At least not yet. Sam cranked film as Avery banked the Jenny, giving Sam a clearer view of the terrain and the animals. When they'd approached the herd's rear, putting the herd between themselves and Jade, Sam turned towards Avery and stabbed his index finger down. He saw Avery's broad grin as he shoved the stick forward and dove to three hundred feet, making a beeline for the animals.

The effect was instantaneous. The terrified beasts wheeled as one and raced away into the dry grassland. Their hooves pounded the parched earth, churning up rusty-red dust. Avery veered a few degrees east and herded the animals from the rear quarter like an aerial sheepdog. As the herd neared the cheetah, Sam trained his camera on the cat. Jade had already moved discreetly out of view, but he knew she was close by, watching. Sam only hoped he'd be able to capture everything on film. Of course, the bigger question was, would Biscuit cooperate?

He did. The sleek, spotted cat crouched for an instant and focused on one outlying animal, a Thomson's gazelle. Then, in a blur of gold and black, the cat bounded after the small antelope. His forelimbs reached out as his rear legs pushed back, extending his body to a long line. As first one, then the other forelimb touched earth and drove down, his hind feet pulled forward until they passed the front legs. With his deep barrel chest, Biscuit was the consummate athlete, drawing in oxygen to power his muscles, pushing himself past sixty miles per hour in his sprint.

The race ended in eight seconds. Biscuit overtook the little antelope and tripped it, sending it sprawling along the ground. In the next instant, he'd clamped his jaws over the animal's throat, suffocating it. Sam only hoped he'd cranked film fast enough to capture the action.

He whirled an index finger in the air in widening circles, signaling Avery to circle out. As they did, Sam's gaze sought Jade. He found her at the end of the third pass.

"What in the Sam Hill is she doing!"

Filming a hunt had been Sam's idea, but the hunt itself had been Jade's. Biscuit had captured small game before, grouse and a few rodents, but soon Jade would be going to Kilimanjaro, leaving Biscuit with Jelani in his Kikuyu village. For the most part, the boy would keep her pet supplied with the chickens she'd purchased, but it would help if the cat could hunt for himself.

There was another, more serious reason for this hunt. Biscuit had been hers for over a year, and he stayed with her by choice. Jade wanted to be certain it wasn't from necessity. If Biscuit desired freedom, Jade wanted him to have it. But that meant fending for himself. Hence, the practice hunt. She'd intended to drive game towards him using her motorcycle, but Sam had decided the hunt would make a great piece of film and offered the use of his Jenny.

Of course, with Sam grinding out film footage, someone else must fly. Jade would have jumped at the chance, but she had to stay with Biscuit in case something went amiss. Avery, on the other hand, didn't need to be asked twice. A former Royal Air Corps pilot, he couldn't wait to get aloft again. Avery, Sam, Jade, and Biscuit rendezvoused at a grassland near Jelani's village. Sam and Avery went aloft while Jade, on her motorcycle, led Biscuit to an open location.

The beautiful cat seemed to sense a game in the works. The white tuft at the end of his black-ringed tail twitched as his eyes surveyed the grasslands. Obediently, he stayed put when Jade withdrew. Then, when the herd raced by, he selected a likely prey and charged, running it to the ground while Jade shouted, "Go get 'em, Biscuit!"

She felt her pulse race and her face flush with more than excitement. It was pride, pure and simple. But as soon as Biscuit had his prey, Jade's sharp vision caught movement in the yellowed grass. A tawny tail, tipped in a black tuft, swished and jittered. Ahead of it, a pair of rounded triangular ears twitched fore and aft. Bits of thin golden mane stuck out at odd angles.

Lion!

The young male had been unsuccessful in his own bid for dinner, probably because he was a bachelor with no harem to support him. When he caught wind of Biscuit's kill, he roared his challenge, fully prepared to drive off the cheetah. And Biscuit was willing to retreat. He might not be completely savvy in the ways of the wild, but he knew he was no match for the four hundred pounds of hunger coming at him, and immediately backed off.

"Oh, no, you don't!" Jade grumbled as the lion strutted over to the Tommy's carcass.

She started her engine and revved out an answering roar before unslinging her Winchester and firing a round into the air.

"Get your own kill!"

The young male looked up from his half crouch, a huge forepaw resting on the Tommy's shoulder. He regarded her with amber eyes, then dismissed her as a noisy curiosity, certainly nothing worth troubling himself over. At least, not with a free meal at his feet. Still, her presence must have annoyed him, for he bent to pick up the antelope and drag it off elsewhere.

When he dipped his head and opened his mouth, Jade fired another round, the bullet striking the dirt a foot in front of him. His head snapped up, jaws empty. The velvety mouth wrinkled back in a snarl, exposing yellowed fangs. But while he didn't reach down for the meat again, he also didn't abandon the field.

That tears it! She revved her bike and gave it the gas, roaring off towards the wary lion.

"Hyah!" she shouted as she charged directly towards him. Jade had little tolerance for bullies, especially one intending to rob her cat of his hard-earned meal.

The lion jerked his head and shoulders back, clearly startled by this new development. Jade slowed and leaned to the side, scooping up a few rocks. Armed, she revved the engine again, letting it give voice to her own challenge. The lion stepped back two paces and snarled. Jade pulled up to within fifty feet and hurled her first missile. It hit the lion square on his nose. She threw another, striking his foreleg when he backed up another step.

Just as she was about to reload and charge again, a drone grew out of the air behind her. The Jenny buzzed both her and the lion, coming within twenty feet of the ground. This new attack was too much for the lion. He gave a parting snarl before turning tail and running.

Jade picked up the antelope carcass and plopped it across the rear seat and the panniers. "Come on, Biscuit," she called, and added a whistle. The cheetah joined her and together they headed back to the landing site and Neville's truck.

While she waited beside the truck, Jade pulled her knife and sliced a chunk of shoulder meat, then tossed it to Biscuit. "It's all yours. But we'd better wait until we get you home before you eat the rest. Our friend or one of his brothers might come back."

The Jenny's engine purred to the east. Jade looked up, shielding her eyes against the glaring African sunlight. As she watched, Avery brought the plane down in a smooth landing. They puttered to a stop, the plane's propellers still idling. Jade expected Avery to climb out and return to the truck while Sam took over using the front cockpit's controls to fly back to his hangar at the Thompsons' farm. But the figure striding towards her was taller by several inches and walked with a slight limp.

Sam!

Jade's pulse quickened. *Uh-oh!* Something about his stride told her that he wasn't planning on sweeping her into a big hug.

"Sam! Did you capture all of that? I even thought of a pissonet just now. Listen." She started reciting. "Biscuit had captured some meat, and just settled down to eat, when the cheetah was cheated, but the lion retreated, and—"

"What in the name of heaven were you doing?" Sam demanded. "Are you nuts? Charging a full-grown male lion?"

Jade opened her mouth to defend herself, to inform him that the lion was an inexperienced young male, that lions were often cowards to begin with, but Sam never gave her the chance.

"If we hadn't buzzed him, who knows what would have happened."

"He was about to run away," she said.

"He was probably about to knock you off your bike and add you to his menu." Sam threw his arms up and out, letting them drop with a smack against his breeches. "I've *never* met anyone so set on getting herself mauled to death."

Jade expected the argument to take its usual turn. He'd grab hold of her, say he loved her, and kiss her.

He didn't. He only pivoted and marched back to his plane.

One ray of sunlight pierced an opening in the mud-daubed walls and struck the toe of Jade's boot where she sat cross-legged on the dirt floor. She followed the beam's path upward through drifting dust motes. The light did little to assist her in seeing the hut's occupants. For that she had to depend on the pitiful, sputtering coals in a sunken fire pit. Much of the time, a hunched figure blocked even that weak light. The beam continued its slow sweep of the room, as though a Kikuyu spirit had an eye to the wall and intended to scan the proceedings. The gloomy interior did nothing to dispel Jade's black mood, created by Sam's anger.

After Biscuit had eaten his fill, Jade had ridden her motorcycle to the nearby Kikuyu village, the rest of the Tommy on the pannier and Biscuit loping beside her. Jelani, the youth she'd befriended on her first African trip, had met her with a message that his teacher, the tribe's healer, wanted to see her. The old *mondo-mogo* puttered around with a handful of bones, alternating between rattling them in his withered hand and tossing them onto the floor. The clacking of bones and the ancient healer's soft mutterings were the most prominent sounds, both unintelligible to anyone not versed in Kikuyu magic and lore. Jade understood a smattering of Kikuyu, but the old man spoke a language known only to the spirits in his head.

From above, Jade heard the delicate rustling of thatch as the hut's other resident shifted about in the roof. Whether it was a lizard, a rodent, or even a small snake, Jade took no chances of it falling through on her. She kept her broad-brimmed felt hat on and did her best to maintain a respectful patience. The latter wasn't easy after half an hour of ritual. She took a deep breath to settle herself and inhaled the hut's history with it. The dominant odor was human sweat, mingled with the scents of animal fat and earth, the last two smeared on the man's body to protect him from insects and the cold nights. Beyond that, Jade detected the more delicate scents of various herbs hanging to dry, coupled with goatskin leather. Missing was the stench of poultry and other livestock. Those animals were kept in the women's quarters.

The *mondo-mogo* ceased his private conversation and straightened. Immediately, a shadow shifted and a slender figure hurried from the darker recesses. Jelani, the healer's acolyte and student, squatted beside his master and awaited instructions. Jade prayed that it didn't involve smearing any more protective ointments on her clothes or giving her any more tattoos. As it was, she bore two already: a lion's tooth on her left wrist and a stylized lion's paw print on her forehead just below the hairline. The latter was a Berber clan tattoo; the former a gift given her by this same healer along with her Swahili name: Simba Jike, the lioness.

While she waited for Jelani to interpret his master's instructions, she studied the slender youth. Instead of the small boy she once knew, she saw a young man of thirteen wearing only an old pair of castoff khaki shorts. His shoulders had broadened and his facial features matured in the past few months. Jelani's perpetually serious expression added to his adult appearance. The laughing boy had disappeared and Jade mourned him in her heart. Jelani had put his ear close to the old man's lips. The healer's voice, weak and cracked, sounded more like a breath to Jade. The youth listened attentively before he addressed Jade.

"My master says he called you here because he dreamed of you," said Jelani. "He saw you near the place where God sits, far to the west."

Jade nodded. The old man must have learned of her upcoming safari to Kilimanjaro, said to be the throne of God by both the Maasai and the Chagga who lived on its lower slopes.

"My teacher grew worried because there are many graves on the mountain. Most do not concern you, but there are some that do. One is very, very old. It is a king's grave. Like you, he walked with a *duma* and let it hunt for him. But this one was different. It resembled a *chui* in its fur, a regal animal fit for a great king. My teacher sees two more graves that are not yet dug."

The old healer continued to touch the bones before him with a soft wand of monkey fur. He interrupted Jelani's tale with a few excited whispers. Jelani listened carefully and nodded. "My master has seen a third grave, but it is open." The youth sighed, and for a moment, his intent look softened with sorrow. "He says it is for you. Be careful you do not fall into it."

As he spoke, Jade felt a numbing cold brush her shoulders, as though death had caressed her while passing by to visit a more immediate appointment.

CHAPTER 2

Kilimanjaro is only one of God's thrones, another being Mount Kenya.

—The Traveler

"YOU SIMPLY MUST TRY THIS RUM PUNCH, JADE. I MUST SAY, YOUR American friends do know their drinks. Rather funny, don't you think, what with that Prohibition nonsense going on in our erstwhile colony?" Cissy Estes reeled and nearly toppled backwards into the tray of canapés. Jade reached for her left arm and steadied her.

"No, thank you, Mrs. Estes," Jade said. "And they're not my friends. I just met them yesterday. I'm seconding their safari to Kilimanjaro."

No doubt about it. It was definitely time to "get out of Dodge." Jade had enjoyed being a godparent along with Sam Featherstone to Beverly and Avery Dunbury's new baby, Alice Merrywether Dunbury. Jade even tolerated Madeline Thompson's noisy little celebration when her third book, *The Kahina's Hand*, was sold and her second, *Ivory Blood*, appeared in the local bookstore. But raucous Nairobi with its silly parties and even sillier concerns made Jade cringe every time she went into town to pick up the mail. When Bev's sister, Emily, sent a wire announcing that she was coming to help with the baby, Jade knew that retreat was in order. Unfortunately, the doorway to freedom led right through the pink-painted Muthaiga Club and another noisy party replete with frivolous gossip.

"I don't know what the colony is going to do without Mr. Clutterbuck," said one speaker. "He's positively a fixture here. Where's he going, anyway?"

"Brazil or Argentina or some such place," came the reply. "Of course, he wouldn't have left if his daughter were still single."

The first speaker giggled. "Well, then, he may have to stay yet. I don't think Beryl's satisfied with being Mrs. Purves. Poor Jock. From what I hear, she's already straying."

"Do you think Nairobi will adopt the daylight savings plan?" The voice came from Jade's left elbow. She turned and found herself face-to-forehead with a round, stumpy man with thinning brown hair and a very white scalp. The line across his brow, white above, russet below, marked where his hat usually sat.

"I have no idea, Mr. Eagan. To be honest, it's stupid. Nairobi's nearly on the equator. The days don't change any more than thirty minutes in a year. Why do you need to save daylight?" The moment she asked what was supposed to be a rhetorical question, Jade regretted it. The postmaster had every intention of explaining his views on the subject.

"I should think it obvious, miss. There is simply not enough time for the local lads to get to their clubs after work and get in any practice for the Saturday meets. Why, our gymkhana—"

"Excuse me, Mr. Eagan, but there's someone waving frantically at me." Jade slipped away and made a beeline for Beverly, who stood just inside the doorway leaning on her husband's arm. Despite her August delivery, Beverly looked as slender and lovely as ever in her newest gown, a soft butter-cream yellow crepe with mother-of-pearl bangles. Jade, still depressed after her argument with Sam, was glad for a friendly face.

"I began to think you weren't going to leave the baby after all," said Jade. "Was there a problem?" She knew they'd recently engaged not only a widow lady to act as nanny, but also a girl from the Seychelles as a maid. But neither had been with the Dunburys for very long.

"Not at all, Jade," said Avery. "Mrs. Armstrong and Shilangi have everything well in hand. It was Beverly's gown that caused all the delays." He chuckled softly as he eyed his wife.

Jade studied her friend's dress. As usual, Beverly wore the latest fashion. "It looks fine."

"*Now* it does," said Beverly. "Before, you could have put two loaves of bread in the bodice with me. I have no idea why the dressmaker thought I was built like a howitzer. I sent her my, er, dimensions." She put a hand to her chest just above the bosom as if to make certain that nothing was exposed.

Jade laughed, her low voice rippling. She touched her own apricot-colored dress, which Beverly had given to her just after the war. "If you didn't get a new dress every time the wind blew, you wouldn't have that problem, Bev."

Beverly opened her mouth to make a retort when their friend Madeline joined them. Beverly embraced her and exclaimed over the farm wife's new blue gown. "Maddy, you look divine! I didn't get to see you before you and Neville left our house."

"Thank you," said Madeline. "I know it's off the rack but it's the first new gown I've had in years. And thank you again for letting us leave little Cyril at your house for the evening," she added, referring to their recently adopted son.

"He's beautiful, Maddy," said Beverly. "You deserve each

other. And you deserve this dress, too. You're becoming quite the celebrity. Two books in print! Now if we could just get our Jade to put on something respectably modern . . . Don't you agree, Avery, darling?"

Avery slipped his wife's hand from his arm and kissed her fingertips. "You are *all* lovely, but I refuse to discuss what Jade should or should not do with her gowns. It's too dangerous. I believe there's a law barring decorated war veterans from any other hazardous combat. If not, I shall propose one." He bowed to the three women. "I shall visit with Neville instead, if you will excuse me."

"He's by the canapé table," said Madeline. She giggled and nudged Jade. "Simba Jike is still to be feared, it seems. By the by," she added, looking around, "where's Sam?"

Jade's voice dropped to a near whisper. "I don't think he's coming."

"What?" exclaimed Beverly and Madeline at once.

"Did you two have a row?" Bev asked.

Jade shrugged.

Beverly grabbed Jade's left hand and held it up. "You *still* aren't wearing his ring?"

Jade shook her head.

"But he proposed back in July," said Madeline.

"Are you going to tell us or must I beat it out of you?" demanded Beverly when Jade didn't comment.

"I really don't care to discuss this here in the blasted Muthaiga Club," said Jade. "But he hasn't abandoned me, if that's what you're thinking. We're just . . ."—she paused and considered the right word—"thinking."

Beverly snorted. "Thinking? My aunt Wilhemina's bustle! You don't *think* about a man's marriage proposal. You accept it or you don't. It's not a call for some ruddy parliamentary session or whatever you have in the States." She put her head down, as though instantly regretting her words. "I'm sorry, love. I didn't mean it. It's just that I had such hopes."

Madeline, never willing to voice her opinion as strongly as Beverly, settled for patting Jade's hand.

"Oh, stop it, you two." Jade jerked her hand away. "Anyway, Sam dislikes the Muthaiga as much as I do. The difference is, he doesn't *have* to be here and I do."

Beverly cocked her head and pursed her lips. "That's what the row was about, wasn't it? Your newest job."

"I don't understand," said Madeline. "You're merely helping as second in command on a safari. It's not even a hunting safari, so you should be perfectly safe. You're going to Kilimanjaro, aren't you?"

Jade nodded. The "row," as Beverly termed it, was less about her job and more about what Sam called her recklessness, but she didn't care to discuss it with anyone, including Beverly, who would only take Sam's side.

"I'll talk to him, if you like, and tell him that he has no reason to be worried," said Beverly.

"Don't," said Jade.

"But Bror Blixen has led many safaris," continued Bev. "He's one of the best. To be honest, I was surprised that he was hiring *anyone* to be a second to him. I presumed you were to be a sort of chaperone."

Jade looked away and pursed her lips. "You're partly correct." Jade took a deep breath. "I *was* hired to take care of the women and their supplies."

"But . . . ?" prompted Beverly, her slippered foot tapping with impatience.

"But Blixen's not in charge. Harry Hascombe is."

Madeline gasped, and Beverly muttered, "Blast."

"I suppose you could still back out of the job," suggested Madeline.

"No," said Jade.

"But . . ."

"No!"

Jade had no intention of breaking her contract with Newland Tarlton Company to help lead the troop of movie actors from California. This venture to Kilimanjaro would pay her twice: once as a salaried expedition leader, and a second time when she sold an article and photos to her magazine. *The Traveler* would expect her next article in another two months, but it took money to get away from Nairobi and all its silliness to find something fresh to write about.

When she was first offered the safari position, she was assured that Baron Bror Blixen was in command. Of course, that changed quickly once she'd signed the contract. Suspiciously quickly. Somehow, Jade suspected that Harry had been in charge all along and had suggested the deception lest she turn down the offer. Sam agreed, and part of their argument last week had grown from there. Jade heard it all again, recalling it word for word.

"I think you should tell Newland Tarlton to take their contract and stuff it where the sun doesn't shine," Sam had said after learning about the change in leadership.

Jade had been riled herself, but once Sam started in on Hascombe being a no-good, lying sidewinder, she immediately tempered her own feelings. "There's no cause for me to quit, Sam. Blixen has a worse reputation with women, and you didn't object to my going with him."

"Actually I did, but I don't trust Hascombe at all. I saw that photograph of you that he carried on Marsabit. He wants you, and out there, alone with him . . ."

"I'm hardly going to be alone with him, Sam. You're going to have to trust *me* or we can't have any kind of future. I can handle Harry *and* myself. When you talk this way, I feel like you're trying to break me."

"I don't intend to break you, Jade," argued Sam. "I wouldn't want to. I love your spirit of adventure. I just want you to temper it a little."

"Temper it," she repeated.

"Right. No more stupid stunts like last July, when you were the leopard bait."

Jade didn't want to be leopard bait any more than Sam wanted her to, but she wanted it to be her choice, not his. "That's what I mean," she countered. "It starts there and the next thing you know, I'm wearing a saddle and tack. Probably where the term 'bridal' came from. Someone misspelled 'bridle.' "

The conversation had deteriorated from that point on.

"What makes you think marriage would be any easier for me?" snapped Sam. "You've been playing nursemaid to me ever since I had that malaria attack." He inhaled through gritted teeth. "I'm not a cripple, you know. I'm a perfectly functioning, red-blooded American man who just happens to have an oak leg."

"I haven't played nursemaid," she retorted.

"Ha! Every time I see you, you're either trying to shove quinine down my gullet or wrap me up in mosquito netting."

And so they'd left it, each one unsure of the other and of themselves. In the end, after tempers had cooled, they'd both apologized. Sam told Jade to keep the ring. He planned to stay on in Africa for a while at least, helping Neville design and build their new coffee washer. Eventually, he needed to return to the States to sell his movie, but it wouldn't be for several weeks.

Jade didn't ask what he'd do if she hadn't decided on his

proposal by then. Would he come back to Africa after his trip to the States? After today's argument, she wasn't so confident anymore. Her confusion left her feeling nervous and sullen. Her indecision didn't stem from a question of love. She cared more deeply for Sam than she had for any man. But she wanted to bolt like an unbroken mustang for the open range every time the subject of marriage came up. She'd explained that the day he proposed. But when she'd handed the beautiful sapphire ring back to him, he'd told her to keep it and think about it. She had. And after today, when Sam stormed off without letting her defend her actions, she worried that *he* was having second thoughts. The fact that it bothered her confused her even more.

"Jade? Jade!"

"Beg your pardon, Maddy. I was daydreaming."

"I want to meet the motion picture director and give him a copy of my latest book." She patted her swollen handbag, larger than the usual evening bag ladies carried to parties.

"You brought a copy of *Ivory Blood*?" asked Jade.

"Clever girl," said Beverly. "Sam should be here to sell *his* motion picture to them."

As if he'd heard her suggestion, Sam entered the ballroom just then, looking particularly handsome in his white tie and black dinner jacket. He saw them and pushed his way across the crowded room to their side. Jade's heart raced.

"Good evening, Jade, Maddy, Beverly." He nodded to each in turn. With each slight bow he made, a mop of his brown hair fell over one eye. He brushed it back. "You're probably surprised to see me here."

"But so delighted," said Beverly before Jade had a chance to reply. "Aren't we, Jade?"

"It's very nice to see you, Sam," she said. She hung back, unsure of her reception.

"I didn't come to punch out Hascombe," he said, in an attempt at humor. "I really did want to see you tonight, and . . ."

"You thought you could tell someone here about your motion picture," Jade finished.

"You probably want the producer, Graham Wheeler." She smiled. "Maddy wants to meet him or the director, too. I'll see if I can find them."

"Don't bother on *my* account, Jade," said Sam. "I looked him up earlier this afternoon. After, er, I got back from our excursion."

Jade felt her face flush. "I'm sorry, Sam. I shouldn't have assumed . . . Was Mr. Wheeler interested?"

"Moderately. Of course, he needs to see the picture first, and he won't have time to view it until he returns from safari." He studied her face in silence for a moment. "I just thought it would be nice to dance with you. But you should introduce Madeline to either Mr. Wheeler or the director first. I'll visit with Avery and Neville until you're free." He made a slight bow and walked away.

Jade watched him for a while, then looked around the room at the people sampling cheese and pastries. "Rex Julian is the director. I don't see him, but I can introduce you to Mr. Wheeler and some of the actors," she told Madeline, and pointed to a small clump of brightly dressed women and tuxedoed men. One woman excused herself from the group and moved towards the door.

"Isn't that Bebe Malta?" asked Beverly as a black-haired woman glided past in a pink satin gown with beaded shoulder straps. Silver lace roses graced the bodice and the lace overskirt. Her hair had been rolled up for the evening and secured with a dazzling diamond-encrusted comb.

Jade nodded. "Yes. I believe she's supposed to have a major role in this picture."

"What's the picture about?" asked Madeline as they headed towards the actors.

"I don't know," said Jade. "I was only told there are four women in the safari and I'm in charge of them."

"Pff," Beverly snorted. "Now I understand." When the others stared at her, she elaborated. "What I mean to say is, I didn't understand why Bror Blixen would hire a woman to take care of other women. If there's *anything* the baron has experience with, it's women. But we all know how *Harry's* experience with those German women on Marsabit turned out." She waggled her finger at Jade. "I hope you intend to open and inspect their boxes. You don't need anyone trying to smuggle guns again."

"I already have. Mostly a lot of costumes. I checked all the more personal female supplies yesterday." She thought about mentioning Bebe's bottle of black hair dye but decided against it. Jade disliked gossip. Each woman had more pots of beauty cream than she could ever recall.

"What about the rest of the equipment?" asked Madeline.

Jade shook her head. "Hascombe's seen to that. I know there are cameras and film cases and one box of blanks. I have no idea what else we're toting. It's a good thing there's a rail line as far as Moshi, because we couldn't feed the porters what it would take to haul this stuff."

"I'm sure Harry knows what he's doing," said Madeline to no one in particular. Jade arched her eyebrows.

"Oh, stop fussing about the safari," said Beverly. She patted her short curls, the color of early morning sunlight. "Introduce us."

Jade approached the nearest cluster of Americans and politely cleared her throat. They turned to her and one of the gentlemen smiled broadly.

"Ah, Miss del Cameron. Glad you could join us. You look ravishing." The speaker was a tall man with brown hair and a square jaw. He resembled a well-chiseled heroic statue.

"Thank you, Mr. Hall. Sorry to intrude," Jade said. She directed her apology in particular to a young, voluptuous, dark-haired woman who had frowned when Jade joined them. The woman's low-cut, ivory silk dress did little to conceal her attributes, and Jade remembered overhearing that she'd been hired as a body double in certain scenes. "I'd like to introduce my friends," said Jade. "They're very eager to meet all of you."

"Of course, but none of that 'mister' stuff. I'm Conrad to my friends. Hope you'll be one of them, since you are one of our great white hunters, protecting us in the wilds."

Jade smiled. "Then you must call me Jade. Or just scream. I generally answer to both."

A willowy, auburn-haired woman with clear hazel eyes twisted her cardinal red lips into a wry smile. "Faster to the latter, I hope." She held out a well-manicured hand to Beverly. "I'm Cynthia Porter. I play an intrepid explorer's devoted wife in this picture."

Beverly shook the woman's hand as Jade continued the introductions. "This is Lord Avery Dunbury's wife."

"Please call me Beverly," she said.

"And this lady," Jade said, indicating Madeline, "is Mrs. Thompson. Madeline is also an author with two adventure books in print and another recently sold."

"*Stalking Death* and *Ivory Blood*," added Maddy. "I'm very pleased to meet you."

Mr. Hall extended his hand to Madeline and Beverly in

turn. "Conrad Hall," he said. "I'm the intrepid explorer that Cynthia mentioned. At least when we shoot the present-day scenes. I'm also supposed to be some emperor from the past." He laughed. "Don't ask me to explain, though. I'm miserable when it comes to history."

"This is Pearl Zagar," Jade said, indicating the voluptuous beauty. "And Henry Wells," she finished, nodding to a younger man with blue eyes and sandy blond hair parted in the middle. Unlike Mr. Hall's block-shaped chin, Mr. Wells' jutted out in a rounded bulb.

"Call me Hank," he said.

"And this gentleman is the producer, Mr. Graham Wheeler." Wheeler nodded, then looked around the room, his expression concerned and impatient. From the corner of her eye, Jade spied Harry Hascombe coming out of the bar and heading in their direction. The last thing she wanted was to risk a confrontation between Harry and Sam, who, despite avowals to the contrary, would love to punch Harry in the face. "If you'll excuse me then, I have someone else to attend to." Jade slipped away and arrived beside Sam's group just as Maddy began her appeal to the producer and Bev inquired about the picture's plot.

"Ah, Jade," said Avery, "I do hope you didn't encourage Beverly to abandon us to become an actress. She's always been rather keen on the idea. I nearly kept her at home tonight."

"I don't believe you and little Alice are in any danger," said Jade with a chuckle.

Avery set his half-empty glass on a nearby tray and smoothed back his fair hair. "Still, I think I shall just go over and make certain."

"I'll go with you," said Neville as he spied Maddy trying to engage Wheeler in conversation.

Jade watched them join their wives before turning back to Sam. "I *am* very glad you came tonight, Sam. I'm sorry I presumed it was for selfish gain. Forgive me?"

"Only if you dance with me."

The band hired for this evening's affair had just finished a set of three fast songs and broke into a slow waltz. Sam had trouble moving his right leg with its heavy wooden prosthesis as rapidly as was required for a fox-trot or two-step, but he managed waltzes well enough. Jade let him lead her onto the dance floor. His ungloved right hand rested lightly just below her shoulder, his touch barely perceptible through her dress and the pocket handkerchief he held to protect the fabric. Jade felt her skin tingle and wished he'd hold her tighter.

She studied his angular face marked by a prominent nose that grew directly from his brow. It was punctuated by a thin brown mustache. A pair of coffee brown, nearly black eyes drew attention away from the nose and lent balance to his features. His brown hair, close-cropped at the sides, was longer on top and fell from a side part over his right brow. Jade compared it to the actors' faces and decided Sam's was the better by far. While not classic like Mr. Hall's or pretty like the Adonis-faced Mr. Wells', Sam's lean, chiseled features bore the stamp of intelligence, honor, and character, which made him far more handsome to her. His eyes especially, which reminded Jade of an African night, could transform his features from boyish devilry to those of a warrior. Looking into them now made her arms tremble ever so slightly.

She felt the need for conversation. She thought of two or three topics and rejected them all. Talking of the safari would create tension between them; she already knew about his work with Neville on the coffee washer and that he hadn't flown his plane but once since he'd run low on fuel two weeks ago. Until the local petrol shortage improved, he was grounded. "I hope Mr. Wheeler makes you an offer on your picture," she said finally. "It would save you an expensive trip home."

"I'll go back to the States soon anyway," he said. "It's an election year. You should come with me, since women have the vote now."

Jade was about to comment when the sound of breaking glass and cracking wood startled everyone. "What in thunder was that?"

"Sounds like it came from the other room."

They ran from the ballroom into the reception room in time to see Cissy Estes sitting on the floor, her rear end in the rum punch bowl. The serving table's thin legs had snapped and splayed under her weight when she fell backwards onto it, spilling the bowl as well as several dozen glass punch cups. Cissy blinked stupidly at the gathering crowd, her right hand still holding her glass.

"I shall complain to the management," she slurred. "The floor is wet."

Most of the guests laughed at her, but the two cameramen, Lloyd Brown and Steve Budendorfer, tried to haul her to her feet. The woman probably only weighed one hundred and fifteen pounds wet, but both these men were slightly built and she was a deadweight. Her shoes kept slipping on the spilled punch, making her legs sprawl at odd angles.

"I should help, I suppose," said Sam. "Can't leave her like that." He hadn't gone two steps when Harry Hascombe grabbed Cissy by one arm, yanked her to her feet, then toted her off to a settee to recover.

"Well, that was certainly exciting," said Beverly, as she and the others joined Jade and Sam. The rest of the crowd dispersed, most going into the ballroom.

"Did you convince Mr. Wheeler to buy your books for a picture?" Jade asked Madeline.

She shook her head. "He was very polite but I don't think he's interested. He's having enough difficulty just getting one movie filmed in Africa and he doesn't want to try a second. But I didn't speak with him for very long. He seemed rather concerned about Miss Malta and went to look for her."

"We've been talking to the actors instead," said Beverly. "Their picture sounds wonderful, doesn't it, Avery?"

"Certainly dramatic enough. It's all based on some legend of King Solomon's son, Menelik, and—"

Avery's account was interrupted by a piercing scream. A woman ran into the room from the back door, her expensive gown streaked with blood.

"That's Miss Malta!" exclaimed Madeline as the actress collapsed in a heap on the floor.

The crowd surged forward and surrounded her, shouting incoherently. Jade pushed past them towards the door and the dark grounds beyond.

"Whatever happened occurred outside," she said as her friends followed.

"A leopard attack?" suggested Beverly.

Jade didn't reply. She hadn't heard any screams or snarls from a big cat, and the actress didn't appear to be hurt. At least, she hadn't seen any cuts or scratches on the woman's face or arms.

The answer lay sprawled on the grass, thirty yards from the door. A man in full evening dress lay on his side, his hands still wrapped tightly around a native's neck. The African was alive, though barely. Before they could get to him, he pulled a knife from the other body and plunged it into his own naked and horribly scratched chest. The native's breath caught in one choking gasp before his head fell back, his dead eyes staring into eternity.

Madeline screamed and buried her face in Neville's shirt. He put his arms around his wife as the others stared horrified at the scene.

"My stars!" Neville exclaimed. "What just happened? Who is that?"

Sam knelt beside the first man and checked his throat for a pulse. Jade stepped to the other side and looked down at the man's face. "It's Graham Wheeler. He's dead."

Avery pulled Beverly closer in a protective embrace. "I guess that means he won't be buying Sam's motion picture."

CHAPTER 3

Distance, or perhaps lack of familiarity, keeps lively parties from skiing and picnicking on Kilimanjaro as they do on God's other seat.

—The Traveler

Sam stood beside Jade and Neville as they guarded the bodies, keeping the crowd back with repeated cautions and mild threats. Avery telephoned the Nairobi police and rejoined them. Harry followed hot on his heels.

"Someone is on the way," said Avery. "At first they told me to ring up the Parklands police station. Said it was closer. Puh!" he scoffed. "I informed them that those chaps are not equipped to handle anything more than a loose dog or a possible prowler. After I repeated the word 'murder' several times, I got someone's attention."

"How is Miss Malta?" asked Jade.

"I just left her," said Harry. "She appears to have recovered from her faint."

"Bev and Madeline are attending her," added Avery, "in one of the ladies' parlors."

"Did any of you see what happened?" asked Harry.

"Only the last part," said Sam, "when this man"—he pointed to the African—"stabbed himself."

"Bloody hell!" swore Harry.

They heard the sound of several motorcars coming up the long drive on the opposite side of the Muthaiga Club. "Harry, maybe you'd better go out front to meet them and bring them here," suggested Jade.

Harry agreed and sprinted around the building to avoid the congestion of people. In a few minutes she heard him return the same way. This time a small crowd followed them, having spotted the police. Snippets of "terrible mess," "blasted natives," and "you will protect us" mingled with Harry's oaths. Finally a commanding voice ordered everyone back inside. Jade recognized that voice.

The group rounded the corner, Harry in the lead, the inspector second, and two constables trailing. "This way, Inspector," said Harry. He'd loosened his tie and unbuttoned his dinner jacket.

Inspector Finch stopped abruptly when he spotted Jade, and a constable plowed right into his back.

"Inspector Finch," said Jade. "Thank you for making such haste."

Finch recovered himself and strode forward. "Why am I not surprised to see you involved in this, Miss del Cameron?" He turned his head towards Sam. "And Featherstone, too. Ah, Thompson. And I believe you're Lord Dunbury, aren't you?"

Avery made a slight bow. "If we are through with the introductions, Inspector, may I suggest that you see to the problem at hand?"

Finch forced a thin smile. "Indeed. Tell me what happened." He bent to examine the bodies.

Avery, Neville, and Harry all looked to Jade and Sam to explain. Sam stepped forward after Jade shrugged and pointed to him. "We didn't witness everything, Inspector," he said. "We were inside and heard a scream. A woman, an actress, ran into the room. Her dress appeared to have blood on it. She fainted and Miss del Cameron and I went outside to see if her attacker was still in the area. We found this man, Mr. Graham Wheeler, lying just as you see him." He pointed to the other man. "The native wasn't dead, although his position suggested he'd been choked to the point of it. He pulled that knife from Mr. Wheeler's chest and plunged it into his own before we could stop him."

"And this actress you spoke of, where is she now?"

"She's inside with my wife and Mrs. Thompson," said Avery. "They took her into a ladies' room after reviving her."

They heard another car drive up. "That will be the doctor," said Finch, rising. He turned to the closest constable. "Go and fetch him. Bring him around here first. We'll see to this Miss . . . ?" He stopped and looked at Jade.

"Bebe Malta," she said. "She's part of a motion picture crew from California. Harry is taking them to Kilimanjaro to film."

"And you?" Finch asked.

"I'm seconding the safari."

"Ah," Finch said, looking at Harry. "You should warn them that she attracts corpses."

"If you're implying—" began Sam, his voice low.

Mr. Finch held up his hand in a placating manner. "I'm suggesting nothing of the sort, Featherstone. So kindly do not take a swing at me, as you Americans quaintly put it."

The doctor, a middle-aged man, arrived and shook hands with Finch. "Dr. Mathews, good to have you back in the colony," said the inspector. He quickly summarized the events as he'd been given them. "It appears to be an open-and-shut situation, but you will, of course, wish to examine these men yourself. Mr. Wheeler, here, has several smaller cuts on his forearms and face, but it is clearly the stab to the heart that killed him. I will, of course, question this Miss Malta, but I imagine the native attacked her, and Wheeler rushed to her rescue, getting stabbed in the process."

The doctor knelt beside the bodies and studied them. "This spot on the native's jaw," he said, pointing with his pencil, "appears to be a developing bruise, possibly where Mr. Wheeler struck a blow while warding off the knife with his forearms. Finally, he grappled with the man, trying to choke him." He separated the two bodies and pointed to the native's neck, where the finger marks showed up as darker impressions on the brown skin. "Unfortunately for our friend, he didn't debilitate his opponent quickly enough and was stabbed. What I find most odd, though, is why the man should stab himself." He looked up at Jade. "You say you saw this?"

Jade and Sam both nodded.

"I expect that this man has a record of violence and didn't care to be captured again," said Finch.

"Possibly," murmured the doctor, "but his pupils are quite dilated. Of course, it is dark outside, but still . . . I should like to run some chemical tests on his blood. He may have enhanced his courage with some drug. Note the numerous scratch marks on his chest. Now look at the skin under his nails. He did this to himself."

Finch agreed and, after a cursory survey of the surrounding area, left the constables to guard the bodies. "Perhaps you had better come with me, Doctor, to see if Miss Malta is uninjured and able to answer my questions."

"I'm going with you," said Jade.

Finch gave her a long, appraising look and nodded. "Very well. Come along."

They found Bebe reclining on a velvet-cushioned settee in the ladies' parlor. Madeline and Beverly had given her a glass of water and sat perched on chairs near her. The poor woman still trembled and her eyes had a wild, glazed look.

"Thank you, ladies," said Finch. "I believe you may go now."

"Certainly not!" declared Beverly. "Miss Malta deserves the courtesy of female protection while she's being examined and interrogated." Madeline punctuated her friend's statement with an emphatic nod.

Finch glanced at Jade, who leaned against the wall, arms folded, and sighed. "I assure you that the lady is in no danger from us, but if it will ease your minds then you may remain. But kindly do not interfere." He motioned for the doctor to approach.

"Miss Malta," said the doctor, "I am just going to check your pulse. There is nothing to alarm you. You are quite safe." He picked up her left hand and felt her wrist with his fingertips.

"He . . . he came at me."

"Who came at you?" asked Finch. "The native? Or Mr. Wheeler?"

"The native," said Miss Malta. "Graham and I were . . . were . . ." She blinked as though she was trying to recall what they were doing. "We were talking. Then that man came out of the shadows holding a knife. If Graham hadn't been there . . ." She shivered again.

"I'll find a shawl or something," said Madeline.

"It's shock," said the doctor, "but yes, something to keep her warm." He looked up at Finch. "Inspector, your suit jacket, if you don't mind."

Finch frowned, but his hesitation lasted for only a second

before he took off his jacket and handed it to the doctor. Jade noted with some amusement that he still wore the same threadbare brown coat with the frayed cuffs as when she'd first met him last August. He wore no wedding ring, so possibly there was no female Finch to urge him into fresher feathers.

"Can you tell me, Miss Malta, what happened next?" asked Finch. When the woman didn't respond, he looked pleadingly at Madeline.

Maddy draped the jacket over the prostrate woman like a blanket and stroked her hair. "Please try to tell us, Miss Malta. You're safe."

Bebe's gaze darted wildly around the room.

"The man who attacked you is dead, Bebe," said Jade. "He can't hurt you."

"Graham killed him?" Bebe started to rise up, but Madeline pressed her back down.

"Please, Miss Malta," said the doctor in his most soothing voice. "I want you to answer this gentleman so that I may get you back to your hotel and give you something to calm your nerves."

"I don't know what happened. I remember screaming and watching Graham fighting. He told me to run inside. I did. I can't recall anything else."

"Thank you, Miss Malta. That will be all," said Mr. Finch. He closed his notebook and absentmindedly tried to slip it into his jacket pocket before realizing that he wore no jacket.

"I'll get some of the crew to escort her to a car, Doctor," said Jade. "They can drive her to her hotel and you can follow her there."

Dr. Mathews nodded and Jade went out the door. She immediately bumped into Sam, Avery, Harry, and Neville holding back a crowd of people all speaking at once.

"I demand to know what's happening!"

"Where's Bebe? Is she all right?"

"The police won't let us outside. Is it true that someone was killed?"

"Where's Wheeler?"

"I'm from *The Leader*. Can I get your story of what happened?"

Saint Peter's bait bucket! A reporter. Jade held up her hands for silence and, when that didn't work, shouted, "Be quiet!" When the din died down, she continued. "Miss Malta is uninjured but in need of rest. And no," she added, glaring at the reporter, "I do not care to talk to you." She stuck her head back inside the parlor. "Inspector, I think you need to come out here."

Both Finch and Dr. Mathews stepped out.

"There's a reporter here, Inspector," said Jade. "We can't send Miss Malta back to the hotel alone. He'll be after her like a buzzard on a ripe carcass."

"I'll take her to the hospital with me," said Dr. Mathews. "*After* these people leave."

"Did you see or hear *anyone* else outside when you and Featherstone witnessed the end of the attack?" Finch asked Jade.

"No," she and Sam replied in unison.

"Then there's no need to keep all these people," Finch said. He raised his voice above the rising din. "Anyone who has something that bears on this incident must stay. Everyone else must leave." No one moved towards the doors. "Or be arrested for violation of police orders."

Suddenly most of the crowd surged towards the front doors, the back ones still under guard by a solitary constable. Jade saw that the actors and the director, as well as their principal assistants, held back.

"All of you have something to say?" asked the inspector once everyone else had gone. He flipped open his notebook. No one spoke. "Then why are you still here?"

A short man with a bulbous nose and curly brown hair spoke up, his strong voice booming. "I'm Rex Julian, Detective."

"Inspector."

"Inspector, then. *I'm* the director. No one has told us what happened to Wheeler. He's our producer. We need to know how badly he's injured."

Finch passed a hand over his brow. "I'm sorry to have to tell you this. Mr. Wheeler was stabbed to death in an attack on himself and Miss Malta."

Murmurs of disbelief and shock followed the announcement. The only person who didn't speak was Cynthia Porter. Jade detected a fleeting touch of shock when the woman's eyes widened and her lips tightened. Then the mood passed and left a blank mask.

"Poor Graham," said Miss Zagar. "What are we going to do, Rex? We're still shooting the picture, aren't we?"

"I'm not sure," said Julian. "The costumes and supplies are all paid for, but there are our guides to pay, the porters, and then there're the costs of editing and advertising and—"

"We don't have the money," said Otto Dimwald, the producer's assistant.

The parlor door opened again, and this time Miss Malta stepped out on her own despite Madeline's and Beverly's entreaties to remain inside. She no longer had the inspector's jacket covering her, and her beautiful gown was streaked with blood, the bodice rose torn and hanging by a thread. The other women blanched visibly. Mr. Wells hurried over to take Miss Malta's hand.

"We have to shoot this movie, Rex," said a slender, carrot-topped young man Jade recognized as Woodrow Murdock. "Too many of us need this picture."

Pearl Zagar emphasized that remark by taking hold of the director's arm and gazing pleadingly into his eyes, her bosom heaving dramatically. "Woody is right, Rex."

"I don't disagree," said Julian, patting Pearl's hand, "but unless you are all willing and able to front the rest of the money, I don't see how—"

"I'll take over the production costs." The room went silent as everyone turned to the speaker, Cynthia Porter. "Of course, I intend to make it all back and receive the same shares that Graham would have gotten."

"Cynthia," protested Hall, "how can you afford it? Graham had some backers, but they'll pull out once they know he's dead."

"No, they won't," she said. "I'm his wife."

A dull thud and Madeline's soft gasp shifted everyone's attention to the parlor door. Bebe Malta had fainted again.

CHAPTER 4

The rail line from Voi on to Moshi was hastily constructed during the Great War. Ironically, the same war eventually gave German East Africa and consequently Kilimanjaro to Great Britain. It's nice that there's already a train to get you there.

—The Traveler

Dr. Mathews patted Bebe's hand, Beverly applied a damp towel to the woman's forehead, and Madeline massaged her feet. Jade left them to it and turned her attention back to Cynthia Porter and the renewed discussion. The actors talked at once, but the director's booming voice cut through them all.

"You're his wife? Why wasn't I told?"

"Because, Rex, we didn't tell anyone. Once you tell one person, it's no longer a secret," Cynthia said. "We felt it was better for my career if we pretended to be single. We even kept separate homes, although we didn't always live in one of them." Her lips twitched. Jade couldn't tell if it was an attempt to hold back a sob or a smile.

Julian turned to the producer's assistant. "Did you know about this, Otto?"

Dimwald shook his head. "Yes. I mean no, Rex. I mean, I saw Graham with Cynthia often enough, but I just thought she was his . . ." He blushed. "Graham was always popular with the ladies." He glanced in Bebe's direction, then quickly looked away.

Prentiss McAvy, an older and rugged-looking actor with a touch of white mixed in his sandy blond hair, chuckled. Jade saw him nudge Murdock. McAvy nodded towards Bebe and then Cynthia with a leer. Apparently he thought that the producer had become friendly with more than one woman at a time. What had she gotten herself into? Jade wondered. Didn't any of these people care that someone they knew, some apparently more intimately than others, had been brutally murdered?

"Poor Graham and poor Cynthia," said Pearl, reaching for the woman's hand. "I hope Cynthia's announcement fixes your decision, Rex." Her voice was hushed and breathy. "Graham would have wanted us to carry on, and at the risk of sounding callous, I need this picture."

Jade heard someone approach and saw Harry standing at her right.

"Remember, Jade, these women are *your* responsibility," he said softly. "And may I say," he added, "that you look as beautiful as ever? That fool Featherstone had better declare for you soon or I'm—"

Jade silenced him with a scowl. She groaned inwardly and, to her left, saw Sam watching her. Why, she wondered, did everything always turn out to be so complicated?

"Stunned as I am to hear Cynthia's news, I'm also relieved," said Julian. "As soon as the proper arrangements can be made for our late friend, we'll proceed as planned." He stopped suddenly and looked at Cynthia. "That is, unless you wish to return to the States with your husband's body."

Cynthia swept her right hand gracefully, dismissing all

concerns and obligations. "Certainly not. My responsibilities are here. I'm sure that Mr. Dimwald will escort the body home and see to a proper burial. We won't have to wait then. You'll take care of everything, won't you, Otto?"

The look she gave her husband's assistant hinted that he had no choice. Jade surmised that the two had not gotten along in the past and that Cynthia felt she was well rid of him.

Finch hadn't budged throughout the entire conversation. When he finally spoke again, everyone including Jade started visibly. They'd all forgotten he was in the room. "Since no one else has anything *useful* to add to my inquiry, you should all leave. Mrs. Wheeler?" he called to the actress.

"Please, Inspector. I have always answered to Cynthia Porter, so I'd prefer you'd continue with that."

"Yes, quite. Well, since you are the *bereaved* widow, I feel it is my duty to inform you that your husband's body has been taken to Dr. Mathews' offices. You should contact him to make arrangements with a mortician when the time comes."

"As I said earlier, my husband's assistant will take care of Graham's remains. Otto has followed after my husband and seen to all his concerns in the past. I see no reason why he should stop now. I'll recompense him very well for his trouble." She turned to Dimwald. "And, Otto, *I* won't be needing your help when I return home, so once you're there, you might want to look for another position. Of course, I'll give you a sterling recommendation."

"Is this case closed, Inspector?" asked Wells. "Did you catch the murderer?"

Jade was surprised no one else had asked that. She'd witnessed the end of the tragedy, but nothing had been said to any of these people except that Wheeler had been stabbed. Everyone, with the exception of Wells, who stood by Bebe's side, seemed unnaturally callous. It made her flesh crawl, and she rubbed her arms to dispel the feeling.

"Very likely so," replied Finch. "The attacker stabbed himself afterwards. He's dead. So you will all be quite safe when you leave . . . now!"

"If you have no objections, Inspector," said Wells, "I'd like to go with Miss Malta to the doctor's clinic. She knows me better than she does Miss del Cameron or any of these ladies and might feel more comfortable."

"I want to go to my hotel room," Bebe whispered. "I'm fine now. Hank can take me there," she added with a nod to Wells. "But I'll need to speak with Mr. Hascombe later." She turned to Harry. "You will come by, won't you?" Harry nodded dumbly.

"That's entirely up to the doctor," said Finch.

Dr. Mathews nodded. "Miss Malta has suffered no physical injuries, and she appears to have recovered from her shock."

Jade turned to Sam. "I guess we should go, too. I came in a motorized rickshaw, but I'm not sure how easy it will be to get one now. Most of the guests are gone, so the drivers will probably assume the dance is over."

"I rode my motorcycle," Sam said. "You'll have to travel back with Bev and Avery."

"Are you going to their house?" she asked, surprised that he'd dismissed her so quickly.

Sam shook his head. "Going back to the Thompsons'." Ignoring Harry, who was still standing nearby, Sam leaned in and kissed her lightly on the cheek. "I'll find you tomorrow, but if I don't, please take care of yourself."

"Remember, the train leaves at noon," she said.

Sam nodded, took two steps to the door, hesitated, and left.

"Trouble in paradise?" asked Harry from behind her.

"Shut up, Harry."

JADE ROSE BEFORE dawn in order to complete her own last-minute packing. Now that the Dunburys were home to stay, she'd moved back into the separate two-room stone building that they'd built for her use. She scanned her list, checking off all the items, including her Winchester, ammunition, canteen, Kodak, rolls of film, a fresh notebook, a leather pouch stuffed with jerky, flashlight, first-aid kit, and a compass. Developing film would wait till her return.

She reached down to her boots and felt the knife hilt poking from the hidden sheath, and put a smaller, folding knife in her left side pocket. She put everything but her Winchester in her day pack. She'd cleaned and reloaded it the night before, after the Muthaiga social. It kept her from thinking about Sam and the upcoming good-byes.

If he would just trust me.

She had looked forward to this safari at first. Finally, a chance to see the "shining mountain" up close, to touch it. And it seemed like an easy job, too. Perhaps shoot a little game for the cooking pot, and keep three American women and one maid from wandering off; what could be simpler? Watching these people make a motion picture would be icing on the cake. Of course, she'd seen Sam make his documentation of a coffee farmer's life, but *African Dreams*, as he called it, was different. There were no trained actors, no elaborate costumes, no scripts or sets.

And no cold, heartless jackals. Inspector Finch had shown more humanity over Wheeler's death than did most of his crew, including his widow. Well, Jade didn't have to like them.

Her essential gear now packed, she turned her attention to her few personal items. She rolled up a second pair of trousers, two spare shirts, a clean camisole, and several pairs of linen underdrawers. Five pairs of heavy woolen socks went into the valise, along with a box of Keating's powder to kill chiggers, one box of aspirin, a bar of soap, and a tube of Colgate Dental Cream. Knowing the nights on the mountain would get cold, especially the higher they climbed, she added a set of Aertex cellular long underwear, a pale green wool sweater, and finished with a fleece-lined coat and a knitted muffler.

Someone knocked at her door. Jade opened it to see Beverly wearing a loose, low-waisted dress in powder blue linen. Jade invited her in, led the way through her sitting room into her bedroom, and closed the valise.

"Is that everything?" Beverly asked. "I understand packing light on safari, but . . ."

"We have enough gear to carry without my adding more to it. Everything must be under thirty pounds, remember? I'll have my day pack myself."

Bev nodded as she perused Jade's list. "What soap did you pack? Nothing perfumed?"

"No, nothing to attract insects, or other pests."

Bev giggled. "Like Harry?"

Jade rolled her eyes. "Please don't say that around Sam."

Beverly leaned against the doorframe and folded her arms across her chest. "You could put his worries to rest by simply accepting his proposal before you get on the train."

"It isn't that simple, Bev." She pulled out her pocket watch and wound it, hoping to avoid further discussion by appearing to be in a hurry.

Bev didn't take the hint. "Explain it to me."

Jade plopped into a chair and picked up her felt hat, playing with the brim. "It's difficult." Beverly's soft snort informed Jade that she didn't believe it. She sat down on the bed. "Do you love him?"

"I think so."

"You aren't *sure*? Let me ask you this. Can you imagine your life without him?"

Jade took a deep breath. "Yes. But I think it would be a lot more . . . empty."

"Then there's your answer," Beverly said.

"No. Because I can also imagine life *with* him and it's more confined." Jade locked her emerald green eyes onto Bev's watercolor blue ones and held the gaze for a moment, long enough to convey the unspoken thought, *Like your life is now.*

Beverly looked away first. Except for Sam, very few people could meet Jade's gaze for long. "You can't leave without breakfast." Bev led the way back to the main house and into the dining area and asked Farhani, her Somali in charge of the household, to serve. "Are you seeing Sam today?" she asked Jade once they were seated.

"Maybe. Thank you, Farhani," she added as the tall man, decked out entirely in white from his turbaned head to his gloved hands, poured coffee into her china cup. He bowed and set the silver pot on the table. "Right now I need to get this valise to the depot and rouse those three actresses and their maid."

"Who *is* their maid? Did they bring someone with them?" Farhani returned with the toast rack, and Beverly helped herself to a slice and the pot of marmalade.

"No," said Jade, buttering her toast. "Well, they did, but she took ill after two days here and had to go back. I hadn't been hired yet, but Harry found this young woman from Zanzibar, a Swahili. Lwiza's her name." She leaned back as Farhani placed a large plate of bacon and scrambled eggs in front of her. "She speaks English well enough and seems to understand what she's hired to do, getting the women in costume, tending their hair, that sort of thing. Very pretty. I photographed her a few times while she was working."

"Arab Swahili or native Swahili?" asked Bev. "You know the Zanzibar Arabs consider themselves to be the only true Swahili."

"I doubt she's an Arab, at least not pure-blooded," replied Jade. "If that were the case, she wouldn't have been allowed free of the women's quarters in whatever household she came from. Her features are delicate, but her coloring is a creamy brown with a golden tint." Jade tasted her eggs, added salt and pepper, and dug into her breakfast.

"Hmm," mused Bev. "Perhaps the child of a slave woman."

Jade shrugged. "I don't envy her her job. Not taking care of those women."

"Are you bringing Biscuit with you?"

"No. I left him with Jelani. If I try to leave him with the Thompsons, he'll just break loose and go looking for the boy or for me."

Jade finished her breakfast and gave her friend a quick hug. "Take care of yourself, Bev, and say good-bye to Avery and little Alice for me."

"At least let Avery help you with your trunk. He's with the horses right now. I can send Farhani to fetch him."

"Don't bother," Jade said. "I can manage it."

Alice's soft cry kept Beverly from protesting, and Jade returned to her rooms to get her gear. She slung her day pack onto her back and her rifle over her shoulder. Then, clamping her hat on her head, she hoisted the valise. Newland Tarlton had loaned Jade the use of a truck, a made-over war ambulance, to help with loading. Avery had been watching for her even without Bev's prompting and took the box from her shoulders as she tried to shut the door. They stowed her personal gear in the truck bed; then Avery cranked the engine. When it sputtered to life, Jade waved good-bye and drove off into town, heading for the New Stanley Hotel. She literally ran into Harry in the lobby. He wore khaki trousers, boots, and a Huck shirt with a frayed collar. The cuffs were rolled to his elbows, and the top buttons undone, making him the picture of easy strength.

"Good morning, Jade," he said, steadying her with both hands on her waist. "Bright and early, that's what I like. How's my cat?"

"Mine now. You gave him up, remember?" said Jade, pushing him away. "I left Biscuit in care of Jelani at his village. Is anyone else up yet?"

"I knocked up the director and those two cameramen. Told them to wake the rest. Haven't heard a peep from the women, but that's your job. Maybe start with that Swahili girl. I think they've put her in one of those back rooms set aside for snooty people's maids." He rubbed a hand over his square jaw. "I did see Miss Malta last evening. Pretty shook up, as you can imagine. Maybe I should try her."

"Suit yourself." Jade asked the clerk for directions and found Lwiza where Harry had indicated. Her tiny, windowless room barely held a cot and a washbasin. A box and a valise, the same size as Jade's, sat beside the cot. Jade knew what was in them; she'd purchased most of the woman's clothes herself, since Lwiza had had nothing suitable for wearing to walk up a mountainside.

The woman seemed serene enough when she answered Jade's knock. She was already awake and dressed in a white, short-sleeved tunic and an ankle-length white skirt. Beautiful red and yellow crisscross diamonds were embroidered on the bodice and ran down the front of the skirt. A long white cotton cloth was draped over her head and tossed over one shoulder. It hid only a portion of her black hair, which was parted in the middle and twisted into a bun behind each ear. Her oval face was a rich, creamy brown, like well-steeped tea with a drop of milk in it. Studying her smooth complexion, Jade guessed Lwiza couldn't be beyond her twenties.

Jade peered past her into the Spartan room. Lwiza had managed to find something to eat, judging by a plate empty of all but a few residual crumbs. Jade inquired politely after her, then asked her if she was ready to begin her job.

"It has begun, *bibi*," she said, addressing Jade with the Swahili word for "lady." "Late last night I tended Missy Malta and left her something to help her sleep after the big bwana left her. I told her I would come to her in the morning with food." She waved a hand gracefully, exposing her arm and the broad silver bangle she wore. The metal was stamped in a filigree, punctuated three times by an ornate cross-shaped design capped with a dome-shaped box.

"Good idea. There may be men waiting to talk with her." Jade hadn't seen the reporter from last night, but that didn't mean another one wasn't lying in wait. If they could keep Miss Malta hidden until it was time to leave, it would be better for all.

"So you know about what happened last night?" Jade asked.

"I heard that the money man was killed. So we will not go to the mountain now?"

"We are still going to the mountain," said Jade. "Only the man was killed, not his money. Do not worry," she added, reassuring the woman. "You will not lose your job. You will be paid." She smiled. "Go and find food for Miss Malta first. Then help her pack her boxes. I will carry your box out for you."

"No, *bibi*," Lwiza said. "I will take it later. I have need of it yet."

Jade nodded. "Then I will wake the other women and get their boxes."

She left Lwiza and headed up the stairs to where the actors were staying. On the way, she met several of the men coming downstairs to breakfast. All were dressed in crisp Huck shirts and jodhpurs, looking like models for the well-dressed hunter. Beyond giving them a friendly good morning, she didn't concern herself with them. They were Harry's problem.

Neither Miss Zagar nor Miss Porter was awake yet. Jade knocked loudly on their doors until both of them opened. The women were still in their nightwear, or at least Cynthia was, since the white gown showed from beneath her blue robe. The way Pearl's silk robe clung to her suggested she'd slept in her altogether. Neither of them appeared very delighted to see Jade. "Down to breakfast in half an hour," she ordered. She met Lwiza coming upstairs with a tray of oatmeal, toast, and tea for Miss Malta.

It took Cynthia and Pearl longer than thirty minutes to get their faces on and their hair arranged. When they finally showed up for breakfast, they wore close-fitting versions of the men's garb, except they'd added colorful scarves around their throats. Jade waited outside the hotel, watching the few early risers walk by on their way to open shops. When she decided her group had had enough time to eat, she rousted them out of the dining area to finish packing. She intended to reinforce the fact that she was in charge. She also wanted to be at the train station early enough to say good-bye to Sam.

As she'd predicted, the women hadn't even begun to pack

their personal belongings and had managed to put their new safari clothing in disarray. Jade noted that Pearl had no sleepwear.

"You can freeze your acting talents off at home, if you choose, but on this safari, you'll need something more insulating than air," Jade announced. "Where's that long underwear I bought for you?"

"I don't know," said Pearl. "I might have tossed it out."

Jade muttered under her breath. "Fold those clothes. I'll be back with another set."

After a fast trip to Whiteaway and Laidlaw to buy the replacement, she took charge of their packing. Both Pearl and Cynthia assumed that Lwiza would pack for them, and kept interfering by removing first one item, then another that they felt they needed before they left. Jade eventually chased them out of the rooms and repacked the boxes to her own satisfaction. Then she directed them all to be taken down to the truck. Harry stared in openmouthed surprise when she said two of the crew were ready. He still hadn't finished with the men. Jade owned that he had more people to deal with and drove her part over to the railroad station to be loaded.

When she returned at ten, she found Sam waiting for her by the old thorn tree near the New Stanley, and a smile came unbidden to her lips. It was checked almost instantly by a nervous twitter in her stomach when she wondered if he'd chosen that spot for a reason. They both knew the tree's history as a message board in the earlier days before the telegraph and telephones. *Well,* she thought, *if he has a message to give me, I'll wait and listen for it.* She greeted him with a truly happy "hello." He responded by slipping his arm around her waist and kissing her lightly on the cheek. Jade asked if he'd eaten breakfast yet.

"Yes, but it feels like ages ago."

"Then we should go inside and find a quiet table to ourselves," she suggested. "I'm hungry, and it will be a long run to Kiu and our next meal." They walked into the lobby together and headed for the dining area. They nearly collided with Lwiza coming out with a pot in one hand and a small pitcher of cream in the other.

"Is that for Miss Malta?" Jade asked. The girl looked slightly harried, and Jade felt sorry for her, having to fetch and carry up the stairs.

"Yes. She will not have tea. She will have *bunna* and cream."

"A bun?" Sam asked.

Lwiza shook her head. "I forget the English word." She paused and thought. "Coffee."

Ah, thought Jade. A woman after her own heart, excepting the cream.

Lwiza left to manage the steps with her long skirt and full hands. Jade and Sam found a table towards the back and ordered chicken sandwiches and hard-boiled eggs.

"I suppose you're all packed," Sam said.

Jade nodded. "Got two of the women packed, too. Lwiza will see to Miss Malta." She saw Sam's frown and reached for his hand. "We won't be gone long, Sam. Two weeks tops. Every day out costs them money. We're taking a train to the foot of the mountain. It's all very . . . civilized now." When he didn't respond she added, "I'll talk to Mr. Julian about your film. Maybe he'll have some ideas or know someone who'd be interested."

"That's not what concerns me now," Sam said. "I don't like this group. Watch yourself."

Jade slid her hand back and leaned forward. "What are you driving at, Sam?"

"I'm not sure," he said. "But something about last night has set my teeth on edge."

"You're referring to the fact that they seem cold and self-centered? I know that already."

"That's not it. It's Wheeler's death. It's not . . . It doesn't make sense."

"Death rarely does. But it seems obvious, doesn't it? This man saw Miss Malta and tried to attack her. Wheeler stepped in and got killed for it. The man took his own life rather than face prison or perhaps execution."

"But Wheeler was already out there with Miss Malta when the attack happened. That man wasn't going after a lone, helpless woman. Hell, he may not have been going after *her* at all."

Jade took a bite of her sandwich, chewed, then swallowed. "So it was a robbery attempt."

"But that doesn't feel right either. Why the Muthaiga, for heaven's sake? The good doctor thought the killer was drugged. So how would he get all the way out there in that condition without someone noticing? If he was just looking to rob someone, why not try one of the darker side streets or shops in town?"

"Because he'd be more likely to get caught?" Jade suggested. "Or he thought that he'd get more money at a rich man's club than in town?" She set her sandwich down. "Really, Sam. You're starting at shadows here." She picked up an egg and salted it.

Sam shook his head. "I don't think so. I think that man was lying in wait out there. Maybe waiting for Wheeler. Why didn't he attack *me* when I came in? I saw someone else leave earlier. Why not them? Why wait for Wheeler?"

Jade paused midbite. "Are you suggesting that Wheeler was *intentionally* murdered?"

Sam shrugged. "Could be. And considering the people you're working with, it could have been any one of them. Maybe that director didn't like how Wheeler was taking control. Maybe one of the actors had a grudge." He poked at his sandwich for emphasis. "Maybe that less than mournful widow wanted his money!"

"And maybe you've been reading Maddy's books, Sam. Sounds like one of her embellishments. How did she describe my old nemesis, Lilith? 'She was as cold as the greed and envy that coursed through her veins.'" Seeing Sam fold his arms across his chest and scowl, Jade sighed and set her egg back down on the china plate. "I've told you, Sam. I'll be fine. You . . ." She paused and collected her thoughts, getting her emotions under control before saying something she'd regret. "I don't feel . . . comfortable with this kind of talk from you. You're trying to get me to quit. To stay behind."

"I'm trying to get you to think about the possible danger."

Once again, she placed a hand gently on his. "Sam, you have to learn to trust me."

They finished eating in awkward silence. Sam stayed around after lunch, sometimes waiting silently in the background, sometimes pitching in to help load the remaining boxes in the trucks. When the train finally pulled out, Jade waved good-bye out the window. Sam waved once, but her last sight was of him standing alone on the platform, his arms folded across his chest.

Harry Hascombe stole up beside her. "He doesn't look too happy, does he? Worried I might steal you away?"

"Shut up, Harry!"

The ride to Moshi passed uneventfully. Jade spent much of the trip to Voi thinking about what Sam had said. Without believing that Wheeler's death was anything more than a bad attempt at robbery or an attack on a lone woman, Jade amused herself with studying the actors' reflections in her window glass. Miss Malta, Jade decided, did have a decent reaction to Wheeler's death. She fainted. That made sense if she'd been having an affair with him.

Rex Julian, Jade thought, appeared more concerned about the loss of money stopping his movie. Now that Miss Porter had the bills covered, he was all business again. As for the two young cameramen, Budendorfer and Brown, they probably just wanted to work and get paid. The same likely went for the minor actors: Hank Wells, Woodrow Murdock, and the extra man, Roland Talmadge. Jade considered Wells again. He'd shown a lot of concern for Bebe. Did he love her? Could he have been jealous of Wheeler? She dismissed the idea.

What about Conrad Hall? Could he have hated Wheeler? Possibly, but at this point she had no way of knowing. The women? Had Wheeler made a pass at Lwiza? No, she had spoken of the "money man" without any shudder of revulsion. Miss Zagar? The woman struck Jade as loose, but that was all. *Unless she wanted more than what Wheeler was giving her.*

Finally there was the ungrieving widow. Cynthia Porter was the most obvious suspect by far. She had the most to gain. But perhaps Wheeler wasn't supposed to die, just get scared? Or maybe Miss Malta *was* the real target? Jade chuckled at her imaginative scenarios, closed her eyes, and dozed until the train stopped at Voi.

After transferring their gear to another train, they spent the night sleeping in a worn-out passenger car parked along the siding. Early the next morning the locomotive to Moshi hooked up and took them on their way west.

Harry joined her early on, his muscular frame settling with ease into the seat next to her. He smelled of fresh air, soap, and witch hazel. "You certainly outshine these actresses, Jade." He held out a hand, palm out, when she opened her mouth to comment. "And I'm extremely grateful to the powers that be to have you under, er, as second in command with this lot. They promise to be a handful."

"Was it your idea to be deceptive about who was in charge?"

"Oh, let's just call it confusion on the part of our employers, shall we?" He opened a roll of magazines and handed them to her. *Cinema Talk* with its cover photograph of Conrad Hall topped the stack. "There are some articles on the movie and some of the actors and actresses in these. You might want to read them and see what we're up against."

Jade took them. "Thanks, Harry."

"Think nothing of it, Jade. Say, as I understand it, your friend Featherstone made a motion picture. Better watch out. He'll be turning daft, too, like these people."

"Shut up, Harry."

He chuckled and left her as Jade opened a magazine and tried to pass the time reading. She worked her way through one interview with the director in which he spoke of the adventure that he'd capture on location. He praised all his starring actors but waxed particularly eloquent over the beautiful Miss Zagar, a rare pearl of beauty in name and fact.

Reading that one article in a rocking train gave Jade a headache, so she settled for thumbing through the remaining pages, marveling at the wealth of beauty ads. The Pompeian ads won hands down over Pond's and Resinol. Their motto, "Don't envy beauty—use Pompeian and have it," came through on full-page picture ads for beauty powder, cold cream, and vanishing cream. She remembered seeing a jar on Bev's vanity, which was surprising, since the product was made in Cleveland, Ohio.

Jade thumbed past photo displays of Pearl in a harem costume holding a boa and another of Hall's new California home in someplace called the Hollywood Hills. They were followed by yet another ad, this time for Pond's massage cream, guaranteeing an end to the double chin and sagging skin. Jade turned the page and saw a final article about the producer, Graham Wheeler, shown astride a horse, his entourage just behind him. The caption described him as making a research journey through Abyssinia. Jade set the magazines aside to look at later and closed her eyes, hoping her headache would disappear. She felt, rather than heard, someone slip into the seat beside her.

"I hope you don't mind the intrusion, but I felt I had to talk with you."

Jade opened her eyes and sat up straighter. "What can I do for you, Miss Porter?"

"Please call me Cynthia. I just wanted a friendly ear, that's all." She fiddled with her hands, twisting them in her lap. "I suppose you think I'm horrid." Jade said nothing, giving the woman time to speak. "The truth is, I don't know how I can face *anything* now that Graham is gone. I did . . . I still do love him." She pulled a handkerchief from a pocket and dabbed at her eyes. "Making this picture seemed to be the most fitting tribute I could give."

"You don't have to prove anything to me, Miss, er, Cynthia. But if there's anything I can do, let me know."

"Just listening and believing me are enough," said Cynthia. "I know I couldn't say any of this to Bebe." She closed her eyes and shook her head. "I knew he was having an affair with her. He did have them, but he always came back to me." She opened her eyes, moist with tears, and turned to Jade. "I'll leave you alone now. Thank you."

Cynthia returned to her seat just as the sun set and the train turned north on its last leg to Moshi. It was as if a magician had covered his stage props with a black cloth, building the suspense before his final trick was revealed. The last Jade saw was forest and garden. What would be revealed when the cloth was pulled away? The expected? Or this time, would the magician amaze his audience with something new and startling? Whatever the outcome, this trick would demand her patience, for Ngai, the Maker, had no intention of revealing it before dawn.

The train stopped at Moshi, and everyone exited the car. Harry's headman, Nakuru, and their cook met them. Harry immediately secured the help of several natives to unload the gear while Jade gathered the movie crew onto the platform. Her efforts were interrupted by Harry's sharp swear, followed by his call.

"Jade! Seems we have a couple of stowaways."

CHAPTER 5

Kilimanjaro often reveals itself to distant travelers, allowing them a glimpse of its majesty, much like some king standing on a high balcony, waving to the crowds far below. But a true audience with this royal mountain is harder to receive.

—The Traveler

"STOWAWAYS?" JADE RAN TOWARDS HARRY. HE STOOD IN FRONT OF the baggage car, hands on his narrow hips, glaring at someone as yet hidden from Jade's sight. She heard a chirp, her first clue to the identities.

"Jelani?" she asked when she beheld the youth. He stood beside the crates, arms folded across his slender chest, face resolute and defiant. Biscuit, a makeshift leather leash tied to his collar, stood beside him. The lad wore the same knee-length shorts as in his teacher's hut, along with a faded brown long-sleeved shirt. The shirt was unbuttoned and the sleeves rolled up to his elbows. His feet were strapped into a pair of leather sandals that had been mended so often little remained of the original work. His black eyes locked onto Harry and, without so much as a glance in Jade's direction, he spoke.

"We are here, Simba Jike, to guard you."

Harry cut loose in a whoop of laughter, then stifled it when he saw Jade's serious expression. "The devil," he said. "And since when does Simba Jike need the protection of a boy? Or anyone, for that matter?"

Jelani did not deign to answer, but turned towards Jade and jumped out of the car. "My teacher sent me," he said.

Harry pulled his hat off and scratched his head. "I thought I saw one extra body when the gear was transferred at Voi. Rascal must have slipped out of the car unnoticed, carried boxes to the new cars, and just stayed in there, though how he managed to get Biscuit past everyone is beyond me."

"Jelani, I'm always happy to see you, but you'll be in trouble again. You don't have travel permits." Jade looked him over. "You must be thirsty and starving, too."

"Do not worry for me, Simba Jike." He held out the metal canister that contained his *kipande*, or documents. "You signed my paper to work for you, remember? I carried gourds of water and bought fruit at the Voi station. Biscuit hunted for birds when everyone ate in the station. I bought a chicken for him when you stopped today."

"You used your hut tax money to buy food?" asked Jade.

Jelani grinned for the first time. "No, I used the money that Bwana Nyati paid me for moving the boxes." He nodded in Harry's direction.

"The devil," repeated Harry. "Well, you're here, so I won't send you back. But I'm not paying you again."

Jelani shrugged.

"Leave him alone, Harry," said Jade. "Jelani works for me. I'll pay his wages." She turned back to the youth. "But why does your teacher think I need to be protected? He already warned me about two deaths. That was over when the African man killed the American in Nairobi and then himself."

Jelani shook his head. "No, Simba Jike. Remember! My teacher saw the graves on this mountain. He also saw a third grave. He said it will open soon and you must not fall into it."

"What the hell is he talking about?" snapped Harry. "We've got enough to handle without him stirring up trouble."

Jade held up a hand for silence. "Harry, Jelani is my responsibility."

"Then you can figure out where to put him."

"I will stay with the *mpishi*," Jelani declared, pointing to the cook. "Muturi is from my village."

"Good," said Jade. "Now, please say nothing more, Jelani. It will only frighten everyone needlessly. Since you brought Biscuit, I'm putting you in charge of him. Now, Harry, what next?"

Harry clamped his hat back on his head. "We sleep here tonight, and tomorrow we get ourselves up the mountain."

Sam had never felt so much like cursing as he did the afternoon after Jade left on the train. The thought of her on safari with Hascombe was maddening enough, but this feeling went beyond jealousy. Ever since Wheeler's stabbing, Sam had felt a gnawing worry eating at him. Something about the death felt wrong. He just couldn't put his finger on what.

Out of fuel for his plane, Sam reviled the ongoing fuel shortage that annoyed the Kenya colony. Unable to sort out his concerns aloft, he did the next best thing and lost himself in something mechanical. An engineer trained at Purdue University, Sam loved machines. He loved the way their parts meshed together and, by their interplay, created a whole greater than expected. He appreciated how they responded predictably to his care. Why weren't women like that? How could they be so much more complicated? His heart answered him.

Because, you dolt, they aren't machines. They're humans. Delightfully soft, unpredictable humans with minds of their own.

And no one, he reminded himself, had a more determined and intricate mind than Jade.

She's right. You'll have to learn to trust her. Unfortunately, trust wasn't the only issue.

Neville joined Sam at midmorning and together they worked on their invention. The improved coffee washer would be more efficient even at high volumes. Once it was finished, they'd patent it. Neville, who had a surprisingly good head for business despite his many half-baked ideas, such as herding crocodiles for leather, had developed a plan to start up a service of washing coffee raised by other farmers. Madeline, who had an even better head for business, had helped them determine the fees.

Maddy brought them lunch and lemonade at two. Little Cyril tagged along and they enjoyed an impromptu picnic. No one talked about the two events uppermost in their minds: Jade's safari and Wheeler's murder.

At sunset, Madeline reminded them of the Dunburys' invitation to dine with them. The men took turns washing the grease off themselves in the tin tub, put on clean clothes, packed Cyril into the old car, and drove into Parklands, just north of Nairobi.

Lord Dunbury's stone house made a splendid showing during the day, with its wide veranda, horse stables, and graceful gardens. Beverly had brought roses from England to replenish the ones that had suffered from neglect while they were away, and trained bougainvillea and other vines up wooden trellises.

By evening, most of the estate's delights were hidden or only hinted at by a perfumed scent or a distant whinny. Neville carried his sleeping son into the nursery to doze next to baby Alice Merrywether, then joined the others in the dining room.

"I hope you don't mind, Sam, but I don't have any coffee

made," said Beverly. "Without Jade to insist on it, it slipped my mind. Such a curious American custom, drinking it *with* a meal instead of after."

Sam shrugged. He found most British customs, such as afternoon tea, odd. At home, you went to the well and took a long draw of water or you guzzled cold lemonade, chilled with ice saved from a previous winter. But you didn't take half an hour to do it. He didn't want to talk about Jade's absence either.

"Don't give it a second thought, Beverly," he said, and changed the subject. "I suppose the papers have reported on Wheeler's murder?"

"Yes," said Avery. "A rather long article in *The Leader*. Mostly writing on the horror of the incident and how the police must do something about the native population lest we all be slain in our beds. That sort of rot."

"There was a second article on the visiting motion picture company," added Beverly. "It included a photograph of the principle actors, Miss Malta, Mr. Hall, and Miss Porter. The story related the topic of their picture and gave some of the details as to the plot."

"What is it about?" asked Sam.

"Very exciting," said Madeline. "It's both an adventure and a love story that takes place in two different times. It's based on a very ancient legend about Menelik the First, the son of King Solomon and the Queen of Sheba. He ruled Abyssinia, but it seems he went on a campaign through East Africa in his later years, conquering tribes and plundering their gold. While he was busy pillaging from the Maasai, he saw Kilimanjaro and felt induced to climb it. It proved more than a match for the old king and he knew he would soon die. So he called together his retinue and told them he would die as befitted a king. He would be buried at the summit."

Beverly, fingers wiggling with excitement, jumped in. "The legend says that he wore jewels, gold, and King Solomon's regalia when he was buried, and that he carried articles of power. Of course, they threw the slaves and concubines in with him."

"Naturally," said Avery. "I'd take mine." Beverly swatted at him playfully.

Madeline took advantage of Beverly's distraction to continue her tale. "There's some twaddle about a future heir finding the regalia and restoring Abyssinia to its former glory. But that's just half of the plot."

"Don't tell me," said Sam. "The actors are the brave explorers searching for the treasure and one of them is a reincarnation of Menelik."

"Very close," said Madeline. "One of them is also a reincarnation of Menelik's lover."

Sam shook his head. "Sounds like some terrible combination of every H. Rider Haggard book ever written."

"I forget. Who plays Menelik?" asked Neville. "And who is his lost love?"

"Conrad Hall is Menelik. He's also the explorer searching for the treasure."

"Then shouldn't he already know where to find it?" asked Neville. "I mean to say, if the chap is the reincarnation, he should already know."

"But he doesn't know," said Madeline. "Don't interrupt me, Neville. Where was I? Oh, Bebe Malta plays Menelik's lover in the past, but in the present, she's a hired servant girl who is looking for her lost love. Of course, the present-day Menelik is married, and that's where Cynthia Porter has her role. She's the explorer's long-suffering wife. Then there's the safari leader, played by Prentiss McAvy. And Henry Wells is a companion who is in love with the explorer's wife."

"Of course," said Avery. "Must have a love triangle. What does that redheaded man do? Woodrow something or other? And there's another man, a big, bulky fellow."

"Woodrow Murdock is the redhead. He's supposed to want the treasure for himself," said Madeline. "Which should mean he'll have to die in the end, I suppose. The other man is an extra as well as a stand-in for the dangerous scenes. I don't know his name."

"Roland Talmadge," said Avery.

"What does Miss Zagar do?" asked Beverly. "I should have thought she would be the lusty servant girl."

"That's most curious," said Madeline. "I don't think she actually has a role. I heard Mr. McAvy explain that they use her body for certain scenes instead of using Miss Malta's."

"I think I can understand that," said Avery. Neville nodded.

"Avery!" scolded Beverly. "You are behaving like a horrid male this evening." She smiled when she said it, and Avery responded with an answering grin.

Sam removed his napkin from his lap and placed it beside his plate. "Sounds like a picture I will miss. I'll stick to Hoot Gibson, if you don't mind. I can tell the bad guys there. But speaking as someone who's been on the backside of the camera, I can't see how they'll manage some of the scenes with Menelik. Shooting everything out-of-doors is very unpredictable."

"I'm sure some of it will be finished back in the United States," said Neville.

"That's right," said Beverly. "Inside in elaborate settings. That sort of thing is generally staged, I believe."

Then it hit Sam what was nagging him about Graham

Wheeler's murder. It was all too convenient and dramatically done to be real.

It was staged!

THE MOSHI STATION was far from lifeless at night. Dozens of African natives lined a wooden barricade. Most carried lanterns and all clamored to carry the luggage. Jade selected one man in a white robe to lead them to what passed for a hotel in Moshi while Harry and Nakuru saw to the baggage. She coaxed and scolded in turn, urging each person to carry his own valise.

The walk there resembled something out of an eerie dream, lit by a swaying lantern that appeared to be detached from the ghostly robe beside it. At times the lantern light caught the swish of Biscuit's tail or the pulsing of his powerful shoulders as the cheetah padded softly beside Jade. A smiling little Greek man met them at the door of his hotel and welcomed them in Swahili. Jade paid her guide before turning to the room arrangements.

"I need rooms for five women and thirteen men," she said, mentally adding up all the crew and assorted personnel.

That was the first difficulty. The man exclaimed that he had only ten rooms and two were already taken. The second problem arose when the proprietor discovered that three of the men were natives. He looked askance at Lwiza as well, dressed as she was in non-European clothes.

"They must find rooms somewhere else," he exclaimed.

"Saint Peter's bathtub!" muttered Jade. She turned and called for Harry's headman. "Nakuru. This man says you and Muturi and Jelani may not stay here."

"It is well, Simba Jike. Bwana Nyati and I have come to Moshi before. The *mpishi* and I have a place to sleep. We will take the young warrior with us."

Jade decided she wasn't sending Lwiza off to fend for herself. Everyone would have to double or triple up to begin with. "We will take the eight rooms," she said. Next came the hard part: convincing the director, actors, and cameramen to pair up. Harry suggested that, as safari leader, he should have his own room. Jade promptly put him with the director. Miss Malta agreed to let Lwiza stay with her, but the other two women refused to share a room with each other until Jade said it was that or sleep outside. In the end, Jade was the only one with a room to herself, primarily because no one else wanted to share it with a cheetah.

The rooms were clean, but Spartan, with creaky beds, sagging mattresses, and cracked cement floors. Each bed leg sat in a shallow tin of kerosene to keep the ants that emerged from the cracks at night from climbing into the beds. Harry urged everyone to stow their personal gear on top of the mattresses by their feet.

"Hell's bells, Hascombe," exclaimed Julian. "When I hired you, I didn't anticipate staying in . . . in a place like this."

Harry touched his hat brim and grinned. "No need to thank me, Mr. Julian. Although I can't promise anything this luxurious once we head up the mountain."

Julian stood by his open door, mouth agape as he stared at Harry.

"Don't worry, Mr. Julian," said Jade. "No ants would dare attack a big bwana's room. You'll be perfectly safe with Harry."

Harry and Jade roused everyone at dawn and herded them onto the veranda for a breakfast of eggs, fried sweet potatoes, and coffee. Jade bolted down her food, found Jelani and Muturi, and headed for the market. They'd brought along potted and jerked meat, but they needed fresh produce and eggs and a lot of chickens if Biscuit was to be fed. Cheetahs needed open space to run down prey, a commodity lacking on Kilimanjaro's slopes. She stepped off the veranda and stopped dead in her tracks, mesmerized by the sight of Kilimanjaro looming in front of her. The lush green of its base gave way to steppes and, eventually, the glistening ice and snowcap, shimmering with a pink blush in the early light.

Jade drank in the serene beauty of this ancient wonder. Born and grown in a violent, volcanic youth, as tempestuous and demanding as any conqueror, the mountain had eventually settled into a serene dignity. Once home only to myriad wildlife, it now tolerated newcomers on its slopes, feeding, sheltering, and watering them with a benevolence that came with old age. It was an elder with wisdom beyond any found in the villages. An elder revered even as the newcomers splattered the hems of its verdant robes with blood from sacrifices and war. It did not matter; a good rain always washed them clean.

Finally, after pulling her Kodak from her pack and trying to capture the mystical sight on film, Jade tore her gaze from the view and gave herself to the mundane task of buying food. They headed past a row of rectangular, mud-brick houses to the open marketplace. Moshi was home to several tribes: Nyamwezi, Swahili, Chagga, and a few Wapare, all of them represented in the market. All spoke Swahili ever since the Arab traders and slavers had made inroads from Dar es Salaam and Zanzibar long ago.

The Arab influence also showed in the men's attire. Most wore white robes and red *tarbooshes*, brimless, flat-topped hats shaped like an inverted flowerpot. Others wore turbans. The white robes reminded Jade of Morocco, and she fingered the silver amulet worn around her neck. She thought about the old Berber woman who'd given it to her, and smiled at the memory.

The Swahili women wore long dresses made by wrapping colorful cotton fabric around themselves and gracefully draping the ends over one shoulder, leaving the other bare. Like the men, they wore *tarbooshes*, but most were heavily decorated with swaths of fabric and dangling ornaments. They sat on the ground next to trays full of flatbread, or walked the market carrying the trays in their arms.

Most of the Chagga lived hidden in the forests on the lower slopes, but some had moved lower and farmed the land near Moshi. A few wore the coastal Arab clothing, but many, including the partially clothed women selling bananas, continued to wear skirts of animal skins.

Indian shopkeepers stood beside their doors, displaying gaudy fabrics, sandals, books, beads, and hoes. They called to Jade as she approached, holding out a particularly bright bit of cloth or a new *panga* knife.

Bananas, sugarcane, sweet potatoes, onions, peppers, flat loaves of bread, eggs, and the occasional chicken were all available, and it fell to Jade to haggle for supplies. Luckily, the cook, Muturi, was an experienced hand at it here. Harry had already brought along ample stores of flour, meal, and other nonperishables. Muturi suggested purchasing a milk goat, and Jade considered the possibility while examining some fresh tomatoes.

Finally, armed with enough food for the next week, a dozen chickens for Biscuit's dinners and six more for the crew, and three kid goats, and followed by six Nyamwezi lads to help carry it all, Jade returned to the hotel. She led a nervous nanny goat, bleating fretfully as Biscuit padded close behind it.

Harry had hired two trucks, one car, and enough Nyamwezi men to act as porters to carry their equipment to their first destination, an old farmhouse. They put the larger crates, goats, and the chickens in the truck beds and seated the men, including Jelani and Biscuit, on top of the boxes. The actors seemed delighted by the prospect of sitting next to the beautiful cat and laughed appreciatively. Harry drove one truck, and Julian drove the other. Jade piled the women and the valises into the old box-bodied car and took the wheel. The house stood thirteen miles from Moshi as the raven flew, twenty miles away as the road struggled to find the easiest path up the rugged, steep track.

Springs and streams cut across their route, the largest being the Una River. Plantain trees, tended by Chagga women, flourished alongside sycamores, olives, and baobabs. Abandoned rubber trees from some past venture scraped the roofs of the vehicles, and tree roots spread across and under the road as though they meant to trip these newest invaders. The route was rough enough to begin with, but it became worse from disuse once they'd passed the moss-covered ruins of a government fort near Marangu village.

Much to the chagrin of the actors, Harry ordered them to walk the last and steepest mile, saying that the engines had enough to pull with the gear. Nearly two hours later, they arrived at their base camp. The porters, led by Nakuru, who carried a sharpened *panga*, took a more direct but narrower route and arrived soon afterwards, the goat in tow.

Harry hadn't been joking when he told the director that their other shelters might not be as nice as the hotel. The farmhouse had been built by a German before the Great War, but he lost it when the territory passed from German hands. It had fallen into disrepair until one of the many Greeks in the area purchased it. He leased it to the occasional botanist or adventurer, not seeing the need to replace broken roof tiles or replace the stolen woodstove. Harry had used the house in the past with other clients and knew its advantages as well as its drawbacks as a base camp. He had omitted talking about the latter.

"There's clean water in the spring, and that's half of any successful expedition," Harry told them. "You can use the brick outbuilding to develop your film if you wish. We have a good cook, and before long, our neighbors will start coming to sell us their food, so we'll eat well."

The Americans stared at the stone bungalow with open mouths. "The windows are broken," said Hall, rubbing his backside, sore from the ride. "Someone could climb inside in the middle of the night."

"There'd be no reason for them to do so," replied Harry, "considering there's no lock on the door. But I assure you," he added hastily when Cynthia squeaked in alarm, "the Chagga have never bothered me before. I fail to see why they would this time."

"But there are women here," said Cynthia. "What will prevent them from . . . trying to accost us?" She sidled closer to Harry as though for protection.

"Begging your pardon, ma'am," said Harry, "but the Chagga rather prefer their own. Still, they might decide to take the fancy costumes, so I brought lumber and hardware to make shutters that we can latch from inside, and a new lock for the door. But first I need the men to make the chicken coop secure."

"The walls look good," said Jade, trying to promote the positive.

Harry nodded. "There's a decent parlor with a fireplace. It will act as our dining room. Then there's the old kitchen, which is empty. It's good for storage. And there are two bedrooms."

"Only two rooms to sleep in?" The complaint came from Bebe. She eyed the other women. "I had expected more privacy."

"You don't have to stay in the house," said Jade. "We brought plenty of tents. You wouldn't have to share one, and I'm sure that Mr. Julian would rather use the rooms for storage."

Pearl folded her arms across her ample bosom and hugged herself. "Is there a bathing room and a toilet facility?"

Harry pointed to a distant, smaller brick building. "The privy is over there. We have a tin tub, which I'll put in a separate bathing tent. The approved practice is to hang something on the pole when you go in so others know it's in use."

Bebe glared at the director. "Rex, I intend to be compensated for these . . . these hardships."

Julian pulled out a cigarette and lit it. "You'll have to take that up with our new producer," he said, pointing at Cynthia. "She holds the purse strings now." He took a long drag on his cigarette and blew out a lungful of smoke. "Anyone who wants use of the house, tell Mr. Hascombe. I presume you can set a cot up in the parlor, too?"

Harry nodded. "We're presently at the end of the dry season, so you could even sleep on the veranda. Nights get cold, but we have plenty of blankets."

In the end, the men and Pearl agreed to the tents. Bebe and Cynthia each took a room, and Jade put Lwiza in the former kitchen. Even with the camera equipment, costumes, and film taking up much of the space, there was more than enough room for her cot. Jade ordered a blanket hung as a screen for Lwiza's privacy.

"What about you, Jade?" asked Harry after the porters arrived and Nakuru had seen to the camp's setup. "You bunking inside or taking one of the tents?"

"A tent," she said as she watched the Nyamwezi men work

and the Americans break into small groups to walk around the area, talk, or just get in the way. Jelani, she noted, had tied Biscuit's leash to the veranda railing and was pitching in with the Nyamwezi. "Preferably not in the thick of things, either."

Harry moved closer beside her and whispered, "Of course, you could just—"

Jade turned and glared at him, her eyes snapping cold green fire. Harry backed off a step and put his hands up.

"I know," he said. "Shut up." He walked off laughing, his broad shoulders shaking.

At the moment, Jade's job consisted of placing the women in their respective rooms or tent and seeing that they each had a cot, blankets, and their personal gear. That and chasing a small rodent out of Bebe's room. She'd screamed for help, and Jade found her standing on her cot, a jumble of papers at her feet where they'd tumbled out of her hand. Jade grabbed a broom and swept the furry beastie outside, then came back to help Miss Malta pick up her papers—an assortment of letters, a Pond's massage cream ad, and several photos of herself.

Jade next went into Cynthia's room to see if she needed any help. The woman was stowing something under her cot's mattress and dismissed Jade with a smile. "I've been in far worse conditions," she said. "I'll be fine."

But many of the men turned to Jade for help. Steve Budendorfer came out of his tent in his stocking feet, a big toe protruding from his sock. "Hey, you wouldn't happen to have a file or scissors, would you? Maybe I could borrow your knife before I ruin another pair of socks?"

Jade shook her head. "You'd slice off your toe. Better ask one of the actresses."

Conrad Hall lost his hair cream, only to find the tube in his hip pocket when he sat down on it. Lloyd Brown went off snickering, leaving Jade to think this was no accident.

Nakuru proved to be an efficient headman, not unexpected, since he'd been with Harry since the Mount Marsabit safari in January and probably before that. This was Harry's second safari to Mount Kilimanjaro, so they already knew the location and the best arrangements. The director ordered a few of the tents to be set farther away, where he could film them without showing the rest of the camp.

Once her charges were squared away, Jade took a few photographs, including the house and Jelani. He'd moved on to assisting Muturi, the cook, who preferred using a fire pit outside to the hearth inside. Then she sat on the steps and took out her notebook and a pencil. She first wrote down her impressions of Moshi, the rough track up the mountain's base to this camp, and the farmhouse. Over the chatter of voices, she heard the spring's gentle burble, and beyond that, the push of water down the nearby Una River.

Jade pulled her knife from her boot and sharpened the pencil. As she did, she listened to some of the conversations and took mental note of the different affiliations. She wasn't motivated by idle curiosity. With this many people to manage, there were bound to be conflicts. The trick was to minimize them before they had a chance to develop and fester. That meant knowing the lay of the land.

Julian wasted no time. He had his assistant, Morris Homerman, as well as the two cameramen in tow, pointing out good places to set the cameras. The man seemed to be all boss and bully. Hall had pulled a sheaf of papers from his valise and was looking over them, sometimes striking a pose or practicing an expression. Another man ready to get to work, Jade presumed.

She saw Prentiss McAvy following Harry as he directed his camp. She assumed he was trying to get his role down as the fictional safari leader. The other men milled around more or less aimlessly, laughing and joking. The bulky Mr. Murdock had found a deck of cards and some chips and was playing poker with Talmadge and Wells. They invited Jade to join them.

"Later," she said. "When I'm sure there won't be another catastrophe calling me away."

Wells' gaze kept shifting from the game to follow Bebe as she wandered about the grounds, examining the clematis vines and the small patches of purple African violets.

"You in or out, Hank?" asked Talmadge, calling his attention back to the game.

"Out, I think," replied Wells, folding his cards.

Most noticeable to Jade was that none of the women gravitated to one another. Like Bebe, both of the others strolled the grounds, sometimes conversing with one of the men, sometimes looking at the scenery. They managed to veer away from one another before their paths intersected. Once, Cynthia's attention was drawn to an iridescent flash of wings as a bronze sunbird flew by. When she turned, she nearly collided with Bebe. Both women forced strained smiles before they continued on their separate ways.

They have to work together, but they don't have to socialize. Jade could almost feel the icy chill roll off them. Pearl, on the other hand, tended to follow the director or Harry. She struck Jade as a woman who collected men as a hobby. At least she and Cynthia didn't shy away from everything that fluttered or skittered, the way Bebe seemed to.

Where's Lwiza? Not seeing her outside, Jade closed her notebook and went in to find her. She felt sorry for the woman.

The hired men had one another to talk to, but Lwiza was essentially alone. Jade wondered if she might enjoy going into Moshi sometime to visit with the Swahili women there. They might not be from Zanzibar, but surely they still would have something in common, if only their language.

Jade found Lwiza in Cynthia's room, laying sheets on the cot. She rapped on the doorframe to announce herself and called *"Hodi?"* the Swahili equivalent of "May I come in?" or "Am I welcome?"

Lwiza looked up from her work and nodded. She continued smoothing the sheets, then turned to open a trunk. She moved gracefully with an easy but erect carriage.

Jade wondered if Cynthia had told her to unpack her things. She knew that Lwiza spoke English, but Jade decided to continue in Swahili to make Lwiza feel less alien among them.

Jade asked her how she was. "*Hujambo*, Lwiza?"

Lwiza straightened and met Jade's friendly smile with a serious look. "I would speak English," she said. "You want something?"

"No," Jade replied. "Only to see if you were all right. I'm supposed to look after *all* the women, not just the Americans. You are far from home. I thought you might enjoy going back to Moshi with me in a few days for more supplies. You could speak with the Swahili women."

Lwiza frowned and her shoulders twitched in what looked like a tightly controlled shudder. "Why? They are not as me."

"No," replied Jade. "I know they were born here in Tanganyika and not on Zanzibar. But I thought—"

Lwiza's delicate lips curved a fraction at the ends. "Thank you, *bibi*. I see you have a kind heart. But I have no desire to speak with those women."

She returned to placing a silken robe on the bed, and Jade had the distinct impression that she'd just been dismissed. "You must tell me, Lwiza, if there is anything you need."

"Yes, *bibi*. Now I must see to Missy Malta's room and Missy Zagar's tent."

Jade left her and, after giving the other rooms a cursory check, went to see how Jelani was faring. She found him assisting the cook at the back of the house. Biscuit lolled nearby and occasionally received tidbits of meat tossed to him from the stew pot. *So much for the hunting lesson.*

Muturi announced that the food was ready, and Harry ordered everyone in line. "There are wooden benches nailed to the floor in the dining room, and Nakuru has set up some camp tables. All very dignified, I assure you."

Jade remembered his penchant for using sturdy tin cups and battered enamel plates rather than the fragile china preferred by many customers. *Very dignified, indeed.* No one seemed to mind, however. The food was excellent and plentiful, including custard pie for dessert. At Jade's insistence, Lwiza joined them at the table. Jelani refused the invitation and ate with the cook, Nakuru, and the six Nyamwezi men retained to help with the work.

"I intend to start filming by nine tomorrow, so everyone should get to sleep," said Julian. No one protested the order. Bebe announced that she wished to bathe in the morning and ordered hot water to be ready for her at seven. After much jockeying for a turn at the privy before it became too dark to see without a lantern, everyone retired to their tent or room. Jade noted that no one had opted to share a tent with anyone else, so the grounds resembled an army encampment.

Her own tent had been set up on the western edge of the others, closer to the house. Harry's was on the eastern side so that none of the safari members were far from someone in charge. As she untied the flap strings and went inside, Biscuit joined her and claimed the spot directly under her cot. Jade slipped off her boots and removed her belt, but true to her habit on safari, she slept fully dressed, her knife and rifle close at hand.

The night passed uneventfully, troubled only by Jade's dream in which she kept trying to find Sam, only to watch him disappear every time she spied him. She woke at dawn, shook out her boots, and put them on. The cook was already up and had a chicken ready for Biscuit. The big cat took it, feathers and all, and retired to a private spot under an overgrown mango tree to eat. Jade rapped on Pearl's tent pole, then stepped inside the house and called at each woman's door to wake up. Next she went back out to consult with Harry about the day's orders.

Twenty minutes later they heard a woman's piercing scream coming from the bath tent.

CHAPTER 6

Kilimanjaro is host to a great assortment of plants and animals, making it a naturalist's dream whether his interest lies in butterflies, orchids, or mammals. Most of the latter are very shy, however, and consequently difficult to see.

—The Traveler

Jade ran towards the tent with Harry hot on her heels. He'd paused only long enough to snatch up his rifle. Jade had already pulled her knife and gripped it in her right hand. Bebe stood just outside the bath tent, wrapped in a knee-length cotton flannel robe. Her face had paled to an ashen white.

"What happened?" Jade asked.

"It's inside. Next to the tub." The actress whimpered. She rubbed the outside of her eye before brushing her finger across her nose. "A horrid black snake!"

Harry ordered her and everyone else but Jade back. Jade adjusted her grip on the knife, ready to throw it and impale the snake before it had a chance to strike. Mambas, for one, were notoriously fast and equally irritable. Harry held his rifle at the ready. He nodded to Jade to slowly pull back the tent flap.

Jade caught herself holding her breath and released it slowly. From farther behind her, she heard Bebe's stifled gasps and sobs. Jade moved the flap just enough for both her and Harry to see the thick-bodied black shape on the floor, tucked in the tub's protective shadow. It didn't move. Dead? Something about the eyes was all wrong. Harry saw it too. He lowered his rifle, and both of them moved forward, nearly colliding in the entryway.

"Be careful!" screamed Bebe.

Jade ignored the warning and picked up the black woolen sock, stuffed and painted to resemble a snake. She held it up for everyone to see. "It's fake!"

Harry muttered several ripe curses. Bebe closed her eyes and swayed. Once again, Wells hastened to her, but not before Harry caught her up with one arm. "It's all right, Bebe," he murmured. "You're safe."

Jade studied the reaction of the rest of the gathering group to gain a clue as to the practical joker's identity. She saw a mixture of relief and disappointment.

"Ah, nuts!" said Talmadge. "I wanted to see a real snake."

"But did you see how dramatic that was?" said Julian. "I want to use that in the picture. Not with that stocking puppet, mind you. Too fake-looking." He rubbed his chin as he thought. "Hascombe!" he shouted. "You could shoot a real snake somewhere. We could use the body."

Harry helped Bebe regain her feet before answering. "If you think I'm going to hunt up a live snake, you're out of your mind, Mr. Julian. I'll shoot one if it slithers into my camp or bars my path, but otherwise, I suggest you make a more believable fake."

"But how?"

Jade tossed the stocking snake to the director. "Mold one out of clay and bake it," she suggested. "That's what the women potters in Morocco do."

"You're joking, right?" said Julian. "I'm supposed to set up a pottery kiln out here?"

Jade shrugged. "Dig a pit, layer dry brush and wood over the clay, light it. Cover the coals with dirt to hold in the heat. Or just let it sun-dry. Maybe someone in Moshi could make one for you. But Harry's right. We're not hunting a real snake."

She slipped her knife back in her boot sheath and walked off, signifying the end of the discussion. As she neared Bebe, the woman grabbed her sleeve. "Miss del Cameron. Have you any idea who pulled this terrible joke?"

Jade shook her head. "None at all. I looked at everyone's faces, but no one revealed anything." Although, she thought, both Budendorfer and Brown looked more amused than annoyed. She remembered the former's ruined pair of socks. "No harm done, Miss Malta. You should take your bath before the water chills."

"I don't think I can ever feel safe bathing here again," she exclaimed. "You will stand guard, won't you? Please? I'd ask Harry, but I'm sure he has more important jobs to do."

Jade sighed, resigning herself to being a nanny for these women. *As long as she doesn't expect me to patrol outside her room at night.* "I'll wait near the tent if it makes you feel more comfortable, ma'am." She found a camp stool and took a seat a few feet away from a front corner tent peg. Harry strode over a few minutes later.

"On the job, I see," he said. Then he lowered his voice. "Better you than me. Now you know why I wanted you hired on. I learned my lesson on Marsabit. Women on a safari can be more work than men. Not," he hastened to add, "that *you* were any trouble in Tsavo."

"Neither was Beverly or Madeline," Jade added, defending her friends lest they be lumped into Harry's category of troublesome women.

"You're right on the mark there, Jade," he said, still speaking very softly so the actress couldn't overhear him. "But you're all a different breed of woman than these pampered dolls. You're a *real* woman, the way they were meant to be."

Jade didn't care for the turn this conversation was taking. She remembered when Sam found her photograph tucked in one of Harry's books. "Harry, I don't think you—"

"Let me finish. I know we've had our differences, and maybe we didn't get off on the right foot back then."

"As I recall, you were drunk and rode your horse into the Norfolk Hotel lobby to shoot it up when we first met. Then you took over my safari and tried to pawn off that bastard—"

"But I'm a *different* man now, and I want you to see that. Now, I'll be the first to admit that Featherstone is a . . . decent sort of bloke, in his own way. But even I can see that he's pressing you. Otherwise your good-byes would have been more, shall we say, congenial?" His voice took on a hypnotically soothing pitch. "*I'm* not that way. I know now that it's the wrong way to treat a woman like you."

He paused and rubbed his chin stubble. "So I just wanted to put you at ease, Jade. I hired you because you're good at the job. I'd be lying if I said I didn't have feelings for you, but you needn't worry about my chasing you around the camp making declarations. You know my mind. If you should ever change yours, you know where to find me."

With that he turned and walked off, leaving Jade feeling slightly stunned. She'd been waiting for advances from Harry and was prepared to deal with them either verbally or physically. She hadn't expected him to behave like a gentleman. *Sam would have a thought or two on that score.*

Bebe came out of the tent, wrapped in her robe, a towel draped over one arm. "I am finished, Miss del Cameron. Thank you so much. You may do whatever it is you need to do with my bath."

Jade stretched out her long legs and crossed them at the ankles. "You misunderstand my role, Miss Malta. Mr. Hascombe hired me to make certain that your needs are looked to and that none of you are smuggling guns or hiding explosives in your lip rouge. If I need to kill a snake, I can do that, too, but I'm not your maid. I will tell one of the hired men that you're finished."

Bebe took a step back and raised her chin a touch higher. "I beg your pardon," she said icily. Then, pursing her lips, she seemed to think better of her words, pulled over a nearby chair, and sat down next to Jade. "I do apologize, Miss del Cameron—"

"Jade."

Bebe smiled. "Very well, Jade. I think I was still reacting from that fright." She chuckled softly. "In retrospect, I suppose it seems silly, doesn't it? Taking fright from a sock puppet, but after that horrid night at the Muthaiga . . ." She covered her face with her hands. "Forgive me. It's just too much to handle." She sat up straighter and sniffed. "I loved Graham so much. And to think he died defending me . . ." She sobbed once and rose. "I think I need to be alone for a while."

Jade wondered if she should follow when she heard a soft, purring laugh nearby. Pearl Zagar stepped into view. The woman walked with a slow, languid movement, accentuating her curvaceous build without the usual hip wiggle that Jade saw some women affect. Her riding breeches hugged her hips like a second skin, and her white linen blouse was unbuttoned down to her cleavage. "Poor dear," Pearl said.

"Good morning, Miss Zagar," Jade replied, wondering who Pearl meant.

"Please. Call me Pearl. And may I call you Jade? It would

be nice to have another woman to talk to out here. One I don't have to try to upstage, if you know what I mean."

Jade nodded. "Have a seat. I seem to be holding court this morning."

Pearl moved the other camp stool and sat down a few feet from Jade, facing her. "Jade," she repeated. "What a seductive name. I wish I'd thought of it. Rather makes us the two gems of the camp, doesn't it?"

Jade's shoulders twitched in a brief chuckle. "I doubt many people would agree with you. At least as far as *I'm* concerned. I'm more frequently associated with annoying animals that people tend to shoot. You're familiar with the term 'varmint,' aren't you?"

"Hmmm. I suppose that is more in keeping with the image you're cultivating," Pearl said. When Jade arched her brows, the young actress shifted her position in the chair and added, "I wasn't implying that you're a phony, Jade. On the contrary. I think *you're* the real deal. But maybe that's why I usually find men so much more agreeable than women. They're less deceptive about what *they* want from me." She crossed her legs and leaned forward. "Tell me *your* story."

"I'm not certain what you mean." First names or not, Jade didn't care to confide her life story to this woman. "I grew up on a ranch. I drove an ambulance during the war, I came to Africa afterwards, and I like it here."

Pearl's lips twitched in amusement. "Succinct. How did you happen to fall into our little party?"

Jade shrugged. "I write stories for *The Traveler*. I plan to write one on Kilimanjaro, so this job gives me a chance to see it *and* get paid for the trip." She decided the best way to shift the conversation from herself was to redirect it to Pearl. "Tell me about your part in this movie."

Pearl rolled her eyes, made more expressive by thickly applied mascara and carefully plucked brows. "*My* part!" She twisted her body in the seat, straining her blouse. "You're looking at my part, if you catch my meaning. Rex didn't think Bebe's body was good enough anymore to play Menelik's seductive lover. But our dearly departed producer was head over heels for her, so she got the role. Though," she added, "I'm not sure she could have kept it." Pearl's lips twitched in a knowing smile. "One overhears things, you know. Trouble in paradise."

Jade pondered this information. "I don't understand what Mr. Julian didn't like about Miss Malta's figure. She's very pretty." She felt uncomfortable engaging in gossip, but she needed to understand what motivated these people.

Pearl's lips twitched again. "Yes, she is rather well preserved for a woman her age." When Jade didn't prod her for details, she continued. "Bebe's thirty if she's a day, no matter what *Cinema* writes about her." She snorted. "Bebe's not even her real name. Not that most of us use ours. Who would want to see an actress named Prudence Schiffenstrasse? Not," she hastened to add, "that she hasn't had a fine career. She's been in pictures since the start, but age doesn't play on the screen. She just won't admit it and accept the older roles like Cynthia has."

"If I'm understanding you correctly," said Jade, "they use you to play some of Miss Malta's scenes, but don't film your face?"

Pearl shrugged. "That about puts the bow on the box. Oh, I'll wear the same wig. And our faces are not all that different when you get down to it. My eyes are a bit more hazel than brown, but that won't show on the screen. Not with the stage makeup we'd wear and the softened blur of the lens." She stretched like a sleepy house cat. "But I still might end up with the part of Menelik's lover all for myself."

Harry marched by on his way to Nakuru, and Pearl watched him intently. "Now, *that* is an intriguing man," she said. "How well do you know him, Jade?"

"He's a good safari leader," she said. "Beyond that, I don't want to know more."

Pearl chuckled. "Hmm. I'd like to add him to my collection. I hear the natives call him Bwana Nyati. What does Nyati mean?"

"Buffalo."

"Buffalo? For his, er, *prowess*, I suppose?"

"More likely for his thick skull," said Jade.

They watched as the director and the cameramen set up the cameras by one cluster of tents. "Looks like Rex is ready to crank film," Pearl said. She smiled. "Lovely talking with you, Jade. I'd better make my presence known, even if they don't need me today. You never know, do you?"

Jade had met her share of cold, calculating women, but this one made her skin crawl. Was that what came from always being in the public eye? She thought about Sam's film. He had cut and edited for two weeks, using the darkroom bungalow built by the Dunburys. Then they'd all congregated at the Theatre Royal to watch it. Sam had bribed the projectionist into letting him use the equipment late one night in return for a ride in Sam's airplane. *African Dreams* was wonderful, and Maddy, a settler's wife, came to life on the screen with warmth, courage, and beauty unalloyed with anything artificial. Jade stood and slipped her rifle over her shoulder. No, Maddy would not feel at home with these people.

A group of Chagga natives emerged from the nearby forest. Jade counted seven men, six with the more traditional leather or rusty-colored cloth wrapped about their waists. One wore castoff khaki shorts. Partially hidden back in the trees were several girls laden with baskets of produce. The man in the shorts, acting as leader, motioned for the others to wait. Then he strode confidently towards Harry. Jade joined him as they exchanged greetings in Swahili.

"This is Zakayo," Harry told everyone. "He speaks Swahili pretty well in addition to the Chagga language, Machame, and a smattering of English, probably more than he admits. I hired him as an interpreter on my last trip. He duly noted our arrival and came back, bringing men with him to hire and some of the belles to sell us food. He's trustworthy enough, although he drives a hard bargain."

"We'll need fruit and vegetables in a few days," agreed Jade, "and I don't relish making the trip back to Moshi often. Do you think we can buy more chickens? Biscuit alone will need at *least* one a day."

"And an extra goat every now and then would be a good idea, too," said Harry. "Hunting's not all that easy here. Too much chance of hitting a passing native in the forest."

"Hascombe!" shouted Julian. "Hire those men to be in the picture. I'll want them here each morning, but I can't guarantee what day I'll actually use them."

"As long as you're paying them, they won't mind sitting and waiting," said Harry. "Something tells me they're going to find this very entertaining. You might end up with the entire village coming in."

"I don't want the village," Julian said. "Well, I do, but I'll go there to film it. Arrange it for me. And make sure that interpreter is with us when we go."

Harry touched his hat brim. "Yes, sir." He turned back to Jade and muttered, "Blasted son of a cross-eyed mongoose. I feel like a ruddy butler." He explained the situation to Zakayo, who listened with a growing smile as the remunerative possibilities dawned on him. The two dickered back and forth, bargaining for the men's time.

"The men have much work to do in the village. Fields to clear, herds to protect," Zakayo said, adding to the litany of improbable chores.

Jade knew that the women did the gardening work and children often tended the flocks. But it made a good story, and Harry, for his part, didn't contradict the little man. In the end, they agreed on a daily wage for the men, as well as a higher one for Zakayo. After that, bargaining for food went relatively quickly.

"He's agreed to a chicken a day unless we ask for more and a set price for every basket of vegetables and fruit. You should see to that," Harry suggested, "considering the women will bring the produce in. Have the cook inspect it all first before you buy it."

"What about your goat?"

"All taken care of," said Harry. "He'll—" Harry stopped abruptly as shouting reached them. "Now what!"

Jade listened to the two voices, trying to identify the speakers. "That's Jelani," she said, and took off at a run.

Jelani stood outside Jade's tent, feet apart, his arms folded across his chest. "No one enters Simba Jike's tent," he declared.

Lwiza stood facing him in an equally defiant pose, both her chin and her hand raised in front of Jelani's face. The woman was two inches shorter than Jelani, but her posture made it painstakingly clear that she did not intend to back away meekly. "It is my duty to see to her tent," she said. "As I see to the other women."

"Stand down, you two," said Jade. When neither of them

shifted so much as an eyelash, she rephrased her order. "Stop it now!"

Their postures relaxed a fraction. Lwiza's hand lowered till it was even with her waist. Jelani's hands went to his hips. Both of them turned their heads a few degrees in order to see both Jade and each other.

"What is this *shauri* all about?" Jade demanded. She was uncomfortably aware of all eyes watching her. As in a pack of dogs or wolves, her status as a high-ranking animal would be determined by Jelani's and Lwiza's responses to her challenge. There was a time when Jade would have bet on Jelani's reaction, but not anymore. Neither of them answered. "Jelani?"

The youth—a boy in her culture, an adult in his—turned towards her, his head high. He matched her for height now, but Jade didn't care if he towered over her.

"This woman"—he jerked his chin in Lwiza's direction—"was inside your tent. I pulled her out. When she would go back inside, I blocked the way."

"Lwiza?" Jade asked, waiting for her version.

"I entered to repair? No, to smooth your cot, *bibi*. I am your maidservant, am I not?"

Jade smiled to soften her next words. "No, Lwiza. You are not. I do not need or want a maidservant. I thank you for wanting to tend to me. But you have enough duties as it is."

Lwiza bowed and turned to leave. Jade let her go, but motioned for Jelani to sit down. With no prospects of anything entertaining, the Americans returned to their spots for their scene. Jade pulled up another folding camp chair and sat facing Jelani. She leaned forward, her forearms resting on her thighs, her hands clasped.

"Now, please tell me what this was about, Jelani," Jade said in a soft voice to prevent further eavesdropping.

"That woman had no business in your tent, Simba Jike."

"Isn't that for me to determine, Jelani?" She sat back and crossed her legs, purposely adopting a more relaxed pose to put him at ease. From behind her, she heard Julian's stentorian bellows for someone to bring him a chair. "I'm happy to see you again, but maybe it is time now for you to explain why you're here."

"My teacher told me to come. He placed a great task on my shoulders. I am here to protect you, Simba Jike."

Jade shook her head. "I don't understand. I'm not in any danger. These people," she said, and waved her arm to the side, "are playactors. You've seen movies at the mission house before. They've only come here to make a movie. They aren't even hunting. Their guns shoot blanks."

Jelani's gaze never left Jade's face. He watched her with the look of a patient grown-up trying to convince a child of what was best. Jade noted the look. "Very well," she said. "From what do I need protecting?"

"From danger."

"I could use something a little more specific, Jelani. Is an animal stalking me? Are the Chagga going to attack? Is a German soldier still hiding here ready to fight the war?"

"My teacher does not know what form death is taking this time, Simba Jike. But he has seen its shadow hugging your trail. He would have come himself, but he is too old. So he sent me. I will guard you, but I will do more. I will use what he has taught me to hold back death."

Jade sighed and examined her hands a moment while she decided just how to respond. "Jelani, I thank you very much. And I thank your teacher. It's good to have people care for me. But I do not . . ." She stopped herself and tried again. "I would prefer not to wear any more of his potions or charms."

"It protected you from the witch and his animals when you first came," Jelani retorted.

It smelled to high heaven and kept everyone away. She held that thought to herself. "I believe in your friendship, Jelani, but you must know that I don't believe in your teacher's magic."

Jelani's brows rose in puzzlement. "But I have heard you and other white people talk of such magic. Do you not say to each other, 'I will pray for you' when someone needs help?"

"Of course, but—"

"And you speak to the Maker and ask him to protect someone or to heal them."

"Yes, but that is not magic, Jelani. That is prayer."

Jelani stood. "The Kikuyu pray to the Maker, too. We pray with beads and plants and our chants. You do not have to believe in magic, Simba Jike. You only have to believe in my prayers. I have come to protect you. And I will."

He walked off, his head high, his step proud. Jade watched him and sighed. Under her breath she muttered softly, "Just no stinky prayers, please."

The second-floor waiting room had comfortable chairs, and the curtained windows let in just enough light to see while holding back the strong afternoon glare.

"Dr. Mathews will see you now, Mr. Featherstone," said the nurse, a woman in starched whites with an expression out of the same starch vat.

"Thank you, Nurse." He followed her into the doctor's examining room.

"Mr. Featherstone?" said the doctor, rising to shake Sam's hand. "The nurse said you would not give her a reason for your call." He observed Sam's slight limp. "Is your leg troubling you?"

Sam sat in a black leather chair and rapped his knuckles against his lower right leg. "No, Still solid. No termites." He took advantage of the doctor's stunned silence and went straight to the point. "I'm interested in that native man that killed the American at the Muthaiga Club the other night. I was there, if you recall, and witnessed the man stab himself in the chest. As I remember, you made an observation to Inspector Finch that the man may have been under the influence of some drug."

Dr. Mathews' right hand went to his clean-shaven chin and stroked it absentmindedly, as one would a goatee. Sam wondered if he'd recently shaved one off. He thought he detected a paler hue from the rest of the well-tanned face. The doctor had the appearance of an outdoorsman, a man of action.

"Ah, Mr. Featherstone," said Mathews, "I am not certain I understand your purpose here. Are you a reporter? Or a criminologist?"

"No, sir," said Sam. "I'm a pilot and an engineer, and neither of those has any bearing on this case. But I am interested in the young lady who also saw the stabbing. She's on safari with the rest of the Americans right now, somewhere up on Kilimanjaro. I want to make sure she's not in any danger."

The doctor's lips twitched. "Ah, Miss del Cameron. Lovely young lady. Naturally, you are interested. Of course. But the native man who murdered the American is now dead. So what harm could come to her?"

Sam ran his hand through his hair. "Well, sir, that would frankly take too long to explain adequately. You'll just have to trust me on that."

Trust me! That was what Jade kept telling him.

Mathews pulled open a drawer and took out a leather-bound notebook. He opened it, flipped past several pages, and paused to read. "It is an interesting case, Mr. Featherstone, although I'm certain there is no mystery here. So I feel quite safe in telling you this. I noticed that the native had very dilated eyes. Of course, it was night, but he was found lying within a bright pool of light from an outside lamp. During that struggle, I would have expected him to stare into that light at least once."

"So his pupils would have constricted then."

"Correct. But that is, of course, hypothetical at best. Still, a man does not stab himself easily. It suggested strong agitation. And he'd clawed at himself. I also noted that he wore only a cloth wrapped around his loins." He stopped to examine his notes again.

"Is that so unusual, Doctor?" asked Sam.

"No. But the white cloth was made of a poor-quality linen. The Kikuyu and Wakamba tribesmen who still sometimes opt for undress despite the law tend to wear a tanned animal skin or a castoff pair of shorts. I have never seen one with a linen wrap."

"So he was not one of the local tribesmen," summarized Sam.

"That was my conclusion. I mentioned as much to Inspector Finch. I believe he was hoping to find the man's identity and has sent a set of fingerprints to Mombassa."

"I still don't understand what any of this has to do with whether or not the man was drugged, Doctor."

Mathews nodded. "Nothing as yet. But something about his garment made me wonder if he'd removed others first. Perhaps with a mind to keeping them free of blood from his victim. The inspector agreed and had his men conduct a search for any clothes. They found a white robe, also cheap linen, but it was ripped at the throat and the sleeves."

Sam leaned forward. "Freshly ripped? Or as if they were just old clothes?"

The doctor smiled. "Ah, you have a clever mind, Mr. Featherstone. You think of alternatives. They *were* freshly rent. The man seemed to have torn them off of himself, just as he tried to scratch his skin off. That suggested to me the poison found in datura. I was in India and the Thugees used it to poison robbery victims. Plucking at one's skin or the air and pulling off the clothes as though they irritated the skin was common, as were dilated pupils."

"Was it datura?"

"My autopsy indicates it was. I found venous congestion of the brain among other symptoms. I have made a sort of study of poisons, you see."

"I'm confused," said Sam. "You said this substance was given to robbery *victims*? But it wasn't the victim, Wheeler, who had taken it."

"No. But in smaller doses, it can make the user feel invincible, render him impervious to pain, and cause erratic behavior. So if this man took it, even accidentally, he was acting under its influence. That is why he killed Mr. Wheeler. We also found a leather flask of sorts with his clothes. Some sort of alcohol inside. I tested it for a vegetable mydriatic alkaloid with a Vitali's test. Very simple. A few drops of nitric acid, evaporate to dry, add potassium hydroxide." The doctor rattled off the steps as though they were known to anyone. "A positive result is a particularly vivid reddish violet color." He finished by clapping his hands together and rubbing them. "The short of it is, Mr. Featherstone, that the man is dead and not on the mountain with your young lady."

Sam leaned forward and fixed his gaze on the doctor's face. "No, sir. There still remains a very important question. Did this native take the poison on his own or was it given to him by someone else? Someone still out there. Maybe even on Kilimanjaro."

CHAPTER 7

Elephants, great gray ghosts, manage to hide their bulk behind moss-festooned trees; at least the ones that they don't pull down.

—The Traveler

"No! You are supposed to be secretly in love with *HER*. You're acting more like you're stuck on her husband." Julian ranted for two minutes over the scene, to the amusement of the Chagga men who'd come every day to watch the antics and sometimes to play in a scene. "Now try it again, Hank, and get it right this time."

"How was I, Rex?" asked Cynthia.

"Not bad, but I need more. Remember, you're conflicted, torn. You love your husband, but you know you're losing him to this illusion of his. You're tempted to collapse into Hank's arms. I want to see that struggle."

Wells and Cynthia took their positions again, she next to Hall in front of the tent.

Jade leaned against an old orange tree and watched. Biscuit lay at her feet, his tongue lolling. Three days had passed since the stocking snake incident and two days since someone had rigged a pot of cold water to dump on the first person who entered the privy one morning. That day it was Harry, and after he'd roared at the crew, not much else had happened short of some items that had gone missing. Bebe and Pearl lost makeup, Hall lost his suspenders, and Homerman's keys routinely disappeared.

Bebe and Pearl were both slobs, so it was no wonder their items weren't immediately at hand. Hall's suspenders had reappeared hanging from a mango tree fork, where some fun-loving person had used them as a slingshot to fire ripe fruit, and Homerman, Jade concluded, was an incompetent boob, pure and simple.

In the end, everyone had settled into the routines at camp and accepted the discomforts without too much grumbling. Jade found herself actually respecting and even liking some of them. Brown and Budendorfer might be practical-joking scamps, but their good-natured personalities made it hard even for Harry to dislike them. Bebe was a consummate professional, but once she was off-camera, she was hopeless on safari. Cynthia, on the other hand, had obviously roughed it before and even lent a hand around the camp. Jade caught the widow with a sad, faraway look in her eyes, and thought she might be attempting to keep busy rather than confront her loss. It was a concept Jade appreciated. Work was often a good remedy for sorrow.

Jade's own work was limited, now that they'd arrived, leaving her time for silent reflection and for poker games with Talmadge, Wells, and Murdock. She felt like screaming from boredom. She longed to attempt the climb to the summit, or even to spend more time in the forest, but there was little need for her to go out of camp, nor did Harry want her to.

"You're not leaving me alone with those women," he'd said.

"Ah, balderdash, Harry," she'd retorted. "I've seen you strut past them. You'd *love* to be alone with them."

At least yesterday's excursion to the French Catholic mission at Kilema had given Jade an opportunity to see more than clusters of tents and overgrown orchards. She rubbed her calves again. The four-mile hike overland to the mission had taken her across bridges of felled timber and along winding trails used by both the Chagga and smaller game animals. On the return trip, Jade had spied a colony of tree hyrax that screamed when she passed by.

Nakuru, more familiar with the mountain than Jade, had accompanied her both ways. Jelani, to her surprise, had not. When she'd asked why, he'd explained that, at present, she was in no danger outside of camp. Now her gaze drifted from the actors to her tent, which was festooned with feather fetishes and marked with charcoal symbols, evidence of Jelani's "prayers."

"That's it, Conrad," said Mr. Julian. "Look off up towards the mountain. You can hear it calling to you."

"You can't see it for the forest down here," muttered Harry as he joined Jade. A scruffy growth of brown whiskers flecked with gray coated his chin, accentuating his strong jawline. He'd unbuttoned the top buttons of his shirt, exposing a tuft of chest hair.

Jade wondered whom he was trying to impress with his rough looks. She shifted a little to make room for him. "I think," she replied, "they'll cut in some scenes showing the mountain."

As they watched, Bebe, dressed in a white robe, slunk beside Hall and pointed up, murmuring entreaties. She kissed his hand and whispered into his ear, all the while casting a triumphant sneer towards the hapless wife.

"Good gad," said Harry. "Bebe's look would curdle milk. She's quite an actress."

"Hmm," mused Jade. "Yes, she is, but I'm not sure she's acting there. I don't think she likes Miss Porter."

"Wonderful, Bebe," exclaimed Julian. "You know you possess him now. Hank, that's your cue. Try to turn him around."

Wells took three long strides towards the mesmerized Hall and placed one hand on his right shoulder. He pleaded, pointing to the stricken wife with one hand, tugging with the other.

"Cynthia, you cannot abide this any longer. Fling yourself at his feet," shouted Julian.

Cynthia did, grabbing Conrad's free hand. "Turn, Conrad," prompted Julian. "Look at the woman at your feet. Look at your friend. You don't know who they are anymore. You're a king! How dare they lay hands on you."

Hall's face underwent the requisite contortions, from confusion to pride followed by fury until he threw Cynthia's hand from him, striking her across the face. Bebe positively crowed with glee as she wrapped her arms around her reincarnated king.

"Comfort her, Hank. You love her. You long to tell her. Great! Cut!" He motioned for Budendorfer to move the camera back. "Listen, people. We're almost finished with this setting. We're going to shoot some scenes in a native village this afternoon. Then tomorrow, we're heading high up the mountain above the forest. Make sure all the Menelik stuff is ready to go. We're going to shoot his expedition first."

He looked around, searching for someone. "Hascombe."

Harry pushed himself away from the tree and straightened. "Wait till he finds out that we can't leave that soon," he mumbled. "What do you need, Mr. Julian?"

"I need that translator. He told me yesterday that there's an old man in one of the villages who can help me."

"There's an old man in every one of the villages," Harry said. "What makes this one so blasted special?" He folded his arms across his chest, peering down at the director in a lordly manner.

"He's had some stories handed down to him for generations. I think he knows something about this Menelik legend."

Harry looked at Jade and half rolled his eyes. "By all means. But I wasn't told about this, so I doubt we'll go today. Do you even know where this village is?"

Mr. Julian shrugged. "It can't be far, can it? We'll simply stop by on our way up."

Harry took off his hat and slapped it against his thigh for emphasis. "It could be on the other side of the bloody damn mountain for all we know." He replaced his hat, turned towards the Chagga audience, and called for Zakayo to join him.

"Did you tell that bwana," he said, nodding to Julian, "that you could take him to see an elder storyteller?"

Zakayo nodded vigorously. "Yes, Bwana Nyati. He asks about an ancient king that came from very far to see the mountain. A king called God's lion. I told him I know a very old man who has heard of this story. The bwana promised much money to take him there."

"Very good," said Harry. "Now, where is this man's village? Is it a far walk?"

Zakayo pointed to the Una River. "We follow water up the mountain. His village is there."

After several more minutes of patient questioning, Harry determined that the village was actually Zakayo's and only a mile upriver. He arranged for Zakayo to take them there tomorrow.

"We'll leave at first light," said Harry. "And we'll come back here afterwards."

Mr. Julian's eyes opened wider in affronted astonishment. "Then we'll go today," he shouted. "It's only a mile."

"It's *probably* only a mile away," corrected Harry. "It could take us an hour to get there, lugging the cameras. And unless you plan to stay the night in the village, you're going to be walking in a very dark forest with a few nocturnal predators, including leopards."

He stood his ground as Julian stormed within a few inches of Harry's face and jutted out his chin. "Mr. Julian," Harry said, keeping his voice calm, "I know these natives better than you. You can't just walk in there, demand a story, and get it. You need to introduce yourself. Bring a gift. Exchange pleasantries. Then, when this elder feels he can trust you, he *might* tell his story, but he'll embellish it, draw it out. A short tale carries no distinction. He'll be all day about it."

The director moved back one step and looked around the camp as though deliberating. Harry waited, his hands in his pockets. "After considering your advice, Hascombe," Mr. Julian said, "I've reached a decision. We'll leave tomorrow right after breakfast."

Harry nodded. "Excellent. How many are going besides yourself and a cameraman?"

"What do you think, Morris?" he asked his assistant. "We might as well make use of the village while we're there. Get some scenes of the present-day safari as though they're asking about the same story, right?"

Mr. Homerman, a quintessential yes-man, nodded in agreement. "Certainly, Rex. You'll want both cameras for different angles. And you'll need everyone but Miss Zagar, I should think."

"I'm not staying here by myself," said Pearl. "I want to see this, too."

"Hmm," mused Julian. "We'll need Hascombe's natives. And that girl we hired for a maid. She should come in case one of the actresses needs her. Hell, might as well bring up everyone."

"We've got to leave some of my men behind to guard the camp," said Harry. "I want the cook and Nakuru to stay here. Nakuru can pick two men to go with us."

"Yeah. I suppose you're right, Hascombe. That's what I had in mind anyway." Mr. Julian started barking orders to everyone. "Listen up. We're all going into the forest tomorrow. So get ready whatever you need to take. We're gonna shoot a new scene. It's not in the script."

He proceeded to explain everyone's role. Jade looked around for Lwiza and Jelani. She needed to tell Lwiza how to dress for the walk and wanted to learn what Jelani's plans were. Lwiza, she noted, was engaged in bargaining with a Chagga woman for a pawpaw. Before she could locate Jelani, Harry joined her.

"Bloody dictator," he said, jerking his chin towards Julian. "Wonder if he plans to tell the Chagga how to act. This ought to be interesting tomorrow."

"I presume we've got something to give to the elder as a gift for his story," said Jade.

Harry rubbed his chin bristles and frowned. "But what? You got any ideas in that pretty head of yours?"

"What about one of the props?" suggested Jade.

"The what?"

"Props, Harry. The stuff they set around in their scenes. They've surely got something they don't need in there. Something for their Menelik tent scenes."

"Good idea, Jade. What's one less gaudy brass vase, right?" Harry jerked a finger towards the director. "Go ask him."

Jade laughed. "*You* ask him. I'm in charge of the women, right?"

Harry shifted his feet and rubbed his jaw. "Man's a bloody nuisance."

"Oh, come now, Harry. You're not afraid of him, are you?" Jade asked, goading him into action. "Who's the big bwana here?"

Harry grinned and puffed out his chest. "I am. *I* give the orders."

Jade saw the glint in his brown eyes and didn't like the turn this conversation was taking. "Now, wait a minute, Harry," she began.

He planted a quick kiss on her cheek, darting back before she could belt him for the impertinence. "And I'm ordering *you* to see to this petty detail," he said. "I've got a camp to run." He pivoted on one heel and strode off, his rumbling laugh drifting back to her.

"You'll pay for this, Harry," Jade called after him. "Me and my big mouth," she muttered, rubbing her cheek. She looked for the director and spied Homerman fidgeting with a stack of papers. Suddenly, she had an idea of her own. Harry had passed on the chore to *his* second in command, so she'd do the same and approach Julian's assistant.

"Mr. Homerman," she called, "I need to speak with you a moment." Jade explained their need for a gift to give to the Chagga elder. "I've seen all the brass- and tin-plated dishes you brought for your historical scenes. Surely you can spare something out of those boxes." As she spoke, she took his arm and guided him towards the bungalow and the stored props.

"Well, I suppose . . ." he mumbled.

"Exactly what I was thinking, Mr. Homerman. Better to

grease the wheels and get the elder to tell his story than traipse all the way up to the village for nothing."

"Oh, yes. I see what you mean," Mr. Homerman said. "Rex would not be happy then."

"Not at all. But he'll be very pleased when you tell him your idea and he sees the results. You do have a key to the boxes, don't you?"

"Of course." He patted his pockets. "Must have left them somewhere." He stopped and put a finger to his mouth, tapping his lips. "Oh, yes, I recall. I hid them in that kitchen. Handier there. Wouldn't have to carry them around."

They went into the house towards the former kitchen and headed towards the back wall. Lwiza stepped out from behind the blanket partition.

"Did you need me for something, *bibi*?" she asked.

"Ah, Lwiza," said Jade. "I did want to talk to you about tomorrow. We're all walking into the forest to a Chagga village. Mr. Julian wants you to come, too. So you should ask the other women what they will need and make sure it's all packed for them."

"Yes, *bibi*."

"It's not here!" exclaimed Mr. Homerman.

"What's not here?" asked Jade. "The keys?" Jade joined Mr. Homerman. "Are you sure you're looking in the right spot?" The man was hopelessly addled. He could have left them anywhere.

"Yes. Well, very nearly certain. I'm almost definitely sure, I think . . ." He pointed to the opening left when the stovepipe was removed from the room. It was above eye level and partly blocked by an abandoned nest of some sort. "I put the keys in that nest. That way I wouldn't misplace them."

"Maybe they fell to the ground or someone borrowed them," said Jade, thinking of their practical joker. "How much of a secret was that spot?"

"Oh, I didn't tell very many people," he said. "Rex, of course. Oh, dear!" he murmured. "If I recall correctly, he was talking with Conrad and a few of the other actors and actresses at the time. Murdock was there. I think Miss Zagar, too. She came to get something out of one of the crates yesterday. I can't think who else."

Jade sighed. *Who else indeed. The entire camp probably knows by now*. "Have you seen any keys, Lwiza?"

"No, *bibi*. If you do not need me," said Lwiza, "I will go see to the packing."

"Yes, good. Thank you, Lwiza." She turned back to Homerman. "I'll go see if anyone has the keys. In the meantime, Morris, look to see if they got shoved farther back in the flue hole or if they fell and got kicked into a corner."

Jade hurried out of the house. She spied Murdock and motioned for him to join her.

"Woody, do you have the keys to the crates?"

Murdock shook his head, his red hair flaming in the sun. "Sure don't. They missing?"

Jade shook her head. "Just misplaced as usual. Mr. Homerman thought you or Pearl might have them."

"Morris is a few worms shy of a full bait bucket, Jade. He's probably put them in a coat pocket."

"You may be right." She sighed. "I'll try Pearl anyway." Jade headed for Miss Zagar's tent and rapped on the tent pole to announce herself. "Pearl? Hello?"

No one answered. Jade pushed aside the tent flap to see if she was napping inside. She wasn't, but the keys lay plainly on her cot atop a jumble of clothes. Jade stepped in and reached for them, then jerked her hand back.

Next to the keys was a lone black stocking, lightly stuffed with packing material. One red eye had been painted on it, a metal tube of lip rouge beside it.

CHAPTER 8

Blue monkeys and colobus, resembling an arboreal skunk, are the most visible mammals. But then, they aren't predators that like to stay hidden, all the better to ambush their prey.

—The Traveler

Jade left the unfinished snake puppet on Pearl's cot and went in search of the actress. She found her coming from the privy.

"Pearl," Jade called to her, "I need to speak with you."

"I'm rather busy at the moment. . . ."

"Now! In your tent." Jade kept her voice low, but firm. Pearl shrugged and followed Jade.

"What's this about?" Pearl demanded.

"Inside, please," said Jade as she pushed aside a tent flap.

Pearl hesitated a moment, her eyelids half-lowered as she studied Jade's face. Then she shrugged and stepped in. Jade followed, not speaking, waiting for the woman's reaction.

"Did one of the natives come in here or—" Pearl stopped abruptly and stared at her cot. "What," she said, pointing to the stocking, "is that stupid thing doing here?"

"You don't know?"

"Well, of course not." She snatched the stuffed stocking

and thrust it at Jade. "I thought you disposed of it when you took it out of the bath tent the other day."

"It's a different one," said Jade. "A work in progress." She held it up to show the one eye.

"Oh, my stars," exclaimed Pearl. "It *is* different."

"Something you want to tell me?" asked Jade.

"What? You think *I* was making one of those stupid things? Try Brown or Budendorfer. They're the comedians. I saw them pour pepper into Conrad's canteen this morning."

Jade kept her gaze locked onto Pearl's eyes and waited. Pearl folded her arms in front of her chest and looked back at her cot. She spied the metal canister of lip rouge and picked it up.

"Ha!" She pulled off the lid and thrust the cream at Jade. "This is not my color."

"That proves nothing," Jade said. "Except that you didn't waste your own cosmetics on the stocking." She picked up the stocking snake, turned, and stepped outside.

Pearl followed. "Hey, just what were you doing in my tent anyway!"

"I was looking for some keys." Jade pulled the set from her pocket and jangled them.

"Oh! Well, I *did* have them. I needed to get out one of the wigs."

Bebe and McAvy came by at that moment. Bebe took one look at the stocking snake and clutched McAvy's arm. "Not another one!" she shrieked. Then she noticed the unfinished eyes and stared first at Jade, then at Pearl. "You!" she said, pointing to Pearl. "You're the one who's been tormenting me. I want her off this set," she snapped.

Pearl rolled her eyes expressively. "Puh-lease!" She gasped. "Why would I waste my time?"

"Then what's it doing here by your tent?" demanded Bebe.

"You were making another one, weren't you?" She didn't wait for an answer. "I'll have something to say about this to Rex."

"Tell Mr. Hall to empty and rinse his canteen while you're at it," yelled Jade after her.

The three watched as Bebe stormed off to find the director. Chuckling, McAvy reached for the toy snake and turned it over in his big hands. "We do have a practical joker in our midst," he said, handing the sock back to Jade.

"And under other circumstances it might be funny," said Jade, "but Miss Malta's a bit too keyed up as it is. I'd appreciate it if you'd help me spread the word that I'd really like this sort of thing to stop."

Jade headed back to the house. She'd wasted enough time already and they still hadn't picked anything to use as gifts for the Chagga.

Harry spotted her and joined her. "Did you choose something the director won't miss?"

"On my way now," she said, and explained the delay, showing him the newest sock snake. "This one's not a mate to the first," Jade said. "I suspect the first was made with one of Budendorfer's socks. He had a hole in one pair. But this one is more like a lady's stocking. I found it in Miss Zagar's tent. She denies making it, of course."

"It doesn't look like one of hers," Harry said. "The ones that she wore two days ago were . . ." He coughed and straightened. "Getting quite a collection, aren't we?" he said, handing it back to her. "So we have two practical jokers. Wonderful. Burn both of them. Er, the snakes."

They went in the front door and headed for the old kitchen. Homerman was still there, crawling around the floor, peering into cracks too small for anything to have fallen into.

"Thank our lucky stars you found them, Miss del Cameron," he said. He snatched the keys and unlocked one of the larger trunks. "Everything for the past-times setting should be in these three trunks."

The first one held gaudy bracelets and necklaces made of hammered tin and bronze and covered with glass jewels. A particularly large crown, like a giant golden pot with ear flaps, lay to one side.

"We can't give away any of this," said Homerman. He unlocked a second trunk and took out a large twelve-by-eight-by-eight-inch metal coffer and set it aside. "Not that. We need that. But we have several goblets and I don't think we're using them except to set around." He pulled out one with ornate scrollwork soldered on the stem. "Would this work?"

Harry took it and turned it over in his hands. "Impressive enough to give to the chief, I'd think. Luckily, Mangi Mlaga, the current chief, doesn't live in that village."

Jade grabbed a brass armband shaped like a coiled snake and handed it to Harry. "Take that, too. Just in case there's someone else we need to honor."

Harry reached for the metal coffer and tossed the items inside. "It will be easier to carry them in this. Make a better show, too. If Julian has his way, we'll be spending the next five days in the village filming everything under the sun. We'll probably have to bring a gift every day."

"As long as we don't give them that box. I need that box," said Homerman.

Harry handed it to the assistant. "You can be in charge of it, if it makes you feel any better."

"And don't forget your keys," added Jade. She wondered if Homerman was related to Julian. She couldn't think of any other reason why the addled little man would have been hired. Jade heard someone walk softly up to her from behind.

"Miss del Cameron," said Bebe, "I wonder if I might speak with you, um, privately? Girl talk," she added when neither Homerman nor Harry made a move to leave.

"Certainly," said Jade. "Let's go to my tent."

"No need," said Harry as he touched his hat brim. "We're done here." His gaze roved briefly over Bebe's form before he turned to go. "If you need *me* . . ."

Bebe shook her head, and Jade waited until the two men were away before turning back to Bebe. "Now, how can I help you?" She was glad to see that the woman had calmed down. She even looked happy.

"I think you can guess," Bebe said with a wink. She rubbed the outside of her eye with her index finger. "I seem to have begun my, er, time." She brushed the finger across her nose.

"Ah," said Jade. "So you're wondering where the female supplies are kept. I thought I gave a set to everyone." She headed for the corner where the women's items were stored.

"You did," Bebe said, "but I had Lwiza put them back. I didn't think . . ." She blushed. "You must think I'm silly or very old-fashioned to be embarrassed talking to another woman, but this is actually quite a relief."

Jade found a box of Hartmann's and passed it to Bebe. "Think nothing of it. It's taboo in many cultures. Dispose of these in the latrine," she said. She didn't add that tossing them anywhere else would likely attract predators. Why frighten the woman now that she was more relaxed, a situation that Jade found a trifle odd, considering most women dreaded this time when they were roughing it? And Bebe did not take well to roughing it. *But it appears that this is good news?* Jade considered the implications as she walked away.

. . .

Inspector Finch was sitting at his cramped little desk hunched over a stack of paperwork when the constable ushered Sam to his door. Seeing the man obviously embroiled in tedious forms made Sam feel a touch more sympathetic towards him. Thinking about how Finch had used Jade in July to hunt down a killer nearly eradicated that empathy.

"In there, sir," said the constable.

Sam rapped at the doorjamb.

"Come in, Featherstone," said Finch without looking up. "Got your message." He scribbled his signature on several sheets and shoved them to the side. "What may I do for you? I trust this is not a social call."

Sam took a seat in the hard wooden chair. "Hardly. I came to find out if there is anything else you can tell me about Mr. Wheeler's murder."

Finch set his pen in the holder next to an ink bottle and clasped his hands together on his desk. "And may I ask why you want to know?"

"Because he was part of the group that Jade has taken to Kilimanjaro. That means his death concerns her well-being and that concerns me."

"Are you suggesting—"

"I'm not suggesting anything, Inspector. But something about the entire mess stinks, and I want to know that you haven't overlooked anything." Sam leaned back in the chair, arms folded across his chest. "I spoke with Dr. Mathews."

"Did you, now?"

Sam waited for Finch to make a comment, any comment. He knew the drill. His statements were being met with questions, inducing him to "confess." It was an old game, a game invented and perfected by interrogators. This time, Sam intended to play the leading role. He settled into his chair and crossed his good leg over his false one.

Finch shrugged, as though sensing there was no point in playing the game. "I respect you, Featherstone. You're a soldier, a warrior. So I won't mince words."

Sam said nothing. Flattery was also an interrogation tactic, as was torture. He was familiar with both and had resisted each in the past. He could resist now.

"If you talked with Mathews, then you know that the murderer had consumed some poison, most likely from the datura plant. In a nonlethal dose, it makes a man superactive, fearless, *and* psychotic. In short, a man like that would be capable of any number of atrocities. So what, in particular, stinks to you?"

Sam repeated his concern that a man in that condition would be more likely found wandering the town, not lying in wait on the spacious grounds of the Muthaiga Club.

"Hmm. Interesting point, Featherstone, and one that, I confess, bothered me as well." He picked up a china cup and wiped the rim with his pocket handkerchief. "Tea?"

"Coffee if you have it."

"Right. Americans don't drink much tea, I take it. Some holdover of that Boston Tea Party, I presume?" Finch stood and went to the door. "Tucker!" he called. "Coffee for Mr. Featherstone and tea for me." He looked over his shoulder at Sam. "How do you take it?"

"Black."

"Black!" Finch ordered as the constable took Finch's cup and scrambled to find a second clean one. The inspector sat back at his desk. "The problem is that we don't have identification on the native. If he's a local chap, someone would have reported him missing from his job, I'd think."

"Don't you have all of the natives' fingerprints on file?"

Finch snorted. "To be sure. Well, the Department for Native Affairs does. But . . . Oh, very good, Tucker. Just set it down on the desk."

The constable put a cup of tea on Finch's desk and handed a mug of coffee to Sam. He took a sip. It tasted as though the pot had perked and bubbled for several days. *Just like home.* "Are they checking the prints?" asked Sam.

"What? Oh, no. One of my men is. An Indian. But it may take weeks. I'm afraid that they haven't cataloged the prints according to any proper indexing."

"Can't you tell something about his tribe? Was he Kikuyu or Maasai?"

"He wasn't Maasai, I can tell you that. Very distinctive hair ornamentation there. Not Wakamba either. They generally file their teeth to make them pointy. Beyond that, I have very little to go on."

"Dr. Mathews suggested that his, er, loin wrap didn't look like something most of the local tribes wear."

Finch sipped his tea. "Quite true. Had more of a coastal look about it, if I had to guess. We have our share of Somali come down from the north. Or could be a Swahili up from Dar es Salaam." He took another sip and replaced the china cup on the saucer. "But I fail to see how this has any import to you. The man killed himself."

Sam took a second swallow of coffee, decided that it wasn't worth a third, and placed the mug on the edge of Finch's desk. "I can't see the man having a motive," said Sam. "And don't tell me he didn't need one because he was drugged. Why take the drug? Was he trying to get his courage up? If so, why?"

"Now it sounds as though you *are* suggesting something, Featherstone."

"I keep thinking everything seemed too staged, too convenient. I wonder if someone gave this native a drugged drink, and set him up to attack Wheeler?"

"Premeditated murder, then."

"Yes," said Sam. "In which case, the murderer is still on the loose. And chances are, he's up on Kilimanjaro."

Finch stood, indicating that the interview was over. "Mr. Featherstone, having met Miss del Cameron, I can understand your, er, attachment to her and, consequently, your desire to protect her. But let me assure you that you're starting at shadows. There is absolutely nothing to suggest that this man was induced to kill Mr. Wheeler."

Sam opened his mouth to protest, but Finch held up his hand to wait. "We will continue to try to identify this man. Beyond that, I can't do much more. However, rest assured that I'll contact you the moment I know anything."

Sam stood and nodded to Finch. "Thank you for your time," he said. As he left the office, he wondered what steps to take next. The police weren't much help, so it was obviously up to him to find the connection between the murderer and whoever had set him in motion.

CHAPTER 9

Even the birds are difficult to spot unless they call out, which they do frequently in a symphony of warbles, chirps, whoops, screeches, brays, grunts, yelps, and coughs. Remember, they have to compete with the olive baboon's loud "wahoo."

—The Traveler

It took three hours to get under way the next morning. First, half the group needed to be roused out of bed. Then they all decided they needed to bring something else with them, a Kodak Brownie camera, a different wrap, something to barter for trinkets.

Bargaining with the Chagga women for woven baskets and clay-beaded necklaces had become something of a sport around camp. Zakayo, their interpreter, assisted more often than not, although Cynthia, Murdock, and Julian had all picked up some Swahili. For some reason, the actors got the idea that this "wilder village" up the hill would have more notable items to keep as souvenirs. Jade could have told them that most of the women who came into camp to sell their fruit and other wares either came from that very village or another one just like it.

Jade brought up the rear, occasionally assisting a straggler. The entire complement of actors and cameramen made the trip, along with cameras, film, camp chairs, and a hamper of food. In the end, they left the metal chest behind and took only the drinking goblet and the snake bracelet, which Jade carried in her day pack. Only Nakuru remained at the camp with Muturi to guard it. Jelani walked Biscuit, and Lwiza followed the actresses.

They crossed a tributary of the Una River on a bridge made of haphazardly stacked stones. Jade noted that the forest here was festooned with moss just as on Marsabit. Vines, some as thick as cables, bound the wild poplar and a gnarled reddish tree with tiny pink flower spikes. Water dripped off the leaves as the crew brushed them, leaving the leaders soaked. Jade was happily drier at the column's tail. The air was rich with decaying humus, and thick moss carpeted their path. Hornbills brayed and quacked from the treetops.

But excepting the birds, the group made so much commotion, it scared away any wildlife. Still, Jade kept her eyes busy searching for a shifting form or shadow that would signify a boar or one of the mountain's elephants. She longed to see one as she had on Mount Marsabit, a ghostly gray giant hidden in the shadows. Deep, round, water-filled footprints and splintered limbs marked the pachyderms' passing.

The forest hid everything well, including the village. Their first hints of its presence were the birdlike voices of the children. The conical huts melted into the tree trunks, making it difficult to ascertain the community's size. Even the gardens imitated the natural forest.

Their group made quite a show entering the settlement. No one was surprised by them, since Harry had seen fit to send Zakayo and one of his men up yesterday afternoon to forewarn everyone. It gave the elder a chance to put on his best furs and for his wives and daughters to prepare a feast. But Biscuit's entrance as he padded softly between Jade and Jelani caught everyone's attention and lent a higher level of importance to the gathering.

Their host, Sina, was seated on a chair of sorts, and Jade knew then what had happened to some of the kitchen cabinets in the farmhouse. His short white hair looked snowy in the dappled sunlight. Harry went first to greet the old man, who rose with all the dignity that age and aching joints could allow. The elder spat on his right hand, then grasped Harry's in the Chagga's traditional greeting.

"Jambo!" Harry said, and proceeded to ask after the man's health and the health of his family and livestock. Zakayo translated into Machame, the Chagga's own language, and gave back the replies. Harry presented Sina with the drinking goblet and the snake armband. The old man accepted them graciously, but without any effusive thanks, as though a man of his stature received such gifts daily. Formalities out of the way, Harry got around to business. He explained the large cameras and received permission for Budendorfer and Brown to film the village.

"I have heard that you know many stories of long ago," said Harry. "Stories told by those who lived here before the Chagga came to the mountain."

Sina nodded, his lids half lowered, a pleased smile gracing his weathered face.

"We would like to hear one of those stories," began Harry.

Julian sat on one of the camp chairs to Harry's right. "Ask him about Menelik."

Harry put his hand out to the side, halting the director's impatience. "In good time," he said. "One doesn't rush these people. It's rude." With a smile, he addressed the elder. "We ask you to tell us of the great king who came and was buried on this mountain."

Sina closed his eyes and tilted his head back, as though pulling deep into his memory and that of his ancestors. "First, I must tell you of how man first sinned against Ngai. Once, God spoke as I speak to you."

Sina uttered a few sentences, then paused as Zakayo translated. Harry, in his turn, translated the Swahili version into English. He hadn't gotten past the tale of the first sin when Mr. Julian interrupted.

"I don't care about sins except to film them. I want to know about Menelik!"

Harry smiled at Sina, who'd opened his eyes to see what this new speaker wanted, and muttered, "Keep quiet, Mr. Julian, or you won't hear anything." Then Harry nodded at Sina to continue.

Sina recounted the wonderful garden God had given and the edict not to eat the yam lest the people die. Jade listened with rapt fascination as the ancient tale of the fall in the garden was retold, but with an authority as if it were a firsthand account. She wondered if this was just the Chagga's version given to them by missionaries or their own, more ancient tale. Whichever it was, Sina quickly followed it with his own telling of mankind's first murder.

"And so even now, when blood is spilled, seven cows, seven goats, and one daughter to be a servant is the price for the death of the man." The old man held out his new cup.

An old crone, probably his chief wife, yelled to two young women, who were barely in their teens. "Rehema, Bahati." The two jumped up and one, Rehema, quickly filled the cup with a banana beer while the other went inside the hut and came back out with roasted plantains and tender yams.

Sina offered the same beverage to Julian and Harry, who both politely declined. None was offered to Jade, who would be considered Harry's woman. Sina barely cast a glance in her direction, but his gaze repeatedly came back to rest on Biscuit, who lay at her feet, his tongue out, panting. Nearly everyone else, except for Cynthia, McAvy, and Hall, who stayed in character, had gone off wandering through the village. Budendorfer kept his camera trained on the actors and Brown filmed Sina.

Jade spotted Lwiza standing off to her left. She seemed more interested in watching the village women. Talmadge and Murdock had both accosted one of the village's young men and were attempting to try their hand at throwing his spear. Murdock's barely stuck in the ground, but the more muscular Talmadge managed to penetrate a plantain tree.

Wells followed Bebe at a discreet distance as she approached one of the younger women. Jade thought she recognized the girl, a bit of a belle with high cheekbones and an engaging smile who'd quickly discovered the American women were willing to pay her for all sorts of ordinary household items. In fact, at least three of the Chagga women who sold produce, woven mats, or fired-clay beads were regular visitors to their camp.

Pearl called to the one who'd brought out the beer. "Rehema." She pointed to the woman's arm wires, coils of copper, and offered her a canister of lip rouge in trade, probably the one Jade had found on her cot with the sock snake. While Jade watched, the girl removed an arm wire and snatched up the paint pot. Pearl mimed how to apply it and Rehema spread a liberal amount on her lips.

Immediately, the other Chagga woman, the young belle, grabbed the metal tube from Rehema's hands and shrieked in triumph. The transformation of Rehema's face was instantaneous as hatred flashed from her eyes. Her reddened lips pulled back in a snarl, the thick color staining her teeth. She resembled something feral and predatory.

Pearl offered her arm wires back, but Rehema would have no part of it. Instead, her right hand shot out, pointing to the thief as she broke loose in a torrent of Machame. Jade had no idea what she was saying, but judging by the horrified looks on the other Chagga's faces, it was not the equivalent of "I'm going to tell." Pearl tried without success to offer the wronged woman something else from her bag as an appeasement.

"Lloyd," yelled Julian to the cameraman, "I want this on film!"

Brown obliged by shifting the camera from the elder and pointing it at the two women. Pearl, frightened by Rehema's rage, backed up until she stood beside the camera.

The belle's face contorted in horror as her eyes rolled back and she fell to the ground sobbing. She crawled to the offended woman and returned the lip rouge, her voice pleading, but Rehema wouldn't take it. The belle, trembling with fear, staggered to her feet and wailed in terror. Rehema stopped shrieking. Her eyes narrowed, and she ran towards one of the warriors and grabbed his knife, slashing at him when he attempted to retrieve it.

"This is tremendous!" shouted Julian. "Real action." He ran towards Brown, who was cranking furiously.

"She's going to kill that girl," yelled Jade. She'd already jumped up and raced towards the belle, shoving her towards a hut.

The warrior wanted no part of the crazed Rehema and left her still holding his knife. Rehema looked around for her enemy and saw her as she ducked into the hut. Baring her teeth in a feral grimace, Rehema started towards the hut, the knife raised. Jade stepped in front of the opening. Rehema laughed and raised her knife higher, a look of triumph in her eyes.

"Biscuit, take her down!" Jade called as she pointed to Rehema.

Biscuit's long legs stretched out as he covered the distance in seconds. He reared up and thrust his front paws on the woman's stomach. Rehema collapsed in on herself, dropping the knife as the big cheetah pushed her to the ground.

Jade started forward. "Stop her, Hascombe!" Julian yelled. "I can't have her in the picture."

Harry grabbed her around the waist and hauled her off her feet.

"Let me go, Harry," she growled, and jabbed her elbow into his ribs.

"Ouch! Dammit, Jade. Stop. They've got her."

By that time, Hall and McAvy had reached the native woman. They each grabbed an arm and pulled her up.

"Cut!" shouted Julian. "Wonderful! What a scene."

Jade jerked free of Harry's grasp and went towards the men to retrieve both her cheetah and the knife. She returned the weapon to the warrior, then took Biscuit by his collar. Rehema immediately comprehended whom she had to blame for stopping her. She shrieked at Jade, hurling her best invectives. Then she stopped as suddenly as she'd begun and hung limp in the men's grasp.

"Set her down," said Harry. "She's quiet now."

"What the Sam Hill was all that about?" asked Murdock.

"I'm not sure," said Harry, "but I think that woman, Rehema, cursed the one who stole her trinket."

"Cursed her?" asked Jade. "What type of curse? No children? Or a face full of pimples?"

"Death curse. Sicken and die. Zakayo told me about this on my last trip here. Gets to be quite a problem with the women," said Harry, pointing to the angry native woman who now sat hugging her knees on the ground. "She probably wasn't going to stab the little thief. No need to. Unless the one she cursed can appease the right ancestral spirits, she'll die."

"How horrid," said Pearl. "I'm sorry I gave her the lip paint and started it."

"Maybe I can make it up to her," said Bebe. She picked up her own shoulder bag and motioned for Zakayo to join her as she hesitantly approached the woman.

"So if she wasn't going to kill that girl, what was she doing with the knife?" asked Jade.

"Ah," said Harry. "Well, that's where it gets interesting. The curse is bad enough, but it can be undone if you have enough time and goats to sacrifice to the ancestors. But if the one spouting the curse should go and commit suicide . . ." He flung his hands out. "Well, then the other one's doomed. That kind can't be lifted. I've heard these curses and suicides happen all too often among the women."

Jade shook her head. "What a tragic situation."

"You don't know the half of it," said Harry. "I may not know any Machame, Jade, but I'd bet my rifle that she just cursed you, too."

CHAPTER 10

Predators exist in all sizes, from insects and snakes to the rarer passing lion.

—The Traveler

"You must block this curse, Simba Jike." Jelani walked beside Jade for the moment, the path wide enough at that point to admit two people.

"I don't believe in curses, Jelani."

"*You* do not have to believe. That is the danger. This woman's anger will reach her ancestors. They will come for you unless you appease them."

Jade stopped and faced the young man. She'd watched him grow from a boy to a youth on the cusp of manhood, eager to prove his bravery, and she'd seen the results of that bravery when he cut his own heel to escape from a slaver's chain. She'd even taken a hand in his education, hoping he'd become a leader, a voice for the Kikuyu. She hadn't planned for him to become a *mondo-mogo*, or healer, but she'd accepted it as a way for him to gain his own people's trust. But Jade drew the line at having him practice incantations over her in a ritual animal sacrifice, the accepted mode of placating tribal ancestors.

"I have enough trouble appeasing my *living* relatives, Jelani. I have no intention of taking on anyone else's *dead* ones." Her stomach rumbled. "I'd like to get back so I can appease my stomach."

The path narrowed again up ahead, and Jade motioned for Jelani to precede her. Biscuit padded between them and Jade brought up the rear, making sure there were no stragglers. She heard the musical rush of the Una's tributary ahead and wished she had time to sit by it and watch the animals come out of hiding so she could photograph them. She'd have to ask Harry, maybe demand it. Most of the time she had nothing to do in the camp. She didn't like being inactive, and out here she needed something to occupy her mind as well. Otherwise her thoughts kept drifting back to Sam and what to do about his marriage proposal. She missed him, but she hated feeling controlled.

Conversations among the filmmakers on the return trip had been sporadic, since it involved calling to someone walking in front of or behind another person. Not the easiest way to exchange confidences. She'd heard Rex Julian wax eloquent to anyone who would listen about the value of today's footage. The fact that a young Chagga woman had nearly died for it didn't seem to faze him. At least it kept him from grousing about having his storyteller interrupted.

As if on cue, Julian pushed his way to the front and badgered Harry. "You should have insisted he tell us the story of Menelik instead of letting him wander like some addled old coot. Bible stories, no less!"

"I told you," Harry replied calmly, "a storyteller's merit is lowered if his audience doesn't want to come back for more. He deliberately held out on us today. He'll tell us tomorrow."

"No more gifts!" ordered Mr. Julian. "He'll milk us for all we've got."

"We need to bring something," said Harry, "but just not as valuable. It will tell him we still honor him, but let him know that we're out of fancy goods."

"You mean we have to traipse all the way back to that village tomorrow?" asked Talmadge. "Fun's fun, but that wasn't it."

"What are you complaining about?" asked Murdock. "You're at least not lugging cameras and tripods and film."

"Neither are you," said Budendorfer, turning around. He had a tripod with the camera attached slung over one shoulder.

"Just speaking up for you," said Murdock. "And watch when you turn around. You nearly clobbered me with that thing."

"Wouldn't want to damage the equipment," said Budendorfer.

"I don't think we all need to go up again tomorrow, do we, Rex?" asked Bebe. "You must have enough footage of us sitting around looking intent. And I didn't have any scenes."

Pearl echoed the sentiment. "My feet are tired, Rex. I'm going to get a bunion."

Cynthia let her eyes speak for her, sending an eloquent appeal to Harry. "Of course, I'll do whatever Mr. Hascombe suggests."

Julian scrambled across the stacked stones that formed a bridge over the river and stopped on the other side, facing his group like some general addressing his troops. Homerman stood beside him as a faithful minion. "You do not have to return tomorrow. And I'll only take one camera, just in case." He didn't have to finish the statement. Jade knew that he hoped something else dramatic would happen in the village.

"Uh, boss," said Brown. "Which one of us cameramen gets to stay put tomorrow?"

"We'll draw straws," said Julian. "Unless one of you wants to be unemployed. Maybe the lucky one can help Roland set up the equipment for the Menelik scene."

Harry waved an arm towards the camp. "We need to keep moving, Julian. You can make your arrangements over dinner. Everyone's tired and a bit on edge."

Harry stayed on the near side of the stream to see that everyone got across safely. The water ran only a foot deep at the end of the dry season, but the rocks were slippery in spots.

"That's it. Here. Hand the camera to the porter. There you are," said Harry. The porter waded into the icy cold snowmelt with the camera slung over one shoulder, just as he'd done on the way up the hill. A second Nyamwezi man followed with the other camera.

"Let me give you a hand there, Cynthia," said Harry. He picked her up and carried her across the stones. Both Pearl and Bebe insisted on the same fun, squealing with glee as he easily toted each in turn. "You, too, Miss Lwiza."

Jade noticed that Harry again treated the Swahili woman with the same courtesy he gave to the Americans. *He may be a horse's patoot, but at least he's not a snob.*

"Need a hand, Jade?" he asked, a huge grin on his face.

"*I* can manage, Harry, but thanks just the same."

He didn't press her, which she also appreciated. Jade waited while Biscuit stooped to drink his fill, sneezing once as the cold water tickled his whiskers. Then the cat bounded gracefully over the stones, electing not to wet his feet. Jade stepped onto the rocks. As on the trip up, she tested each rock before planting her booted foot on it.

When she was halfway across the bridge, the sound of rushing water turned into a buzzing hum, like a hive of bees in her ears. Her chest constricted in one sharp gasp when she felt her balance totter as a rock that had seemed secure suddenly shifted. It slid into the cold stream, and Jade heard the plunk and felt the splash as though from a distance. Her vision faltered and she heard voices, but they spoke no dialect she knew. The only creature she saw with any clarity as she struggled to maintain her balance was Biscuit. Yet even now, the cat seemed larger and the spotting on his golden coat resembled a leopard's more than a cheetah's.

"Easy, Jade," said Harry. "I've got you."

Jade felt a strong arm around her waist and the dizziness passed. Biscuit was once again on the far side by Jelani, and Harry stood directly beside her.

"I'm fine, Harry. You can let go of me now."

"Not until you're across. I can't risk your twisting an ankle or breaking a leg in a fall." He let go of her waist and took hold of her left arm instead.

Jade didn't fight him. The sooner she got off the bridge and onto solid ground, the better. "One of the rocks came loose with all the foot traffic," she said by way of explanation. "We should shore up the rest."

"I'll leave the men to do that," said Harry, and he directed the Nyamwezi to repair the makeshift bridge. Then in a lower voice he added, "Is that all, Jade? Your face got sort of queer-like. I'd have suspected you were about to faint, but you're not the type."

Jade scowled. "I just lost my balance when the rock slipped. That's all. I'm fine." She pulled away from him and motioned for him to go on.

Harry watched her face for a moment longer. Then, satisfied that she was in fact all right, he led the way back to their base camp. Jade again took up the rear guard and started down the trail, but not before catching Jelani's watchful gaze. She read in his eyes that he didn't believe her for one moment. Curiously, she didn't either.

"This pipe still isn't fitting right," said Sam. He stood up and wiped the sweat and grease from his face with his kerchief. "It needs to be ground down a bit more."

"Shall I take another go at it?" asked Neville.

"I'll do it," said Avery. "You chaps take a break."

Sam shook his head, his brown hair flopping over one eye. "Thanks, Avery, but I'd just as soon do it myself."

Neville wiped off a wrench and put it aside. "He's been that way all day," he said, nodding towards Sam. "Surprised he's letting me do anything."

Avery shrugged and puffed on his pipe. "That's what comes of being a pilot, Neville. Once you start working on your machine, you're not going to trust her to anyone else."

"Naturally," said Neville. "But your life would depend on that. *This*," he continued, patting the jumble of metal, "is just a coffee washer."

"Not *just* a coffee washer, Neville," said Sam. "This invention is going to make your fortune and revolutionize the coffee industry. Every farmer will want one."

"*Our* fortune," corrected Neville. "This was as much your idea as mine. Maybe more so."

"I presume you are applying for a patent," said Avery.

"Yes," said Neville, "and Isherwood and Sons in Nairobi is going to manufacture them."

"Indeed!" said Avery. "There's a feather in the colony's cap."

A clanging bell interrupted the men's conversation. "Ah, Maddy has our supper ready. This will have to wait until tomorrow," said Neville.

Avery accompanied the others to the well pump, where they lathered up their hands and scrubbed the grease from them. Maddy met them with clean towels. "Hello, Avery. I didn't know you'd stopped by. You'll stay for supper, won't you?"

"Thank you, Maddy. That is, if you don't mind. Beverly has taken it in her head to attend a meeting of the Ladies' Pistol Club, of all things. The nanny has the baby in hand, so I'm a bit of a bachelor tonight." He knocked the ashes out of his pipe and stuck it in his pocket.

"Good for her," said Madeline. "Beverly, I mean. What fun. Jade should join that club, too, shouldn't she, Sam?"

He dried his hands and tossed the towel over his shoulder. "Not sure Jade's interested in pistols as much as rifles."

"Or roping," added Avery with a laugh. "I still wish I could have seen when she threw—" He stopped abruptly when Neville elbowed him and shook his head. One glance at Sam's profile told Avery that Jade's recent escapades were topics to be avoided.

Madeline helped her friend recover by skipping over the recent time when Jade had captured a murderer by lassoing him, and mentioned one of her earlier, less hazardous adventures. "Sam caught Jade roping that zebra on film, Avery. I thought you saw that."

"Ah, yes," he said. "Indeed. I did see that."

"There's no need to pretend in front of me," said Sam as he sat down at the table. "I'm perfectly aware of all the wild stunts Jade has done."

Madeline set a platter of steaming ham slices in front of the men and added bowls of boiled potatoes, fresh garden greens, tender boiled corn on the cob, and a loaf of warm bread.

Neville led them in the blessing and everyone tucked into

the meal. After a few minutes of silence, Avery broached the forbidden subject again. "Have you heard any word from Jade, Sam?"

His brows furrowed. "No. Should I have?"

"I thought she might have sent a wire back from Moshi saying she'd arrived," said Avery.

"I doubt there was time," suggested Madeline. "But I'm sure she's fine and—"

Sam leaned back in his chair. "May we talk about something else?"

"No, by thunder!" said Avery. "We won't. Sam Featherstone, you're not fooling anyone. You're in some terrible, gloomy mood, and while I normally make it a point to stay out of another man's business . . . er, this time, I'm breaking my own rule for a friend. You're not jealous of her being off with Hascombe, are you?"

"No," said Sam. "Jade's dislike of him is too strong. And if he tried anything . . ."

Neville laughed. "Our Jade would probably shoot him a right jab to the jaw."

"Or just shoot him," added Avery with a chuckle. "Then are you still worried about Jade having a murderer in with her crew?"

Sam folded his napkin and plopped it next to his barely touched meal. "Since you insist on discussing it, yes, I am. I've talked with Dr. Mathews and that blasted Finch and they agree that it is odd, but they can't find any connection to that lot from California. Not that they're looking for any, either. I've asked anyone else who was at the Muthaiga that night if they'd ever seen the native before. Of course, either they don't want to talk to me or they have no idea what the native looked like."

"And there's no other clue to the man's origin?" asked Madeline.

Sam recounted what he'd learned so far.

"In other words, the man probably came from Mombassa or wandered up from Dar es Salaam, looking for work or trouble," summarized Avery. "He bought some bad *tembo* from one of the local native brewers and had a murderous fit."

"You're leaving out the part about the poison in the native beer," said Sam. "The natives around here don't do that. At least, not that I've ever heard of."

"Sam's right there, Avery," said Neville. "Maddy and I have lived here since before the war, and I've never heard of *tembo* being tainted with . . . what was it again?"

"Datura," said Sam. "Sort of a morning glory type of flower. Seeds and root are all poisonous. Mathews sent the drink down to a chemist friend of his in Mombassa. Thought he might be able to isolate something from it, but as far as he knows, it's just ordinary *tembo*." Sam fidgeted with his napkin for a moment. "I wonder if you'd do me a favor, Avery."

"Certainly. You need only to name it."

"Send a telegram to that women's prison, the one Lilith Worthy is in. See if she's been up to anything."

"Sam!" exclaimed Madeline. "Do you think she's behind this?"

He shrugged. "She's tried to kill Jade before and she's got connections in Africa. I'd just like to be certain, that's all."

"I'll send it tomorrow, but chances are, old chap," continued Avery, "that the man had this brew already with him. Gave him Dutch courage, so to speak. Took too much of it this time. Delicious meal, Maddy."

Madeline beamed. "It's so nice to have you here with us, Avery. Even if you were abandoned for a pistol club."

"Actually, I had another motive for dropping by," he said. "An old school chum of mine whom I haven't seen in years has wired me. Fascinating fellow. Traveled all over the Sudan and the Nubian Desert. Actually wandered into Aby—"

"Mummy?" The querulous call came from an adjacent room.

"I'll get him, my dear," said Neville, rising. "Little tyke probably wants some water." He left the room and returned a moment later carrying their recently adopted son. "Look who's here, Cyril. It's Uncle Avery."

"Hello, little man," said Avery. "I was just about to invite your mummy and dad to come and dine with me and Aunt Beverly this Saturday. You must come, too, and keep little Alice Merrywether company."

"How delightful," said Maddy. "We'd love to."

"And, of course, you too, Sam," added Avery. "Especially you."

"Why especially me?"

"Because I want you all to meet this old friend of mine whom I was telling you about. Get your mind off your troubles."

"You mean off Jade, don't you?"

Avery laughed. "She's fine, Sam. A lot of silly playactors are no match for Jade. Any sign of trouble and she'll be right in there setting it aright."

"That," said Sam, "is *precisely* what I'm afraid of."

For all her bravery and wisdom, she is still foolish about many things. Jelani sat cross-legged on the ground inside the tent he shared with the cook. Muturi liked working for Bwana Nyati. He took care of his men and paid them well, not only with money but also with good blankets and plenty of meat. And that last part was good, because Jelani needed a goat to sacrifice if he was going to save Simba Jike.

Getting the goat would take some time, but he needed that time anyway to find out where to make the most propitious sacrifice. At home, Jelani and his teacher would go to one of the sacred groves of trees where their ancestral spirits lived. But this time he was not appeasing his ancestors' spirits. He needed to mollify the Chagga's ancestors. Would they accept his offering in Simba Jike's name?

She sat by the house now, laughing and playing a card game with the white men. Now was his time to act. From his own animal-skin bag, Jelani took out a dried gourd sliced along one side to form a dipper. Next he retrieved a sprig of wild thyme and walked to the nearby spring. He filled the gourd with water and took it to Jade's tent. Then he dipped the thyme into the water and sprinkled Jade's tent on all sides, chanting as he went.

"*Ngugwitia*, Ngai, I plead, oh, God."

Going around the tent he continued to sprinkle the water and chant. "Protect, oh, God." Finally, he returned to the front and stepped inside, sprinkling Jade's cot and belongings before marking her tent with pieces of clay and charcoal.

It was not enough, but it would have to do for now.

Jade sat outside her tent the next morning, writing in her notebook for want of anything better to do. She regretted not accompanying Harry and Julian and a few of the actors back to the village, but Harry had insisted that she stay behind to watch over the women. Of the three actresses, only Cynthia had opted to return up the hill, most likely because Harry was going. Jade had noticed how Cynthia had gravitated to him these past few days. Was she looking for male solace to replace her husband? Or was Cynthia less bereaved than she'd said? *It's none of my business.*

As she finished recording the Chagga's creation account, Jade set aside her book and looked at the black and ocher stripes and starbursts that Jelani had added to her tent. He wasn't the only one trying to protect her. Harry was concerned about her making another trip across the stream so soon after yesterday's mishap. He thought she might be coming down with some illness and wanted to be sure she was rested. Only he didn't say it in so many words. What surprised Jade the most was that Jelani had returned to the Chagga village. After yesterday's slip, she expected him to follow her constantly, warding off whatever curse he felt she was under.

Still, staying here wasn't entirely pointless. She'd been interested in seeing if any of the Chagga women involved in yesterday's fracas came into their camp to sell their wares again. In particular, she hoped to spy the one who'd issued the curse. Jade feared Rehema would renew her efforts to kill herself after they'd left.

But Rehema showed up at the fringes of the camp around midmorning, just before Harry and the others went up to the village. Jade toyed with the idea of greeting her, letting her know that she carried no grudge. Then she rejected the idea. For all she knew, it would set the woman off again. Jade kept out of sight until the young Chagga woman had gone.

Find something useful to do while you're hiding. Jade decided to clean her as yet unused Winchester rifle. Her father had given her a new one, a model 95 with better range and stopping power. Once they were on the saddle, they'd need to hunt for meat. Even an unfired rifle collected grime. Biscuit lay at her feet, one eye closed, the other keeping watch on a rodent that darted nearby. When Jade put away her rifle an hour later, the camp seemed quiet. She decided that could mean trouble as much as noise could.

Reasoning that a patrol of the camp seemed in order, she called to Biscuit. The cheetah stood up and stretched, his front limbs extended, his rear upraised. He fell in beside her, heeling like a well-trained dog. Jade spotted Budendorfer, the lucky cameraman who hadn't had to climb the mountain with a heavy camera today, heading out of their makeshift darkroom and into the house. Talmadge stood in front of the more opulent-looking tent, draping fabric from tall poles to create the illusion of an interior. The man seemed to be a jack-of-all-trades in this movie, filling in as an extra or as a double for dangerous scenes as well as acting as all-around handyman.

Lwiza knelt beside the tin bathtub, hand-washing someone's clothes. Jade noted that she had set aside her more traditional garb for the shirtwaist, split skirt, and tall boots Jade had purchased for her. Pearl reclined in a chair outside her tent, reading a book, though she watched Lwiza's progress as much as anything else. Bebe sat on the veranda, fanning herself to keep away insects. She held her script and, judging by her changing expressions, seemed to be holding her own private rehearsal. *The consummate professional.*

Jade decided to visit with the cook and see if he needed anything or had a cut of meat to spare as a midday snack for Biscuit. Halfway there, she noticed the cat's head jerk to the northwest. Biscuit chirped once and nudged Jade's knee with his head.

Ah, Harry's back.

Jade heard them before she saw them.

"Of all the dag-blasted nonsense, Hascombe! I'm telling

you right now, I won't put up with any more of this bull shine. If you can't exercise some control, then—"

"Then what, Mr. Julian? You won't find another safari leader out here on a moment's notice. I'll grant you Miss del Cameron could handle the job just fine, but Nakuru would leave with me and then where would you be?"

"Are you threatening me, Hascombe?"

They emerged from the tree line and into the clearing. Harry turned and put his hands up in a placating gesture. "I'm not threatening anything. I'm just telling you the facts, Mr. Julian."

"What happened?" asked Jade, hurrying over to them.

Brown staggered out of the woods and, after carefully placing the camera and tripod to one side, collapsed in a heap on the ground. The others followed him and gave Jade surreptitious looks behind the director's back, rolling their eyes.

"Your boss man did not fulfill his promise, that's what happened," bellowed Julian.

Jade placed a hand on the director's arm and kept her voice low. "Sir, please calm yourself. It's not good for your health out here to get too worked up."

"He told me that the old man up there would tell us Menelik's story today," ranted Julian. "And he didn't! Instead, all I got was some damned long-winded yarn about a giant magic snail that brings dead warriors back to life with his slime. I want to hear about Menelik and all his grave goods!"

Jade looked to Harry, her brows raised. "A giant snail?"

Harry shrugged. "Called Kikorwi. Actually a morality tale about not trusting women."

"Interesting," said Jade. "I'd have paid a quarter to hear that one myself."

"What?" Julian shouted. "This is intolerable. You should

have insisted that old coot tell me what I wanted to know. He's bilking us for more gifts."

"What did you give him today, Harry?" asked Jade.

"Two handkerchiefs. A white one and a red checked one." Harry took a deep breath and faced the angry director. "He promised he'd tell us about that old warrior king tomorrow. It's just one more trip back up. We have to give him what he wants."

Jade heard Brown groan from behind Harry. Something in Harry's voice told her there was more to the story. "And just *what* might that be, Harry?"

"You."

Jade folded her arms across her chest and locked her eyes on Harry's. He looked away first. "Actually, not you, per se, but Biscuit. He said he'd only tell the story in front of the . . . What were his exact words?" Harry paused, pulled off his pith helmet, and rubbed the sleeve of his forearm across his brow. "Only in front of the golden cheetah and the lioness that walks with it." He clamped his hat back on his head. "How the hell he knew your nickname is Simba Jike is beyond me."

"Probably heard Jelani or one of the men say it. I'd bet he speaks at least some Swahili."

"Well, Hascombe," sputtered Mr. Julian, "you are going to demand that she goes with us tomorrow, aren't you?"

Harry's eyes widened as he shot an alarmed look at Jade. "Mr. Julian," he said, "I'd as soon wrestle a croc as demand that Jade—"

"Biscuit and I would be delighted to come," broke in Jade. "On one condition."

"Oh?" asked Harry and Mr. Julian simultaneously.

"I really want to hear about the giant magic snail first."

Mr. Julian sputtered and stormed off to bully someone else. Harry grinned, his teeth flashing in his tanned face. "Ah, Jade," he purred. "You really are a little devil. You know that, don't you?"

She smiled.

CHAPTER 11

Leopards like the forest. The trees afford them ample opportunities for pouncing.

—The Traveler

"War went on for as many years as men have fingers. Men fought as they eat or sleep. They knew no other way. The Una ran red with the blood of slain warriors."

Jade sat cross-legged on the ground near Sina. Biscuit had dined on a scrawny hen that was presented to him as a gift from the old man. Now he lay contentedly at her side, his hindquarters wrapping around to her back. Zakayo sat to her right, in between her and Harry. Most of the others sat on camp chairs behind them, but because so many had elected to stay in camp, including all of the women, Harry had left Nakuru behind with the Nyamwezi men as guards. Jade looked for Rehema but didn't see her.

"Ngowi fought against a powerful chief. But most of all, Ngowi fought against the magic of Kikorwi, who could bring slain warriors back to life. In this way, Ngowi's army grew ever smaller while Mawache's army sprang back fresh each day. Ngowi's people used to hide in the long caverns here by the Una to avoid slaughter. But they could not hide forever."

"This is taking even longer than yesterday," muttered Julian from behind Jade. She shushed him with a sweep of her hand.

The elder continued to tell of Ngowi's plan to send a beautiful girl into the enemy camp as a spy. He elaborated on her travels into the rival chief's lands, how she followed the herdsboys and was admitted to the royal harem. Eventually, the woman was shown Kikorwi's lair among the great rocks. "Then came the dawn when Mawache went to Kikorwi's den and found the great snail had been slain. When Mawache questioned everyone, he learned of the girl's trickery. She'd killed Kikorwi and fled." The elder passed his gaze over Biscuit and Jade. "The treachery of a woman can burn you in fire."

Jade didn't know if this was meant as a warning to her, to Biscuit, or to Harry and the men not to trust her. But then, she recalled, she was the one who'd requested this retelling. The elder had demanded her presence and Biscuit's for Menelik's story.

The end of this tale was marked with refreshments, reminding Jade of intermission at a theater. Woven banana-frond mats heaped with cooked meat and roasted plantains were passed around the group. Jade accepted a plantain for herself but gave her portion of the meat to Biscuit, who suddenly seemed to find the proceedings interesting again. Jade took the opportunity of stretching her legs, taking Biscuit with her as she wandered off into the woods for a few moments of needed privacy. Her head hurt and she wished she'd brought some aspirin.

A decent night's sleep would help more than anything. Last night's had been broken badly, and when she did sleep, it was riddled with bizarre dreams. She'd had this problem before, often reliving her ambulance runs during the war. But this one was about Kilimanjaro, and for some reason, the first syllables kept getting emphasized. Almost as if she was hearing "kill a man." She kept seeing a retinue of ancient warriors climbing the mountain, wailing and moaning. Gold and gems flashed from their heavy burdens. As they disappeared into the mountain's clouds, one of them beckoned her to follow, but somehow, Jade knew if she did, she'd be sacrificed along with the slaves.

Biscuit rubbed against her knee, a raspy purr issuing from his throat. Then he lifted his head and stared up the slope and his body tensed.

"What is it, Biscuit? What do you see?" Jade searched the forest for some movement, a monkey or a bird that might have attracted the cat's attention. *He did that in the dream last night.*

And she'd followed him. While she did, his coat changed until his spots resembled a leopard's. She followed up the mountain, above the tree line and the saddle, always climbing. After he, too, disappeared into the clouds, she woke up in a sweat. That in itself was odd, because in the dream she'd felt cold: the penetrating, numbing, soul-chilling cold of the grave.

A similar chill ran across her shoulders now. She shivered and tugged on Biscuit's collar. "It's time to get back, fellow. The old man won't start the next story without you." On her return, she passed by a grove of banana trees. Human skulls, the remains of long-dead ancestors, lay among the trunks. Nearby a horde of flies buzzed around a goat head.

Ancestor worship. She wondered if this had anything to do with the recent curse. If so, the cursed woman had wasted no time trying to free herself. *Just how much time do you get with a curse?* At that moment, her ears buzzed as they had at the river with the low hum of whispering voices. The sounds were more than all around her; it felt as if they were coursing through her, sizing her up, plotting against her. They buffeted her face, her ears, crept across the nape of her neck. Jade shook her head and swatted at the air to be rid of them.

Harry noticed and hurried to her side. "Come away from here, Jade. Ruddy insects will drive a person crazy around these corpses." He tugged on her arm and the voices vanished.

Jade followed Harry and Biscuit back to the elder's hut. This time, Biscuit sat like a sphinx between Jade and Harry, his forepaws neatly together. From the front, the cheetah was a picture of docility and contentment. Jade knew better. She felt his tail twitching in irritation, the white tip beating a staccato rhythm in the small of her back. She reached her hand around and stroked him gently, grounding herself in the real touch of his fur.

"I will now tell the story of the old king," began Sina. "It is a story told to me by my father, and by his father, and so back through my ancestors. Back to the time when we first came to the mountain."

Jade watched Julian from the corner of her eye. He leaned forward in his chair, forearms on his thighs, hands clenched together. His eyes shone with an intensity she had seen before when people were consumed by greed, whether for money, power, or lust. The sight oppressed Jade as she saw behind it the root cause of all the destruction and death she'd witnessed in her life. She felt her temples tighten and wondered if that greed lay behind Wheeler's death.

"This story lives in the memory of the ancestor spirits. And so it resides in the sacred groves where they are buried."

Julian wriggled, and Jade knew he was growing impatient at all the preliminaries. To Harry's credit, he gave a brief warning to sit still or they might not hear the story at all.

"I tell this story again so my sons will hear it and know it when I go to my ancestors and my bones sleep in the banana groves."

Jade drifted into the account. She'd always appreciated a good storyteller, whether it was one of the cowboys spinning a tall tale on her father's New Mexico ranch or her own father recounting his adventures. On rare occasions, even her mother would relate a story told to her by the Gypsies. Half the pleasure was in appreciating the teller's style. This one had the singsong rhythm of a memorized legend, told by rote.

"A king, mighty in warriors, mighty in land, mighty before God, came from the east. He wore shining garments stronger than spears, and carried weapons that shone as the sun and could cleave a man's head in two. He rode in a chariot pulled by wondrous animals that snorted fire. Beside him walked a great cheetah, his coat more golden than sunlight." Sina looked at Biscuit. "His spots were as the leopard's, and great stripes ran down his back. Every day he let the cheetah hunt, and every day the king's cheetah took two antelope, one that he ate and one that he brought back for the king.

"His warriors and slaves were more than man could count, his maidens more beautiful than the flowers. They rode in litters carried by men whose arms were as tree limbs for strength. Even the slaves wore metal and stones that shone like the sun and glittered as light sparkles on water. Men and maidens held double bows that seemed like the horns of antelope and were covered in this shining yellow metal they called gold. Strings fastened to these bows made music when their fingers caressed them. They sang of the king's glory. The king himself wore a purple robe, woven with threads of gold. It was held in place by an ornament made of clear shining stones the color of water, fire, and sky. Rings of gold and stones flashed on every finger.

This king came from a land far to the north and east seeking to increase his kingdom. He fought many wars, each time growing in strength and wealth. His scepter was mighty and could kill a man just to look upon it.

"The Maasai fought with great strength against this king, for they hold their cattle as gifts from the Maker. But the king told them he would leave their cattle, taking only what he and his army needed for food, if they would give him their gold. This they did, but the king looked with wonder at the great mountain. 'What is this mountain?' he asked the Maasai. 'It is the mountain of God,' they told him. 'I am God's lion,' he said. 'I will climb this mountain and talk to God.' So he went through this forest, he and all his great army. He went beyond the forest to the wild land where the antelope run."

The Chagga elder paused here to drink and regain his voice. No one, not even Julian, interrupted him. Jade again looked across to the director and saw the gleam in his eyes. His mouth was parted slightly, as though he wanted to take in the words through his breath and not just his ears. Biscuit, she noted, had closed his eyes and a deep, rumbling purr churned in his throat. She closed her own eyes and let herself be swept away into the vision of majesty and glory that belonged to the time of Solomon.

"This king felt God's hand on his chest. He could not breathe. His limbs weakened. 'It is for this that God called me to climb his mountain. I am old and I shall die. But I shall die as befits a king and be buried on God's mountain with all that I have won.' So he dressed himself in his greatest robes and ordered the leaders of his army to stay where they were. Then his slaves and some of the army carried him and all the gold up to the top of the mountain. So much was their burden of treasure that their backs bent low under the load. Only his warriors came back to the leaders. The slaves were slain and all were buried with his riches inside the mountain. The leaders told the Maasai that they must not disturb the grave. Someday, it is said, it will be found by this king's descendant and his glory will shine again. But not," he added, "until the end days."

When Jade opened her eyes, she felt disoriented. The village, Harry, Sina, all seemed out of place. Gone from her vision were the richly armored troops and an aging king who had seemed to look at her in her imagination and beckon to her to follow. Only Biscuit felt real to her in both times and places. A sharp hand clap by Julian rousted her out of her reverie.

"It is true!" Julian said. "The king *must* be Menelik to be known as the lion of God."

"And how does this help you make your motion picture?" asked Harry. "I thought you knew this story already, since you came here to Kilimanjaro instead of Mount Kenya or some other mountain that the natives consider holy."

"Well, it verifies it. And it will help me make the dialogue for the picture when we show the old man telling his tale." He rubbed his hands together. "Can you imagine that treasure? A pharoah's tomb would be nothing to it."

Jade motioned for Zakayo's attention. "Please ask the elder a question. Ask him what happened to the king's cheetah."

Zakayo repeated Jade's question. For a moment, Jade thought she'd committed some breach of etiquette, because the old man stared at her as though he was surprised to see this woman sitting close by. Then his gaze passed over her to Biscuit. He stopped purring for only a second and blinked at Sina. Then he butted his massive head against Jade, for all the world as if he was introducing her. Sina answered.

"He says that the king's great cheetah walked up the mountain with him but would not leave his master," said Zakayo.

"The warriors say that he sat beside the grave guarding it and that he still watches it today."

"Why did you ask that?" asked Harry, but before Jade could answer, they heard a shrill scream from one of the huts.

A young Chagga woman ran out, her eyes wild and staring. She pawed at her cloth wrap and her skin as though trying to divest herself of both, leaving long red gashes on her neck and arms. The girl stumbled blindly through the village, crashing into cookpots and people. Then, after colliding with and tripping over a goat, she collapsed on the ground, convulsing.

Jade and Harry rushed to the woman's side while the Chagga looked on with a mixture of wonder and fear. Harry took hold of the woman and turned her over.

"Get some water," he ordered.

"Toss me that canteen," Jade shouted to Julian.

He shook his head. "We can't let her drink from our canteen. What if she's contagious?" Jade snatched up a hollowed gourd from a nearby cooking fire and waved it. "I'll use this. Now toss the canteen."

Julian did as she commanded. Jade poured some water into the gourd and held it to the woman's lips. The young woman's mouth opened to drink and she struggled in vain to clutch the gourd. Her movements reminded Jade of someone who'd been dying of thirst, desperate for water. Her dilated pupils made her staring eyes look feral.

The native woman's convulsions lessened, but she seemed to be slipping away from any chance of recovery. Her eyes rolled back, revealing the whites. Jade felt for a pulse. She found it, but it grew weaker even as she held her fingers to the woman's jugular vein.

"We're losing her," she said.

"No. We've lost her," said Harry. He laid her head on the ground and stood. "Do you recognize her?"

Jade nodded. "She's the one who was cursed two days ago." As she spoke, she felt the ground jiggle softly under her feet. *Earthquake!* The Chagga felt the tremor, too, and ran towards their huts. Jade turned to see how Julian fared and spied him directing the camera's placement to film the dead girl. Jade cleared the distance in four long steps and positioned herself directly in front of the lens.

"Move out of the way, Miss del Cameron," bellowed Mr. Julian.

"No! And if you or your crew cranks so much as one frame of that poor girl's body, I'll personally dismantle the camera and toss the parts in the Una. Do I make myself clear?"

Biscuit, hearing the tension in her voice, moved between her and the director, one paw on the man's ankle.

"You must be joking," the director said. "This is too good to waste. I already have the woman cursing her. Showing her lying there later is—"

"I said no!" Jade didn't budge except to pull her knife from her boot and direct the hilt at the lens. "So help me, you'll respect her death and leave her in peace or I'll smash it."

Julian exhaled loudly. "Have it your way, but I'll have you know, miss, that I don't care to be crossed."

"Neither do I," said Jade, but she took careful note of the hateful fury in the director's eyes as he turned away.

CHAPTER 12

Death is no stranger to the mountain. Kilimanjaro itself was born in violence.

—The Traveler

JELANI PADDED CLOSER TO JADE'S TENT, A BRAIDED VINE ROPE HANGING from one shoulder and a fetish, a cowrie shell and a blue feather, strung from a leather strip in his right hand. He was about to drape the fetish over the front tent pole when he felt something simultaneously hard and soft butt his thigh. He put his free hand on the cheetah's head and stroked it while he hung the protective charm.

"Guard!" he whispered in a voice barely louder than a breath. But Biscuit recognized the word and positioned himself in front of the flaps. Jelani nodded approval and slipped away towards the livestock pen. Jade's situation was worse than he'd feared. It was only because Simba Jike herself possessed great power with the guardian spirits that she was still alive.

But it was only a matter of time. He'd seen her slip on the way down the mountain that first day. Normally her step was as sure as a cat's. No, this was no accident. The avenging devils or ancestors or whoever that woman had called on had been merely testing Simba Jike. Even the mountain had sent a warning. Bwana Nyati said such shaking—earthquakes, he called them—were common here, but Jelani knew better. The mountain, a spirit, or Ngai himself was displeased.

Jelani took the rope from his shoulder and made a loop in one end. He slipped the loop over the neck of a kid goat and led the animal out of the pen. The kid *maa*ed softly but no one in the camp stirred. Jelani had seen to that when he put a sleeping draft in last evening's meal. It was not very powerful—if real danger threatened the camp, Bwana Nyati or Nakuru would wake up—but it allowed him to leave the camp with the kid without anyone stirring over a small noise.

Once free of the camp and in the trees, Jelani headed up the Una River. Originally, he'd intended to sacrifice the animal in the Chagga village's banana grove to appease the angered ancestors. But after the other woman's death, he knew that these spirits wouldn't be easily pacified, especially by an outsider. No, he needed to take a different tack.

Since he couldn't turn back the wrath of the Chagga spirits, he would build a defense instead. He'd sacrifice to his own ancestors, calling on a long line of *mondo-mogos* to protect Jade. He wondered if he should try to call on some of her own protective spirits, the ones she called saints. There was one in particular, he recalled, that she invoked most often, a Saint Peter, and something that he carried. *A bait bucket!*

But somehow, he didn't think this man or any of the others would respond to the death of a goat. He'd once heard about the death of a special lamb from some missionaries, but he hadn't understood what they meant. No, this kid goat was a good one and his ancestors would be mightily pleased. When he was done, Simba Jike might not be completely out of danger, but she would have a fighting chance.

. . .

"Bebe, you're going to have to accept my decision," said Julian in a firm voice. "We've been over this already several times."

"Graham told me that *she*," Bebe said, pointing across the camp to Pearl, "was only going to be my body double for certain scenes. Now you're telling me that she's actually going to take my best role?" Her voice, controlled at first, rose in pitch. "You're shooting *her* in this scene?"

"Graham approved this. I thought you knew that. But you still have a very dramatic part," Julian said. "You're the reincarnated lover. It's a powerful role."

The pair argued near Jade's tent, away from the other actors. Since they probably didn't know Jade had gone inside a few moments ago, she was reluctant to come out and embarrass them. Better, she thought, that they maintained their sense of privacy. *Not that they'll have it much longer if they don't keep their voices down.*

Privacy! That was almost amusing, considering this morning's scene. Pearl's gossamer costume left very little to the imagination, even with a well-placed fringed sash draped down the front, especially once she'd immersed herself in the Una River. When she'd emerged a moment later, the fabric pasted to her skin and nearly disappearing into it, Jade had wondered why she was the only one blushing. No one else seemed to think anything of it.

At least Harry hadn't been there. Somehow that would have embarrassed Jade more than the other actors' presence. But he'd left that morning to climb up higher to hunt. For some reason, their second-to-last goat, a kid, had disappeared. It left them short of meat. Jade had looked around for Jelani and, not finding him, had assumed he'd accompanied Harry as gun bearer.

"You wouldn't be doing this if Graham was alive," Bebe exclaimed. "It's Cynthia's fault. She hates me because she knows he loved me, not her. I was all ready for this scene."

"Bebe, you're getting hysterical," said Julian. His voice was growing less controlled and would soon approach his usual dictatorial bellow if the actress didn't watch herself. "I don't know why you're getting mad now, Bebe. I told Morris to tell you this a week ago."

This is not helping my headache. I'm having too many of them lately as it is.

Jade had woken with one to begin with, feeling groggy. A good stout cup of coffee would have helped, but Muturi had overslept and only just gotten the cook fire started. Jade went to the spring and splashed icy cold water on her face to wake up, Biscuit at her side. The big cat didn't seem to want to leave it either, not even when she'd set out the remains of last evening's stew, which she'd tucked away for his breakfast. So she'd sat on a stump nearby while he ate and tried to figure out why she felt so awful. And while she thought, she watched the others.

The loud yawns told her that the entire camp had slept heavily, enough to make her suspicious. When she'd told Harry about it, he'd dismissed her notion that they'd been drugged.

"There's nothing missing," he'd said after a quick check of the storeroom. "We just had a trying day yesterday, that's all."

He'd been right about the trying day. He'd been wrong about nothing missing, but no one seemed to make too much of the absent kid goat.

"Something ate it," Harry said.

"There's no blood," Jade countered.

"Something scared it then and it ran off." He shrugged and flashed his toothy grin. "You worry too much," he said, crooking a finger under Jade's chin. Then he left camp, whistling.

She finally decided Harry was right and they'd just been overly tired from the hikes and from the distressing scene in the Chagga camp. The ones who hadn't made the trip weren't necessarily the earliest risers anyway.

And I feel like something passed from the south end of a north-facing mule.

She'd piled on an extra blanket, but for the life of her, she hadn't been able to shake the bone-penetrating cold that had enveloped her again last night. Even when Biscuit had plopped down beside her it hadn't helped. And when the blessed cup of coffee hadn't appeared as planned, she'd resorted to the aspirin in her tent. Now she was stuck in here until either those two stopped arguing, or she decided she'd had enough and she let them know she could overhear them. At least Biscuit seemed content to nap at her feet while she waited.

"You can say Graham agreed to this all you want, but I don't believe you. And my name had better appear on the screen before hers, and in bigger letters," said Bebe. "I may have to watch that harlot do my scene now, but I refuse to take second billing to her. She's not an actress. She's a second-rate circus sideshow."

"You have my word, Bebe. Now come on. I need to get your, er, her scene shot."

Jade listened to a moment of silence while, she presumed, Bebe made her decision.

"I have your word, Rex?"

"Cross my heart and hope to die."

"Well, we wouldn't want *that*," said Bebe. "All right, but I want *my* scenes punched up."

"Don't get your drawers in an uproar, Bebe. Your part is still bigger than hers."

Their voices diminished in volume as they walked away.

Jade waited a discreet moment before she slipped from her tent, Biscuit at her heels. The actors had clustered on chairs near the set, eating sandwiches for lunch. Some were dressed in modern safari clothes. Others wore flannel bathrobes over their period costumes. The mix of old and new looked comical.

Jade wondered where their Nyamwezi men were and spied them standing by a tree. They were decked out in colorful striped kilts that looked rather Egyptian. Gaudy breastplates of shiny tin and bronze covered their muscular chests. One wore a tall helmet that Jade thought looked like an upside-down metal pot. The *panga* that they'd used on their arrival to slash away the undergrowth hung at his side.

"Ah, there you are, del Cameron," said Julian. "I need that cat in my movie."

Jade noticed his choice of words. Not "want" or "would like to have" but "need." His tone suggested it was an order rather than a request.

"Why?"

Julian stared at her. "Why?" he repeated. "You heard that old Chagga man's story. Menelik traveled with a cheetah. It's vital to the picture. He's already in the scene with that crazy native woman. I can't just have him disappear from the story."

Jade wrapped Biscuit's lead around her hand.

"He won't do anything dangerous. He's a prop," said Julian. "That's all. I'll pay you twenty dollars."

"What can I do with American money out here?"

"It's all I have except a bit of Tanganyikan coins. Exchange it when you get to Nairobi."

"He won't do anything dangerous," Jade echoed.

"Cross my heart and—"

Jade flipped a hand in the air. "Spare me the histrionics,

Mr. Julian. Put it in writing and make it fifty dollars, cash up front."

"Done." Julian pulled out his wallet and peeled off five ten-dollar bills. He handed them to Jade. "Morris!" he yelled.

His assistant, standing right next to him, jumped. "Write up a contract for Miss del Cameron authorizing me to put her cheetah in the picture." He glanced over at Jade. "Put in a clause that the cat won't do anything she deems dangerous."

"Right away, Rex." The harried assistant ran off to his tent and Jade soon heard the sound of clacking typewriter keys.

Jade pocketed the money. *That should keep Biscuit in chickens for a while.* Suddenly the picture seemed more interesting. *Wait till I tell Sam that Biscuit had his second role in a motion picture.* She thought about the cheetah's first part in Sam's movie, herding a zebra stallion. "Lunch is over," declared Mr. Julian. "Everyone in their places for the next scene."

Cynthia sat down by the camp table, fluffing her hair. "I'm ready. This is where I find that coffer that has my husband all worked up, and I open it and confront him, right?"

"No, Cynthia, I changed my mind. We're shooting your scene later today. I want to get this scene first while it's in my head. It's where Menelik's lover puts the necklace in the box."

"But Conrad's already in costume," she replied.

"We don't need him in this scene. I just want the lover and her maidservant. The sets are all made up." He pivoted around. "Where is that woman?"

Jade assumed he meant Pearl, who'd gone to her tent once her wading scene was over.

The director looked at Jade. "What's her name, that African woman we hired?"

"Do you mean Lwiza?"

"That's her. Lwiza!" he bellowed.

The maid came from the house wearing her embroidered white dress and sandals.

"Ah, there you are. I need you in this scene," said Julian.

Pearl emerged from her tent, no longer wearing the wet gown. This time she had on a pale blue linen robe wrapped around her chest, leaving her shoulders and arms bare. The ends of the fabric were tied under her bosom and hung down the front. While less sheer than the other gown, it still clung seductively to her curves.

Lwiza studied the effect for a moment, then shook her head. She hastened over to the actress and fussed with the arrangement, untying the knot and rewrapping one side so that it draped over one shoulder.

"Hey, I like that," said Julian. "That's good. It looks more exotic."

"It is the right way," Lwiza said with a shrug.

"I think it looked better the first way," said McAvy.

"You would," Julian said, "but *I* think the native's got the knack. Just like she did with the men's getup. So we're going with it. Now take your places." Using gestures and pantomime, he directed the Nyamwezi to stand stiffly at attention in the background.

Jade wondered what they thought of all this, but decided it was probably the easiest work they'd been hired for so far.

"Okay, Pearl, this is *your* scene now. Do it like I told you. You know that you're going to lose your king, your love. You're agitated. He's going up the mountain to die. You want something of his to treasure. You've taken his royal pectoral from his tent and you're going to hide it in your jewel box. Understand?" He pointed to the broad, jeweled collar that nearly resembled a breastplate in its size.

Pearl watched him from under heavy lashes and smiled. "I understand perfectly." She shot a sidewise glance at Bebe, standing to her left, her arms folded across her chest.

"Good." Julian turned to Lwiza. "All you have to do is stand here"—he pointed to a side table—"and look like a servant. When Miss Zagar asks for it, you bring her the jewel box and set it on the table." He didn't wait for her to reply. Instead he turned to Jade. "Put that cheetah there." He pointed to a fringed rug in front by the table.

"Come on, Biscuit," Jade coaxed. "Time to go to work." She led the cheetah to the rug and unhooked his lead. "Lie down. Stay." Biscuit stretched his long form out on the rug, half reclining, his great head and barrel chest upright, his forelegs extended.

"That's fine. Now . . ." Mr. Julian stopped and studied the set. "Where's the damn box?" he snapped.

Jade wondered how anyone could find anything among all the clutter of the set. The great tent, open in front, was festooned with hangings and pillows and incense burners. Large wooden props, cut and painted to look like giant urns, stood next to each of the Nyamwezi.

"Morris!" yelled the director. "Where's my jewel coffer?"

Homerman ran out of his tent, a sheet of paper in his hand. "Here I am, Rex. I finished that contract for you."

"Hang the contract," shouted Julian. "I need that jewel box for this next scene. Why isn't it on the table where it's supposed to be?"

"I . . . I don't know, Rex," stammered Homerman. "I guess I don't remember what—"

"Well, you'd better remember," roared the director. "I can't waste all day on your incompetence."

"I swore I had it out already," Homerman muttered. "I'll go look for it, Rex." He trotted off towards the house to search the supply room for the missing prop.

Jade pulled a pencil from her shirt pocket and handed it to the director. "Might as well sign this while we're waiting, Mr. Julian," she said. The director groused but he signed his name to the paper and handed it back to Jade.

By the time she'd folded it and slipped it into her pocket, Homerman returned, carrying the needed prop. "This is heavy!"

"Set it over there," ordered Julian, pointing to a small stand near Lwiza. "All right. Places, everyone. Ready to roll film. And action!"

Jade watched while Pearl went through all the theatrics of clutching her bosom while looking up at the ceiling, then again with her head dropped. She recited lines of undying passion for the sake of lip-readers. Jade noticed that Pearl was much less skilled than Bebe, who used more expressive facial movement and far less chest heaving. Pearl pulled the pectoral from under her pillow and kissed it three times. After clutching it to her chest and kissing it again, she called to her maid.

Biscuit's movement caught Jade's eye. He stood suddenly as Lwiza approached with the coffer and set it on the low gilded table in front of her mistress.

What's wrong with Biscuit?

The cat uttered a high-pitched, staccato growl. Jade edged around to the side, keeping out of view of the camera. Her left knee throbbed as it always did when death was close by.

"Mr. Julian," Jade called, "there's something wrong. Stop the scene."

Pearl turned her head for a moment, looking at Jade.

"Get back in character, Pearl," ordered Julian. Biscuit stepped between Pearl and the box. "Jade, tell that cat to move."

"I'm telling you something's wrong. He knows it." Jade edged forward. She'd slipped her knife from her boot and held it ready. "Pearl, don't open the box."

"Cut!" shouted Mr. Julian. "Look, del Cameron, I'm telling you to get out of the way." He walked up to the set and to the coffer. "I'll prove to you that there's nothing wrong."

"No!" shouted Jade.

Julian ignored her. He reached out and lifted the hinged lid from behind. Pearl's piercing scream ripped through the air.

CHAPTER 13

Now that the mountain's warring youth is finished, it has settled into a benevolent old age, feeding and sheltering its inhabitants.

—The Traveler

JELANI HAD HEADED UP INTO THE MOUNTAIN'S FOREST, KEEPING west of the Chagga village. The kid goat trotted obediently behind him, pausing only on occasion to nibble some greenery. A slight tug on the rope brought the animal back to the trail. A few blue monkeys slipped quietly past him in the trees, but all else was silent.

The young healer kept his eyes and ears sharply alert, observing every shifting shadow and each noise. Leopards were more nocturnal, but one still might decide that the goat looked too tempting to pass up. More important, a Chagga warrior might decide he was trespassing and relieve him of both the goat and his life.

Jelani also studied the trees. The forest held many giants, some that he recognized, others that seemed different to him. Many carried branches draped with a long, feathery moss, like the chin fur of the wildebeest. Each ancient tree probably held many spirits, but none of them would have listened to him.

Because I cannot speak their language.

What he wanted, what he *needed* to find was a *mokoyo*, a type of fig with an orange bark that peeled away in thin strips, like a snake shedding skin in patches to reveal a fresh new yellow skin underneath. Ngai had instructed the ancestral Kikuyu man to make his sacrifice at this tree, preferring it to all others. It was even more critical now, when Jelani was far from his own village and ancestral spirits. Would they hear his call? Would they come to him? Or would the Chagga ancestors keep his own away?

They sacrifice in their banana groves, not in the wild forest.

Above and to his right, Jelani heard a low, croaking purr that increased in volume. *"Rurr, rurr, rurr, rurr."* He looked up and spied a male black-and-white colobus singing. A few females sat in a second tree, browsing on leaves. When the male jumped to another branch, a trogon yelped before flying off, his scarlet breast disappearing into the dim light. *"Yow, yow, yow."*

Jelani took the bird as an omen and left the main trail as it crossed one of the smaller streams, and followed the water uphill. The *mokoyo* liked water. It gave life to the spirits within. If one of his sacred trees grew on this mountain, he would find it close to flowing water.

There must be one here. This is a holy mountain, one of many that Ngai chooses to live on when he visits. Mount Kenya, Jelani knew, was one, but both the Maasai and the Chagga said this was another. He had walked on Mount Kenya once with his teacher and had felt the holiness seep through the soil and into his bare feet. When he stopped, he could feel the mountain's very pulse, and his own slowed to match it. Jelani stopped and closed his eyes. *Yes, it is the same here.*

He opened his eyes, and a glint of bloodred flashed before

him. He followed the trogon until it settled on a branch. Whether or not the bird was a spirit, Jelani couldn't say, but it directed him to the very tree he sought.

The ancient tree stretched straight up higher than four men standing on one another's shoulders. At least twice that number would be needed to span it, with their arms outstretched. In a forest where the great gray *tembo* easily uprooted trees with their tusks or pulled them down with their trunks, the *mokoyo* resisted them. Ngai had given the tree a heavily fluted stem that allowed it to brace itself against all onslaughts. It was proof of the Maker's wisdom. Why have a tree for the ancestral spirits to live in if it was only going to be torn down by a hungry animal?

Jelani approached the tree with reverence and with caution. Those same buttresses made deep recesses, places for a wild pig or a snake to hide. It would not do to disturb either one. As he gently caressed the sycamore fig's peeling bark, he cleared his mind of all but his prayers. This task would prove to be his greatest challenge yet. It was one thing to sacrifice near your village; it was another to call on ancestors from a great distance and induce them to come to a strange mountain. But Simba Jike's life depended on him. Now more than before.

He knew this to be true, for last night, he'd heard the Chagga interpreter talking to the cook as he prepared rations for the Nyamwezi men. The interpreter frequently brought gossip to the men in return for food. This time he told them that the angry woman who had cursed Simba Jike had just been found dead, blood draining from her nose, her arms and legs swollen. That meant that her curse was now a death curse, and nearly impossible to throw off.

Jelani took hold of the goat and pulled out his knife.

. . .

The screams continued as a sequence of shrill blasts, punctuated by gasps for air. And when Pearl wasn't shrieking, Bebe was. It reminded Jade of the hand-cranked air-raid sirens she'd heard during the Great War. She edged in closer towards the box and its writhing contents.

The slender green snake had been secured in a cloth sack, partly visible from Jade's vantage point. But the snake had managed to insinuate itself out of the loosened drawstring. It raised its head above the rim, its eyes oversized for its egg-shaped head.

"Move out of the way," yelled Jade. She needed a clear line of sight. Pearl stayed rooted to the spot in her terror, Biscuit in front of her.

"Biscuit. Herd. Away. Now!"

The cheetah responded immediately and butted against Pearl's legs, pushing her backwards. When the woman still didn't take any steps, Biscuit nipped her thigh lightly. Pearl reacted almost instinctively to what appeared to be a new threat and backed up until she bumped into the Nyamwezi wearing the pot helmet, a man named Fundikira.

The jostling coupled with the confinement irritated the snake. It raised its head and inflated its neck, giving Jade a slightly bigger target. She raised her right hand even with the top of her head.

In one blinding motion, she hurled her knife down towards the low table. The blade impaled the snake through the throat, affixing it to the coffer. But the snake wasn't dead, and Jade had no sidearm. She spied the *panga* hanging from the guard's belt.

"Fundikira, the *panga*!"

The Nyamwezi untied it and skimmed it across the ground to her feet. Jade snatched it up and, with one clean stroke, decapitated the snake. Its green head tumbled to the floor, rolling towards Pearl. Her screams resumed. Fundikira quickly moved out of the way, his hands over his ears.

"It's dead," said Jade. "You're safe now."

Pearl minced sideways until she was clear of the offending head and ran out into the open. "What was that horrid thing?"

Jade retrieved her knife and lifted the snake's body from the coffer. "Boomslang."

"Boomslang!" exclaimed McAvy, coming forward to get a better look.

Jade handed the corpse to him and wiped her knife blade on the grass.

"Is it poisonous?" asked Murdock, who joined McAvy.

"Yes," said Jade. "Hemotoxin. Breaks down your blood cells. Destroys your organs."

"How horrid," whispered Cynthia. "But how did it . . . ? Who could have . . . ?" Her eyes opened wider and she backed away, hugging herself. "It was meant for me!"

"What do you mean?" demanded Julian.

Cynthia pointed her finger at the snake's body as she stepped back. "We *were* going to shoot *my* scene with the coffer, remember? If you hadn't changed your mind . . ."

"What are you jabbering about, you insensitive bitch?" snapped Pearl. She'd channeled all her fear into anger now and directed it at her colleague for want of a better target. "*I'm* the one who nearly got killed. If I had opened that box, I'd be dead now. Thank my lucky stars that Biscuit stopped me." She dropped to one knee and hugged the cheetah around his neck.

"The boomslang is a pretty timid snake. It rarely bites unless you make a grab for it," said Jade. "The fangs are in the rear of its mouth. Chances are, you would have escaped. And even then, it takes a long time, hours, before anyone ever gets sick. So, you see, you wouldn't be dead now." She'd meant the speech to be reassuring, but it only enraged all the women.

"No, *she* wouldn't be dead because *I* was supposed to be playing this part," shrieked Bebe. "That was *my* role and everyone knew it! I suppose I should be grateful to that slut," she yelled, pointing at Pearl, "for stealing it; otherwise *I* would be dead."

Pearl's head jerked as though she'd been slapped in the face. "Who are you calling a slut, missy? I know how you got this part. Everyone knew Graham liked the ladies." She stopped and ran her gaze up and down Bebe's body. A wicked sneer crossed her lips. "I just didn't know he liked them so long in the tooth."

"Oh!" Bebe's face contorted into a snarl, her teeth bared and clenched, her brow furrowed. She lunged at the younger woman, her arms outstretched like claws.

Jade, who was closer to her than anyone else, grabbed her by one arm and swung her aside. Bebe wasn't as strong as Jade, but her fury nearly made up the difference. The actress scratched ineffectually at Jade's arm and face, forcing Jade to pull Bebe's arm behind the woman's back. Once Jade had the arm pinned, she shoved her knees into the back of Bebe's knees, forcing the woman's legs to buckle. Bebe dropped to the ground with a shriek of pain.

"Stop it! All of you," shouted Jade. "You're all acting like a bunch of pissy tomcats."

Budendorfer and Brown both snickered behind her, and she wheeled to face them. "That goes for you, too. None of you is helping here. Mr. Julian," she said as she turned to the director. "I expect you to control your crew. If you can't, then I'll think of something."

Julian stared at the snake's head, seemingly indifferent to

anything else around him. "This is tremendous," he said to himself. "How much of that did we get on film?" he asked Brown.

"All of it, boss. I kept cranking the whole time."

"That's great! Here's what we'll do. We'll cut out the parts where del Cameron is in view. We'll get one of those natives," he said with a sweep to include the empty tent where the Nyamwezi guards had stood, "to draw a knife. Then we'll cut to the dead snake and the head."

"But why would there be a snake in the box?" asked Budendorfer.

"What? Are you crazy?" Julian slapped the second cameraman alongside the head. "I'll think of something. I'll write in a scene about a curse or something. I tell you, this is priceless."

Jade clenched her fists, itching to plant one on the man's jaw. Instead, she helped Bebe to her feet. "You're all overwrought," she said. "All of you need time to simmer down." She gave Bebe a gentle nudge in the direction of the house. "Go lie down."

Jade nodded to Cynthia and Pearl. "You, too. Both of you go to your respective rooms."

She felt like a parent chiding children after an explosive temper tantrum. *It's a good thing that Pearl and Bebe aren't in the same building. At least Cynthia and Bebe should manage.* Then she remembered that Bebe had just been accused of sleeping with Cynthia's husband. "Woody, why don't you go with Miss Malta and Miss Porter and stand guard outside their doors. Make sure they're all right."

Murdock touched his hat brim in a mock salute and escorted the two women to the house. Seeing four of his actors leave the set finally got Julian's notice.

"What? Where are they going? We aren't finished yet!" he demanded.

Jade took a deep breath, trying to curb her own rising temper. Before she could say anything, McAvy stepped in.

"Rex, Jade's right. The ladies have all had a shock. They need to rest for a while. Frankly," he added as he swiped an arm across his sweaty forehead, "I could use a drink."

"Has it occurred to you, Mr. Julian, that someone tried to harm one of your people?" Jade asked.

Julian's mouth opened and stayed that way. Jade wondered if it was the first time the man had ever been rendered speechless. "But . . . but . . ." he stammered.

"She's right, Rex," said Hall. "This was no accident."

"Nonsense," Julian declared, having found his voice again. "The thing must have crawled into the box. Probably went after a rodent." He waggled a finger at her. "We do have those around here, you know. *You* even chased one out of the house, as I recall."

"How did it get in the box?" asked Jade.

"How should I know? Damned thing crawled in."

Jade shook her head. "Boomslang are arboreal, for one. Tree dwellers," she explained when she saw everyone's confused looks. "It had no business in our storage room or this tent, for that matter." She picked up the coffer and turned it over in her hands, examining it. "There's no hole for it to crawl through."

"It pushed up the lid," argued Julian. He took the box and demonstrated. "See. It's very simple." The heavy lid fell back on his index finger. "Ouch!"

"If it's so simple, then why didn't it push its way back out?" Jade asked. "And," she added before he could reply, "how did it manage to end up inside this bag, too?" She held up the cloth drawstring sack.

"It's just a sack," said Julian. "Why shouldn't it be in there?"

Jade grew impatient with the man's obtuseness. She stepped in closer until she was within two inches of his face. "I saw this box a few days ago when—"

"What were you—" began Julian.

Jade silenced him with a raised hand. "We were looking for trinkets to give to the Chagga elder so you could hear your precious story." She lowered her voice, packing purpose into every word. "I looked inside. There was *no bag* in this box. There was *no snake* in this box. This box was in a *locked* crate. And unless the damned snake had the key, someone put it in there!"

"Put what in where?"

Everyone turned to Harry as he and Nakuru strode into camp, two bush pigs strung on a pole carried between them. With his shirt unbuttoned at the throat, and his sleeves rolled up, he looked the epitome of strength and coolness under fire.

"Hascombe. About time you got here," said Mr. Julian. "What do you mean running off and leaving us unprotected in this wilderness?"

"Unprotected?" Harry handed off his end of the pole to one of the other hired men. "What's he talking about, Jade?"

She retrieved the boomslang's headless body and handed it to Harry. "This somehow made its way into one of the set boxes." She pointed to the head, still lying on the rug. "That's the rest of it."

"You?" he asked, not needing to finish the question. Jade nodded.

"But how . . . ?" Harry didn't get a chance to voice his question. The three actresses spilled forward as though on cue and ran for him.

"Oh, Harry," they shrieked in unison.

"Protect us, please," added Cynthia.

Harry nearly went down beneath the combined force of three very nervous, very grateful females.

Jade shook her head and motioned for Biscuit. "Come on, boy," she said as she walked away. "No hero's welcome for us."

Jade stirred the campfire and added another log.

"Once again, from the top, Jade," said Harry, his deep voice soothingly low. He'd bathed and shaved and the scent of witch hazel drifted towards her.

She carefully repeated the day's events, beginning with the director's change in plans and ending with Harry's entrance into camp. They sat alone outside. Though it was only seven o'clock, still early by their normal routine, no one seemed in a social mood. The usual poker game on the veranda, played by lantern light, had been called off for the evening. None of the men sat around swapping good-natured yarns of past movie productions. The actresses stayed in their own quarters, and Lwiza saw to their needs, going from one to the other as they called for her. Even Julian had stopped haranguing his assistant and cameramen.

Not that he hadn't worked them later that afternoon. He'd let the women rest for a short period while he reenacted the snake's demise, using Fundikira. Then he insisted on calling out Pearl to finish her scene, followed by Cynthia to film the modern finding of the pectoral.

Both women had approached the coffer with trepidation. They had had to be shown repeatedly that there was nothing inside before they would even touch the box. Harry stood guard off to one side, at their insistence. After his initial stifled, "Bloody hell," when he saw Pearl in her revealing costume, he stood sternly at attention, watching everyone and everything lest another incident occur. Cynthia more than any other stayed close to him, and he put a protective arm around her waist.

The only person who didn't make an appearance was Bebe. Finally Jade went to check on her and found her lying on her cot, staring at the cracked ceiling. When Jade asked if she needed anything, she declared she only wanted to be left alone. Lwiza brought dinner to her when they broke at six o'clock.

Jelani, who hadn't been with Harry after all, wandered back into camp around five thirty. His clothes looked wet, as though he'd fallen in one of the streams. When Jade asked him where he'd gone, he merely regarded her like a doctor scrutinizing a patient.

"I had business, Simba Jike," he'd replied before walking off to get something to eat.

Now, after her own quick bath, she and Harry had gathered on camp chairs for a council of war. Biscuit reclined at Jade's feet, his forepaws touching her boots. Dirty plates lay on a folding table, and Jade cradled a mug of steaming coffee.

"Well, I'll admit," said Harry, "the whole thing has me stumped. A boomslang!"

"So you agree that someone must have put it in the box?" She missed Sam's solid, no-nonsense logic, but was grateful that Harry took her seriously.

Harry removed his hat and ran one hand through his graying brown hair. "Looks that way, doesn't it?" He shifted his chair closer to her for a confidence. The scent of witch hazel grew stronger. "Any ideas who?"

Jade shrugged. "I've been thinking about it. Remember that fake snake? The one made out of a stocking?" She sipped her coffee, letting the hot liquid caress the back of her throat and the fragrant aroma cleanse her mind.

"The one in Bebe's bath? You found another one, didn't you? In Pearl's tent?"

Jade nodded. "It was unfinished. But what I also remember is how excited our illustrious director got over that idea. He wanted you to find a real snake for him."

"I remember. The bastard." Harry leaned forward, resting his forearms on his thighs. His shoulder brushed Jade's. "It would be like him to hire one of the natives to get a snake for him. Just so he could have his dramatic scene."

"Right," agreed Jade, "but somehow I can't see him risking any of his people with a poisonous one."

"Maybe he didn't expect a venomous snake," Harry suggested. "Maybe he just ordered a snake. Thought he'd get a rock python or something."

Jade shuddered.

"You're shivering, Jade. Are you cold?" He edged closer.

"No. I'm fine."

Harry put a hand on her shoulder. "I'm a ruddy idiot. *You've* had a worse scare than the others. You had to actually kill the bloody thing."

Jade knew there was an element of truth in his statement. She did feel like collapsing, and for a moment, Harry's gentle concern nearly did her in. She felt the attraction of having a man's strong arm around her. But it was Sam's she wanted. Jade took a deep breath and twisted aside, putting inches between them. "I can't figure out how *anyone* would risk their life catching something poisonous. What would motivate someone to try it?" She drained her mug.

"Money's usually a good incentive," said Harry, withdrawing his hand. "But boomslangs are the least aggressive of the lot, unless they're agitated. I heard stories of one collector who came out here a few years ago, a biologist of sorts. He found out that they like to curl up and sleep in birds' nests when it's cold. So maybe someone took advantage of the cool nights here and caught one that way. Still, it's not something I'd want to try. Strangest venom."

"Oh?" prompted Jade.

"Right. You see, it breaks down your blood. But it waits for a day or two."

"You're joking. I knew it could take an hour or two, but days?"

"It's true. I knew of a chap who got bit. His companions kept him absolutely still for well over a day. Man said he felt fine and assumed he didn't get any real dose of venom. Two hours later some nasty-looking bruises developed on his legs and blood started coming from his nose. Fell down dead a good twenty-eight hours after he was bitten."

"Hmm, I wonder." Jade set her cup down and jumped up from her chair. Biscuit raised his head inquiringly. "I'll be right back," she told him, and hurried to her tent, where she'd tossed the fabric bag, and brought it back to the fire along with her flashlight. "There is something else in here," she said. "I can feel it crackle under my fingers." Jade handed the light to Harry. "Hold that for me, please," she said. Then she opened the bag and peered inside. Biscuit sat next to her.

"What is it?" Harry asked.

Jade reached in and pulled out the remains of a bird's nest.

"So was it Julian?" asked Harry. "Should we confront him, do you think?"

Jade thought for a moment. "No. He'd only deny it. And somehow, it doesn't feel right. I can see him buying a snake, but surely he'd be careful enough to get a dead one at least. We need to keep our ears open, though. Talk to the crew, but keep it easy."

"An interrogation of sorts," said Harry.

"In a way, but not so open," said Jade. "This was probably a single incident, but . . . but after Wheeler's death, I don't think either of us wants to take any chances with this lot."

"You think his death was related?"

Jade heard the skepticism in Harry's voice. She watched the fire, seeing Sam's concerned face in her mind's eye. "Maybe we should pack these people up and get them back."

Harry shifted in his chair. "Can't do that, Jade. I'd get fired and probably never get another safari. But I can't see that it's that serious. A stupid prank at best, but whatever it was, no one was hurt and I doubt anyone would try another stunt like it."

Jade frowned. "You're the boss."

Harry reached over and touched her arm again. His voice dropped to a husky rumble. "You're not a flighty woman. When you see danger, it's generally there. I respect that. But you have to see my position. Still, just because I'm not willing to pack them in doesn't mean I'm not taking this seriously. No, ma'am. I can ask some questions. Since I wasn't here for the excitement, I think I can get away with it."

"Fine," agreed Jade. "I'll leave the questioning to you. I'm going to call it a night."

Harry studied her for a moment. "Are you sure you're all right, Jade? You've had a damned harrowing day, you know."

"Really, I'm fine, Harry. Thanks for your concern, but I'm just tired."

"Wait," he said softly. He stood, too, as she rose from her chair. "In case I forgot to mention it, I'm particularly grateful for your quick thinking and good aim today. You saved some lives. I knew I picked the right person to second this group. Someone I could trust to take care of camp when I'm out of it. I wish you'd let me show you how glad I am that you're here."

Jade felt his body heat radiating out to her, carrying his musky, male scent. She remembered over a year ago in Tsavo when he'd kissed her after the rhino attack. She recalled that he tasted of Africa. Then she'd brazenly taken the kiss as her due. But not now. Not this time. "Your trust is enough," she said, and walked off to find Jelani, trying to think of something else. Her brief comment on Wheeler's death came to her aid. She hadn't thought about it for a while, but now everything Sam had said came back to her. She wondered if he might not have been right after all. Did he trust her judgment as much as Harry did? Then she wondered why it mattered so much to her when she hadn't said yes to his marriage proposal.

The lantern's soft red glow seemed deceptive. It illuminated without letting one really see. Sam always needed more time to adjust to his night vision than he liked to admit to anyone. He repositioned the lamp so that it was level with his shoulder, casting its glow from behind. That helped. He avoided thinking about what Jade's reaction would be when she found he'd made prints from her negatives.

I can always blame it on Finch.

No, that wouldn't work. He didn't have the face for bluffing. It made him a rotten card player, but an honest man. His best defense if Jade started into a hissy fit would be the truth. He needed evidence that something peculiar was going on, and he thought he might find it in her candid shots of the actors. If she didn't like it, well, she'd just have to lump it. He had to do something.

Maybe if I replace all her developing stock, she won't even notice I've been in here.

He hung the last picture by a clothespin to dry on the line.

It was one of that Swahili lady standing to the side, watching while the three actresses posed for a newspaper reporter. Jade had captured not only the woman's serene face, but also the details of her costume. The fingertips of one hand rested lightly just below her throat, the long white sleeve falling back, exposing an intricate silver band halfway up her forearm. In the background, the American women with their heavily painted eyes and plucked brows pretended to be chummy.

Who was he fooling? He'd taken a hand lens to the other pictures, hoping to see that African man who'd murdered Wheeler lurking somewhere in the background. So far, nothing. According to Jade's note cards, these pictures were taken two days before Wheeler was killed. He wished she'd taken pictures the morning of his death.

He found his growing anxiety hard to explain, even to himself. Call it intuition, or just horse sense, but he *knew* something was wrong. He likened it to that sense the livestock had just before a storm or a temblor. Sam had had the same feeling when someone had tried to bilk his father out of his life savings years ago. On the surface, everything seemed fine and dandy, a good business opportunity. But Sam had picked up on subtle nuances in the crook's behavior. His dad just said that he must have a good nose for bull crap.

And I smell it now. Only this time, it wasn't money at risk. It was Jade's life, and the thought drove him into a frenzy. She was hell and away from him now. The gnawing conviction of something terribly wrong nearly drove him to distraction. He hadn't slept a wink last night.

Sam picked up one of the dry photographs, one with Wheeler and that actor who played the safari head. *What was his name again?* Sam consulted Jade's notes. *McAvy.* Like many of Jade's photos, it was a candid shot of the two men relaxing.

At least, McAvy seemed relaxed, leaning back in his chair, arms folded across his broad chest. Wheeler, on the other hand, appeared to be studying someone else, someone off to his right. A trace of a wistful smile graced his lips. Sam peered more closely, again using the hand lens.

Miss Porter! So he was watching his wife.

Sam wondered who else had seen that look. Whoever it was, they weren't in the photo.

CHAPTER 14

Kilimanjaro might be settled, but the earth is not. Tremors still remind visitors and residents that the rift is active. It never pays to become too complacent.

—The Traveler

The next morning, Jade found Jelani at his usual spot near the back of the house, assisting Muturi in preparing breakfast. Biscuit padded beside her and, seeing an unwashed pot that had held cooked meat before Muturi mixed it with the eggs, stuck his large head into the cast-iron kettle and licked the bottom, a contented raspy purr rumbling from his barrel chest.

"I need to talk with you, Jelani," Jade said. "About what happened yesterday."

"Muturi *mpishi* has already told me of the snake," he said, "and how Biscuit protected the woman from opening the box."

"Good. Then you know about this latest *shauri*. But that's not what I came to talk about." She waited to see if Jelani volunteered anything on his own. He didn't, reaching to take a used plate from Mr. Wells. "Where did you go yesterday?"

"I went to . . . pray, Simba Jike," he said. "Just as you did last Sunday at the mission."

"You went to the mission?"

Jelani shook his head. "No. My ancestors do not live there. I went to a holy place in the forest. To a *mokoyo* tree."

Jade didn't need to ask any more. She knew just enough about the Kikuyu spirituality to know that sacrifices were made at these trees. Her suspicions about what had happened to the kid goat were correct. Chiding him would be tantamount to an insult.

"I trust your prayers were heard," she said.

"Let us hope so," said Jelani.

Jade noted the intensity in his voice just then. *What is he keeping from me?* "Is there something I or Bwana Nyati should know about?"

"The Chagga woman is dead," he said.

"The one who made the curse? Rehema?" asked Jade. "She's dead?"

Jelani opened his mouth to answer, then stopped when Lwiza came by, followed by Cynthia and McAvy.

"Someone died?" asked Cynthia, her voice tremulous. She surveyed the camp's occupants. "Who?"

Her outcry was overheard by several others, and soon they were joined by still more. Repeated questions of "What happened?" and "Did someone get hurt?" swelled to a din.

"Quiet, all of you," ordered Jade. "None of us is hurt."

"But I distinctly heard you," said Cynthia. "You said, and I quote you, 'She's dead?' "

By that time, Harry had joined the group. "What's going on now?" he demanded. He glanced at Cynthia briefly. She dropped her gaze and stepped closer.

Jade looked at Jelani. "Suppose you tell all of us, Jelani."

"I overheard the Chagga man, Zakayo, tell Muturi *mpishi* that the woman who made the curses in their village was gone," said Jelani.

"Gone is not the same as dead," said Jade. "Did Zakayo give you this news, Muturi?"

"It is so," said the cook. "He told me that she walked back from this camp having sold many yams. Then she went to fetch the water and fell. Blood came from her nose and mouth, and her legs and arms were fat as a rock python when he has swallowed a pig. The woman she went to for help sent her away and she left the village. He came to tell me."

"Then we still don't know that she's dead," said Jade.

"Simba Jike," said Jelani in a tone one used to teach a particularly slow child, "she was sent away because it was certain she would die. Better that she not die in the village."

"Probably ran her out because they thought she had some disease," said McAvy.

Jelani nodded. "So now her curse is a death curse."

"Considering the girl she cursed already died before her, I'd say she went to a lot of trouble for nothing," said Wells.

"I suppose," added Bebe, "that it's tragic, but I imagine those natives die all the time, don't you think? Do you really think it was some horrid disease?"

"Oh, gawd," said Pearl. "We're probably all doomed then. She sold food to just about everyone, didn't she?"

Harry rubbed his freshly shaved chin. "It doesn't sound like any disease I know of. It sounds like snakebite."

"Snakebite," whispered Jade. "Then maybe she—"

"My thoughts exactly," said Harry. "We may have to go back up to the village and ask around. See if anyone knows anything."

"We could have Zakayo interview people for us," Jade suggested. "Then report back. They're more likely to talk to him than to us."

"Good idea," said Harry. "I'll ask him when he comes in. What *are* the plans for today, does anyone know?"

Talmadge nodded. "Rex says he's hired some Chagga to pretend to attack our camp."

"So Zakayo should probably be with them," said Jade.

"Right," agreed Harry.

Bebe hugged her stomach. "Excuse me. All this talk of blood makes me ill. I'm going to get some bicarbonate." She ran off to the house.

Cynthia clutched Harry's arm and looked up into his face with large, pleading eyes. "Are we in danger, Harry? You'll protect us, won't you?"

He puffed out his chest and patted her hand. "Don't fret your pretty head, Cynthia. We're simply following up on how that snake got into the box. If that Chagga woman wanted to make certain that her curse on Jade took, she was probably crazy enough to plant the snake there. We want to make sure. But the woman's dead now, so she can't hurt anyone else."

"Oh, I do hope so," said Cynthia. "It's good to know that *you're* here to protect us." She stood on her tiptoes and planted a kiss on Harry's cheek.

"Now that I think on it," said Harry, his voice low and husky, "there were more questions I wanted to ask you. Is there someplace we can talk? Privately?"

"Perhaps after breakfast," Cynthia said as Bebe returned.

Jade rolled her eyes. Harry might do well enough with the women, but somehow, she wasn't sure how his interrogation skills would work if he ever talked with the men.

SAM SAT IN Dr. Mathews' waiting room until the patient, a man with gout in his big toe, hobbled out the door. He was surprised to find that the doctor kept Saturday hours.

"Actually, I don't," said the doctor as he offered Sam a chair in his study. "I rarely keep any regular hours, as I travel a great deal. Missions, and some of the King's Rifles' encampments, you know. I started coming in on Saturday mornings just to have a chance to read or look over my cases in peace and quiet. But someone always manages to find me."

"And I'm as guilty as the last man, aren't I," said Sam. "My apologies."

"Oh, no," said Mathews, "I didn't mean you, Mr. Featherstone. Good heavens, how very rude of me. No, *you* had the decency to ring me up and make an appointment. I thought this would be a better time for all concerned. Fewer interruptions, don't you see."

"And I appreciate it," said Sam. "I won't take up any more of your time than necessary."

"I take it this is still about that knifing at the Muthaiga?"

Sam nodded. "I'd hoped that you'd heard something back from your friend in Mombassa. The one who was examining the drug-laced drink."

"Indeed. I heard from him yesterday. One of the papers I intended to study today. Most curious case, but I'm afraid I haven't much more to tell you than we already know. My colleague verified that the seeds found in the drink were a variety of datura. Common enough plant. I believe it even grows in your country. Jimsonweed, I think it's called?"

"That's right. Devil's Trumpet is another name for it. Terrible when the livestock get into it. If it doesn't kill them, it gets into the milk and poisons the calves."

"I would imagine the effect would be similar to that on humans: irrational behavior, temporary blindness, an inability to carry out basic bodily waste functions."

Sam sat up straighter. "We used to know a rhyme for that

back home. How did it go? Can't see, can't spit, can't pee, can't . . ." He stopped. "I imagine you can work out the rest."

The doctor laughed. "Indeed. But the effect, of course, depends on the dosage. In this instance, some of the seeds were actually crushed and steeped in the alcohol. That made it more potent, and the alcohol, naturally, enhanced the overall influence."

"So this man probably didn't go out to the Muthaiga already intoxicated?" asked Sam.

"I should think it highly unlikely. No. I imagine our crazed friend arrived at the Muthaiga, then partook of the drink and became hallucinogenic and crazed."

Sam studied the doctor's face for a moment, searching for some insight as to what the man made of all this. "I don't know about you, Doctor, but that just sounds like a load of—"

"Indeed." Mathews clasped his hands on his desk and leaned forward. "Mr. Featherstone, I am inclined to agree with you. It is just all too bizarre."

"Was there anything unusual about the alcohol?"

Mathews shrugged. "Not that my friend could detect. Seemed to be the basic native-brewed beer, *tembo*, they term it. Like the elephant. But he did say that the practice of putting datura seeds in alcohol is not practiced by our local tribes. However, it is sometimes done in the northern countries."

"So our murderer came from up north?"

"You'll have to ask the inspector about that. One of his men took a photograph of the corpse and sent copies by train down to Mombassa and north to the outlying towns. Hoped someone might recognize the man." He reached into his top desk drawer. "Left one with me. Might assist you in finding answers."

Sam stood, took the photograph, and extended his hand to the doctor. "Thank you very much, Dr. Mathews. You've been very helpful. I guess I should call on the inspector next."

Mathews shook Sam's hand. "My pleasure, Mr. Featherstone. As a student of native pharmacology, I'm quite intrigued by this case myself. Er, you might just keep my giving you that picture a secret. The inspector does not always—how shall I put this?—tolerate amateur investigators questioning him."

Sam scowled. "He should have thought of that last July before involving Miss del Cameron and myself in one of his cases. He owes me for that."

"A most interesting young lady, that Miss del Cameron," said the doctor.

"You don't know the half of it."

Whatever Julian had planned for the morning, most of it was wasted. Even Harry's plans were foiled. First Cynthia reported feeling nauseous soon after breakfast and spent much of the morning retching by the stream. Lwiza attended her, bringing her damp cloths to wipe her face. Jelani offered his services as a healer, pointing out several natural remedies for stomach discomfort readily at hand, but Cynthia would have none of it. Finally, Lwiza got her to take honey in warm water.

Pearl announced that she would be in her tent if anyone needed her. Jade saw Harry head in that direction a few minutes later. More interrogations? Jade wondered. Unable to film his dramatic attack scene, Julian did the next best thing. He made his men rehearse it.

"Cynthia already knows her part. She'll be sitting by her tent, cleaning her weapon. Wells, McAvy, Hall," Mr. Julian called. "I want you all sitting outside of McAvy's tent."

"What are we doing?" asked McAvy.

"Visiting, talking. For cripes' sake, use your imaginations!

Wait! Play one of your poker games. That'll look good." He watched them set up the folding table and chairs. "No, none of you have your rifles with you. Just Murdock. You have to scramble to your tents for them."

"Where am I, Rex?" asked Murdock.

"I want you standing over there." Julian pointed to a spot by the edge of the overgrown banana grove. "That will give you a clear view of everything going on. You're watching them all, remember? This is your chance to take over the safari and get the treasure for yourself."

Murdock nodded. "So you don't want me to fire, right?"

"That's right. Pretend your rifle's jammed. But when you see the native creeping around the side of Cynthia's tent, knife raised, then you shoot. You shoot to save her."

Bebe laughed. "Oh, that's original. Poor little woman has to have some man defend her life and virtue. How corny is that? She should take care of herself."

"That's what I meant to say," said Julian. "You'll try to get a bead on him, but she's in the way, so you can't shoot or you'll hit her. Got it? I'll tell Cynthia that she sees the native, loads, and fires just in time." He rubbed a hand across his chin and mulled over the idea. "Yeah, that will be dramatic. Glad I thought of it."

"Where do you want me?" asked Bebe. "Don't I get to do anything in this scene?"

"Yes, you know that Murdock set up this whole attack, so you need to stay by him. I have it." Julian slapped his hands against his temples. "You see this as a chance for Cynthia to die. Then you can have Menelik reborn for yourself."

"Of course," Bebe said. "But I see he's going to shoot Hall, so I push his gun aside and he shoots Hank instead." She studied the setting for a moment. "If you don't mind, Rex, I'm going to take a walk. I want to think about my role in solitude. Become my character."

"Hey," Julian shouted after her, "those Chagga men are supposed to be here soon. They're just going to get in the way and expect to get paid twice if I make them wait until this afternoon to film. So if you see them, tell them 'come back, sun high.' That should do it."

Bebe flapped a hand at him and walked into the woods on the main trail to the village.

Jade had been watching and listening from the porch. When she saw Bebe leave the old orchard, she decided she'd better bring her back. "I know Miss Malta takes her part seriously," she said, "but I don't think she should go off alone, Mr. Julian. I'll go after her."

"Then *you* tell the Chagga to come back later." He wandered in a circle, waving his hands in the air. "What am I paying these people for?"

Jade snatched up her Winchester and trotted after Bebe. But Homerman stopped her before she made it to the orchard.

"Ah, Miss del Cameron. I'm glad I bumped into you." He wrung his hands together and mumbled through his fears. "Terrible fix. The devil to pay."

Jade took hold of his shoulders, wondering if Cynthia had gotten worse. "What is it, Morris? Spit it out!"

"It's a disaster," he moaned. "Looked everywhere."

Jade was about to slap him when he finally spilled out, "I still can't find one of the rifles. I was hoping we might borrow yours for—"

"No!" Jade tried to sidestep the man but he held the main path, his hands clasped in front of him. She pushed him aside. "You'll just have to look a little harder. Now if you'll excuse me, I have to be going."

She hurried into the orchard and headed for the trail to the village. *The trail should be safe. The Chagga are friendly, and there hasn't been any spoor from a large predator.* But the thoughts didn't quiet her concern. There had been too much trouble already, and Jade didn't want to take any chances. *Silly Bebe might take it into her head to eat something poisonous.*

She hadn't gone more than twenty yards up the trail when she saw Bebe returning. "There you are. You shouldn't wander off alone like that."

"I'm fine now that you're here," Bebe said. "I heard those horrid natives coming, and I told that interpreter man to go away and come back later. But I'm so glad you're here. I don't know what I was thinking, walking off alone like that. And I thought I heard something in those trees over there." She pointed off to the right.

"Oh," Jade said. "Probably just a bush pig." She had hoped to use the chance to question Zakayo now rather than waiting until Mr. Julian was done with them for the day. "You should head back, but I'll find Zakayo and make sure he understands. I wanted to talk to him anyway."

Bebe grabbed Jade's arm. "Don't make me walk back alone. I really would feel safer with you along. Did I tell you how simply swell you were the other day when you killed that hideous snake? I wish I could be more like you, but this entire safari is almost more than I can endure."

Jade turned back with her, putting her obligation to the women over an opportunity to speak with Zakayo. *Might as well talk with her while I have her alone.*

"And how *are* you doing, Miss Malta? That was a pretty bad scare yesterday. I'd imagine everyone is still rattled."

Bebe dabbed at her forehead with a linen hankie and

smoothed an errant strand of hair. "Of course I'm rattled. Who wouldn't be after a second attempt on her life?"

Jade assumed the first attempt was when Wheeler was murdered. "So you really think that snake was intended for you?"

Bebe, who'd moved a few steps ahead of Jade, snapped her head around and glared at her over her shoulder. "Who else? That was *my* part. Everyone knew I was supposed to play the emperor's lover. If that idiot Rex hadn't changed his mind at the last moment, *I* would have been opening that box."

"Granted, but I understood that Miss Porter was supposed to be shooting her scene instead: the one in which *she* finds the pectoral in the box."

Bebe waved away that notion with a flip of her hand. "Cynthia should check her schedule more than once a week. Rex is always making changes. Or maybe she's just getting old and addled. Look at her today," she added, her voice laced with scorn. "Setting back the entire production for a bout of nervous indigestion. She should've taken a bicarbonate like I did."

Jade didn't think Cynthia was much older than Bebe, but didn't remark on their ages. It appeared to be a sore spot with the women. But then, in a make-believe world where glamour and beauty reigned supreme, she wasn't surprised. And both Cynthia and Bebe took their jobs seriously, devoting a lot of time to their parts.

"I've got to admit that I'm still baffled by how that snake got into the box to begin with," said Jade. "If it *was* meant to hurt you, then who would have done that?"

Bebe tossed back her head and sniffed. "Any number of people, I imagine. Pearl is desperate for my role. And Cynthia hates me because Graham loved *me*, not her."

"Pearl is the one who nearly opened the box," argued Jade. "Why would she open it if she had put a poisonous snake inside?"

Bebe waggled a finger at Jade. "But she *didn't* open the box, did she? She *knew* what was in there. But once Rex made the change, she couldn't do anything about it without giving herself away."

"But how would she manage to get a snake to begin with?" asked Jade.

"Ha! You're joking, right? Don't you know about her?" She rubbed her eye, brushing the finger across her nose afterwards. "She used to work in some circus sideshow before Rex discovered her. She danced a hoochie-coo with some big horrid constrictor." They'd reached the edge of the house's old banana grove. "Thank you for keeping me safe, Jade."

Jade nodded but Bebe didn't wait for her to answer. "If you'll excuse me, I need to get ready for what's left of my role." Sarcasm put a sharp edge to her voice.

Bebe walked off, heading straight for the director. Jade watched her and considered her statements. She'd seen Pearl's photo in one of the cinema magazines depicting her with a four-foot boa constrictor draped across her shoulders. But this was no constrictor, and Pearl's screams were those of a terrified woman. It was true, Julian did change his mind a lot, but Jade noticed it was often after someone put an idea into his head.

Who did he talk with earlier? Maybe Harry's found out something. Jade decided to look for him and compare information. Not seeing him outside, she headed for his tent when Homerman ran into her again.

"Pardon me," he said. "I wasn't looking where I was going, I guess." The little man fluttered his hands and twitched his head in short, jerky motions, like a fidgety bird.

"Don't apologize, Morris," Jade said. She felt a little guilty for shoving him aside earlier. "You look like you're in a hurry. But then, you seem to carry a large responsibility around here."

"Rex is very exacting," he admitted, "but sometimes it doesn't help."

Jade wondered if something else had happened or if he was still looking for one of the rifles. *Sweet Millard Fillmore. Can't these people be left alone for more than five minutes without someone having a hissy fit?* "Is something else wrong that I should know about?"

"Only that I still can't find parts of the set," he said. "I could have sworn I left all the boxes against that back kitchen wall," Homerman mumbled to himself.

"What boxes?" Jade asked. By now she wondered how anything was ever found. This little man was the most absent-minded assistant imaginable.

Homerman twitched, as though he'd already forgotten Jade's presence. "What do you mean?" he asked. "Is something else missing?"

Jade took a deep breath and shook her head. "You said you couldn't find some boxes for the set. And earlier you'd lost a rifle. I asked what is missing."

"Oh! A hat, footstool, a box of . . . Maybe they're in Rex's tent." He scampered off and Jade laughed softly. *What a crew.* Individually, they were personable, but collectively? She continued on towards Harry's tent when she heard him call to her from the cook's fire.

"Where were you, Jade? I've been looking for you." He handed her a mug of coffee.

"Thanks," she said, taking it in her hands. "I've been running herd on Miss Malta. She took it in her head to trot up the trail to head off the Chagga until this afternoon. Then, when I caught up with her, she decided she probably shouldn't have done that and insisted I protect her." She took a sip of the coffee, savoring the taste. Strong, but not overpowering. She'd have to tell Muturi to toss an eggshell into the pot to take out some of the acidity.

Harry waited for Jade to continue. "And did she need protecting?" he prompted.

Jade shook her head. "But after she witnessed that attack on Wheeler, I guess I can't blame her for being jumpy. She insists that the boomslang was meant for her. She's blaming Miss Zagar." Jade took another swallow, giving Harry the opportunity to add something.

"Probably because of their rivalry," he said. "But Pearl was the one almost bitten."

"Miss Malta says it was a chance whim of our illustrious director that made the switch. She said that Miss Zagar used to handle snakes before she became an actress."

Harry's laugh sounded more like a snort, giving credence to his nickname of Bwana Nyati, or buffalo. "She didn't handle *venomous* snakes. That's an entirely different situation."

"Did Miss Zagar tell you about it? Or have anything useful to say?"

Harry peered into his coffee and swirled it around. "I talked with her. Like you and I agreed," he added. "This motion picture is her first big chance at fame, apparently."

"So she'd have reason to want to hurt Miss Malta."

"No!" Harry said quickly. "According to her, she already knew the role of old Menelik's lover was hers. It was something Wheeler and Julian had bantered about for a while. She says that Bebe's just fooling herself. That she's not accepting getting older."

"Older?" Jade scoffed. "What is she? Twenty-nine? Thirty?"

"Thirty-one," said Harry. "At least according to Cynthia. But you could have fooled me. Her body is still very . . ." He glanced at Jade through lowered lids and cleared his throat. "Er, she doesn't look it to me."

Jade finished her coffee in two gulps. "No one's going to admit to putting that snake in the box, Harry. You and I both know that. If what Jelani said is true, then Rehema was the one who caught the snake to begin with and probably died as a result of it. You said it might take over a day before anyone would feel sick from the venom."

"Yes, and by then it's too late to bleed it out. But how would she have gotten the snake into that box? And why?"

"How?" echoed Jade. She pointed to Homerman, scurrying around looking for misplaced articles. "That's how. He's always losing the keys. As to why? Maybe Rehema thought it would bite me. I'm the one she cursed."

"Right," agreed Harry. "I'll keep my eyes and ears open anyway, and once they get finished with this attack scene, the two of us can talk to Zakayo and see if he knows anything."

An exultant shout interrupted them. "There they are!" exclaimed Homerman.

"Morris must have found whatever he lost," said Harry. "Wonder what it was."

Jade shrugged. "Box of something." She watched as Julian walked the men through their upcoming scene. He shoved them into the right spots, stared at the sun as though gauging where the light and shadow would be in another hour, and pushed them into new positions. Next he placed little squares of dark paper on the ground, markers for where the Chagga men were to stand. Bebe hung by his side. *Probably hoping he'll drop her an acting crumb.*

"Ought to be an interesting scene," Jade said. She wished Sam had a chance to watch this. She knew he'd find it intriguing. Should she tell him about the snake incident when she got back to Nairobi?

"Harry?"

"Yes?"

"You don't think Wheeler's death has anything to do with that snake in the box, do you?"

Harry put a hand on her shoulder, then quickly removed it. "Absolutely not. That was just a robbery by a crazy native. Don't *you* go jumping at nothing now. I'm counting on at least one clear head here."

"Is everyone in position?" shouted Julian. He didn't wait for a reply. "Does everyone have their weapon?" It was past noon and as hot as a sauna, but the director insisted on shooting then rather than wait for the following morning. His drive to film resembled an addictive need.

"You told me to put the rifle in the tent," said Wells. He sounded irritable.

The heat's getting to everyone, Jade thought. *They're not used to working in it.*

Julian scowled. "Does everyone who is *supposed* to have their weapon at hand have it?"

Since that meant only Murdock and Cynthia, they were the only two who responded in the affirmative. Cynthia still looked pale, but Julian considered that to be an asset for this scene. "We found mine in the tent," she said. "I have it now."

"Good. And everyone else has their rifle stacked by a tree or in their tent." This time it was an edict, not a question. "Now, I want this in one take. No wasting film, you hear?"

Budendorfer waved a hand tentatively, as though afraid to speak out.

"Well?" demanded Julian.

"Rex, the Chagga men aren't here yet."

"Of course they're not here yet. Do you think I can't see that they're not here? But we might as well shoot the climax while we're waiting."

Budendorfer glanced at Brown, who shrugged. "Uh, boss? Which one of us do you want to film that?"

"Both of you!" roared Julian. "I need two angles." He studied the setting and the light. "Steve, you keep your lens trained on Cynthia's face. Lloyd, you take a broader shot, but get tight on Wells in his death scene."

Jade tapped Wells on the shoulder. "You die in this scene?" He nodded. "Does that mean you're almost done with the movie?"

"No," he explained. "We're just doing location scenes here. There's still a lot to shoot on the set back in Los Angeles."

Jade had already noticed that the story was often filmed out of sequence. Sam had done the same thing and explained the importance of taking advantage of lighting as well as not wasting time changing costumes if the same ones would be worn in a later scene. While she understood the concept, she found it confusing and wondered how the actors kept it all straight in their heads.

"Why are you supposed to die?" she asked.

"I'm supposed to be in love with Cynthia's character," Wells said.

Jade nodded. "But she still loves her husband?"

"Right. Now Murdock is obsessed with the treasure. He wants it all to himself. So he's arranged this native uprising in an attempt to kill off Hall. Only the servant girl interferes. That's where Bebe comes in."

"The reincarnated lover, correct?" asked Jade.

"That's right. She doesn't want Hall killed. She sees him as Menelik reincarnated. So when Murdock intends to shoot Hall, she pushes his hand away; his gun shoots wild and kills me, as I'm busy rushing in to save Cynthia." He moved his hands back and forth as though he had little puppet figures attached to them. "See?"

"I see." Jade frowned.

"But you still look confused," said Wells.

Jade shrugged. "I suppose it's tragic and will bring tears to the eyes of the audience. But I expected that in the end Mr. Hall's and Miss Malta's characters would be reunited in death on the mountain, and you and Miss Porter would go back together."

Wells stared at her, mouth agape. "Why, that's brilliant, Miss del Cameron," he said.

"Jade," she corrected. "Just call me Jade. After several poker games, it's permissible."

"Yes, Jade." Wells blinked a few times without speaking. "Um, excuse me for a minute, um, Jade." He trotted off towards the director. "Rex, I have an idea."

Movement at the edge of camp caught Jade's attention. Zakayo and the Chagga men had arrived. Mr. Julian noticed them as well, for he motioned for Wells to stop for a moment.

"Hascombe!" Mr. Julian bellowed. "Go tell those men to sit down out of the way and watch. Oh, and try to explain blanks to them while you're at it."

Jade watched Harry pull the Chagga men aside and saw the confusion on their faces as he tried to explain a gunshot that didn't kill. She thought this would be a good opportunity to ask Zakayo about Rehema and see if he knew anything about her death or about the snake. The director's next edict squelched that idea.

"Del Cameron! I need you." Mr. Julian slapped Wells on

the back. "Good idea, Hank. Glad I thought of it. Talmadge, clutch your arm or something when you do the fall for Hank. We'll put his arm in a splint for the final scenes. Del Cameron!" he shouted louder.

"I'm right next to you, Mr. Julian," Jade said.

"Good. I need that cheetah in this again. Think he can run in and alert Cynthia to her danger just in the nick of time?"

"Probably," said Jade. "But I didn't think Biscuit was in any of these contemporary scenes. Isn't he supposed to be Menelik's pet?"

"He is, but I thought maybe his reincarnation should come in to save his master's wife. Should add a mystical touch. Very big with audiences. Besides, he already knocked down that native woman."

"But cheetahs don't live in these forests. It wouldn't make any sense."

He let out an exasperated sigh. "That's the exciting part. Where did this cheetah come from, right? Trust me. It will work." He turned his back to her. "Listen up, everyone. A few changes. I'm not killing Wells. He's just going to get a wing clipped."

"Why?" asked Hall.

"Trust me, Conrad," said Mr. Julian. "I've got a great new idea. Just came to me. Now. Let's show these natives how to act. Men, get in your places. We're going to film you firing first so we can get your faces. Then we'll do the scene with Woodrow and Bebe. After that, we'll shoot the action again, this time focused on the natives."

Budendorfer and Brown hauled their heavy equipment to the spots picked out for them while Bebe argued some point with the director.

Harry joined Jade as she knelt beside Biscuit and stroked his sleek sides.

"Did you ask Zakayo about the snake?" she asked him.

"No. He's too excited about this pretend attack right now. Besides, it's going to get pretty noisy in a moment, even shooting blanks."

As if to punctuate his statement, Julian yelled, "Action!" and the actors leaped into motion. They dropped their playing cards, jumped up from their chairs, and sent them clattering to the earth. After they ran to their tents and grabbed their rifles, the clearing burst into a cacophony of noises. In addition to the rifle fire, several birds and a nearby troop of olive baboons screeched in fear. Two minutes later, Mr. Julian yelled, "Cut!" and silence reigned again.

The Chagga men were clearly impressed by the display. Two of them inspected the trees that were directly in the line of fire and marveled that they weren't marked in any way.

Next Mr. Julian directed Murdock and Bebe in their scene. Budendorfer covered them while Brown trained his camera on Wells' anguished face. Then they shot Talmadge as he stood in for Wells and made a dramatic fall backwards, rolling in and out of the smoldering campfire. This time, the Chagga men held back, clearly disturbed when Cynthia rushed to his side and cradled his head in her lap. But when Talmadge moved aside and Wells took his place on Cynthia's lap, they cheered as the double stood and brushed himself off, obviously uninjured.

"Now, the final take. I hope," Mr. Julian added as he stared at the Chagga. "Hascombe, did you explain what they're supposed to do?"

"They know they're supposed to fall," Harry said, "but not when."

"Tell them to fall when they see the man shoot at them,"

Julian ordered, his voice heavy with exasperation. He pointed to McAvy and Wells. "Show 'em how it's done."

Wells walked twenty paces from McAvy and turned to face him. McAvy aimed his rifle at Wells' chest and fired. Wells dropped, clutching his rib cage. Then he stood again and showed the Chagga that there were no marks on him. The Chagga nodded appreciatively.

Harry repeated the instructions to Zakayo, who already understood most of it. Zakayo, in turn, explained to his men, who nodded. They fairly bounced with excitement, finding themselves a part of something unusual. Jade assumed it would give them a fresh story to regale the village with for many months to come.

"And Hascombe," shouted Julian, "tell that interpreter I want *him* to creep up in front of Cynthia. Explain lurking to him. Might as well use the one man who can understand."

Mr. Julian grabbed a Chagga man and hauled him by the arm to his spot. After he pointed to it, stood the man on it, then pointed to the American aiming at him, each man understood what was required of him and followed the director to his own mark. In the meantime, Harry explained Zakayo's part to him.

Julian interrupted with more orders. "I'm going to yell 'action' and I want them to start waving their spears and knives in the air. Tell them to shriek, too, Hascombe. But tell them not to leave their spots. Then I'm going to point to you men," he explained to the Americans. "Fire in turn. Count three before the next man fires. That way these natives won't all fall at once. Hopefully."

Zakayo again passed on the instructions and the Chagga all nodded their understanding.

"Del Cameron!"

"Still here, Mr. Julian." Jade walked up, holding Biscuit's lead.

"Get your cat ready. When I yell, 'Now!' you call to him or do whatever you need to do to get him to run in front of Miss Porter."

"He'll come when I call to him. Don't worry."

"Cynthia," continued Julian, "that cheetah's going to race by. That makes you look up at the last minute so you can fire and save yourself. Then you run to where Hank is lying, wounded. Does everyone understand? Brown, I want you covering that part only. Got it?"

Jade unclipped Biscuit's lead and removed his collar. "Stay," she ordered. Then she trotted around to the other side of the set, making sure to remain out of camera range.

"And action!"

Julian pointed to McAvy and he fired his rifle. On cue, the Chagga man across from him clutched his chest and fell screaming. One by one they fell, down the line like ducks in a shooting gallery, each one trying to outdo the others in drama. Clearly, Talmadge's fall had impressed them.

Jade watched as the Chagga men threw themselves wholeheartedly into their roles. If Julian wasn't happy with this, then nothing would please him, she thought. The display certainly impressed her, and she noticed that even McAvy's and Murdock's faces blanched at the realism.

"Now!"

"Biscuit! To me!" Jade shouted. Immediately the cheetah raced towards her. Jade had chosen her position so that the great cat could just see her behind the tent on the side nearest Cynthia. Zakayo stalked on the opposite end of the tent, out of Jade's view.

Her faith in her pet's intelligence and obedience wasn't

misplaced. Biscuit tore in front of Cynthia in a flash of creamy gold and black, leaping a tent peg on the way. The actress, who'd been working to quickly load her rifle from a box of cartridges, jumped up and fired.

"And cut," yelled Julian. "That was damned good! Budendorfer, Brown, did you get it?"

"That cat's probably going to be a blur, Rex, but—"

"But that makes it eerier," Mr. Julian said. "Hascombe, tell those natives they can get up now."

Harry took the nearest Chagga by the arm and hoisted him to his feet. He clapped him on the back and grinned. The other men jumped up on their own, chattering to one another with a lot of laughter. "Come on, Zakayo," called Harry from a distance. "You, too."

Jade walked around the tent, Biscuit at her side. She took one look at the hole in the interpreter's chest and the growing pool of red liquid underneath him and dropped to her knees beside him, her heart racing. "I need the first-aid kit, now!" she shouted. But in her heart, she knew it was already too late.

CHAPTER 15

The earliest human occupants on Kilimanjaro were Wakonyingo pygmies, who knew how to smelt iron ore.

—The Traveler

The call for the medical kit came out as an automatic response, as did Jade's subsequent actions. Her left hand seized her own pocket kerchief and pressed it against the wound to stanch the blood while her right fingers felt Zakayo's neck for a pulse. But her mind saw other scenes.

For a moment, she was a mile from the front lines in France, kneeling beside a young corporal. She could almost smell the gunpowder and decay, hear the blasting shellfire. A medic's station had been shelled only a few minutes before she arrived in her ambulance to retrieve the wounded. From her position, she saw part of the corporal's face, complete with the peach fuzz of youth. The other half had been blown away.

Then the scene shifted, dissolving until only Zakayo's body lay before her. All voices, all the outcries diminished, becoming nothing more than the rush of blood coursing past Jade's ears. A faint wail, like a newborn, rose up from the ground. It built in strength, joined by more keening moans. She saw the blood spread, covering the ground, felt the countless numbers of Chagga who had died in battles and feuds on this mountain press in on her.

Where's Kikorwi when you really need him?

As if in answer, the cries ceased, replaced by a crooning whisper. It took the form of the Una River first; then the wind in the treetops joined it in harmony. Kilimanjaro was singing a lullaby to its dead, soothing them as a mother might. With the singing came another sensation: the overpowering feeling of being stalked, of eyes boring into her vulnerable back. She could almost smell the hot, carrion-laced breath on her neck and tensed against the inevitable attack.

Something warm pressed against her shoulder, and a rasping tongue caressed her hand. Jade jumped crablike to the side, still keeping low to the ground. Her hands seemed to be tied to something in front of her. But instead of the expected leopard or lion, she beheld an enormous cheetah in front of her, his bronzed coat and unusual spot and stripe patterns glinting in the near-blinding sun. *Where am I?*

"Jade."

Harry's voice jolted her back to the present. To her surprise, she held a neatly folded pulp bandage in her hands, firmly pressed over the chest wound. Her bloody handkerchief lay to one side. Biscuit leaned against her thigh and Jade drew strength from his warmth.

"Let go, Jade," said Harry softly. "He's gone. That went right through the heart." He gently pried her hands loose from the bandage. There was very little blood on it. Most had soaked into her kerchief or drained out the larger wound in his back and seeped into the soil.

"Someone shot him," she said, her voice foreign in her ears. "Someone had a live round."

Jade pushed the bandage against the wound and continued to apply pressure, unwilling to admit the uselessness of the action. Slowly, she became aware of the others around her. First Harry's presence, solid and businesslike. It served as a foundation to ground herself on. A cacophony of noise and smells assaulted Jade's senses. Damp, molding earth, acrid sweat, sweet blood, and the residual smoke from the blanks all blended into one cloying scent. The actors jabbered nonstop, debating how this accident could have happened, while the Chagga men muttered fearfully and angrily among themselves. A series of hysterical, gasping outbursts dominated the noise.

"But I didn't mean . . ." "I can't understand . . ." "You have to believe . . ."

"Someone take care of Miss Porter," Jade said, startling herself with her own voice.

"I have her," said Pearl. She knelt beside the shocked woman and put her arm around her in a rare show of sympathy and compassion. Bebe joined them and added her own soft reassurances.

Maybe there's more to them after all, Jade thought. "Mr. Murdock," Jade called. When she caught his attention, she nodded towards the women. The man went to Cynthia's side and spoke to her, trying to lead her away.

"Can you say something to those Chagga men, Harry? Before this turns ugly?"

"That was my next move," he said. "Once I knew you were all right." He stood and, with palms out to the side to show that he meant no harm, walked slowly but steadily in their direction.

Jade rose to her feet, her immediate gaze on the Chagga. Her Winchester leaned against a chair beside her tent, about twenty paces from where she stood. Harry's own Mauser was slung across his back. She kept her side vision and her ears alert for any movement, any sound. That sense of being stalked hadn't diminished, and, other than her knife, they were an unarmed group open to attack.

Well, most of them are unarmed. Cynthia's rifle had held at least one live round. It might have a second. Jade was close enough that she could snatch it up if she needed it. She prayed she didn't. But they'd just promised these men that everyone would be safe, and now one of them lay dead. Add to that the difficulty of communicating with them without Zakayo. Jade hoped that at least some of them knew a smattering of Swahili. Judging from how well they followed the director's edicts, possibly most of them did. Still, Jade didn't like to think what would happen if they decided on retribution instead of some other method of recompense.

Harry spoke to them, loud enough for Jade to hear. Words for "mistake," "sadness," "peace" were repeated again and again. She heard him offer to carry Zakayo back to the village with gifts. When Jade glanced away for a moment to find Jelani, she saw him return from the spring, a hollowed gourd in hand. He began sprinkling water, first on Zakayo's body, then on Jade, and finally on the camp in general.

If the Chagga noticed the young Kikuyu's prayers, they didn't react. However, they did cast nervous glances at Biscuit. The cheetah still stood by Jade's side, head up, regally standing guard beside her and Zakayo. Did these men remember the old storyteller's tale of Menelik's cheetah? Did they hold her pet in awe, thinking he was part of the past come to revisit them?

"Biscuit," Jade said softly. "To Harry. Greeting."

Biscuit rubbed the side of his head against Jade's hand, then walked off towards Harry. His shoulders pumped up and down like pistons, accentuating his square head and barrel-shaped chest that tapered into a lean body. He held his tail out behind him, the white tip raised like a banner. Biscuit took his place next to Harry's side and rubbed his head against Hascombe's knee. Then he chirped a greeting to the Chagga.

The effect electrified the Chagga. As one, they stretched out hesitant hands for Biscuit. When the cat didn't move, they grew a little bolder and touched his broad head. Biscuit only raised it higher, like an imperial lord allowing his minions to approach. After a few moments, Jade made a low clicking sound with her tongue. The cheetah turned and strode back towards the body, the men following.

"Pay them, Mr. Julian," said Jade. "Give them Zakayo's wages, too."

"Why should—"

"Do it!" snapped a woman's voice.

Jade turned to see Cynthia, Murdock still trying to persuade her to come away. Her previously ashen face had taken on a flush of anger.

"Do it and be generous," she said.

Mr. Julian opened a bag containing the German rupees, still the currency of Tanganyika, and counted out the coins.

"Just give them the whole damn bag, Rex," snapped Cynthia.

The two larger men picked up the body by his shoulders and feet and started back to their village, the other men following.

Jade picked up her woven Berber bag, shouldered her own rifle, and called to Biscuit.

"Where do you think you're going?" demanded Harry.

She tipped her head in the direction of the Chagga men. "With them." When he started to protest, Jade stopped him. "Harry, I need to visit their village. I'll be back in time for dinner." Harry's eyes opened wide and his face flushed as he struggled visibly to control his next words. "Why for the love of . . . No!"

Jade stood her ground. "Yes, Harry. It's important for two reasons. One, with Zakayo dead, I need to find out what I can about that boomslang and if that woman did in fact catch it. Someone else might know something. And," she added, signaling him to wait, "if we leave without seeing the elders and giving some show of regret for Zakayo, we might find a nasty surprise in the morning."

Harry opened his mouth to respond, hesitated, then nodded. "I don't like the idea, but you're right about that last part, at least." He took hold of her shoulders in his big hands. His jaw worked as though he struggled for words. "You know I wouldn't even consider letting any other woman try this, but I believe you can do it. Still, I'd feel much more at ease if you took Nakuru with you."

"You'll need him even more while I'm gone. I'll take Biscuit. They seem to respect him. Maybe some of that feeling will rub off onto me."

The Chagga men appeared to accept Jade's company. Perhaps Biscuit's solid presence helped. Or maybe the last goat, a black male kid, which she led as a goodwill offering, did the trick. She hoped the animal would be accepted in the right spirit. As she'd told Harry, it would have to do, since they didn't have seven cows, seven goats, and a daughter to offer for the blood debt. She'd read a few accounts of Chagga tribal life, enough to know that human sacrifice, while rare in the past, was no longer practiced. At least, she hoped not.

That would really prove Sam's point about my being reckless.

On the path up to the village, Jade considered the difficulty of her task. She didn't speak Machame, the Chagga tongue, but she knew from watching the old storytelling elder that he understood some Swahili. It had also become apparent from the daily bargaining for produce that many of the women knew some as well. It stood to reason, living as close to Moshi as they did, that they'd have dealings with the people there.

Twice, Biscuit stopped and looked over his shoulder at the trail behind them. Once, he chirped. Jade waited each time, expecting to see Nakuru or even Harry catch up to them. Finally, when it was clear that no one was following, she and Biscuit continued after the Chagga.

Their entrance into the village was met by stunned faces and a momentary silence, quickly rent by the wailing of every woman present. Two women, one older and another at least ten years younger, hugged each other. The eldest shrieked and moaned louder than all the women, and Jade assumed she was Zakayo's wife. That much seemed likely, but whether the younger woman was a daughter or a secondary wife, she couldn't tell.

Three men, two who were part of the group that brought his body back, went to a nearby banana grove bordered by dracaena shrubs with their cornlike leaves. They stepped carefully among the skulls that lay between the trunks. First the oldest broke off a dracaena branch, then the younger men.

His sons? They went into the older woman's hut and remained. Jade longed to see what was happening, but didn't dare intrude on their ritual. The women, in the meantime, had taken the body and stripped it. They placed it onto a sleeping hide and bent Zakayo's body until it was doubled up, chin to knees. The older woman took long strips of rawhide and bound the body into this new position. Dull thudding from inside the hut and the occasional puff of dust led Jade to believe that the men were digging a grave inside. No one paid any attention to her. She didn't know whether to be relieved or not. Finally, a slow movement from her left caught her attention. The old storyteller, Sina, moved towards her with a slow dignity.

"Shikamo," Jade said, choosing the more formal greeting for an elder. Literally it meant, "I grab your feet," an indication of subservience.

Sina nodded. *"Marahaba,"* he replied, giving the Swahili blessing in response.

He motioned for Jade and Biscuit to follow him. She expected him to return to his hut, but instead, he led her to the banana grove, where he took a seat on a log. Jade sat at his feet, the kid goat on one side and Biscuit on the other. Next, the old storyteller called to one of the other men who'd come back from her camp and motioned him to join them. The man did, but he looked warily at Jade, his expression shifting between fear and anger.

Sina spoke to the man, who replied at length, pantomiming firing a rifle, falling and rising again, and finally falling completely. Jade noticed that Zakayo's name was not mentioned. She wondered if it was taboo to speak the name of the dead. The elder next pointed to Jade, his brows raised in a question. The man shook his head.

Ah. Now he knows that I didn't fire the killing shot.

Sina nodded and turned back to Jade. He cocked his head slightly and spread his hands. The movement conveyed a question. Why?

Jade took a chance and answered, "*Ajali*, accident." The elder nodded. He pointed to the goat, and Jade handed over the rope that served as a leash. Sina looked at the kid's coat and nodded approvingly. It appeared that the apology had been made and accepted. She wanted to ask him about what had happened to Rehema, to see if anyone knew about the boomslang, but now, in the midst of the villagers' grief, it suddenly seemed insensitive to ask. She fidgeted and shifted position, debating with herself about staying or leaving.

But the elder sensed her agitation and opened the conversation, using the man beside him to assist when pantomime and his own limited Swahili failed him. "You know that woman who cursed you is dead," he said. "She ran from our village, bloated with blood."

Jade nodded. Rehema had been part of his household. She wondered if Sina grieved for what was either a new wife or one of his daughters.

"Your life is in great danger now," he continued. "More than before."

Jade frowned, but didn't reply. To contradict the elder might close the discussion. She noted the old man's concern but, more than that, the expectant gleam in the younger man's eyes. Clearly, she thought, this was good news to him. Time to assert herself.

"I do not fear death. It has stalked me before and not won. And when Ruwa," she added, using the Chagga's name for God, "wants me, then it will be time enough."

Sina smiled, the gaps between his teeth showing. "Perhaps if you left the mountain and returned on the iron snake, you would escape. Perhaps the curse only stays on this mountain. But you could never return."

"I will go north again," she said, pointing the way to Nairobi. "But not yet. I do not run from fear. I am Simba Jike, and now it is time for me to lead those others on this mountain. When my job is done, I will go home then."

Sina nodded. The other man scowled, but held his peace. "And this goat?" asked Sina.

"The man who was killed may have need of it," Jade said. It made no difference to her if the family ate it or if it was considered a sacrifice to his ancestors. She intended only to show good faith and forestall any reprisals.

"It is good. We will have peace between us," he said.

"Elder, I would know how this woman who cursed me died."

Sina arched his brows in surprise. He spoke to the younger man, who argued back for a moment before a wave of the old man's bony hand silenced him. "Come," he said. "See."

Jade helped him rise to his feet and followed a half step behind as he led the way out of the village and into the surrounding brush. He pointed to a slender path, nearly hidden in a clump of low-growing shrubs, but Jade didn't need his directions to know that was where at least one corpse lay. The stench was overpowering. Biscuit, who'd walked beside her, sniffed the air, opening his mouth to taste the scent. Jade took hold of his collar, lest he get too familiar with the remains.

"The woman is here?" She'd understood that Rehema had been driven out. Had she died here in the brush?

Sina shook his head. "The girl she cursed is here."

"Why here?" she asked. "Why not in the ground?"

"She bore no children," the younger man said with a sneer. "Childless women are not buried." The way he stared at Jade made it clear that he put her in the same class: useless and not worth the trouble of digging a grave. Jade had an inkling of what he was trying to tell her.

"And the woman who made the curse," she asked. "She also had no children?"

Sina shook his head no. Jade understood. If she was going to die anyway and simply be tossed out for the scavengers, better to run her out of camp before she could curse someone else.

"How?" she asked.

"She went into the forest one night with a bag, and took it to your people. When she came back, blood came from her." The old man pointed to his mouth and nose. "She went to the women for medicine, but there was none for this. We saw the marks on her hand." He used his index and middle finger to point to his right wrist, hooking them like fangs as he tapped his wrist.

"Snake," said Jade.

The old man nodded.

The next question was harder to phrase. "Did anyone see whom she gave the bag to?" She pantomimed the action to help carry her meaning.

The elder looked at the younger man, who shrugged. "She spoke with your people here," he said. "And she sold eggs and fruit to your cook."

Jade sighed. That much she knew. Well, at least she knew where the snake came from. Most likely, the woman was just vindictive and wanted to carry out her curse. *Good thing she didn't know where I slept.* She thanked Sina and the younger Chagga as well, then left, Biscuit padding at her side. A sudden word from the elder stopped her.

"*Ku-ngoja*, wait."

Jade turned and faced him.

His aged face, so pliable with its wrinkles and loose skin, twitched and shifted around his mouth as though he struggled with some inner thought that resisted being spoken. Finally, with a deep sigh, he managed one word. It was a word Jade knew very well.

"Hatari!" Danger!

She nodded, indicating that she understood, and left the village.

. . .

Jelani had seen her argue with Bwana Nyati and knew that the big man, no matter how strong, was no match for Simba Jike. She would have her way. A lioness did not yield readily to any male animal, even a buffalo. And Bwana Nyati was not her mate, though Jelani could tell by his eyes that he wished it. So Jelani watched her take Biscuit and head into the forest. He knew where she was going: to the village with the Chagga men. Straight into the mouth of the curse waiting to swallow her.

Immediately, he ran to his sleeping area and pulled out his woven bag. Throwing it over his shoulder and taking up a stout walking stick, he slipped from camp. The only one who would miss him was the cook. Except for Simba Jike and Biscuit, the others barely noticed him. He took no offense. If anything, it suited his purpose, making it easier to follow her, to add what protection he could. Unfortunately, it was very little.

Jelani had been to the mountain the English called Mount Kenya once with his master. But *this* mountain, though a home for Ngai, felt different. It had its own power, just as the mountain of the elephants up north had felt different to him then. His ancestors didn't reside here and the others, the ones who did, did their best to block his prayers. Sometimes he could almost hear them, shouting to drown his words and thoughts. He wondered why the others didn't hear it.

To this day, the only spirit that had answered his call was that of a cheetah, but unlike any he'd ever seen. His golden coat was mottled with broad, dark splotches. Three dark stripes ran down his back. It had come to him in a dream the night after he'd sacrificed the goat.

But did he come to protect or to harm? Somehow, Jelani didn't think he was there to harm. Cheetahs rarely attacked people. But then, this was no ordinary cheetah. It resembled the one described in the old storyteller's tale, the one that walked with the ancient warrior king. But if he came as a protector, did he come to protect Simba Jike or only Biscuit? He wished his teacher were here to tell him.

Simba Jike continued on her way up the slope to the village. Twice, Biscuit stopped, and twice Jelani fell back lest the cat give him away. When they resumed their trek, he followed slowly, searching for a protective spirit to send after her. Then, just outside the village, he felt a presence. It was the weight of the woman Rehema's curse, hovering like wet, heavy smoke.

Jelani closed his eyes and chanted to force this danger back and away from Simba Jike's path. In his mind's eye, many of the dangers took form, shadows flitting through the smoke. He saw her walking amid the shadows and most, such as the snake and the elephant, pulled back from her, the snake from fear, the elephant with respect. A shadow that might have been a lion drifted away as though it had no purpose on the mountain.

But one shadow hovered and, as the smoky pall coalesced, a form took shape. First four legs appeared, then a long tail and a powerful chest. Jelani watched, his own eyes closed, as a pair of yellow eyes emerged. They glowed with a deep hatred and a desire for vengeance. He felt the spirit creature's strength and knew he could not control it with his own prayers. He turned and ran back to camp. He needed Bwana Nyati's help.

Jade left the village with little more than a backward glance. No one, including the man who'd acted as her interpreter, seemed to pay any more attention to her. They were too occupied with the process of mourning and the accompanying rituals. Biscuit padded softly at her side, his tongue lolling and his shoulders rising and falling above his expansive chest. She found herself keeping step to the cat's rhythm.

The beautiful orchids, moss, and balsam flowers were lost on her. Fatigue set in, the aftermath of shock, fear, and physical strain. Jade's hips and lower back ached from the squatting sit she'd adopted in the village. Her mind felt dull and she tried to sharpen it by paying closer attention to the sounds around her. But the chatter of blue monkeys and the songs of many birds faded into the background. All she heard was the Una, rushing along, but at times it came back with an echo.

The Chagga's hidden cave. Jade was seized with an inexplicable need to find it. Kilimanjaro had been born of volcanic activity and, consequently, was riddled with old lava tubes through which snowmelt flowed and issued forth in springs along its slopes. Most of these were small, but Jade recalled the larger tubes in the Chyulu Hills. It stood to reason that there were larger ones here as well. Even the tale of the magic snail told of villagers hiding in one.

She slid her rifle from her shoulder and walked into the forest. Immediately, she slipped into the pattern of a hunter, stepping on the balls of her feet to avoid undue noise, slowing her breathing, and most important, training her ears to listen. This time, she didn't listen for an animal. She listened for the hollow rush of water flowing through an underground channel. Biscuit fell into step behind her, not knowing what his mistress was doing, but accepting the need for silence with that uncanny ability that all animals have at sensing their human's mood.

Every third step, Jade stopped and turned her head from side to side, trying to pinpoint where the faint shushing sounded louder. Twice she changed direction. Finally, she noticed a small tributary, no wider than a foot. Jade followed it upstream and was rewarded for her efforts. There in front of her stood a partially collapsed opening, almost completely covered in vines and creepers. She'd found the exit to the Chagga's ancient hiding spot, the one Sina had spoken of in the Kikorwi tale.

Jade pushed aside the creepers with her rifle and peered inside, keeping the rifle at the ready in case an animal was using the cave for a den. Considering the stench of carrion that wafted out, it was very likely. *Or maybe . . .* She felt into her bag and pulled out the flashlight she kept there. Switching on the beam, she let it play over the black inner walls, which did their level best to suck up all the light. Only the water reflected any back at her.

"Coming, Biscuit?"

The cheetah took a step back and sneezed.

"I guess that means no." She held a hand out, palm down. "Sit. Stay."

Biscuit responded as a well-trained dog might and sat down, his tongue lolling.

Jade shouldered her rifle again and slid her knife out of her boot sheath, wishing that she had a better way of carrying her light without occupying one of her hands. Playing the light along the floor, she stepped slowly into the old cave, her ears attentive to any sound. Only the gurgle of water reached them.

The tube was wide enough to admit several people walking together or a person alongside a cow. But if the Chagga had used this cave to escape from their enemies, they hadn't put it to use for a long time. She found some evidence in the form of scat that smaller animals had ventured inside, but nothing fresh. Only the stench of decay told her otherwise. About twenty feet into the cave, she found the smell's source and Rehema's final resting place.

So, this is where you ran to. Jade felt a pang of pity for the poor girl. Cheated out of a trinket, she'd resorted to cursing her rival, intending to kill herself to make it stick. Then, deprived of that, she'd resorted to a deadly game of revenge, using a poisonous snake as her weapon. Had she intentionally let the snake bite her in an attempt to again make her curse against Jade a death curse? Or had it been a terrible accident?

Whatever the answer, the girl in death was again cheated, this time out of a proper place among the banana groves and her ancestors. Knowing that, she must have remembered the old stories and run to the one place outside of the village that had some connection to her people.

Jade reached for her kerchief and remembered that she'd left it bloodied back at camp. She held her shirtsleeve over her nose. Then, slipping her knife back into her boot, she knelt beside the corpse and played her light over it.

Rehema still wore the same cloth wrap that Jade had last seen on her. The body itself was bloated, and dried blood encrusted her mouth and nostrils. It matched Sina's and Harry's descriptions of death by boomslang.

Jade started to rise when the beam of light caught a braided cord clutched in Rehema's right hand. Using her knife, Jade carefully pried the fingers open and retrieved the small woven bag made of split banana fronds. It felt surprisingly heavy.

"Let's see what you have in here." The bag had no flap or catch. Jade opened it and shone the light inside. She expected to see the usual trinkets a girl might carry: a pretty stone, some beads, perhaps some useful household tool. She didn't expect to pull out a small round purple box. The writing was abraded, but it was a modern lady's compact complete with rouge powder and a thin padded cloth for applying it.

Biscuit's chirp from outside reminded Jade that she was alone in here and needed to get back to camp. She slipped the compact back into the bag, noting the crackling sound it made when it hit bottom. There were still other things in the bag to see.

But not here.

With a whispered apology to Rehema's body and a muttered prayer on her behalf, Jade grabbed the bag and hurried out of the cavern. Biscuit greeted her with his usual head butt against her thigh along with repeated pacing two yards down the trail, then back to her.

Her curiosity tugged at her to investigate the bag, but she settled for stowing it and her flashlight in her own bag. "I'm coming, Biscuit. I know you're probably hungry."

But he didn't act hungry. His pacing and raspy growls held all the earmarks of a nervous cat. Jade took a quick look all around her, his anxiousness infecting her. She felt an uneasy tingle along her arms and the unmistakable sense that eyes were watching her. If something was out there, running down the trail would only make her look more like prey and, if the stalker was human, like an easy target.

She slowed her breathing and listened. Again, only the Una's ongoing flow came to her, but now the sound took on a murmuring voice, whispering to her, taunting her with menace. Biscuit noticed something, too. He stopped and his eyes searched the woods. A low growl rumbled from his throat. Like an angry house cat, he hissed and spat. Jade felt an icy chill caress her shoulders and brush her spine.

She shuddered and unshouldered her rifle, working the lever to chamber a round. Both of her knees ached from the day's strain, but the left, the one that always warned her of death, now pulsed with a slight stabbing throb. She heard the old Chagga's warning repeat itself in her ear.

Hatari!

CHAPTER 16

The Chagga people migrated into the area, fleeing cruel leaders. The Maasai told them that this was God's home, and he was a good and benevolent god. So the Chagga moved closer to the mountain, seeking protection.

—The Traveler

"MADDY, NEVILLE, I'M SO GLAD YOU COULD COME." BEVERLY HUGGED the former and accepted a kiss on the cheek from the latter.

Neville, who was carrying Cyril, shifted the toddler to one side and shook Avery's hand.

"Let me take him," Madeline said, extending her arms for her son. "I'll carry him into the nursery so you men can visit." She looked around the room. "Where's Sam?"

"Here I am," he replied, coming into the parlor from another door. He carried a large brown envelope under his arm.

"I don't know why you didn't wait to ride with us," said Madeline. "Whatever did you need to come into town for anyway?"

"I went to see Dr. Mathews again," he answered, placing the envelope on an end table. "And I wanted to do a little darkroom work."

"And we have the better darkroom setup," said Avery. "But hurry back, Maddy. I want to introduce you to the guest I mentioned earlier, Major Anthony Bertram. He should be arriving any moment now." Madeline and Beverly left the parlor, taking Cyril with them.

"I thought this chap was staying here, Avery," said Neville, accepting a scotch and soda.

"He is, but he wanted to drop in on Edmunde Colridge at the Nairobi Club. Seems his father knew old Lord Colridge, Edmunde's father. Who doesn't?" he added with a chuckle. "Man's a living legend."

"We might never see him then, if the elder Colridge joins them," said Neville. "His lordship can talk the ear off a deaf man." Beverly and Madeline emerged from the nursery wing, and Avery indicated chairs to his guests. He sat down on the leather sofa next to his pipe stand, Neville chose a spot on a facing sofa, but Sam continued to stand. The women took seats next to their respective husbands.

"Well, he'd jolly well better come back," said Avery. "I loaned him the use of my motorcar. Point of fact, I should have considered how long his usual treks off into the unknown take." He swirled the ice in his glass. "We might never see him or my Hupmobile again."

"I took a liberty, my love, to ensure that wouldn't happen," said Beverly. "I told Major Bertram to bring Edmunde back with him if he wished. Matthew, our *mpishi*, has prepared dinner for seven and there's already a place set. Besides, I'd like to get to know Edmunde. If my sister, Emily, does visit, I plan to introduce them. Keep her busy."

"Very clever of you, darling," said Avery as he set aside his glass. "Well," he said, taking out his pipe and filling it. "Since we won't have another opportunity once our guest or guests of honor arrive, tell me how your new invention is coming along."

"Nearly completed, I should say," said Neville. "Testing it tomorrow. Looks very promising."

"Even if the coffee washer only sells within the colony," said Maddy, "we'll do very well for ourselves."

"And then what will you do next, Sam?" asked Beverly. "More inventions? Or another motion picture? You'll have capital at your disposal."

"I haven't decided," he said. He paced back and forth from one sofa to the other.

"Please stop that, Sam," scolded Beverly. "I feel I'm watching a tennis match. For heaven's sake, sit down."

"No, thanks, Beverly," he said. "I'm sorry. I will try to stand still."

"Well, you have to sit during dinner," she replied. She tried another tactic. "How is your plane? I know Avery so enjoyed flying it. He's told me—" She stopped abruptly when Avery nudged her ribs with his elbow.

Sam's entire body stiffened and his lips clamped tightly. "The plane is fine, Beverly. I'm out of fuel, though, and it doesn't appear that this shortage will end anytime soon."

"I believe you're wrong there, Sam," said Avery. His pipe dangled from one side of his mouth, and he puffed at it between sentences. "Governor Northey is taking steps to ensure the resolution. Give it a month perhaps."

"I hope not that long," added Neville. "Deucedly hard on the farmers coming into town. Have to go back to ox wagons otherwise."

"What's in the envelope, Sam?" asked Madeline. "You said you'd been doing some darkroom work. Are those photographs?"

"I didn't know you took stills," said Avery.

"They're some of Jade's. I was hoping to spot that crazed native in one of them. See if one of the actors had been seen with him."

"Oh, my," murmured Madeline.

"And did you find him?" asked Avery.

Sam shook his head. "No."

"Then why—" Avery broke off when he heard his car pull into the porte cochere. "Ah, our guest has arrived." He set his still-smoking pipe in a tall ash stand and went to the door.

"Is he alone, or did he bring Edmunde with him?" asked Beverly.

"He's not alone, but he didn't bring Edmunde," replied Avery as Farhani opened the front door.

"Then who?"

"Point of fact, he brought his lordship."

"Where is it, Biscuit?" Jade whispered.

Biscuit stared into the forest and hissed again. Jade followed his line of sight and saw the yellow eyes before anything else.

Oh, hell!

"Biscuit, to camp!" she ordered. Biscuit gave one parting growl before racing down the trail. Jade raised her rifle and, keeping her eye on the leopard, inched slowly backwards. She wanted the cat to just slip away, to decide she was too big to be prey. But for every step she took back, the animal took one forward, head low, eyes locked on hers. The vegetation hid his vital spots. Jade remembered some advice her father had given her in case a black bear followed her. "Make a lot of noise and make yourself look as large as you can."

She stood up straighter, still keeping her rifle trained on the cat. "Shoo! Get out of here!"

The cat hesitated just before emerging from cover, but it didn't back down. Jade didn't want to kill it, but she wasn't going to have a choice. She could shoot at the ground just in front of the leopard as she had with the lion, but if she didn't scare it away it would be on her before she could fire again. Her best chance for survival was to kill it now. The cat took another step. Its head and chest were exposed. Jade took a bead on the chest and squeezed the trigger.

Nothing.

She tried to work the lever and chamber another round, but the mechanism wouldn't move. It was as if someone had glued it into place. The full danger of her predicament dawned on her in the same instant it did the leopard, for the cat took two quick steps forward onto a flat rock before freezing again.

Jade slung the useless rifle over her shoulder and pulled her knife, holding it ready to meet the inevitable attack. The leopard wriggled its hindquarters, bunching its muscles for the brief charge. Jade knew she'd have only one decent chance. There would be no deflecting it now. Wounded, the cat would only fight harder. She gripped the knife's hilt with both hands and braced herself.

When the shot came, she jumped backwards, colliding with a tree. The leopard ran off.

"Jade!"

"Harry," she answered. She heard his heavy tread as he ran forward to meet her. He held his Mauser at the ready, anticipating an attack.

"Are you all right?" he asked.

"I'm fine. Thanks. I think you scared it."

"Scared what? I couldn't see anything, so I shot right into the forest in the direction you were looking."

"It was a leopard." She pointed to the rock. "Right there. It may have smelled that goat I'd brought along and followed me. Or it may have smelled carrion. I found Rehema, Harry. Her body's lying in that hidden cavern that the Chagga used to use as a hideout."

Harry didn't seem to notice her last revelation. He scanned the area for tracks. "A leopard tailing you?" He scratched the back of his neck. "Be damned if I can see any sign. You'd think there'd be a wet paw print on that rock, at least. The men will really think you're jinxed now. Why didn't you shoot it?" He continued to study the ground.

"My rifle jammed."

Harry scowled. "Jammed? Haven't you cleaned and oiled it recently?"

"Of course I have. And I don't leave it lying around, so no one could have gotten to it."

"What happened to it?"

"It didn't fire the first time. And I know it was loaded. I tried to throw that first cartridge out and load another but the lever wouldn't budge."

Harry studied her with an expression of concern, his brows lifted and his head cocked. "Are you certain you saw this leopard? Maybe you had a hallucination and thought you did. You imagined that you'd fired."

"No! It was right there. Biscuit saw it, too. And my rifle jammed. Look." Jade put her knife back in her boot's sheath and took hold of her Winchester. She aimed up into the forest and squeezed the trigger. The rifle went off, snapping a small branch off a tree. "What the . . . ?" She pulled down the lever and it moved smoothly, ejecting the spent cartridge and inserting another.

"I don't understand. It was completely locked before. If you hadn't shown up when you did . . ."

Suddenly it dawned on her that he'd just run up to her rescue before Biscuit could have made it back to camp. She heard more heavy footsteps and considerable panting. McAvy and Murdock, each carrying Remingtons, stumbled into view.

"Ah," said Murdock, "you found her." He leaned against a tree to catch his breath.

Jade nodded to them both and turned back to Harry. "How did you get here so soon? Were you hunting?"

"No. That native stowaway of yours, Jelani. He ran into camp about twenty minutes ago claiming you were in danger. I thought the Chagga had you. We came on the double quick." Harry twitched his head towards the still-panting McAvy. "Well, I did, at least. Then I met Biscuit on the way. Sent him back down with Jelani." He took off his hat and scratched his head. "The entire affair doesn't make a great deal of sense. It's as if he knew there was trouble before it happened."

Jade didn't comment. She had no answers to give. "Let's get back before there's more trouble in camp."

"LORD COLRIDGE," SAID Beverly as she hastened to her husband's side. "What a lovely surprise." If her smile seemed a touch forced to Sam, at least she managed one.

"Major Bertram," Beverly said as Avery's former schoolmate followed the old settler into the room. "Please come in."

Bertram laughed. "You're the essence of politeness, madam. Most hostesses would simply kill me for bringing someone else." He handed his hat to Farhani.

"I trust I'm not intruding," said Colridge. "Edmunde wanted

me to meet young Bertram, but he had a prior commitment this evening and had to decline your gracious offer for dinner, Lady Dunbury. Knowing that would disappoint you, I came in his stead. Must represent the family, you know. Of course you do." Each edict was punctuated with a puff of air that sent Colridge's bushy white mustache fluttering like a banner.

Colridge headed straight towards the Thompsons, who'd risen from their seats as soon as they saw him enter. "Mrs. Thompson, lovely as ever. Africa agrees with you. Of course it does. Why wouldn't it? Thompson," he said, shaking Neville's hand and clapping him on the shoulder with his left hand. "By thunder, I've heard tremendous things about you. Tremendous! Inventing a new machine. You do Kenya proud. Er, what does it do?"

"Thank you, Lord Colridge. It—" Neville was too late in adding any explanation. Colridge had already turned to Sam.

"By thunder, I know you. American. Making some sort of motion picture. Filming that fair. Of course you were."

By this time Avery had sufficiently recovered. He cleared his throat, signaling for attention. "Yes, well. Allow me to introduce everyone. I believe you all know Lord Colridge." He next indicated his friend with a slight turn of his hand in his direction. "And please allow me to present Major Anthony Bertram. These are our friends, Neville and Madeline Thompson, and Sam Featherstone. Sam is a pilot. He flew for the Americans in the war."

Colridge, who hadn't known about Sam's flying, puffed through his mustache and studied Sam as the latter shook Bertram's hand.

"I understand you have a plane," said Bertram.

"Yes," said Sam. "A Curtiss JN-4, a Jenny."

Beverly's majordomo, Farhani, stood in the doorway leading to the dining room. Dressed all in white, he added a touch of elegance to the room. "*Mpishi* says that dinner is ready, memsahib."

"Thank you, Farhani," said Beverly. "If everyone will please follow him into the dining room, we may begin dinner."

Sam watched the others go in before him, noting Major Bertram rolling his eyes and spreading his hands when Colridge insisted on sitting between Madeline and Neville so he could expound on his knowledge of machinery to both of them. He saw Beverly's graceful response, a sweet smile, and noted Avery's broad grin.

Why the devil am I here? Sam thought, and immediately wondered if he meant just at this dinner party or in Kenya in general.

Madeline came to everyone's rescue during dinner by engaging Lord Colridge in conversation. Essentially this meant he talked and she listened, adding copious smiles of encouragement sprinkled with intelligent questions. With the old settler so happily occupied on one side, the others were able to listen to Major Bertram describe his travels across Egypt, up the Blue Nile, and eventually into Abyssinia.

"Wild country," Bertram summarized as they waited for their dessert. "The outlying tribes are terribly fierce. Ruled by chieftains or warlords or whatever you wish to call them. They answer only to themselves and the regent. I carried a special pass from Empress Zewditu countersigned by her cousin, the Regent Ras Tafari Makonnen. Even then, there were times I was held a virtual prisoner until they felt I was no threat or, more likely, had nothing of value to steal."

Farhani distributed glass dishes filled with a pudding laced with chunks of fresh mango and pawpaw. Bertram took a taste and smiled at Beverly to express his enjoyment. "It is certainly good to be back in a land with decent, law-abiding citizens and a sane government."

"Don't be too certain, Tony," said Avery. "I mean about the law-abiding citizens."

"Indeed," added Neville, "not but a week ago we had a brutal murder and suicide just outside of the city by the Muthaiga Club."

"The Muthaiga? It's a good job that you didn't make me stay there, Avery. I'd have wondered about our friendship. Tell me about it."

Sam listened while Neville and Avery described Wheeler's stabbing and the eventual suicide of the attacker.

"As I understand it," said Neville, "the police haven't identified the man yet."

"I thought all the natives were required to carry documents now," said Bertram. "Wear them around the neck."

"Their *kipande*, yes," said Avery. "This man had none."

"But the inspector has sent photographs to the outlying areas," said Sam. "I think they assume he was a drifter and someone in Mombassa or elsewhere might recognize him. I have one myself. Mathews gave a copy to me this morning."

"Sam!" said Beverly. "Whatever do you plan to do with it?"

He shrugged. "Show it around to some of the natives who work at the Muthaiga, perhaps. No one seems to ask them, but they're more likely than a white man to have seen him."

"May I see it?" asked Bertram. He cast a sheepish grin at Beverly. "I suppose that sounds macabre, doesn't it, but I'm rather curious to see what a Nairobi murderer looks like. Sort of a student of physiognomy, you see."

Sam excused himself and fetched the envelope with the photos he'd developed that day. Included was the print from Dr. Mathews. He pulled out all the pictures, and found that picture at the back. Before he could hand it to the major, Lord Colridge snatched it from his hand.

"I know this fellow. Why didn't that fool inspector ask me?"

CHAPTER 17

The Chagga promptly drove out the
Wakonyingo, but only after they learned how to smelt iron, too.

—The Traveler

A PALPABLE RELIEF SWEPT OVER THE CAMP. JADE WAS BACK, AND IT seemed that there'd be no reprisals. More than one, "That was close," was exchanged. Jade had headed for the bath tent, taking a bucket of warm water with her, and quickly attempted to wash away more than grime. The cold chill still clung to her.

When she was done, she gave her rifle a thorough going-over and couldn't find anything wrong with it. She didn't understand it, and Jelani's silence and knowing looks unnerved her as well. What she regretted was that she hadn't had time to thoroughly inspect Rehema's bag again. For that she wanted complete privacy, which meant by lamplight in her tent tonight. Only then would she reveal her full findings to Harry. She looked for him and found him by the washbasin.

Harry dried his hands on a towel and held Jade's gaze for a few seconds, silently expressing not only his relief, but also his admiration.

"Excepting the leopard *shauri*, that was well-done," he said finally. "What made you think of taking Biscuit with you to the village?"

"I saw how the Chagga had watched him," she said. "Almost reverently. I think old Sina's saga affected them more than it did our esteemed director." She took a deep breath, and released it, willing her tension to go with it. "I hoped they might see him as some sort of omen and accept the death as something bigger than any of us."

"Just the same," said Harry, "I think precautions are in order. Nakuru," he called. The headman joined him, silently awaiting orders. Harry clapped him on the shoulder. "Double the guard tonight, just to be on the safe side. Be especially wary right before dawn. Sorry, Jade," he said after Nakuru left to inform the other men. "I know tomorrow's Sunday, but you're going to have to stay here with us instead of traipsing off to the mission in the morning. I need all my eyes and hands in camp."

Jade nodded. "I understand. I'll take the dawn watch if you like."

"Good. We'll take it together. I don't expect anything, but I don't want to take chances." Muturi rang the dinner gong and they joined the actors and crew in line.

"What happened, Harry?" asked Jade as they hung back at the line's end. What with one demand or another on her time, it was the first opportunity she'd had to discuss today's horrid tragedy. "It was Miss Porter's shot that killed Zakayo. Everyone was supposed to have blanks."

"They were. Homerman had small boxes for each person. I even test-fired one out of each box earlier to be sure. All I can think is that some of my ammunition accidentally got mixed in."

Jade frowned. "It wouldn't be your ammunition, Harry. They're all firing American-made rifles, mostly Remingtons."

"That's right. What was Cynthia firing?" asked Harry.

"A Winchester .30-40."

"Then did some of your ammunition get in there?"

Jade shook her head. "Mine is .303 British." She remembered McAvy and Murdock coming up the trail after Harry's rescue. They'd had Winchesters with them, and surely they hadn't loaded them with blanks. She said as much to Harry. "You saw their crates. Did they plan on doing any hunting? Would some of their own rounds have gotten mixed in?"

Harry shrugged and suddenly looked every bit of his forty-plus years. "There was no hunting planned except for game that you or I shot. They have no permits. I didn't . . ." He let his words dangle. Jade knew he hadn't searched every crate, every personal item. Who would? "So either someone back in their movie studio made a mistake or one of them mixed their own ammunition with the blanks," Harry concluded.

And if the latter, was it an accident? Too many coincidences! A movement caught her eye and she suddenly saw a two-horned chameleon resting on a window ledge. It blended so well that only the snap of its tongue for a fat millipede gave it away. It'd chosen its spot well, planned and executed its ambush perfectly. Jade watched it, her mind busily reviewing events.

"Harry, don't you find it odd that Zakayo was killed? The person we both wanted to talk to about the boomslang?"

"It could have been any of the Chagga," Harry countered. "Zakayo just happened to be the one by Cynthia's tent. And she happened to have the box with live rounds."

Jade sighed. Sam would have known what she meant. Sam *had* suspected already but, like Harry, she'd been too dense or bullheaded to listen. Now, in light of the past incidents and near accidents, she suddenly saw the truth, just as a movement suddenly revealed the reptile that might have been on the ledge since their arrival. Someone in this camp was a murderer.

"Harry, I know you don't believe me, but just think about it. You agreed that the snake had to be placed in that box by someone."

"Yes, by that crazy Rehema. Hell, we know that fact because she died from what certainly sounds like a boomslang bite. We just wanted to ask Zakayo if he saw her in camp with that bag. To put a lid on the case."

"No, Harry. To see if she gave the bag to someone here. Julian, Homerman, Miss Porter."

"Well, *not* Cynthia," Harry protested. "That makes no sense. She's the producer, for cripes' sake. She's got money invested in this bloody enterprise."

"Then someone else," said Jade. "Whoever it was made sure we couldn't talk to Zakayo."

"Very well. Then Julian's your man. He's the one who put Zakayo in that spot."

"Have you learned anything else from the actors?" asked Jade.

"No. Homerman says he took care of loading the rifles. Cynthia's about done-in with guilt even though she only fired the shot. I'll talk with her more later, see if I can learn anything. Right now Bebe won't even speak to me beyond a curt hello, and Wells has turned into some kind of gloomy Gus and won't talk either."

Jelani filled their plates, and Harry insisted Jade join the others to eat. Jade had very little appetite, but she knew she had to keep an eye on the actors. Besides, it might be a chance to pick up some information. She watched Cynthia make a beeline for Harry, while McAvy and Hall sat on opposite sides of Pearl. Bebe returned from the privy, took a plate, and, ignoring

Wells' call to her, joined the director and the cameramen. Jade chose a seat with the poker-playing group of Murdock, Talmadge, and Wells, who had already made a place for Lwiza.

"Evening, gentlemen, Lwiza," Jade said as she sat down. She forced a smile, especially at Lwiza. Jade's mood was being carefully watched after the day's events. It wouldn't take much, she realized, to get everyone's nerves in a frazzle again. "You can all relax," she said. "We're in no danger. The Chagga aren't going to attack."

"What was all that ruckus before?" asked Wells. "When Harry suddenly lit out of camp with that stowaway kid. Who is he anyway?"

"Jelani is my friend," explained Jade. "He's a Kikuyu healer. I've known him since I first came to Africa. As to the ruckus . . ." She paused to consider how much she should tell them. "There was a leopard along the trail. Jelani must have seen its spoor." Facing four perplexed faces, she explained. "Signs. Paw prints, droppings, claw marks on a tree trunk. Knowing I was alone with Biscuit, he decided I needed a man's protection and went back to get it."

The three men and Lwiza accepted her explanation and devoted more of their attention to the roasted pork in front of them. "Being on safari has one thing going for it," said Talmadge. "The chow is great. I don't eat this well when I'm back at the studio."

"That's because you have to do your own cooking then," said Wells. "Fried bologna gets a little old after a while."

"What did you eat when you went with Mr. Wheeler to Abyssinia?" asked Jade.

"Oh, we didn't go on that trip," said Murdock. "Never even heard of the place until I got hired for this picture."

"You're joking," said Jade as she buttered a slab of flatbread. "Didn't *any* of you go? Doesn't that have something to do with getting into your roles?"

"I'm just a stuntman and a glorified extra," said Talmadge. "Remember? I'm the man in the scene when they need another man in the scene. Or the one who takes the dive for a star."

"Hall and I are the only two who really needed to know anything about this emperor stuff," said Murdock. "Graham just made us read all his notes and study every photo he took."

"You actually read all that bunk?" asked Wells. "I couldn't make it past the history, much less the native customs. Not that Rex hasn't told us enough. All I ever hear from him is bunk about gold and jewels."

"What about the ladies?" asked Jade. "I'd have thought some of them would need to know some of the history."

Murdock shrugged. "Well, maybe Cynthia. Her character is mainly the understanding wife. But I'm sure Graham made all of them read the same stuff he gave me."

"Do you still have those notes with you?" Jade asked.

"Yeah, maybe. Wait. I might have left them back in Nairobi with the rest of my personal belongings that I didn't need out here. You know, dress clothes, good shoes."

Talmadge nodded towards Lwiza, who'd sat quietly eating her meal with dainty manners. "Miss Lwiza has been a big help to some of us. She's the one who showed me a good way to hold my spear at attention when I had to play Menelik's general."

Lwiza ducked her head shyly. "I only showed what I saw in a picture once before," she said. "In a book. I wanted to be of help."

"Well, you've been a jim-dandy big help," said Talmadge, reaching over and patting her hand. "She's the one who finally found old Homerman's keys today." He laughed. "You can tell that man is Rex's brother-in-law. Sure didn't get his job being qualified."

"Did he mix up the ammunition?" asked Jade. "Is that why Miss Porter's rifle had live rounds?"

The men all shrugged. "Beats the dickens out of me," said Wells. "It's a sad mess and that's the truth. I heard one of those hired chaps talking before. Couldn't make out what he said, but I heard him say, 'Porter.' "

Murdock's head jerked up. "What?"

Wells nodded. "It made me wonder if someone had mixed up Cynthia's name with their job. You know? Porter, porter? Maybe they thought that was a gun for a gun bearer to carry."

"I can't believe that's what they meant," argued Jade.

"Well, Rex thinks it explains everything," said Wells. "As far as he's concerned, the matter's settled."

Wonderful. Of course he wouldn't dwell on it. Just another native man killed. Jade's disgust put a dank taste in her mouth. She pushed her plate away. "I want to thank you again, Woody, for coming to my rescue. I hope you didn't come up with blanks in your rifle, though."

"My pleasure, Jade. McAvy and I had live rounds in our gear in case we went hunting. Just took us a while to load those rifles." Just then Julian called for everyone's attention by clanking his spoon on his tin cup.

"Everyone needs a good night's sleep tonight," he said. "Tomorrow we're going to break camp and climb up the mountain. We're going to the crater!"

What little appetite Jade had fled as a sudden cold, stabbing fear gripped her stomach.

"You recognize him, sir?" asked Sam.

"Of course. Used to work for me." Lord Colridge handed

the photograph off to Bertram. "Hired him to replace my other Somali. The one your Miss del Cameron stole away."

"Pili?" exclaimed Beverly.

"Precisely," said Colridge. "After she sent my best lad off to some university somewhere, I had to find another, you know. Somali are generally quite good with horses, so, naturally, when Bahdoon came looking for work, I hired him."

"But you didn't report him missing?" asked Madeline.

"No, for the simple fact that I'd *fired* him a month ago. Never actually caught the man stealing, but when missing articles coincide with a man's addition to the household . . . well, it's simple. Told him to collect his possessions and cut out."

"Did he have references, this Bahdoon?" asked Bertram.

"Yes, forged, I should imagine," said Colridge. "But to answer the question as to why he had no *kipande*, most Somali are not required to have them."

"Thank you, sir," said Sam. "I'll tell Inspector Finch tomorrow."

Colridge waved his hand in dismissal. "Think nothing of it, son. Very glad to help. Should be happier if I had Pili back. Is there, er, any chance . . . ?" He looked to Beverly, his brows arched, the picture of hope.

Beverly cocked her head and smiled. "I think not, my Lord Colridge. After an intensive tutoring in the basic sciences, he's deeply invested in his studies of animal husbandry. It's possible that we'll see him some holiday, and we're hoping he'll come to work for us when he's completed his courses. He has some hope of eventually earning a veterinary degree."

Colridge pulled back in surprise. His eyes widened and his lower jaw dropped. "The devil," he said, then hastened to add, "My apologies for such language, Lady Dunbury. I was . . . I mean to say . . . Well, he always was a clever lad." The old man puffed his chest out and preened his brushy mustache with his fingertips. "Taught him everything I knew about horses."

"And he couldn't have had a better teacher, sir," said Avery, feeding the man's pride.

"At what university is he studying?" asked Colridge. "Edinburgh, I should imagine."

Avery shook his head. "Sorry, sir, but we keep that a very tight secret. When Pili inherited part of his father, Gil Worthy's, estate . . . How shall I put this? Worthy's widow made an attempt on Pili's life. Lilith might try again. We've already moved him once. And after finding some letters opened, we take extra steps. She may yet have a spy in Nairobi."

"Indeed? Hmph, well." Colridge pursed his lips and his gaze shifted from side to side as he looked to the others for confirmation or refutation. But any further commentary was brushed aside as Bertram, who'd been leafing through the other photographs, remarked on them.

"I say, these are very interesting photographs. Did you take these, Mr. Featherstone?"

"Please call me Sam, and no, I only developed them. I'd hoped to spot our erstwhile Somali friend in them." He thought about explaining why, then decided against it. At this point, his theory sounded far-fetched even to him.

"The photographer did a marvelous job," declared Bertram. "Look how well he captured this Abyssinian woman."

"The photographer is a young American lady," corrected Madeline. "She's on safari on Mount Kilimanjaro with these very people, but you're mistaken. There are no Abyssinians in her group." She ticked them off on her fingers. "A British hunter, his Nyamwezi man, American actors, and their Swahili maid."

"I assure you, Mrs. Thompson, I'm not mistaken. The Swahili—the *pure* Swahili, mind you—are mostly transplanted Arabs. There's a distinctive cast to their noses and faces. This woman has the look of one of the Abyssinian nobility. I can see it in her cheekbones and the hairstyle, the way she's parted it in the middle and rolled up each side."

He turned the picture to better catch the room's light. "Of course, in the blacks and whites of a photograph, one misses the buttery walnut skin tones so characteristic of the upper class." He tapped the arm in the picture. "But even if I *was* mistaken about the face, this armband would decide the issue. I've seen these before. The highborn ladies who serve as ladies-in-waiting wear them. Design represents either the ark or the temple." He set the photograph on the table atop the others. "Most curious. I can't imagine one of these ladies leaving court."

While the others exclaimed amongst themselves, Sam sat quietly trying to recollect something he'd heard the woman say. *Bun? A bun?* Bunna! "Major Bertram," he said, trying to keep his voice even as he fought the gnawing anxiety that grew within him, "what is the Abyssinian word for coffee?"

"*Bunna*. Why do you ask?"

CHAPTER 18

Rival branches of Chagga fought each other for control,
the blood of the fallen mingling with the blood of sacrificial goats.
Once again, Kilimanjaro knew violence.

—The Traveler

"Is this a good idea, Harry?" Jade asked. "Taking this lot up the mountain?"

"I don't have a choice, Jade. It's what I was hired to do. And the sooner we get up there, the sooner Julian will finish his motion picture, and"—he poked his chest for emphasis—"the sooner *I* can get them on the train and back to Nairobi. But Julian's mistaken. We're *not* going to the crater. I'm engaged to take them as far as the saddle, that heath at the edge of the ice field."

He looked around at his own men standing in a cluster talking in low tones. "Nakuru's all right, but the rest of the men are getting nervous. They're starting to take this whole tale of a lost, buried king seriously. Think we're jinxed."

"Jinxed?" echoed Jade. Behind her, Lwiza passed by on some errand.

Harry pushed up his hat brim. "That's right. First you slip on that little bridge, then some bloody boomslang appears in a box. Next Zakayo gets killed and your rifle jams as you try to shoot a leopard that left no prints. Add to it that bloody Chagga curse on you, and they're starting to *invent* mishaps. Scorched posho at breakfast, a box that slipped and hit someone's arm, it's all evidence to them right now. It might do them good to move up higher and find out that we left our troubles behind us. If we turn tail and leave, that will only reinforce their superstitions, and I'll never get men to work for me here again."

Jade pondered that idea for a moment. "You're probably right, Harry. But are we ready to go up? Don't we need to pick up more supplies in Moshi?"

"Don't worry yourself on that score, Jade. We have enough of the staples: flour, meal, jerked meat, that sort of thing. I'll hunt. Or you. Game's good up higher, especially above the forest in that heath they call the saddle."

Jade frowned as she listened to the others prattle away at their private conversations. Most were subdued, but Julian waxed ecstatic. "Look at him," she said. "A man died today, shot by their rifle, and he acts as if nothing happened. He probably considers himself lucky to have a genuine death scene caught on film." She noticed Pearl and Bebe staying close to Cynthia and was glad to see the other women make an effort to support her.

Harry took hold of her right elbow. "I'm as disgusted as you are, Jade. But we *are* heading up the mountain tomorrow. We need *all* our strength. *I* need you to be at your peak. One sign of hesitation from you would send the new men into a superstitious panic."

"New men?" she asked. "You hired some Chagga porters? Is that wise, considering what just happened? We could go into Moshi and hire more if we waited two more days."

"I might have, but you did an excellent job of placating the

Chagga. Elsewise we could have had a hornet's nest descending on us. Giving these men jobs will smooth differences even further."

Jade let out a deep breath. "You're the boss, Harry. I just hope these men weren't related to Zakayo."

"Jade," he said softly, stepping closer to her. "You don't have to take it that way. *You're* my right-hand man, in a manner of speaking," he added, running his gaze over her body. "I trust you. I'd rather hoped you felt you could trust me." His voice held a note of hurt.

"Harry, I'm the last one to question your ability to run a safari," said Jade, stepping back. "But another day's notice would have helped. You underestimate the amount of time it takes to get these actresses together. That's one of the reasons you hired me, remember? Now, what's your plan?"

He studied her face and hair for a moment and released a deep breath. "Right! On to business. We roust everyone up an hour before dawn. My men will take down the tents and start up the trail ahead of us with Nakuru leading. When our lot has had their breakfast, we'll start up for Bismark's hut. It's only four hours' walk, not difficult. Hell, our men will make it in three. We'll stay the night there. Give them a chance to acclimate to the higher elevation. But Nakuru and some of the men will continue on to Peter's hut after dropping off a few supplies."

"They can make that in one day?"

"They have before. It's another six hours at most. And it gives them a full day's rest before they set up camp on the other edge of the saddle. We'll be there a day after them."

"What about the supplies? Are they all going to be a day away from us, too?"

"Not all of them. Nakuru will leave our essentials and

enough food stores at the first hut along with a few men to carry everything the next day. But the Americans will have to carry their most personal gear themselves."

"This group thinks *everything* is essential, Harry. Especially these women. They'll have Lwiza running ragged, sorting. I'd better give her a hand." She turned to go.

He snatched at her sleeve. His voice dropped to a husky whisper. "When you're done, why don't you join me at my tent for a cup of coffee? We can plan together."

"A little late for that," she said, brushing his hand aside. "Besides, if we've got the watch from two until dawn, I'll need a few hours' sleep." She walked away.

"Don't you see? That's it!"

It was all Sam could do to stand still. Any attempt by Beverly or Avery to get him in a chair was pointless. He'd sat long enough, holding back his revelation until Colridge's son, Edmunde, came for his father. But even then, he couldn't spill out his discovery. Instead they had to endure another twenty minutes of Edmunde. And now that the father and son had gone, no one believed him.

"Look," Sam said, holding his hands out in front of him. "It's very simple." He made a fist with his left hand and extended the index finger. "First off, the native that stabbed Wheeler was not only intoxicated, but drugged to the point of mania with datura. Mixing datura seeds in alcohol is done in Abyssinia."

He looked to Major Bertram for confirmation and received it in the form of a perfunctory nod. A second finger extended. "This movie is about an early Abyssinian emperor. And lastly," Sam said, punctuating his statement with his ring finger,

"Major Bertram has just pointed out that the woman everyone thinks is some simple Swahili maidservant is from Abyssinia." He spread his arms like some performer waiting for the applause after a performance. His audience stared at him with tilted heads and upraised eyebrows.

Avery stood up and joined Sam. "I'm sure that's sterling logic, Sam, but I think there's another explanation."

"Of course," said Beverly. "That girl likely bought that armband from a trader. And even if she is from Abyssinia," she added quickly when Sam opened his mouth to protest, "she's probably just someone Wheeler hired to help with authenticity."

"Right," agreed Avery. "Think about it, Sam. Why would some girl leave the empress's court just to wreak havoc on a movie? It makes no sense. It's a coincidence. It has to be."

"Coincidence," echoed Sam flatly, his disbelief and disappointment evident.

Avery immediately changed tactics. "I do see what you're saying, Sam. And I must admit it is a bit of a stretch to think there's no connection. But isn't it more likely that she was hired by Wheeler when he did his research?"

"And she waited until they were all in Nairobi to kill him?" asked Sam. "Why not kill him then? You've assumed Wheeler hired her in Abyssinia. Remember, they had some American maid to begin with. One who suddenly took ill, no less."

"But why would she kill him?" asked Neville. "I still don't understand the motive."

"And we have no connection between that murderer and this Lwiza," added Madeline.

Sam ran a hand up the back of his neck and into his hair. "I'll admit, it's all very sketchy, but let me try to explain my gut feeling. Wheeler wants to make a film about this Menelik and his supposed treasure. He goes to Abyssinia to research the legend. This woman who calls herself Lwiza hears about him. She makes her way to Nairobi and, after the regularly hired maid *conveniently* gets ill, agrees to work for him. She wants to stop this safari. So she finds someone to kill Wheeler. Who better than a recently fired African with no papers?"

"But why?" asked Beverly.

Sam shrugged. "Maybe there's more to this legend than we know. A grain of truth. Maybe she's out to protect the secret."

"Or the treasure," said Madeline. She blushed when the others stared at her. "Well, it could be."

Avery turned to his guest as he filled his pipe. "What do you think, Tony? You're the expert among us. Ever hear of this legend of Menelik's treasure?"

"Yes, but not from court," said Major Bertram. "Any stories *I* heard came from some outlying chieftain, drunk and boasting around the campfire. Outlandish yarns supposedly passed on from one of Menelik's generals. Of course, with each telling, there was more gold and more slaves, enough to have stopped up several volcanoes. What is most important, however, is that this king was buried with Solomon's regalia, all signs of power. Regalia that would restore the kingdom's glory: a scepter, a certain ring, and a crown."

"Then why," asked Neville, "haven't the Abyssinians looked for it?"

"Good question," said Major Bertram. "If you were to ask anyone in court about it, which I did, they would either laugh at you or ignore you as an uncouth foreigner, depending on whom you asked. That would suggest it's all a myth. Menelik the Second *did* make the pilgrimage but he had no luck. Interestingly, I did hear a version from one old priest that finding the regalia would happen only at the start of the end days."

"So when someone finds it, the world ends?" asked Beverly.

"No. Finding it too soon wouldn't force God's hand, but it would destroy the promise of restoring the kingdom's glory. The tomb should not be found *until* the start of the end days."

Sam paced back and forth across the room. "Well, someone on that safari is willing to kill to find that treasure now."

"Sam," scolded Avery, "if it were Beverly out there, I'd be frantic, too. But you'll wear yourself down, man. Sit!"

"Surely after you tell Inspector Finch what you know, he'll do something," said Neville.

Sam grunted and resumed his pacing. "You forget. Tomorrow is Sunday. Finch will be off for the day, and you can be certain that none of his subordinates will pass along any message. The train won't even be running."

"I know," said Madeline. "You could fly out there and warn her."

"No fuel," said Sam and Avery simultaneously.

"I don't quite understand," said Major Bertram. "Is this young lady in some sort of predicament? I understood you to say there's a man in charge. Surely he'll protect her."

Sam wheeled in midstep, pivoting on his wooden leg. "Major Bertram, you have no idea what she's capable of. Why, just before she left, she actually charged a lion. Rode her motorcycle straight for him like she was chasing off the neighborhood tomcat."

"Oh, dear. I see," said Bertram.

Madeline's face blanched. "I didn't know about that. Did you know?" she asked, turning to Beverly.

Beverly shook her head, her lips pursed. "She always was too brave for her own good. Even during the war. Always the first one to volunteer for the more dangerous ambulance runs."

Avery tapped out his pipe ashes and hung his pipe in a

nearby stand. "Sam," he said, rising, "you won't rest easy until you know you've warned her properly. And you probably won't trust our friend Finch to see to it. So I suggest you compose a telegram and send it to Moshi. Tell them to deliver it posthaste to their camp. Someone will know where they are."

Sam shoved his hands in his pockets. "I will. As soon as the blasted telegraph office opens Monday morning. Then I'll see Finch before I take the train to Moshi and find her."

"That's the spirit, Sam," said Neville. He clapped his friend on the back. "With any luck, they'll still be somewhere at the base."

JADE COLLAPSED ON her cot fully clothed, keeping even her boots on her feet. Her edict to pack only the essentials followed by her explanation of what she considered essential had gone over about as well as she'd expected.

"A change of clothing if needed, good socks, your canteen full of water, your hat, a jacket. That's essential. Any female hygiene items you need. That's essential. Face paint, filmy sleepwear, woolly half slippers, those are *not* essential. So pull those items out and pack them in a crate for storage."

"Why do I have to carry any gear?" demanded Cynthia. "I thought that's what I was paying all those natives to do."

"All those natives will be carrying food, cooking equipment, cameras, film, ammunition, tents, blankets, not to mention all those movie props *and* walking farther than you will have to travel tomorrow. We're going up over two thousand feet in elevation. Another three thousand the next day. You'll find it will get much colder at night. Pack your thermals and your coat in the box to be left at the first hut. Lwiza and I will help you."

"No, she won't," grumbled Cynthia.

"What?" Jade asked.

Cynthia stood with her arms folded tightly across her chest. "Bebe demands all her time to begin with. Always having her carry and fetch for her. Pearl, too. After that, Rex is constantly using her to get those two prima donnas ready in their historical scenes. Apparently my simple safari matron role doesn't warrant any special attention." She sniffed. "Between the lot of them, I hardly get any use of her time. And for some reason, I think she's avoiding me."

"Did you say something to offend her?" asked Jade.

"Certainly not!" snapped Cynthia. "Not that I should be expected to beg anyone I'm paying. If she doesn't want to help me, so be it."

"I'll help you repack."

"Thank you, but that won't be necessary. I've been able to take care of myself in uncivilized areas before."

"Oh?" Jade raised her eyebrows in an expression of obvious interest. "Where?"

"Here and there," she said, not meeting Jade's eyes. "I've camped a lot." With that, she hurried off to her room and Jade offered her assistance to the other women.

Pearl declined Jade's offer with a lazy smile. "I'm already packed," she said. "I heard Rex giving the order to Harry two days ago, you see. Besides, my previous job required enough traveling that I've learned to keep everything stowed to begin with. So," she added with a low purr, "I can occupy myself otherwise this evening."

At least those two understand responsibility. Jade found Lwiza also had her meager possessions ready to go, which was good, considering Bebe's room looked like it had been the scene of either a tornado or a bargain sale booth at a street fair. Bebe issued one order after another while Lwiza, Jade observed, calmly ignored most of them and set to work quietly and methodically sorting and packing. After checking with Jelani and Muturi, Jade picked up Biscuit and collapsed in her tent to write in her notebook.

Only then did she remember Rehema's pouch, principally because it was presently an uncomfortable lump biting into her spine. With a groan, Jade hauled herself off her cot and pulled the pouch from under her blanket. She relit her lantern and set it on the box that served as a nightstand.

"Let's see what we have in here."

Jade opened a clean handkerchief and spread it on the bed. Then she spilled the contents onto the kerchief. The main item that caught her attention was the lady's compact. Jade picked it up and examined it. "POM" and "Bloom" were painted onto the lid in gold along with part of a heart. The rest was badly scratched and unreadable. There were no initials inscribed anywhere.

She pushed the little lip to release the catch. The color was a soft red. Jade couldn't recall seeing this on any one actress in particular. As far as she knew, they all wore it. She'd given their boxes only a cursory look in Nairobi, enough to see that no one was smuggling anything. *It should be easy enough to ask around and see whom it belongs to.*

But only if the compact was stolen, she reminded herself. Not if it had been given to Rehema in return for something. What then? Would the previous owner admit it?

Saint Peter's little fishes. It might have been traded for a bunch of fruit, for all you know.

Jade set the compact aside and fingered the remaining items. As she expected, there was a small drop spindle for spinning fibers, a needle fashioned from a thin bone, and a pretty stone polished by a stream. Jade felt a pang of sympathy at such simple treasures and a life lost. She started to put them back into the bag when she noticed all the black seeds on the handkerchief. If her memory wasn't mistaken, they looked a lot like the seeds of jimsonweed that plagued sections of her family's New Mexico ranch back home in the States.

Jimsonweed was just a common name for datura, and it went a long way towards explaining how Rehema had fulfilled the first part of her curse.

CHAPTER 19

The Chagga tales are full of passion and betrayal. But now their violence is spent in animal sacrifice to appease restless ancestors.

—The Traveler

When Fundikira rapped at Jade's tent pole to signify her turn for the dawn watch, she was already awake and ready. Harry met her at the cook fire, a banked heap of glowing coals, and handed her a mug of coffee. He looked particularly pleased with himself, a broad smile on his scruffy face. Neither of them really expected the Chagga to attack them, but a show of readiness was still good diplomacy in case a few were watching. Only the bravest would risk the trails at night, when leopards prowled the forest tracts and foraging elephants were easily startled.

Jade took her position at the northeastern edge of the camp, with Harry at the opposite side. Biscuit padded up to her and yawned, exposing large, slightly yellow canines and plenty of tongue. She stroked his head and felt his warmth as he wound about her legs. Then his head jerked to one side and he chirped. Without looking, Jade knew who had attracted his attention.

"Go to Jelani, Biscuit," she whispered. Biscuit gave her one final rub, then strolled to where the Kikuyu youth had taken it upon himself to keep watch from the south.

Another sound, that of booted feet, reached Jade's ears. She turned and spied Cynthia, her arms hugging herself against the predawn chill. The woman walked quickly, head down, towards the old farmhouse where she slept. But the direction she came from didn't match a nocturnal visit to the privy. Jade wondered whose tent she'd been sharing. But she saw no dimly glowing lamps and heard no other sounds to give her a hint. *None of your business anyway.*

She gave her eyes and ears the job of sensing danger and turned her mind over to the problem of Rehema and the poisoned seeds. Jade had witnessed the Muthaiga attack and the suicide at the end. That native had obviously been out of his mind. His actions had matched those of the cursed Chagga woman. Both had clawed at their skin, eyes glazing over. And the woman had staggered like a drunk. Jade had witnessed a sheep do something similar when it had eaten some jimsonweed on the ranch. While she couldn't be sure of the Nairobi man, at least the Chagga woman's death was caused by datura poisoning. The seeds in Rehema's pouch confirmed it. Jade didn't hold much with coincidences. This stretched the realm of credulity. So who was the connection? Someone in their party had to be involved. But who and why?

Wheeler's death lent itself to several "whos," each with its own "why." Julian wanted control of the motion picture and had an eye for treasure; Cynthia wanted control of the money or revenge for Wheeler's affairs. Any actor might have borne a grudge. But unless Julian knew that Cynthia was Wheeler's spouse, he took a risk of being left stranded without any money.

The Chagga woman's death could be attributed to that boomslang snake. Someone had witnessed Rehema's outburst and offered her a more certain mode of ridding herself of a rival without having to kill herself to put a curse in effect. And the price? One poisonous snake.

Jade shivered. The boomslang didn't work. Whoever it was intended for didn't die. Did that mean there would be another attempt on someone here? Where did Zakayo's death fit in? Was he killed because he knew something about the transaction? Or had that rifle and bullet gotten into Cynthia's hand by mistake?

Ah, Sam. You were right all along. Where the heck are you when I need you? Jade longed to be able to talk to him about this, hear his logical ideas, feel his strength near her. *Well, you're on your own.* Some part of her deep inside mocked her. *Isn't that the way you prefer it?*

Another corner of her brain reminded her that she wasn't completely alone. She had Harry. She should make use of him as an ally and quit thinking of him as an enemy, as she had in the past. And to his credit, he had changed. *Well, at least a little.* Jade noted that Harry now treated her like a trusted business partner. In place of a lover's empty flattery, he'd complimented her on her levelheadedness. True, he'd admitted earlier that he still cared for her, but at least he hadn't chased her like a rutting elk.

Even when I stood outside of his tent last night to tell him about my newest discovery.

She'd expected him to invite her inside. To her surprise, he'd come out, shirt half-buttoned, and suggested they take a walk, listening intently to everything she'd said.

"That tops it and no mistake," he'd said. "I've got to hand it to you, Jade. You've made me see things in a different light."

"So we ship these people back?"

Harry had shaken his head, rubbing a big hand across his

scraggly chin. "Can't. Might lose my license. But we will keep a closer watch from now on. Nobody fires a rifle that we haven't checked. Instead of that idiot Homerman, we keep the keys to the boxes. I'm trusting you with that. And we oversee everything they set up or put out for their scenes. No surprises."

"Do you think it's Julian?" Jade asked.

"Seriously? I'm not sure. Maybe Hall or Wells. Wells has had an eye on Bebe."

"I've been thinking. There's another person who's been on this trip whom we've overlooked."

"Not Nakuru!" said Harry.

Jade shook her head. "No. Lwiza. For the life of me, I can't figure out any motive for her to do any of this, but she certainly has had access to a lot of boxes and she overheard where Homerman stashed his keys. I wonder if Lwiza took one of the women's rouge compacts and used it to barter for that snake. She could have put it in that coffer."

"Then *you* keep an eye on her. I don't know anything about those women's paints. I'm trusting you. Good night." He'd hurried back to his own tent.

Trust. That old bugaboo kept popping up a lot lately. Now, as she stood guard, watching the trees for movement, she wished Sam trusted her as much.

Is that why you haven't accepted him yet? She had no answer to that, just a longing ache.

Before sunrise, they roused everyone out of bed. Nakuru directed his men in taking down the tents while the Americans stumbled off to eat breakfast. Before they'd finished their oatmeal and bush pig ham slices, Nakuru and his men were ready to leave. They headed up the trail first, without waiting for the others. An hour and a lot of fussing later, the Americans were ready, too.

The hike to Bismark's hut should have been a stroll in the park. The path climbed gently and steadily through a green canvas. Long, feathery moss from a few trees and their shorter cousins coated every rock or fallen log. Impatiens in scarlet, violet, and yellow speckled the green, along with lush white begonias. They stepped over or around many trees, uprooted by elephants, providing more canvas for the moss to paint.

"Ouch!" yelped Homerman only twenty minutes into the walk. "I stepped on something sharp."

"Hold up, people," called Harry. "Let's have a look." He pulled his knife and probed the boot heel. "What the . . . ? It's a ruddy nail." He pulled it and tossed it aside.

Jade picked up the nail and noticed that it wasn't rusty. She shoved it into a side pocket and continued up the slope. Gray-faced monkeys followed them in the treetops, and yellow orioles flashed among the leaves. Jade longed for a way to capture the beauty and vibrancy but the light was too dim to enable a photograph. This called for a painter's touch. She made mental notes to record later in her journal.

But despite the beauty, Jade couldn't shake the unnerving sense that something was following her. She trailed the column, Harry taking point, and kept her eye on the forest for signs or sounds of approaching Chagga warriors. Once, she caught a glimpse of an elephant, a shadow moving in shadow. For a brief moment, the sight swept her back to another mountain and another forest: Marsabit. With it came memories of her first meeting with Sam. She sighed. But except for long columns of ants carrying what looked like yellow pollen, she saw little wildlife.

Jelani hung towards the rear of the column as well. Jade heard his low, crooning chant drift back to her and wondered if he, too, sensed something. Even Biscuit kept casting sidewise glances into the forest. But if the Chagga or something else followed them, they stayed well hidden. Jade put it down to tension and an overactive mind and continued on.

Their path paralleled the Una, which graced them with views of trickling waterfalls that would swell to engorged torrents after a rain. At other times, they crossed it or one of its tributaries along a more shallow riffle, using logs or rocks placed at convenient stepping points by Chagga, who used the trail to maintain their aerial bee barrels, cultivated hives set high in the trees. After nearly two hours and yet another stream fording, the trail grew rockier and steeper.

The forest changed with the trail. Now great buttressed trees dominated the landscape, and tangled masses of bearded moss hung from every one, as if passing women or ancient warriors had snagged their hair and left it to hang.

Alas for Absalom, thought Jade.

Tree ferns twice the height of a man grew out of rich, black soil. When the group trod on the path, the dirt released an aroma of fertile humus, the mountain's accumulated memory held within it. Club moss and gray lichen clung to everything. The air grew damper, and the women complained that it was ruining their hairstyles.

"Not much farther," Harry coaxed. "We're nearly to the hut. Nakuru left us some food there before continuing on up to tomorrow's stop."

Forty minutes later, they spotted Bismark's hut, a rectangular stone building. Five windows and a door faced the downward slope. The ground in front of the house was cleared of brush, while a row of tall trees stood sentry over the rear. Jade pulled her Kodak and snapped the party as they plopped on the ground or on the steps up to the door.

"Where's the latrine?" asked Julian.

Harry pointed to the trees. "I told you that you shouldn't

expect anything quite as nice as our base camp," Harry said. "Jade will stand guard for any of you ladies."

"You must be joking," said Bebe. She opened the door and stared at the empty hut. "Where's the furniture? What are we to sleep on?"

"Your blankets," said Jade. "But we can collect dried lichen from the forest for bedding. It's soft."

"I have no intention of gathering anything or sleeping on something that might have bugs in it," said Pearl. Hall echoed her sentiment.

After the group had picked out and claimed their spots on the floor inside the hut, Jade tried to coax the women into exploring the area. They each declared themselves positively unwilling to take another step and lay down on their blankets to nap. Jade set one of the hired men as guard while she collected lichens for her own bedding. She deposited her load inside near the door and arranged her blanket on top. Then, unwilling to leave her charges, she resigned herself to staying in camp and joined some of the male actors.

"Anyone game to try their luck at cards again tonight?" she asked.

"You cleaned me out the last time, Jade," said Talmadge. He grinned. "My daddy taught me to keep an eye out for female cardsharps."

"I'm hardly a cardsharp. And," she added, "you only lost two dollars and thirty-seven cents to me. Come on. We'll use coffee beans for chips. Penny a bean. Five-card draw."

The foursome sat on the ground and Jade dealt. As she handed round the cards, she felt Kilimanjaro jiggle under her.

"What the . . . ?" began Talmadge.

"Just another little earth tremor," said Harry. "Don't worry. Kilimanjaro isn't active."

"There's the first good news I've heard today," said Talmadge, looking at his cards. "I'm in for another cent," said Talmadge, upping the ante.

"One lousy cent?" scoffed Murdock. "Shoot, man, you must have a full house and are trying to hide it from us." He tossed in a bean. "I'll see it."

As the hand progressed, Jade kept her cards close and watched the other players with a practiced eye. Her father's foreman, Dody Higgins, had taught her that most people gave away information with some telltale sign, called a tell: "You don't need to be a cheater and mark cards to read their hands. Just watch for that twitch or nose scratch. I knew a man who coughed every time he had three of a kind or better."

He was right. She'd played poker only twice before with these men, but in that time, Jade had already picked up on some of their signs. Talmadge pulled his cards closer to him and pushed in ten more beans. Wells saw his raise, but Murdock chewed on his lip and folded. As Jade saw the raise and added ten more beans, Wells dropped out of the hand. Soon only Talmadge and Jade remained.

"What d'ya got, lady?" asked Talmadge.

"Pair of nines," she said, laying those two faceup on the ground. Then, just as Talmadge's grin broadened, she set down the other three. "And three jacks."

"Full house," exclaimed Wells. "Damn. That sure beat my pair of tens. Glad I folded."

Murdock shrugged. "I had a two, three, five, six, and a king. Turned in the king hoping for a four. Got a nine."

Talmadge grinned. "Going for an inside straight, huh? I had a lousy pair of twos. Thought I could bluff you all into folding." He looked at Jade and shook his head. "You *are* some kind of cardsharp, lady."

Murdock laughed at Talmadge. "Hell, Roland, it doesn't take a sharp to tell when you're bluffing versus when you've got a full house. You get all protective when you've got a good hand. Me, I've got the perfect poker face."

Jade didn't bother to contradict him. He always pursed his lips when he had a good hand.

"You just must not be as good an actor as we are, Talmadge," said Wells. "That's why you get to do all the action-man roles instead of act."

Jade chuckled along with the others, but wondered how much truth was in that simple statement. *Just how good are these actors?* She decided she needed to start watching for tells when she talked to them. Had someone already revealed a lie and she hadn't caught it?

"I hope you gentlemen are good for all this loot," Jade said. "I—"

A string of angry curses interrupted her. *Harry.*

"Deal me out, fellows. I think I'd better see what's amiss."

She left them and hurried over to Harry and Muturi. They stood beside a fire ring and a heap of sticks. Jelani stood a few steps in the background with the remaining porters.

"What's wrong?"

Harry held out a tin for her to take. "It's the matches. They're soaked."

"Soaked?" Jade opened the tin. Sure enough, the matches swam in a pool of water, their sticks swollen and wet. "How?"

Everyone shrugged. Everyone but Jelani, who stood with arms folded across his chest and a scowl on his face.

"And that isn't all," said Harry. "Muturi opened the box of

mealy meal and it's half-empty. I found a hole in the bottom. It's been trickling out all morning."

Jade remembered the nail and the trail of ants carrying flecks of yellow. *Then that was meal and not pollen.* "Do we have enough for the porters for tonight and tomorrow?"

"Yes, but it's going to cut rations a bit tighter farther on," said Harry. "Especially if we consume any of it for griddle cakes for breakfast."

"Then we do without griddle cakes," said Jade, knowing that the African men relied on the meal as a main staple in their diet. It was also part of their hire. If they didn't receive it, Harry would be in violation of contract. "Save the meal for the porters. We've got jerked meat, right?"

Harry nodded. "And dried fruits. Muturi will soak it all and make some sort of fruited stew concoction." He scowled. "Once we get the ruddy fire going. Looks like I'll have to waste a cartridge and use the gunpowder."

"Save your ammunition," said Jade. "I can help." She instructed Jelani to gather more dried moss and lichens while she searched the fallen debris for a flat block of dry wood. When she located one, she carved out a small bowl and cut a notch near it, releasing the wood's fragrant resins. Next she fashioned a bow from a green branch and a spare bootlace. The lace wrapped once around a dried and pointed stick.

"Voilà," Jade said. "A bow drill." She slid a leaf under the board's notch, pushed the pointed end of the stick into the shallow bowl near it, and sat on the ground, her feet planted on each end of the cedar plank to hold it in place. Then, using the match tin lid and her handkerchief as a loose cap on the drill, she pushed and pulled on the bow. Each movement rotated the drill in the cedar, heating it with the friction of rubbing. After several minutes, she checked the leaf for a tiny glowing coal worn from the wood. Jade slipped the coal into Jelani's bundle of dried mosses and cupped it in her hands like a nest. She blew gently on the nest, coaxing it to burn. After smoking a moment, a small flame shot up and soon the entire bundle was aflame. Jade gently placed the material in the fire ring and carefully fed it small twigs until the fire grew strong enough to support larger twigs and small branches.

Muturi and the remaining porters nodded appreciatively. They could have done the same, but they were tired from carrying the cookpots and stores. Jade's exertions went a long way towards smoothing ruffled tempers. Jade watched the fire blaze away with a feeling of satisfaction. "There you are, Harry. Our troubles are over for the day. We're here and—" The sound of running feet coming from up the trail interrupted her.

"Hold that thought, Jade," said Harry as he went out to meet the two men who'd just broken out of the trees and raced towards them. Jade recognized them as two Chagga men hired from the village of Zakayo to act as porters on this climb. Harry held up his hand for them to halt and addressed them in Swahili.

"What's wrong? Why have you left Nakuru and your duties?"

"Bwana Nyati," said one man, "we will go no farther up God's mountain. It displeases him and he has cursed us."

CHAPTER 20

There are a lot of ancestors and more coming each generation.

—The Traveler

HARRY'S VOICE RANG OUT LOUD AND ANGRY, EFFECTIVELY BREAKing up the rest of the poker game and attracting all but the napping actresses to find out what was happening. Since Harry's conversation was in Swahili, the Americans looked to Jade to translate and explain.

"What's the commotion about?" asked Julian. "Are we under attack?"

Jade shushed him with a wave of her hand while she listened.

"What is this foolishness about curses?" demanded Harry.

"We go up too high," exclaimed the pair's spokesman. "The boxes come apart. When the headman tells us to go higher, blood comes from our noses. The ground shakes. Ruwa is angry."

"Ruwa is not angry," said Harry with all the authority he could muster. "But I am. I hired men, not frightened women."

Jade stepped forward, letting the men see that she, for one, was not afraid. When the spokesman saw her, he rolled his eyes and pointed. "She is the reason for this trouble. She was cursed. Now the curse follows us."

"If I was cursed," said Jade, "then the curse is on *my* head, not on yours." She took another step closer. "Does a box break only when it is cursed? Your nose bleeds because it does not like to be high. It will stop in a day or two."

The two men glanced at each other, then ducked their heads and shifted, apparently feeling a little foolish now that they were face-to-face with the big bwana and Simba Jike. Their gazes darted towards the cooking fire and the now bubbling pot for posho.

What will they think when they discover that we've lost half the mealy meal?

Harry must have had similar thoughts. "I will not stop you if you wish to return to your village now. But I will not spare food for you if you go. If you stay to eat, then you must go up with us tomorrow. And I do not want you spreading your lies around the camp."

Jade worried that the two men would choose to return to their village. There were still a few hours of daylight left. She decided to sway the decision in the group's favor.

"Biscuit," she whispered, "greet."

The cheetah, which had stood at her side during the proceedings, padded forward until he was in front of the two men. From his throat erupted a loud, raspy purr. He rubbed his broad head against their hands one at a time before stepping back to Jade. His pose appeared so stately, so regal, that they couldn't help but be affected by his notice.

"We will stay," said the spokesman. "And go up with you tomorrow."

Harry waited a moment before responding, letting the men

know that whether they stayed or left was ultimately his decision. "Since memsahib Simba Jike's *duma* has made you welcome, I will let you stay." He turned aside and walked away, putting an end to the discussion. "I'm going to see if I can hunt down another wild pig," he said. "You've got the camp, Jade."

"Now tell me what happened!" demanded Mr. Julian as Harry left.

Jade briefly recounted the incident of the frightened porters, being careful not to stress the broken supply boxes. One didn't have to be an uneducated native to have superstitions. She knew that they ran deep within some Americans as well.

"The nosebleed frightened them," she said. "And they thought it was a warning from Ruwa to keep them from climbing his mountain. But it's hard to explain thinner air and changing pressure. That's why Harry has us staying here tonight instead of going up to Pete's hut. You need to acclimate to the changing altitude."

"Nosebleed!" exclaimed Hall. "Look. I'm not a sissy or anything, Julian, but do you really think this sort of risk is necessary?"

"Of course it is," snapped Julian. "Think of the realism of seeing Kilimanjaro as a backdrop to the climax scenes. Why, it's essential. We should be there tonight and filming tomorrow. This lollygagging around is wasting my time. And think of what's up there!"

"Mr. Julian," said Jade, "if we hurry up the mountain, nosebleeds will be the least of the problems. Altitude sickness is a very real danger. I'm sure Harry told you the risks." She gestured towards the porters, Jelani, and Lwiza. "These people can't go any higher than the saddle."

Julian waved his hand, dismissing the problem. "Yeah, sure. Headaches, dizziness."

"No, Mr. Julian. Those are the first warnings. People die at high altitudes. They don't breathe right. The air's thin up there. And cold," she added. "There's frostbite, too."

"Risks exaggerated by safari companies so that they can increase their fees," said Julian. His lips curled in a sneer. "Name one person who's died climbing Kilimanjaro."

Jade studied Julian for a moment; then a faint smile played across her own lips. "Well, there's your precious Emperor Menelik, for starters. Careful, Mr. Julian, as you strive for accuracy. You might get more than you bargained for."

She turned to walk away and caught Lwiza's eye. For once the woman was alone. *Maybe I can talk with her privately.* Here was someone who had access to all the women's personal items. She would know which one of them had owned that compact. But Jade couldn't ask outright. *For all I know, she stole it from one of them.*

She decided to ask each of the women indirectly by inquiring what beauty line they would recommend to her. Then she'd ask what the other women used. Hopefully, by cross-checking answers, she'd find out who was telling the truth. The concept was laughable, considering Jade didn't wear any creams or paints. She found a good broad-brimmed hat did as much as anything against the sun's ravages. *Now we'll see how good an actress I am.* There was one problem, though. What if *all* the women lied? She'd have to learn their individual tells and see what they did when they prevaricated. *I'll ask them their ages.*

Jade plastered a big smile on her face. "Lwiza," she called. "May I talk with you?"

"Yes, *bibi*. In what may I serve you?"

"With advice, Lwiza." She took the young woman's arm by

the elbow and led her aside to stroll with her out of earshot of the others. Not that the men would bother them, but she wanted to create a feeling of privacy, to exchange confidences. "I'm finding this safari is not agreeing with my skin. Yours is so smooth. I thought you might tell me what you put on it?"

Lwiza's eyes opened in surprise. "I have a special cream that is made from many ingredients. It is a recipe handed down among the ladies of my family for generations."

"Ah," said Jade. "You have lovely skin. Then I imagine you are only nineteen years old."

Lwiza didn't respond beyond a faint smile and a graceful inclination of her head. Jade tried a different tack. "Do you give any of your cream to the American ladies?"

"They have their own, but I do not know what they are made of. They keep such things locked away from me." One side of her mouth curled up in disdain. "As if I would wish to take any of their trinkets."

Jade could tell that she wasn't going to get very far with Lwiza. The woman was too reserved. But as Jade walked with her, she detected a faint spicy fragrance that intrigued her. "Whatever you use, Lwiza, it certainly smells pretty. It reminds me of something sacred, a scent I smelled as a child in church."

Lwiza arched her brows and tilted her head, her dark eyes watching Jade's face. "Yes. There is oil from myrrh in it. A gift of the magi to the Lord. It has healing properties as well."

"Old recipes are usually better than modern ones, aren't they?"

Lwiza smiled and nodded. "I can bring some to you later if you like. Is that all, *bibi*?"

"Not quite," said Jade. "I am very curious about you. You are educated. At least, you've read some books, considering your help with the costumes. How is it you came from a home in Zanzibar to do maid's work in Nairobi?"

Lwiza held her head a trifle higher. "Is there dishonor in working, *bibi*?"

"No, there is not, but—"

"Excuse me, *bibi* Jade." Lwiza pointed to the other side of the camp. "Bwana Hascombe has returned with his kill. I must wake the other mistresses to prepare for their meal."

Jade followed Lwiza's hand as she saw Harry hand a young wild pig to Muturi. When she turned back, Lwiza was already halfway to the stone hut. As Jade watched her, her mind turned over two facts: Lwiza hadn't answered her last question, and most Swahili were Muslim, not Christian.

Private conversation had been impossible during dinner, but Jade paid attention to everyone's faces as they talked anyway, observing expressions and mannerisms. Most of them met their listener's eyes when they talked to just one person. Both Cynthia and Hall always managed to look beyond the others, as though they were playing to a distant audience. *Probably some deeply ingrained acting technique.* Julian didn't look up from his food when he said anything. And both Budendorfer and Brown had a tendency to punctuate statements with a laugh. Homerman rarely spoke at all. The other men mostly just ate, sometimes pausing to share a joke. Jade did manage to talk to each of the women alone when she went along to guard them during their necessary visits into the woods.

"I swear by Pond's cold cream," said Pearl, her lids half-closed in her usual sultry fashion. "But I use Joncaire powder." She touched her face, currently devoid of makeup. Her youthful skin glowed. "At least, I do for the camera. Wouldn't want a shiny nose." She laughed. "But if you think I'm going to reveal my age, then you've been in the equatorial sun too long."

Pearl had no idea nor even cared what Cynthia or Bebe used. One of them, she thought, had worked for or advertised for somebody. "I'm not certain of the fact. But they're both getting so long in the tooth that it's probably ancient history."

"I understand you used to work in a circus sideshow," said Jade. They'd reached the edge of their clearing and she wanted to milk as much information out of the woman as she could. "That sounds exciting. How ever did you find your way into that?"

"Easy when you grow up in Florida. Half the circuses winter down there." Pearl moved away from Jade and headed towards the men. She turned and spoke over her shoulder. "Thank you for the escort, Jade. Let me know if you want to borrow some of the cold cream."

Bebe advised Jade to wash her face with a resin-based soap and, in general, danced around all of Jade's questions regarding her life. "We spent so much time in my girlhood on the Italian Riviera that I nearly consider it my home, and that's why I now use Italian creams, powder, and rouge. Ciprie Gi Vi Emme. *Very* fine quality. However," she added, "if you *do* find out what Cynthia uses, let me know. I want to be sure to avoid it."

"You probably don't need anything special at all," said Jade. "You can't be more than twenty-four or twenty-five years old. And I'm only guessing that because of the number of pictures you've been in."

Bebe looked at Jade. "I'm twenty-seven and not ashamed to admit it."

Cynthia swore by Pompeian creams, and chose La Dorine face powder for her personal use. "I think my husband brought it back for me from Paris one time. Told me that a Swedish actress, Martha Hedman, endorsed it." She scoffed. "I don't know why she managed to get a contract to advertise for them and not me. She's only made one picture that I know of."

"It looks like most of you ladies prefer foreign powders. Pearl has some French-sounding brand, too. And Bebe fell in love with an Italian brand that she picked up during her summers on the Italian Riviera."

"She told you that nonsense about living in Italy?" Cynthia stifled a laugh that came out more like a snort from a bull. "Excuse me, but her Italian experience comes strictly from her immigrant grandmother's stories. Bebe's from Cleveland, for heaven's sake."

Jade decided to jump in completely and learn more about Cynthia's relationship with Mr. Wheeler. "You appear to be holding up better after your husband's death, Miss Porter. But I imagine you still miss him a great deal."

"Actually I do," she said. "Graham was a good man in his own way, but a bit of a philanderer, as I told you before. One tires of that. Still, there were enough times when I had him to myself." She sighed as though recalling happier times. "We traveled a lot together. He would have liked this safari." They stopped at the side of the stone hut. Cynthia surveyed the camp until she saw Harry. "*He's* certainly an interesting man, and very kind."

"He's all yours, dearie," said a voice from behind them. "I pass him on to you. *You* can have leftovers for once."

Jade and Cynthia both wheeled around. "Bebe!" snapped Cynthia. "What do you mean, sneaking up on us and eavesdropping?"

"I wasn't eavesdropping," Bebe said, eyeing Cynthia as a snake might watch a mouse before striking. "I was stretching my legs and I heard you mention Harry." She smiled sweetly, forming small dimples. "But I thought since you're no longer grieving for Graham, you might as well have him. I'm done with him."

"What?" shrieked Cynthia before regaining control of her voice. "What do you mean, you're done with him and I can have him? It's not as if I . . . want him."

"Oh, puh-lease, Cynthia," said Bebe. "I've seen you leave his tent and sneak back to your bed. As if I wouldn't notice. But you don't need to sneak anymore on my behalf." She rubbed her outer eye, then brushed her finger across her nose. "I only wanted him for some insurance, in case Graham and I . . ." She let that thought trail off suggestively and examined the other hand. "Jade knows. I don't need him anymore—or anyone. I'm off the hook."

Bebe continued her stroll, waving her hand at them over her shoulder. Cynthia stormed off in another direction, and Jade pondered how to keep those two separated that night. A few moments later Harry walked up, rubbing the side of his face, which glared red in the shape of a handprint.

"What in the world got into Cynthia?" he asked.

"Shut up, Harry," Jade said, and walked away.

"And this Major Bertram was certain that the woman in the photo was not a Swahili?" asked Finch.

"Positively," said Sam. He'd gone to the police headquarters early Monday morning and parked himself by the door in the waiting room, ready to pounce on the inspector first thing. He'd taken the dead man's picture as well as Lwiza's and spent his entire Sunday badgering the staff at the Muthaiga and the Norfolk and New Stanley hotels for information. Had Bahdoon applied for a position there? Had anyone seen him with this woman? Sam had discovered from the natives that Bahdoon had been turned away for work at each of those establishments. No one had recognized the woman except at the New Stanley, where she'd stayed in the maids' quarters.

Finch shifted in his chair and rubbed his hand over his chin. "This does make matters a bit more interesting." He picked up a folder, opened it, and leafed through the pages, pausing to read a few notations.

"Then you agree with me that this Lwiza could be behind that native's death and, consequently, Mr. Wheeler's as well?" asked Sam.

"Hmmm," said Finch, without looking up.

Sam inhaled through clenched teeth, and Finch closed the folder with a slap. "I will admit," Finch said, "that this case has its peculiarities. And his lordship's identification of the native in question is certainly helpful. Bahdoon, you said. And he is a Somali." He leaned back in his chair. "Frankly, Mr. Featherstone, I'd find this more interesting if this Lwiza was a Somali, too. Then there would be a connection, you see."

A constable knocked on the door. Finch called him in and was handed a folded sheet of paper. Finch read it, frowned, and stuffed it into his suit coat's inner pocket. "It seems we have had a curious event in the Indian district that you might want to know about. We've found where your man Bahdoon was staying. He had a room in the back of Navrang Chopra's shop. Mr. Chopra recognized the photo that my lads took around to the shops and houses. He's quite put out that the man is dead. He owed him rent. He's even more put out with us that we confiscated Bahdoon's effects."

Finch held up the paper. "This," he said, "is the list of those effects." He proceeded to read down the list. "A leather pocket-book, rather worn, possibly stolen. No identification. Containing five American dollars and eight rupees. Hmm," he added, "we shall have to run that against any theft reports. Also one brown paper parcel, contents of which are six biscuits and one very dried bit of bread. A frayed khaki shirt, and that completes the list." Finch put the paper into the folder and pushed the folder aside.

"Really nothing much there to go on," Finch said. "The man was unemployed, took to pickpocketing, probably from that acting troop, and Wheeler's death was a robbery gone bad."

"And what about the datura seeds mixed in his alcohol flask?" asked Sam. "According to my sources, that is a tradition in Abyssinia."

"And in India as well," said Finch. "The Kali cult has used that as a murder weapon. Possibly he got some from the Indian district to screw up his courage. Took too much. But," he added quickly as Sam made another teeth-gritting gasp, "I do agree that this Lwiza is a suspicious person. If she's passing herself along on false identity, then she needs to be brought to book. I shall send a telegram to Moshi and tell the officer there to watch for the safari's return. He can apprehend her at the station."

"Mind if I wait to hear their reply?" asked Sam. "They may have some news of their own." Since Finch planned to send a wire, there was no need for his. *One less thing to rile Jade.*

"Be my guest. I shall even ask for an immediate reply."

Finch wrote out a missive and sent one of the constables to the telegraph office with orders to wait for the reply and bring it right away. Half an hour later, the constable returned bearing a message, but not the one Sam wanted to hear.

"Sorry, Inspector, but the message never got as far as Taveta. Seems some of the wildlife took it into their heads to butt down one of the telegraph poles. Snapped the line. But they promised to transmit the rest of the way once it was mended. Should only take a few days."

Sam muttered a curse under his breath and felt his stomach stab at him. This worry over Jade's safety was eating him inside. He got up and extended his hand to Finch.

"Thank you for your time, Inspector. If you find out anything else, please leave word with Lord Dunbury for me."

"Oh? And why not with you?"

"Because I'm taking the next train down to Voi and then on to Moshi."

CHAPTER 21

In 1848, Johannes Rebmann asked his Chagga guide what he called the white material capping the mountain. The guide simply called it "cold."

—The Traveler

MONDAY MORNING JADE TAILED A SILENT TROOP. NEITHER BUDENdorfer nor Brown tried any practical jokes, and McAvy didn't pester Harry about a bwana's role. No one even grumbled aloud. That fact alone gave Jade cause for concern. Lack of sleep coupled with the more strenuous walk had taken a toll on the actors.

Jade blamed more than the closely cramped quarters for her own rough night. A leopard had patrolled around the hut. She'd heard it chuff near the door, and once something large had brushed the window shutters. But no one else had heard it, thanks to the tree hyraxes. They called all during the night, their high, piercing notes sounding like a woman crying out in pain or horror.

Kilimanjaro exacted another price with the increased altitude. Even the porters didn't carry on their usual banter or sing their marching songs. When they woke early Monday, the two porters who'd joined them the previous evening were gone. They'd urged their comrades to come with them, but the other hired Chagga men had stayed, whether from loyalty or fear or because they wanted their pay, they didn't say. But the mood of the runaways had been infectious. The renewed sensation of being followed made the hairs of Jade's neck and arms prickle.

Early into their walk, they'd startled a herd of elands. Their large dun-colored bodies and flapping dewlaps soon blended into the mists over the high heath. Papery-petaled anemone bloomed among the rocks and grasses along with tall, spiky red-hot pokers. A fragrant lemon scent rose as her boots crushed some everlasting leaves. The combined scene should have called to Jade's heart, to her sense of Africa's beauty, but Kilimanjaro laid a cold hand on her. All she felt was a bone-numbing chill that had nothing to do with the outside air.

As if to emphasize this caution, the ancient mountain allowed them to see only the distant, smaller Mawenzi Peak to their right. He kept his highest seat, Kibo, veiled in cloud and mist. He seemed to be telling them that their search was in vain unless he granted an audience. Jade motioned for Jelani to join her. She needed the sound of intelligent human speech.

Jelani seemed to read her mind. "The mountain hides from us today."

"That will make bwana Julian unhappy," said Jade, keeping her voice low. "He wants to film the peak from the saddle."

Jelani glanced at her through half-lowered lids. "Is that all he wants?" he asked.

Jade put her finger to her lips to caution silence. Voices carried far in the cool air. "Are you warm enough? You only have sandals and socks on your feet. And why aren't you wearing that extra shirt I gave you?" Jelani shrugged, a typical teenager's reply to a nagging parent's query. *Well, he won't be in the glacier line, so he should be all right*. But the altitude concerned her as well. "How is your head?"

Jelani smiled. It wasn't the boyish grin she fondly remembered, but his newer, more mature and serene half smile. "I am fine, Simba Jike. It is *you* that I am worried about. There is something that follows you."

Jade started and nearly tripped over a rock. When she looked to see what had caught her boot toe, she spied another nail amongst the rocks. "Harry," she called. Harry called a halt and went back to join her. "Is there another supply box cracking up?"

Harry took the nail in his hands and nodded. "There must be. Damn!"

Harry let everyone rest for fifteen minutes and passed around one of the spare canteens to the porters. "We get into some ravines ahead," he said as he urged them up. "Lots of loose lava chunks hidden in the heath, too, so watch your step."

Jade waited for the rest to precede her so that she could again guard the rear. Jelani and Biscuit moved up the column behind Muturi. As she stood aside, Jade scanned the lower slope for any sign of movement in the feathery heath: a sound, a grunt, the scuttle of dislodged gravel.

Nothing. Only an eerie silence. She surveyed the upper slope, noting a few odd-looking trees that wore their dead leaves like shaggy shirts on the trunks. They rose out of the damp ravines, their trunks black as though they'd sprung from the volcanic rock. In form they reminded Jade of the huge saguaro cactus that dominated the southern Arizona desert, except these carried a spray of lance-shaped leaves at the end of branching limbs, as though some large fork had been speared into a salad. On the ground, more white everlastings lent a splash of brightness.

If it's that leopard following us, he's going to run out of trees to ambush us from. If it's a Chagga . . . She again looked behind her. *Anything could hide in some of these ravines.*

After a while, they turned west to work their way around a large knoll.

"We should be going up, not sideways," said McAvy. It was the first time any of the actors had spoken beyond a simple gasp or groan.

"Patience," counseled Harry. "Unless you want to try your hand at going over that outcrop, I suggest we continue around it. Besides, the view is splendid this way."

Harry was right. They were well above the tree line. Before them lay the entire vista of the wide plains south of Kilimanjaro. It staggered Jade to realize how high they'd climbed. By the time they'd crossed the second stream on narrow wooden planks, their director shouted out, "My stars! I need some footage of this. Morris, break out the cameras."

No one groused as Julian ordered a halt and the cameras set up. They all found some agreeable rock to plop themselves on to rest while Brown ground out the film.

"I need some action here," Julian said. "Hall, Cynthia, Murdock, Wells, McAvy, I need you in this, the valiant explorers climbing up to find a glorious fortune and fulfill your destiny. Morris, put a sling on Wells. He's supposed to be shot in the arm."

Julian ordered everyone to get into character and pushed Harry, Jade, and Lwiza out of the way. He sent Budendorfer across the ravine with one camera to film the advance and left Brown to follow from behind. "McAvy, get in front," Julian ordered. "You're the big bwana here." He grabbed Jelani by his shirtsleeve. "You, boy. Carry one of those crates."

Jelani folded his arms and stood his ground.

"Jelani's not paid on this job," said Jade. "He's here as my friend, so I don't think you can order him to tote anything."

"All right," conceded Julian. "I'll pay him. I need more porters or it won't look right."

With Jade's encouragement, Jelani settled for the high salary of fifty rupees. When Biscuit wanted to follow Jelani, Jade grasped the cheetah's collar and held him aside.

"They don't want you in this scene," she said.

Harry came back to watch. Biscuit butted Harry's leg in greeting. "Well, at least someone is glad to see me," Harry said.

"Has something happened to make you think someone's mad at you?" Jade asked with as much innocence as she could muster.

Harry sat down next to her. "Do you mean outside of Cynthia slapping my face last night, and both she and Bebe turning their backs on me when I said good morning?" He cleared his throat and shifted his backside on the rock, trying to get more comfortable. "Do you know anything about this?"

"What? That you had a fling with Bebe earlier and with Cynthia more recently? I might have heard something about it."

"I can explain," he said, clearing his throat again. "Bebe *sent* for me back in Nairobi the night of the murder. Said she was terrified to be alone after what she'd seen. I'm telling you straight; she *threw* herself at me. Then Cynthia and I . . . well, I was, er, interrogating her like you asked, and she was so lonely after losing Wheeler that one thing led to another and . . ."

Jade didn't reply. In truth, she was trying not to laugh out loud. *Why is he telling me this?*

"You're probably hurt, too, Jade," he began.

"Harry, I'm not your confessor. I don't care to know about all your peccadilloes. But you ought to know that Bebe used you. She thought she might be pregnant with Wheeler's child. I don't think she wanted anyone to know that, especially after she found out he was married. From what I've read, that scandal would ruin her career."

Harry's eyes widened as the conclusion dawned on him. "She was going to blame me? Why, the little vixen!" He reached for one of Jade's hands. She pulled it away and scowled. "But, Jade," he said, "you can see that neither of these were my fault. I care about *you*."

Jade stood up. "Harry, you're a rounder; you'll always be a rounder." She took out her Kodak and walked away, shooting pictures of the vegetation and the vista. At one spot, she peered down into a small ravine and spied the remains of a box. She climbed down and retrieved it, reading the words painted on the broken board.

"Tinned beef." She'd tell Harry later. Right now she didn't want to talk to him.

Julian wanted the stream crossing to be shot and reshot from different angles. After the third trip across the same ravine, he decided he'd gotten all he could out of that one spot. The caravan proceeded another half mile and faced yet a third stream. This time the porters protested when Julian wanted to repeat the filming.

"Peter's hut isn't far," said Harry. "Less than a half mile. The men are tired and everyone needs to eat. Then, if you still want to film that last stream, you can come back for it. Empty a few of the boxes and let the men carry those."

"Fine," groused Julian. "We'll dump some of the gear and come back here after we eat."

Harry urged everyone forward with repeated coaxes and promises. "That's the ticket. Looking sharp. Not far to the hut and a nice luncheon. Lots of fresh, clean water to drink."

The trail took a sharp turn north and climbed a rocky patch of heath loaded with the bottle brush–shaped lobelia, whose pointed upper leaves lay matted downward while the bottom ones flared out like a ballerina's tutu. Tucked amongst the rocks and purple heather stood Peter's hut, a concoction of wooden slats, a few windows, and a decent roof. One tent was set up to its right and a beautiful little brook tumbled between stones on the left.

Jade took scant notice of the hut. Her eyes were locked on the newly revealed Kibo, the high point of Kilimanjaro, and Ruwa's throne. Shining white ice and snow draped over its top and sides, coating it like an ermine mantle. She appeared to be the only one with eyes for the glacial peak. Everyone else was staring at the plain little shack and the lone tent set up beside it. Everyone but Julian. Jade saw his gaze feasting on the summit with a palpable hunger.

"It's smaller than Bismark's hut," said Murdock. "How are we all going to fit in there?"

"Ah, well, there are a few bunks slatted into the walls, so we don't all need the floor. There's a dugout that the Chagga men sleep in. And Nakuru set up . . ." Harry's words dropped into silence as a tall, black man strode towards him from the dugout.

"And Nakuru is here," finished Jade.

Sam's patience had all but disappeared. The train's downhill run towards Mombassa was certainly faster than the reverse, but it still never managed to exceed twenty-five miles an hour. And there was no comfort here. No food was served. The car jolted and the air inside was oppressively hot and stale. It stayed that way, too, since every time he opened the window, red dust swirled inside. Not long after that, a lady would insist that he shut the window before her hair, hat, traveling dress, or complexion was ruined.

Apparently swooning from the heat is preferable.

Sam complied. Maybe he could sleep and wake up at Voi. But his brain kept nagging at him, teasing him until his head throbbed with all the little details he'd learned.

At least you know Lilith isn't behind this. At Sam's request, Avery had telegrammed the women's prison where she was incarcerated, and asked for an update on the woman's activities. The reply had come back late Saturday. She hadn't had any outside communication for over a month, and that was from a visiting minister.

Sam thought about swallowing some aspirin, chasing them with warm water from his canteen. *Better not. They're not making your stomach very happy.* So for the second time, he tried to divert himself by surveying his fellow passengers and guessing their reasons for this trip. They appeared to be the usual assortment one expected. The two dignified-looking men, Sam thought, were government appointees on their way to England for a few months "away from the equatorial sun and the altitude." A pair of middle-aged women, he decided, seemed bound for a fancy-goods shopping trip in Mombassa. A younger man, browned and hardened by the sun, kept fidgeting with a pocket watch that contained a picture inside.

He's a farmer and he's going to meet his bride, newly arriving from England. The last pair, a moonstruck couple, were easy to read. *Newlyweds off on a honeymoon trip. Perhaps Zanzibar.*

That was when Sam remembered why he didn't enjoy playing this game of identifying the passengers. It reminded him of two facts: one, Jade had yet to accept his marriage proposal, and two, he now had his own serious doubts. He felt them now as they attacked his throbbing head and riddled his stomach with sharp pangs. For all that he loved her bravery and heroism, her recklessness drove him mad.

How are you going to live with the constant fear that she's about to race after a lion, an elephant, or a murderer? Hell, being leopard bait was bad enough, but she had been in a cage there. This latest stunt chasing the lion off Biscuit's kill was too much.

And what about now? Is it this Lwiza you're worried about? Or is it really Hascombe?

It was both. Sooner or later, Jade would find out that Lwiza was an impostor and she wouldn't leave well enough alone. She'd charge right in and force the woman's hand. She'd done it in Tsavo, on Mount Marsabit, in Morocco, and, most recently, on an isolated Kenyan farm. She wouldn't hesitate at ten thousand feet. *You'll still worry about her even if you leave and go back to the States.* Would he? he wondered. *Out of sight, out of mind?* Well so far, every time she was out of his sight he felt like he was out of his mind.

The train slowed to a stop, the brakes screeching in a pitch that sent shivers up Sam's spine. He opened the window to stick his head out and call to the engineer, but the rolling and choking dust cloud stopped him. He shut the window as hundreds of zebra raced past in a snorting, swirling, black-and-white blur. Several squealed in pain or terror.

Finally the herd cleared the track and raced off into the distance. Still the train stayed motionless, huffing and breathing steam. The whistle blew twice. Their car jolted forward about a foot, then jerked to a halt. After five minutes and no progress, Sam opened the window and hailed the engineer. "Why are we still stopped?"

"Obstruction on the tracks, sir."

Sam imagined a fallen zebra, left by the herd and as yet unseen by the pursuing lions. "Do you need a hand clearing it?"

"Wouldn't advise it, sir. Lions. Five of them."

"Lions?" murmured all the other passengers. Immediately, their own windows were opened as heads popped out to glimpse the beasts.

"Four females and one male, to be precise," continued the engineer. "Seems one of the zebra caught a hoof on an exposed sleeper and the pride brought it down where it stood. They're feeding right now. Best to keep your heads inside."

"Can't you run them off?" asked Sam.

"Tried. Blew the whistle, even bumped one of the females. She just snarled and slapped the engine. And if they moved off a bit, we'd still have the carcass to deal with. Wouldn't want to derail on it, and I wouldn't advise trying to lift it off the tracks as long as the lions are about. Best to wait a bit. They won't be too long at it."

Sam plopped back down in his seat. The delay wouldn't matter in the end. He'd be spending the night at Voi anyway before the train to Moshi left. What was another hour more or less? But it felt as if nature were conspiring to keep him from his goal.

And what are you going to do when you get to Moshi? Climb the blasted mountain looking for her? Sam closed his eyes and fell asleep. He dreamed of zebra and lions, but every time the lions had a kill, he saw Jade's body under their feet.

HARRY LED NAKURU aside so they could speak in private while the actors battled it out for prime sleeping spots. Jade tagged along without an invitation.

"What are you doing here, Nakuru?" asked Harry.

"The men are up by the ice line with the tents, bwana, as you wished," said Nakuru. "I came back only to warn you. They are not happy. Another box broke on our walk to this hut. This time potted meat spilled out. The tins scattered like frightened antelope."

"Were you able to find them all?" Jade asked.

"Not all, memsahib. Many fell into deep ravines. But we have some. It is enough if we do not baby our stomachs."

"That box was reinforced with leather straps," said Harry.

"The leather had been broken. I looked at it, bwana. The cuts were clean. They were not the marks of old leather that cracks. The Chagga men that stay, they speak of a curse. Even my own men are listening. I will not stay here. I will go back to keep them at peace." Nakuru looked around at the porters. "The two men who went back," he said, "they did not find you?"

"They found us, and promised to come up with us, but they ran away early this morning."

Nakuru shrugged. "It is well. Two less mice gnawing at the meal."

"Still, I'd better make sure we have enough food and save the rest of the tinned meat for when we can't get anything else," said Harry. "Did you spot any game on your way here?"

"The animals do not like the wasted area where the tents are," said Nakuru. "But I saw the fresh spoor of the eland not far from here." He pointed to the northeast. "I also saw the spoor of an elephant. The Chagga men, they say that the elephant goes to the mountaintop to die so that the white man cannot take his tusks."

Harry chuckled. "The old elephant-graveyard story again. No, Nakuru, I think *tembo* was just passing through to the other side of the mountain. He'll be in his forest before long."

He shrugged his shoulder, hitching his rifle. "I'll take two of these Chagga men with me to hunt. You rest, my friend. When I return, we'll have a feast."

Nakuru shook his head. "I must go back to the men to keep peace there. We will meet tomorrow." He nodded his farewell to Harry and then to Jade and marched off across the highland to the more barren saddle.

"He can't go on, Harry. It's another six hours at least. Make him stay."

"Five for him, I'd guess," said Harry as he watched the figure stride rapidly away. "He's got that much daylight left. And he's right. If those men are spooked, they can't be trusted alone. Any one of them might take it into his head to bolt for home this evening and be caught exposed on the mountain overnight. Temperatures drop to freezing here."

He called to two Chagga men to join him. "Don't fret your pretty head, Jade. We'll be with them tomorrow and all will be well. You've got the camp. Try to keep them all here."

Since Harry took most of their porters, and since everyone else was too fatigued to hike back to the last stream, Jade had no trouble keeping the crew rounded up. It helped that Julian wanted to film everyone arriving at Peter's hut. The man became a veritable dictator, bullying them first through a short, cold lunch of jerked meat and dried fruits, then ordering the actors through their scenes. It worked. Their exhaustion and anxiousness came through without their having to act at all.

"Tomorrow when we get to the saddle, we'll film all the Menelik scenes, showing his dying wishes and his entourage carrying him up to the heights to die," Julian said.

"Tomorrow when we get to the saddle," countered Jade, "you all need to rest. You need to do that *now*, before anyone takes sick from the altitude. There's an old Swahili proverb that applies here. *Hakari, hakari haina baraka*. Hurry, hurry is without blessing. We're hurrying too much as it is. Poor Mr. Homerman is about done-in."

"That's a lot of hooey and poppycock," said Julian. "I'll grant that the *climbing* wears on a body, but the height? Old wives' tales."

Jade knew better than to argue with the director. The man had blinders on, blocking everything but his precious picture.

"My head feels like there's a miner inside digging his way out with a pickax," said McAvy.

"Mine, too," said Hall.

"My head doesn't hurt *that* bad," said Cynthia, "but I'm so dizzy."

"Me, too," said Bebe. She looked at Jade and gave her the full benefit of her tilted brows, parted lips, and pale face. But Jade noted that she walked perfectly steadily.

Cynthia frowned at her colleague's interruption and sat down on a rock. "You must listen to Jade, Rex," she said. "As producer, I insist. You know the symptoms of altitude sickness as well as the rest of us." She rubbed her fingers in circles around her temples. "Heaven knows, Graham certainly warned us all before we took these roles."

"Sleep is what you all need," said Jade. "By morning you should be used to this altitude. Tomorrow we'll take the climb more slowly. Lots of rest breaks for water."

"How high do we go tomorrow?" asked Murdock.

"The last camp is at fifteen thousand feet, give or take."

"And after that?" asked Pearl.

Jade shrugged. "No higher. Just forays to the snow line, I think. We can't ask the Chagga porters to go into the snowfields. They don't have the proper footwear."

"That's their problem," said Julian as the rest filed into either the hut or the tent to sleep. "Harry should have insisted that they wear real shoes instead of those preposterous sandals. I have to get to the top!"

"Take that up with him," said Jade. "But as I understand it, Harry's contracted to go only to the edge of the saddle." She waited for Julian to answer. When he didn't, she persisted. "Did you tell Harry that you intended to go up to Kibo Peak or not?"

"Not in so many words," said Julian. "I said we needed to film on Kilimanjaro. But I have to get to the crater. That old Chagga man said that the tomb—"

"Mr. Julian, I don't know what you expect to find, but the crater is huge, and the whole tomb is a myth." Jade turned to see how Jelani and Lwiza fared. Biscuit, she noted, panted a bit more, but if his appetite for jerked meat was any indication, he felt fine. Jelani, who was again assisting Muturi by peeling some of the last fresh vegetables they'd carried up from below, assured Jade that he was in good health. She was more concerned about Lwiza. The woman made so few requests that there was a tendency to overlook her.

Jade found her behind the dugout, quietly loosening nails from the crates.

CHAPTER 22

Kilimanjaro's conquest included a fair list of people who attempted the summit, only to be beaten down by cold, wind, and the altitude.

—The Traveler

"WHAT ARE YOU DOING!" JADE KEPT HER VOICE LOW, BUT FIRM. She didn't want to alarm the camp. Still, she didn't care to be alone facing this small woman armed with a crowbarlike implement. "Jelani!" she called, and added a sharp whistle. Soon both her Kikuyu friend and her cheetah stood beside her. She heard Jelani's breath hiss when he realized what Lwiza had done.

"I need rope," Jade said. "Biscuit, guard." Immediately, Jelani ran off to find rope and Biscuit padded around to stand at Lwiza's flank.

"Do not try to run away," cautioned Jade. "That would be very foolish up here."

All this time, Lwiza didn't say a word. She simply froze in her kneeling position by the crates, her black eyes watching Jade's face. There was no fear in that gaze, and Jade saw the quick intelligence behind it.

Jelani returned with some rope. "Tie her hands, please,"

Jade said. "No, not behind her. Keep them in front so she can eat." She pulled her large kerchief from her side pocket. "Here, tie her wrists with this first. It will keep the rope from burning. Make it snug, but do not hurt her."

"You pay her too much kindness," said Jelani.

"She may not deserve it, but I don't know that yet," said Jade. "But," she added, staring directly into Lwiza's eyes, "I mean to find out."

Lwiza managed to meet Jade's cool stare for ten seconds before she had to look away. It was longer than most people could, with the exception of Sam, who appeared to be immune. Jade started by ticking off what she'd already surmised.

"You eat pork. You have worshiped as a Christian. You know much about Abyssinian dress. You would not speak with the Swahili women in Moshi, saying they were not like you. You told the truth then, didn't you? You are not a Swahili. Who are you?"

Lwiza held her chin up proudly. "I am Abeba Negash," she said in English. "I am of the royal house of Abyssinia."

"A princess?" asked Jade, doing her best to keep her face and voice neutral.

"No. I am a . . ." She paused to think of the words. "I wait on the empress."

"Ah. A lady-in-waiting. Why are you here?"

Lwiza—or, more correctly, Abeba—pursed her lips. "I was hired to wait on *these* ladies." She said the last word with a sneering tone.

Jelani shook Abeba's shoulders. "Do not play games with Simba Jike," he said. "*She* is descended from royal blood."

Abeba twitched her shoulder to shrug off Jelani's hand. "I have heard of *bibi* Jade. I did not know she was a princess, but I saw she was woven from finer threads than the others."

Jade ignored such idle flattery. “You gave drugs to the man in Nairobi and told him to kill Bwana Wheeler, didn’t you? And you gave those drugs to the Chagga woman so she could kill her rival. In return she gave you a snake to hide in the box.”

Abeba shook her head vigorously. “No! I have killed no one.”

Jade continued her accusations. “You put real bullets in Miss Porter’s rifle to kill the Chagga man so he could not tell what he knew.”

“No!” Abeba, already on her knees, held out her bound hands as if to plead with Jade. “I have not done these things. I only broke the boxes. I am not here to kill.”

Jade leaned forward. “Then why *are* you here?”

Jelani watched on the side while Simba Jike questioned the false woman.

Ah! So she is the one who brought the troubles to the camp. Jelani knew that a sorceress did not need to be old and wrinkled to be skilled. Nor did she need to resort to magic. Obviously, this one was also content to use her own hands and tools to create her mischief. Still, it would be a good idea to know what else she was capable of. Perhaps he should search her belongings. He knew all the women were supposed to sleep in the hut, so perhaps she had put her pack inside. Unfortunately, some of the American women were already in there. Then Jelani had an idea. He slipped away from Simba Jike and the maid and went to the cabin. He rapped on the door and waited until one of the women, the one named for the pretty white stone, opened it.

“What do you want?” Pearl asked in a pleasant enough tone. She fought back a yawn. “Is it time to eat?”

"No, memsahib," said Jelani. "Your maidservant sent me to fetch her bag. I do not know which one is hers."

"Oh. Let me get it." Pearl went to the far side of the hut and returned with a plain-looking rucksack made of heavy canvas.

Jelani thanked her and took it to the side of the cabin opposite most of the activity. There he opened the sack and rummaged through it. He found a photograph of some white man he did not recognize, gloves, three long black socks, and a few other items of clothing. There was also a small pot with a heart on it. When he opened it, he found it half-filled with a sweet-smelling white ointment. Nothing that looked dangerous. Disappointed, he stuffed everything back inside and plopped the bag on the steps. He saw one of the women, the older one who played the hunter's wife, returning to the hut from some sheltered ravine. Jelani left the bag and hurried back to Jade before the woman saw him.

Harry returned by three that afternoon, the porters toting the carcass of a yearling eland. Muturi immediately fell to cutting the meat, allotting several tender chunks for Biscuit. He had made a long fire pit and slid larger cuts along a thin metal pole to roast over the coals. For a moment Harry watched him work.

"Where's that young Kikuyu fellow?" he asked Jade as she joined him.

"Guarding Lwiza."

His lips tensed. "What the bloody blazes has happened now? Can't I leave camp just once without—"

"Temper on safety, Harry," said Jade. "I'd rather not rouse the rest of the camp. They need to rest. The altitude hasn't hit hard, but they're still feeling the strain."

He took off his hat and ran one hand through his graying hair before plopping the hat back on his head. "Very well. What happened this time?"

Jade briefly summarized how she'd found the woman weakening the crates, and her own immediate reaction. "Lwiza isn't her real name. It's Abeba Negash. She's some sort of lady's maid to the empress of Abyssinia."

"The devil you say! Don't tell me Wheeler hired her there?"

"That's what I assumed, someone to help with authenticity. But not according to her. She claims she saw Wheeler and his entourage when they entered Addis Ababa during his trip there, but he never met her. She learned what he intended to do by eavesdropping. She joined the group when they came to Nairobi."

"Is she behind any of these deaths?"

"She says not, although I'm not sure how much I can believe. According to her, she's mostly guilty of making the original lady's maid sick so she'd go home and Lwiza—I mean Abeba—would be hired. That and causing those crates to break up."

"Did she say why?" asked Harry.

"Something about 'he must not find Menelik's grave,' but by then she was pretty excited and she went in and out of English to her own language. I didn't catch the half of it, but I think she's trying to keep us away."

Harry snorted. "We're not looking for Menelik's grave. Its existence is a myth." He waved a hand, gesturing to the hut and tent. "They're making a motion picture about people looking for the grave. Doesn't she understand make-believe?"

"Does Julian?" asked Jade.

"Well, of course he does," said Harry. "The man's a bloody director. It's his business."

"Maybe. But I noticed how his eyes lit up when old Sina recounted the legend of the great king. The man looks like he really believes. And while you were hunting, he was very demanding about climbing to the summit. He insists on entering the cone."

"We never contracted for that," said Harry. "The agreement was to take them as high as the saddle."

"Who made the agreement?" asked Jade.

"Wheeler and Newland Tarlton Company."

"And Wheeler's conveniently dead," murmured Jade half to herself.

"Wait a minute," said Harry. "Are you suggesting that Julian had Wheeler killed so he could go after treasure?"

Jade thought about it for a moment before replying. "No. For the main reason that I don't think Julian has the imagination to pull it off." She held up her hand. "I know, he's the director. But I'm not sure he's had an original thought since we've been here. Think about it, Harry. People are always giving him ideas and he claims them as his own. I'll bet the entire picture was all Wheeler's idea. Julian wasn't even with Wheeler in Abyssinia."

"Then Julian's only taking advantage of Wheeler's death to get to the cone," said Harry. "If that's true, and if Lwiza or whatever her name is—"

"Abeba Negash."

"Right, if she's telling the truth, then someone else is still responsible for that snake."

"The snake, Wheeler's death, Rehema's and Zakayo's deaths—"

"Rehema's and Zakayo's deaths were accidents, Jade."

"Open your eyes, Harry! I find that many accidents a bit too hard to swallow." *Blast it. Sam would understand.* She stifled that thought. *Sam's not here, so it's up to you.* "The trick is going to be finding out who is behind them."

"Do you want me to question any of them again?" he asked. "The women?"

"Good heavens, no! Just keep your eyes and ears open."

"You can count on me, Jade."

She wasn't sure she could, but right now, Harry and Jelani were all she had.

Jelani. Maybe she could put him to work, but how? She called him over and explained her dilemma.

"I have already looked in the lying woman's bag," he said with a nod towards Abeba. "There was nothing in it that looked bad. A woman's beauty pot, clothes, black socks—"

"Black socks?" With everyone wearing boots, Jade hadn't been able to see what socks Abeba wore.

"Yes, three," said Jelani. "Very long."

Three long black stockings! So maybe Abeba had made that second fake snake. But why leave it on Pearl's bed? To incriminate her? To cause dissention in the ranks and break up the safari? "Thank you, Jelani. You've been a big help."

Jade watched everyone closely during supper. Cynthia, Hall, and McAvy didn't have much appetite, a symptom that matched their previous headaches. Still, they seemed less haggard than earlier, and Harry expressed his opinion that they'd be right as rain in the morning. Even Homerman ate well. Jade took supper to Lwiza, who was under guard in the dugout. Only Bebe inquired after her, wanting her help with her boots.

"She's a bit indisposed right now," said Jade. She wondered what to do about Lwiza during the night or in the days to come.

"We're going to have to tell the others," said Harry. "They're bound to notice her tied up. And I don't trust her loose."

"If we keep her under close guard, we can untie her later," said Jade. "There's very little here for her to use as a weapon. Most everything is already up at the saddle. I'll put her in between Biscuit and myself tonight. She can't slip past both of us."

Harry grinned. "Biscuit always was a clever cat."

"Right. And tomorrow we'll be on the march. Once we make camp, I'll have Jelani keep an eye on her when I can't."

But how was she was going to manage that and watch for anyone who might be behind this *shauri*? If Abeba was trying to keep them off the summit, it could explain everything. Wheeler's death should have stopped the safari but hadn't. When that didn't work, Abeba attempted to scare them away with the snake. Rehema and the other Chagga girl were unintentional victims, but victims nonetheless. And Zakayo? Well, if he knew what Abeba had done, then he'd had to die. Finally, she resorted to sabotaging the boxes to force them to go back down. Would she try something else?

But what if she's telling the truth? What if she's only guilty of weakening the crates?

Then they were still in trouble. *Find the pivoting crime.*

The answer came quickly. Everything sprang from Wheeler's death. *The others, Rehema, Zakayo are. . .* Jade stopped herself. *Wait. Those deaths aren't about Wheeler; they're about that damned snake in the box.*

Her head ached and she massaged her temples. *There must be some connection.* The problem was that everyone was connected in some way. She needed some quiet place to sit alone and think this out. Harry was no good at it, and once again, Jade found herself wishing for Sam. He'd have ideas to share with her.

And a warm, reassuring hug.

Loneliness washed over Jade like a cold, wet rain. She'd grown up on a ranch surrounded by male ranch hands, but she hadn't had much experience socializing with men. Her mother wouldn't have tolerated her stepping out with one of the hired hands, who by and large were older than her father. Instead, they'd treated her like a little sister, teaching her how to toss a knife or sling a lasso.

The few men she'd been introduced to as prospective husbands at heavily chaperoned parties had looked on her like a prize to be won. David Worthy had been the first man she'd actually known socially, and the war took him before she could sort out her own feelings for him. Others, like Harry, had proven untrustworthy in some way. Consequently, Jade had long ago come to depend on herself, shying away from attachments. Most of the time, she enjoyed the freedom. Tonight she didn't. She felt adrift.

I don't want to feel this way anymore.

She escorted the women off to do their duty away from camp behind a blanket, took her turn, and led them back to the hut. The sun was setting and, in the shadowy growth far below, Jade thought she detected the slinking form of a large, four-legged beast. *Maybe it's your imagination.*

Harry took the watch from nine until midnight, followed by Muturi, who watched until three. His soft rap at the hut door woke Jade, and she stepped out in the frigid air to take the dawn watch. She wore a thigh-length wool coat, gloves, and her big felt hat clamped firmly down over the tops of her ears. She went to the little stream beside the hut and knelt on the frozen ground to splash a little water on her face. The icy water shocked her into wakefulness, and a mug of the strong coffee that Harry had left brewing by the fire helped restore her.

Jade welcomed the watch. Her sleep had been fitful at best.

Each time she slept, she dreamed about her near fatal encounter with a leopard last July, and that recurring, bone-numbing cold crept into the blanket like some reptile. Each time she woke, she felt as though her ribs were constricted and she couldn't inhale deeply enough to ever catch her breath. Now, with her Winchester on her shoulder, she walked around the perimeter of their camp and let the morning air clear her head. Above her were more stars than she'd ever seen before, even when tending sheep in the high summer pastures of home. *Here* was Menelik's treasure. The old man had surely cast everything into the sky before he died. She stretched her left hand up, half expecting to brush the stars and send them rippling in waves.

Keeping watch here was easy. The starlit sky provided plenty of illumination over the surrounding moorland. Her main concern was to keep an eye out for nearsighted wandering wildlife or, more likely, a pack of the African wild dogs that roamed this area and the upper steppes. A few snores from the tent told her that at least two people were sleeping well. A sudden thump followed by a querulous "snark" told her that a bunkmate wasn't and had just tried to do something about it by rousting the noisemaker.

Her ears caught soft footfalls accompanied by the fragrant scent of crushed heather. She waved to Jelani to come closer to the fire. As Biscuit padded next to him, puffs of his frozen breath made him look more like a fire-breathing beast than a cheetah.

"What are you doing awake?" she asked as Biscuit pressed close to her thigh.

"We came to keep the watch with you, Simba Jike."

"Thank you, Jelani, but I've taken watches alone before."

"Your spirit did not labor under as many concerns before," he replied.

Jade took a deep breath, the frigid air stabbing at her lungs. She shuddered and told herself that it was only the cold. But Jelani's words sounded as if they should have come out of her old French confessor at the mission and not from a thirteen-year-old youth.

"Yes, but at present your well-being concerns me the most." She picked up the blanket that Harry had left for her and handed it to Jelani. "Wrap this around you before you freeze."

Jelani did as he was told and sat down near the fire, his blanket also draped over Biscuit's back. "Did the servant woman kill the Chagga man, Zakayo?"

Jade remained standing, scanning the perimeter for any danger. "I don't know." She stopped and listened, not trusting her eyes alone for the watch. She kept her own voice a hushed whisper. "She lied about who she is. But her killing him doesn't feel right."

"Why?" he asked.

"Why indeed," said Jade. "The crates breaking didn't hurt anyone," she said after thinking.

"But the snake and the other problems, they were deadly," said Jelani.

"Yes. Exactly. Two different types of trouble."

"From two different types of people then," said Jelani.

Jade spun around and knelt beside her friend. "That's it! There must be a second person behind the deadlier attacks. Otherwise, Lwiza—I mean Abeba—would have continued on by poisoning one of the porters rather than just spilling the mealy grain."

"Does this help you know who is evil?" asked Jelani.

Jade shook her head as she rose and continued her watch. "No, but it helps me sort out what I do know. I won't have to try to make sense of these new problems."

There would be little time once the day began to make notes or try to draw connections between people. *Maybe I should have paid more attention to those magazines.* It was possible that the articles held some clue to an as yet hidden relationship between them. *Blast it! They're in my supply box at the upper camp.*

"These people are very good at making stories seem real," she said. "It is very hard to tell when they are lying because they are so skilled at it."

"Then," said Jelani, "you must observe them when they tell the truth."

Jelani's wisdom shone through like the stars overhead. "Yes," said Jade. "I will do that. You should really get some sleep now."

"No," said Jelani. "You are still under a curse."

Jade smiled at him. "But that was way down the mountain. It can't reach me up here."

Sam reached Voi nearly three hours later than anticipated. After eating an overcooked meal of charred yams and boiled beef that would've choked a hyena, Sam located the telegraph dispatcher at the station. "Inspector Finch of Nairobi and I sent a telegram to Moshi this morning. Has a reply come through yet?"

"Nothing's come out of Moshi, sahib," said the Indian. "The lines went down. They have a great deal of trouble with the animals that way." He stretched his hand up high. "Giraffes go snapping the lines. Elephants use the poles as back-scratchers. Not to worry, though, sahib."

"Oh? And why's that?" asked Sam.

"Well, sahib, you are going on to Moshi yourself. You can deliver the message and pick up the response."

Sam thanked the man and went to his bunk in the side-lined railcar, wondering what other news or reports he might find waiting for him in Moshi.

BISCUIT LEFT JADE's and Jelani's sides at first light and spent an hour making breakfast out of the innumerable striped mice that lived near the hut. Muturi *mpishi* also rose before sunrise and renewed his cooking fire with a bundle of heath. While Jelani fetched water from the stream, Jade broke the skin of ice from the water bucket outside the door and washed her face. Within half an hour, Jelani and the cook had mixed dough and spread large flatbreads on hot stones to bake. Jade roused the women as well as Julian, Hall, and Wells, who'd also opted for sleeping in the hut. From behind her, she heard Harry coax and bully the remaining men out of the lone tent.

"How are they this morning?" she asked Harry when they were all seated on rocks and eating their breakfast.

"Better. No complaints so far. And what about your group?"

"Cynthia is much improved. She says she feels short of breath, but her head doesn't hurt and she's hungry. No one else has answered me, but they appear fine. Just tired. We need to take this last leg slowly, no matter how much Julian bellows."

"I agree. Ideally, we should spend another day here before going on, and I'd have enough food to allow for it. But with our meal supplies a bit lower we don't have that luxury, and I'm not risking our men or my license." He studied Abeba, who sat slightly apart from the others under Jelani's watchful eye. "What about her?"

"Very quiet," said Jade. "But I'm inclined to believe what

she said. She's only trying to keep them from looking for Menelik's burial spot."

Harry snorted. "As if we were wasting our time on fairy tales." He surveyed the unusually silent group. "You might be right, Jade. But I still plan to keep her tied up when we're on the march. I don't care to have her attack anyone while our backs are turned."

"Harry, I'm not sure that's a good idea. What will you tell the others?"

"The truth."

"And have a panic or a mutiny on our hands?" Jade's lungs felt a little tight, and she paused to inhale deeply and calm herself. She mustn't get upset up here, not at this altitude. "I know I tied her hands before, but I was more worried that she'd try to run off and die on the mountain. Where we're headed, no one in their right mind would head out on their own. If we just watch her, she can't do anything."

Harry shook his head and folded his arms across his broad chest. "Who's in charge of this safari? There's no other way to handle it, Jade." He stepped away from her and raised his voice. "I need everyone to come here and listen to me."

Jade groaned and hurried over to stand beside Abeba, both to ensure that she didn't bolt and to protect her from the others' reactions.

"We have discovered a thief and a troublemaker in our group. The person behind the broken crates. Someone who has deceived us the entire time. Jade found someone's face powder on the dead Chagga woman, which she stole from one of you, as well."

"Millard Fillmore *mwenziheri juu ya baiskeli*," murmured Jade to herself as Harry went on. But he had their attention, even the Chagga porters. Jade heard whispers of "Studio spy?"

among the mutterings. *We don't know that. He's as bad as they are with theatrics.*

"Well, who is it?" demanded McAvy after Harry paused. He looked first at Jelani and then Muturi.

Harry pointed a finger at Abeba. "Her. She's not a Swahili and her name's not Lwiza. We caught her trying to break apart the supply boxes."

"Did she put the snake in the coffer?" asked Wells.

"We don't know—" began Jade, trying to keep a lynch mob from forming. She was interrupted by Bebe's shriek.

"*She's* the one who stole my makeup. She probably killed Graham, too. She's been through my things. I know. My bag . . ." Bebe sprang at Abeba, snatching at her hair and face. "Murdering witch!" Bebe screamed.

Harry lunged for her and grabbed her around the waist before she could claw Abeba. "Settle down, Bebe," he said, as he struggled to hold her back.

Finally Harry lifted her off her feet and carried her tucked under one arm to Wells and McAvy. Bebe, seeing her prey slip out of reach, turned her anger on Harry. She squirmed in his grip and kicked at him. One blow connected with his groin and he doubled over, dropping her on the ground. Before she could renew her attack, both McAvy and Wells took hold of her arms.

"Damn it, woman," Harry squeaked after a moment. "You didn't need to do that."

Bebe shook her head, flinging off her scarf. She rubbed her eye and brushed her nose. "I told you I didn't need you anymore," she said, not deigning to look at anyone.

Cynthia took a half step forward, saw Harry's dark look, and stopped. "*Did* she have my husband killed?"

"We don't know that," said Jade, standing close to Abeba.

"We don't know *anything* except that she did weaken our supply boxes. Everything else is speculation." *Good heavens, Harry, what have you unleashed here?* "There are some things that just don't make sense to me yet," Jade finished.

"What are you going to do with her?" asked Murdock.

"Take her with us," said Harry. "Unless you want to go back now."

"No!" shouted Julian. "Absolutely not. The picture isn't finished yet."

"Tie her up and leave her here," said Hall. "We'll get her on the way back."

"Who is she, really?" asked Pearl, her gaze running up and down the other woman.

"Her name is—" began Jade.

"No," said Abeba sharply. "I will defend myself." She held her head high, tilting her chin upwards. "I am Abeba Negash, handmaid in the court of the Empress Zewditu of Abyssinia."

Everyone spoke at once, variations of, "What? Impossible? I knew she wasn't real."

"You are an Abyssinian?" asked Julian.

"I am."

"No wonder she knew so much about the robes and helmets," said Talmadge.

"This is wonderful," said Julian to himself. "Absolutely wonderful."

"Oh, Rex," said Cynthia. "Stop thinking about the picture for a moment. All of you need to pay attention. Why is she here?"

All eyes stared at Abeba as everyone waited for her answer.

"You must not look for the tomb," she said. "To open it will mean death to us all."

CHAPTER 23

The most eminent of these climbers is reported to be Menelik, the son of King Solomon and the Queen of Sheba.

—The Traveler

SAM JERKED TO THE SIDE IN THE SHABBY LITTLE PASSENGER CAR AS it clanked around a sharp turn. Except for a Greek man and a Lutheran missionary, he was alone and tired. He looked out the window. They'd passed Serengeti station fifteen minutes ago. Sam had been glad to learn that the telegraph line repair was nearly completed and, after relaying government and military messages, the one from Finch would finally take its turn in the queue. Thirty minutes, they'd said.

The train continued around the curve, the bumps shaking him and the others like rag dolls. From his window, he spied two immense bull elephants sparring for dominance. Their trunks locked around each other as first one, then the other pushed his opponent backwards, raising great clouds of red dust. Their massive heads shook from side to side, their ears flapping. One bull broke free moments before ramming his rival.

Sam opened his window and stuck his head out for a better view. The behemoths' trumpeting bellows rose in pitch, reverberating in the still air. Both of them screamed, but whether from rage or pain, Sam couldn't tell. The shrieks took on an unreal quality, coupled with sharp, cracking snaps. The bull on the right dug his tusks down into the ground and wrenched them back and forth. When he hoisted them back up, it was to the accompaniment of groans, cracks, and scraping screeches. Sam was so engrossed in watching them that he didn't immediately notice that the train had stopped. That fact registered at the same instant as another.

"Holy smokes! They're fighting *on* the track!" Sam slid the car door open and ran to the locomotive. He was joined by the engineer and the native man who tended the firebox.

"They're on the tracks," he repeated to the railroad men.

The engineer nodded. "And there's not a blooming thing we can do about it either, mate. When two bulls take it in their heads to fight, they aren't going to pay a mite of attention to this train. Even if we tried to push them aside, in the mood they're in, they'd derail us."

Sam leaned against the side of the engine. Was all the wildlife conspiring against him this trip? "How long will this go on?" he asked.

The engineer shrugged. "A few hours. A day. Who can tell? This is a rare sight. Both of them must be in musth; otherwise they wouldn't be this serious."

"Musth?" asked Sam. "Is that like rut in elk?" The breeze shifted, and he waved his hand in front of his nose. "Phew. They reek. I can smell them a quarter mile away."

The engineer nodded. "I don't know anything about your American animals, but if it means some old bull going mad to trample everything, then that would be it. There's no telling when a bull hits it or how often. No season, so to speak, and it might last a month, maybe two."

"It is their madness," said the fire tender, a tall Kikuyu man. "They cry out their pain, too." He ran his fingers down his cheeks from his eyes. "All very bad. We wait here."

"We'll probably wait here for a good long while after they go away," said the engineer.

"Why?" asked Sam, though something in his mind told him he knew the answer.

"Did you hear that cracking and screeching a moment ago?" he asked. Sam nodded. "That was the sound of teak sleepers getting snapped like so many matchsticks and the rails pulled out of alignment. Had problems already with the heat swelling the rails, pushing them askew."

"Sun kinks," said Sam.

"That's right. One of those bulls must have found a kink with his tusk. By now, I imagine they've completely wrecked the track. Not much in the way of ballast on them," he added.

The second bull, the one on the left, shook his head and bellowed just before charging the other. As the three men watched, the two collided with a solid thud. This time, the bull on the right was shoved backwards, slowly but inexorably. Right into the telegraph pole behind him. The pole held for a moment. Then, with a groaning creak, it began to bow as the bull straddled it and forced it back and down. Finally, the strain was too much for the wires at the top and they snapped with a high, singing whine. One of the wires struck the straddling bull on the rump.

The effect was like cracking a whip on a mule. The bull screamed and trumpeted, startled by this new and unexpected assailant. Then it bolted and ran away from the tracks. The other bull followed in hot pursuit. Once the two elephants were gone, Sam climbed aboard the locomotive with the engineer and the fireman, and they crept forward until they reached the damaged track. Sam jumped down first and surveyed the wreckage.

"Blast and damn!" he swore.

"That would be my account of it, mate," said the engineer. "They bent those rails as easily as if they were thin copper wires instead of forty-one-pound-per-yard steel."

"Forty-one?" asked Sam. "I thought the rails were all fifty or sixty pound per yard."

"They are on the main line, but this side line was constructed in a hurry during the war. That's why these ties are creosoted teak instead of steel. Some've been replaced as the white ants or dry rot work through them, but not here. This line is still under military control, and they don't maintain it as well as I'd like." He sighed and looked back down the way they had come. "Looks like a trip back to Serengeti station. Hopefully they finished repairing those telegraph lines."

"And then what?" asked Sam. "Do they have replacement rails and ties at the station? I'd be glad to lend a hand and fix the track."

"Very good of you, friend," said the engineer, "but truth be told, they'll have to telegraph Nairobi and have equipment sent down from there. They could be down here by morning. More likely by midday. But I'm afraid we won't get into Moshi until Thursday at the earliest."

Sam limped back to the passenger car. As he settled into his seat, the locomotive hissed and chugged; then the car jolted backwards. They inched back down the line at a painfully slow pace. The feeling of helplessness swept over Sam and settled in his stomach like a burning fire.

No one spoke the rest of the way across the barren saddle to the final campsite. No one had the air for it. With the biting temperatures and the blustering wind, trying to do anything besides walk was out of the question. The cameramen had the cameras wrapped in protective blankets. Harry kept Abeba beside him at the front, and Jade again brought up the rear as they headed east-northeast across the lava wastes.

The wind bore what sounded like a flock of seagulls to Jade's ears, and she stopped to find the source. Down the slope she spied a pack of wild dogs, calling to one another in high-pitched hoots. Something seemed to frighten them, but Jade couldn't discern what it was. She looked to Mawenzi Peak and studied the few storm clouds that attended it. In a month, perhaps less, the rains would come. Then Kibo, as if jealous of Jade's attention to the lesser peak, revealed itself in all its blindingly white, icy splendor. Rust-red walls, like dried blood, rose up beside them. Immediately underfoot, all was gray. Gravel-sized weathered lava carpeted the ground, the bleakness interrupted only by lava bombs, great balls of rock where the mountain had spat out a viscous magma.

At noon Harry called a brief break for a cold lunch of smoked eland sandwiches on flatbreads, chocolate, and cold water. They ate in silence, hunched against the wind. Only Julian appeared to be in good spirits, and Jade caught him humming softly. Two hours later, they reached their campsite. Most of the sleeping tents were clustered together near an upthrust of volcanic rock, but the tent for the Menelik scene sat apart, a glacier and Kibo as its background. Nakuru and the porters had taken up residence in one of several small caves formed by air pockets in the lava flows, and dubbed *Chumba a Mungu*, or God's parlor room. Muturi built up their small campfire using wood and brush they'd carried with them from below and heated water. He poured in some powdered milk and melted chocolate bars and everyone, including the porters, revived themselves with the hot chocolate. Julian bullied them through their break and filmed the modern climax, ending in Hall's death.

"No time to dawdle," bellowed Julian. "I want to film Menelik's final scene. Bebe, Hall, get into costume. Harry, get your man Nakuru and all those other men in the guards' costumes. Talmadge, you're his general. So move. I want this now, while the light is at the right angle."

"Really, Rex," said Murdock. "We're all done-in and my dogs hurt. Can't this wait?"

"No. Who knows what the weather will do tomorrow. Might not be able to see the peak. I need that peak! Besides, I *want* you all tired. You've climbed all this way and now your emperor is dying. This will make it more realistic."

"Why her?" asked Pearl, a sharp edge to her voice. "*I'm* playing the emperor's lover."

"I decided to give the role back to Bebe," Julian said. "After careful consideration, I think she will give me the pathos I need."

Pearl shot Bebe an evil look, her jaw clenched, her eyes snapping. "You bitch! Did you sleep with him, too? Do you have to use every man you see?"

Bebe put a hand to her breast and returned the stare with a look of wounded bewilderment. "How can you say such a thing?"

"No arguing!" yelled Julian. "Everyone get to work."

No one dared contradict him. As far as Jade was concerned, the sooner they finished this blasted movie, the sooner she and Harry could haul them all off the mountain and back to Nairobi or Mombassa or Outer Mongolia.

Fatigue and the cold wreaked havoc on the actors and, true to Julian's prediction, lent verisimilitude to the scenes. Not that Bebe needed it. She threw everything she had into her roles, proving herself to be the better actress. She poured out her heart over her dying lover's breast, whether it was Hall as the reincarnated lover or Hall as her emperor, going so far as to thrust a knife through her own heart in each scene. Naturally, Harry and Jade both checked the knife before they filmed to make certain it was rubber. And Jade kept close watch on Abeba, waiting to see if she made any sign hinting of trouble.

Julian pestered the Abyssinian relentlessly. "Which direction should the men go to carry the body? Did they climb up to the cone on this side? Where in the cone did they put him? Hascombe, make her answer me!"

Harry ignored Julian, and Abeba refused to answer anything, choosing to sit near the cooking fire, away from everyone except Jelani and Muturi. But she watched every move the actors made, especially when they struggled off across the loose debris that littered this upper slope. Finally, as the sun sank lower and threw long shadows behind every rock, Julian called, "Cut!" The sky glowed like liquid gold above the soft purple and blue glacial shadows.

The porters dropped the bier and Hall with a plop and staggered back to their rocky den while the actors hurried to their tents to put on warmer clothing. Muturi served a thick stew of eland meat along with the last ears of corn, which he'd roasted in a bed of coals. Jade noticed that appetites flagged again, and several people retired complaining of headaches.

Harry checked with his own men to see that they kept their woolen socks and gloves on to prevent frostbite, and Jade made the rounds of camp with arnica ointment to ease aching legs and stop chilblains. At first, the Nyamwezi and Chagga men would not let Jade examine their fingers or toes or apply the salve, but after Jelani insisted, they let the young healer tend to them.

Harry called to Jade and pointed to a few purple clouds

building over Mawenzi. "It's early in the season, but it looks as though we could see storms soon enough. Probably just as well our director friend finished today."

"Yes. Two of the Chagga men need to go down. I suspect they haven't kept their feet properly covered. They might even lose a few toes."

"Nakuru said they had their woolies on when everyone went to bed, but they take them off during the night." He surveyed the sky again. "I fulfilled my end of the contract. I got Julian here to make his blasted picture." He walked over to the director, who was still badgering a silent Abeba.

"Mr. Julian," said Harry as Jade stood by Abeba's side, "tomorrow morning you can have one hour to film scenery, but I need to take your people back down. We'll leave by eight. I mean to get everyone back to base camp. If we have to, we'll stay a night at Bismark's hut."

"But my picture!" demanded Julian. "What of my picture?"

"We can stay another day or two at base camp if you need it. But you got your funeral scene on the mountain. That's all I was signed on to do."

"The crater! It's your job to—"

"It's my job to keep everyone safe!" bellowed Harry within an inch of Julian's face. "We've had too many deaths associated with this project of yours. I'm not waiting for more."

Harry's roars had stirred the others and, one by one, they poked their heads out of their respective tents and stared. Julian was not about to back down and lose face in front of his crew.

"We will go when I say so," he said. "And not before. Not unless you"—he paused and poked Harry in the chest—"want to lose your license for breach of contract."

Jade decided to intervene before the two men came to blows. "Harry, Mr. Julian. Stop it, both of you, before one of you ruptures something." She shoved her hands between the two and forced them apart. "Mr. Julian, you should listen to Harry. That's why you hired him. It takes a professional to know when your people are in danger."

"That's right," Harry said in a loud but calmer voice. "And Jade thinks your people are still in danger. You may have an unknown killer in your midst."

"Harry," said Jade softly between gritted teeth. "No."

He ignored her. "Jade's very quick. I trust her judgment implicitly. If she's not certain that Lwiza or Abeba, or whatever her name is, is responsible for the boomslang or Zakayo's death, or even Wheeler's death, then I'd listen to her. What if you've hired a killer?"

"Harry, for Pete's sake, shut up!" said Jade, as she watched the eavesdroppers inch out of their tents. Her tone of voice must have carried some weight, because Harry did, in fact, shut up long enough for Jade to say, "This conversation is ended. Mr. Julian, you'll have to comply, because we'll have all the tents and the food. Harry, I'm keeping Abeba with me in my tent tonight. For her own safety as much as everyone else's. Good night."

Jade told Biscuit to stay with Jelani, hoping the cat's body heat would protect the lad. She'd given the youth another pair of her own socks and an extra blanket, but they had no other spare boots or gloves. Biscuit uttered a soft growling bleat, a discontented, worried sound that Jade rarely heard.

"Go to Jelani," she repeated. Biscuit reluctantly stepped away. "Abeba, you are sharing my tent tonight." She led Abeba there as the sun set and ordered her cot to be installed while Jade herself lit a lantern. Next she tied Abeba's wrists to the cot. If the woman tried hard enough, she could work loose, but by then, Jade would have heard her. She rummaged through her own box, found Rehema's bag, and pulled out the compact.

"Do you know this little box?" Jade asked, studying Abeba's response.

Abeba strained to see in the dim light. "Yes, it is a beauty case." She reached for it, stopping when the short rope reached its limit.

Jade held it a little closer and moved the lantern so the light fell more fully on the purple rouge box compact. She said nothing and kept her own attention on Abeba's face.

"I once saw one of that design in Missy Malta's room, but it was gold and not the royal purple. Missy Zagar has one the color of a blushing rose. I stayed away from Missy Porter, though, lest she recognize me."

"Recognize you?" asked Jade.

"Yes, *bibi*. I saw her when she came with the money man to court. I did not think she saw me, but I was not certain." She looked at Jade. "This case is not yours. You do not paint your face as they do." The statement held a note of inquiry to which Jade didn't reply. "You found it with the dead Chagga woman," concluded Abeba. "You are thinking I stole it."

"That had occurred to me," said Jade. "Did you?"

"No," she said, her eyes meeting Jade's gaze, unflinching. "I cannot tell you which woman's it is. But all of them still wear their beauty. Even if this one belonged to one of them, the woman must have more."

That would explain why this compact was nearly empty. Someone disposed of a pretty case, mirror, and puff.

"What will happen to me?" asked Abeba.

"I'm not sure," said Jade. "When we return, we will have to report everything to some commissioner. But if there is no other evidence, I suppose you will be sent back to Abyssinia and told never to return."

"I have heard that you have talked with spirits who warn

you of death. You carry marks on your forehead of an ancient tribe. You must understand it is important to protect this tomb and the ancient things. They must not be found until the time is right. The tomb is prophesied to be opened *only* at the start of the end times. To open it sooner will cause it to lose its power."

At the mention of the Berber tattoo on her forehead, Jade's hand went to the small, intricately worked silver box around her neck. The amulet contained a protective talisman, but she wore it not for that, but for its ties to her own Berber ancestry and the mended relationship with her mother. "So we *won't* all die," she said. It was a statement, not a question. Jade had never believed it to begin with.

Abeba hung her head. "I said that to frighten that man, Julian. But no. It would mean that my country would never again rise to its glory."

"Do you actually know where the tomb is?" asked Jade. "This is a big mountain and the crater is vast. I can't imagine finding anything here."

"I know enough," she said. "My ancestors were among the priests who buried the emperor. My mother came when Emperor Menelik the Second tried to seek the tomb. But it was not for him to find. She led him to the wrong places until he went home. Do you believe me? Do you believe that I *only* mean to protect the emperor's tomb and his treasure? To kill is a sin. I would not do that."

Jade studied the woman's face in the lamplight and examined her own feelings. The woman's expression spoke of honesty, and Jade wanted to trust her. But there had been too much deception already. "It doesn't matter what I believe, Abeba. Now get some sleep."

Abeba pulled the blanket over herself, and soon Jade heard her breathing slow to the deep inhalations of sleep. She was tired herself, exhausted, and her head ached. But something was nagging at her thoughts and she wanted to examine those movie magazines again. They'd been stowed in her personal box and brought up to the camp for use as fuel if nothing else. She also wanted to look into Abeba's bag for that extra black stocking to see if it matched the one used to make the second fake snake. Jade carefully pulled out the rucksack bag, one of several purchased for the crew members to use. Some had written their initials on the flap. This one had none.

Jade opened the bag under the lamplight. She found a tortoiseshell comb and a silver pot with a stopper. Jade opened the pot and smelled myrhh. *Her beauty cream.* Under the pot lay Abeba's white cotton blouse and long skirt. No stockings! *Spitfire! Jelani looked in the wrong bag. Whose was it?*

She replaced the rucksack and opened the magazines, looking at each story again by lamplight. She started a story about a scandal involving extramarital affairs, but ignored it when she didn't recognize any of the names. Instead she read about Talmadge's ability to fall and Hall's litany of accomplishments, all while looking handsome. Pearl's article told little about her, mainly showing photos in sequined vests and harem trousers. Cynthia's story of her world travels related her past trips to Egypt and Spain and Tunisia. Nothing Jade hadn't read already. She turned pages, searching for anything. She found an ad for the Pompeian company.

Jade looked at the ad more carefully. It depicted a color picture of a woman at her vanity, massaging the area around her eyes. The woman's wrists were pointed inward, obscuring much of her face. The headline "Pompeian Massage Cream" covered her reflection. The caption below the picture stated, "Don't envy beauty—use Pompeian and have it." Along the side were small depictions of the various products. At the bottom right corner was a picture of a purple box with "Beauty Powder" in a gold label. Below that was a smaller image of a jar of day cream and a little gold case with a heart atop it and the words "Pompeian Bloom" in gold paint.

So bloom is different from powder. Shows what I know.

Jade rubbed her own temples, trying to squelch the headache. Her eyes were tired, her vision blurring. The face in the ad looked familiar. *Who? Miss Malta?*

That's it! It *was* Bebe, posing for a cream made in her own hometown of Cleveland, where the cosmetics were made. It was no great leap to assume that Bebe actually used it since she posed for the ad. *But why deny using it? And does she use the rouge, too?* Jade wished she'd asked about rouge more specifically and chalked it up to her own lack of knowledge of these vanities. She turned to the last magazine and flipped it open to where she'd dog-eared a page. It fell to the advertisement for the Pond's cold cream and soaps. She'd seen this same ad before, and not in the magazine.

Where? Her head, tired and achy, refused to give her an answer.

She turned the page and read the article on Graham Wheeler describing his trip to Abyssinia to research ideas for a motion picture.

"Producer researching tales of treasure. Producer Graham Wheeler has once again shown that he will stop at nothing to find a good story for whatever picture he is backing. After Spain, Tunisia, and Egypt, this time, he dared the wilds of Abyssinia."

Wait! These are places Cynthia went to, and Abeba said she saw Cynthia at court. Look at the photo! Jade stopped reading and stared more closely at the photograph of Wheeler astride a horse and studied the people in the background. Sure enough, there on another horse, her face just visible in profile, sat his wife. Suddenly Jade remembered where else she'd seen the Pond's ad on the reverse side. It had been at base camp while shooing a mouse from the house.

Why did she keep that Pond's ad? She doesn't use that brand. The answer came slowly into her tired, oxygen-starved head. *She didn't keep it for the ad.*

It started to make some small amount of sense, and Jade went to her cot knowing that she had made progress towards understanding. In the morning she'd tell Harry, and together, they'd confront all the women and search their things to sort out the answer.

Jade fell asleep and dreamed of Sam. He was standing on the plains surrounded by wild game, but every time she called to him, he walked off. She tried running, only to trip over a body and end up where she started. Or she'd run and find herself trying to cross deep ravines to get to him. By the time she'd finally made it to the other side, he'd flown away.

The dreams repeated over and over again until a few hours before dawn, when she again entered the dark dream with its gravelike cold. Her left knee throbbed and, as happened in some dreams, Jade found herself wishing that she'd wake up. Somewhere in a distant corner of her mind, she heard a low growl and hiss followed by a muffled yelp.

That soft sound startled her awake and she struggled to rise off her cot. The stab in her knee continued. She tried to get out from under the twisted blankets, but not in time to escape the blow.

Something struck her on the head and she fell.

CHAPTER 24

Of course, Menelik did achieve the summit, but he was dead at the time.

—The Traveler

Jelani listened to the soft snores and deep breaths of the men beside him. Their combined body heat along with the carefully tended fire and their woolen blankets made the shelter comfortable enough, but Jelani could not sleep. Not even Biscuit's warmth and rasping purrs lulled him into drowsiness.

Something will happen soon. Tonight!

He called to Biscuit with a soft chirp. "Go to Simba Jike," he ordered. "Guard." Biscuit slipped away and headed towards Jade's tent.

For an hour afterward, Jelani took his turn feeding and protecting the cave's fire. And while he watched, he listened. Not for wild animals or for human sounds, but for the voices of his ancestral spirits. He sprinkled a few drops of water from the last spring onto the fire. The liquid hit with a soft sizzle, sending up tiny puffs of steam. But as Jelani prayed that these spirits would alert him to the dangers facing Simba Jike and help protect her, sleep overpowered him.

Something startled him a little later. It was as if he heard a noise that hadn't been made or had been made in his soul. Jelani sat up and blinked, trying to focus. Beyond the fire stood a form, and for a moment, he thought Biscuit had returned to him. Then Jelani saw that this cheetah was larger, more commanding than Biscuit. The new cat had spots in a curious rosette pattern and long dark stripes running along his spine.

"Marahaba," whispered Jelani, blessing the animal. *"Karibu,"* he added, inviting the cheetah inside. The newcomer stared at him, unblinking, then strode away. His shoulders rose and fell like pistons atop his great barrel chest.

Jelani jumped up and ran out of the shelter, but the cheetah was nowhere to be seen. He called for Biscuit, hoping that one cheetah would be able to see and follow the other. But the cat didn't come. Jelani hurried first to the cooking fire, then to Jade's tent, and finally to Bwana Nyati's tent. At each spot, he chirped, listening and watching for the response that should have come immediately.

Biscuit was gone.

Jade woke in the dark to the sound of voices raised in argument. There was no mistaking Harry's bellow. And the other?

Jelani?

She tried to get up and fell back against the cot. Her head felt as if someone had reenacted the Great War in it, firing howitzers from one ear to the other. Small white spots played in the corners of her eyelids, remaining when she tried opening them, something she couldn't do for long. After two attempts, she gave up and listened instead.

"If you will not let me see her, then you must waken her," said Jelani.

"No! And that's final," snapped Harry. "It's not even dawn yet and you want to disturb her? Bad enough you wake me up."

"I'm awake, Harry." Jade groaned, her eyes still shut. *What the hell happened?* Vague memories of an outcry followed by painful blackness came back to her.

She tried again to open her eyes and endure even the dim light from the campfire outside. *What the . . .? There's another cot in my tent.* A moment's reflection told her it was for Lwiza. *Not Lwiza. Abeba.* Then she looked again. *It's empty!*

Jade forced herself to her feet, stumbled to the doorway, and gripped the tent pole to support herself. "Harry!" she called. "Abeba's gone."

Harry and Jelani both ran to her side, calling to her in unison, "Simba Jike."

"Jade!" Harry helped her to the folding camp chair at the other end and gently pushed her into it. "Are you all right?"

"Yes—I mean no. Oh, hell! Someone hit me."

"That woman," said Jelani. "She has gone."

"And good riddance to her," said Harry, his voice a low growl. "Let her find her own damn way back."

"We need to find her," said Jade. She struggled to rise against Harry's hands pushing on her shoulders. "Have you checked on the others?"

"No," said Harry. "Let them sleep. We'll wake them soon enough and . . . Why?"

"Because Abeba might be in trouble. Somehow I don't think she went willingly. Before you pushed me back inside, I thought I saw drag marks on the ground outside the tent."

Harry hurried back to the opening and studied the ground. Sure enough, the loose scree and the night's frost had been raked in two lines.

While Harry busied himself examining them, Jade turned

to Jelani. "Go to the bwanas' and *bibis'* tents. Quietly! See who is missing."

"Simba Jike. You must listen—"

"Go!" ordered Jade.

Jelani ran off and stuck his head in each tent in the circle. Harry went back to Jade.

"There are footprints in the frost. At some point your Abyssinian spy walked next to one other person at least, maybe a man by the size of the marks."

"Once the sun comes up, those frost tracks are going to disappear," said Jade.

Jelani ran back into the tent, clutching the blanket around his shoulders, his breath coming in white puffs. "Bwana Julian is gone," he said. "And there are only two of the memsahibs. The one they call lady is gone."

"Lady?" asked Harry. "Who calls . . . ? Ah, I understand."

"Right," said Jade. "Bebe sounds like *bibi*."

"Damn! Looks like our director friend went off after Menelik's grave after all and either took hostages or convinced them to tag along for a share," said Harry. He spied Jelani shifting from side to side with impatience. "Jelani, get some coffee for Simba Jike." After the youth left, grumbling audibly, Harry turned back to Jade. "Can you stand now?"

Jade nodded her head a little, careful not to set off another explosion of pain. The spots in front of her eyes had vanished and the headache had settled into a dull throb along the temples.

"Any idea of when Julian hit you?" Harry asked.

"Not sure it was Julian. But no. Maybe an hour, two hours ago? I can't really say."

"Oh, it had to be Julian or that Abeba woman," said Harry. "He's determined to find that grave and she's determined to stop him. Although how he expects to find it beats the hell out of me." He pointed to the back of her tent in the direction of the huge glacier not far from them. "This mountain changed from when Hans Meyer made the peak in 'eighty-nine to when he returned in 'ninety-eight. That glacier moved back a good hundred yards in those nine years. Imagine where it was in biblical times."

"Harry, don't discount—" Jade was interrupted by Jelani's return with a steaming mug of coffee, which Harry took from him and thrust into her gloved hands.

"Drink," he ordered. Harry kept one arm around her to steady her.

Jade took a tentative sip, winced as it scalded her throat, then took another. "Harry, you need to get the others off this mountain while I go after them."

"The last time I checked, I was still the big bwana here," said Harry.

"And that's why *you* need to stay in charge and get them down. Two of the three people missing are women and they were my responsibility, right?" She took another swallow of coffee and felt the heat revitalize her. "I'll take Biscuit to help me track them. I know cheetahs aren't scent trackers, but he did all right finding Jelani—"

"Biscuit is gone!" shouted Jelani.

"What?" asked Jade and Harry.

"That is why I needed to wake you," Jelani said with an angry sidewise glare at Harry. "Last night after you slept, I sent Biscuit back to keep watch over you, Simba Jike. At first this morning, I thought he was still in your tent, so I chirped for him to come. But he did not come and I cannot find him."

"Well, that tears it!" Jade said. "Of all the low-down, bush-whacking tricks!" She grabbed her woven Berber pouch and tossed in a flashlight and first-aid kit before handing it to Jelani. "Fill this with all the jerked meat you can." As he ran out of the tent to get the supplies, Jade checked her rifle and shoved more cartridges in her trouser pockets. Then she set the loaded Winchester on her cot and tied a woolen scarf around her head.

Harry watched her, his brows getting lower and lower as her intent hit him. "Just what the blazes do you think you're going to do, woman?" She started past him and he grabbed her arm above the elbow. "You're not running off anywhere," he said.

"Don't make me hurt you, Harry. Because I will. Now get out of my way and let me do my job. You go do yours."

Jelani returned with her pack. Jade slung it over her head and one shoulder, and hefted the rifle. "I will go with you, Simba Jike," Jelani said.

"No."

The young man didn't budge. Jade noticed Jelani's face, saw the set of his jaw, and recognized the same expression she'd seen when he'd been arrested for fomenting a rebellion last July. Both he and Harry blocked her exit, and getting past them would be like evading two bulls in a pen, with them guarding the stall gate.

Reinforcements came from an unexpected quarter. McAvy stumbled to the tent, hollering for Harry. He held a handkerchief, sodden with blood, to his nose.

"Harry. My nose. It won't stop bleeding. Murdock and me, we heard someone at our tent and we got up to investigate. Then my nose turned into a gusher. Murdock's is the same way, only he passed out."

Harry the leader and Jelani the healer both moved almost instinctively to help the man. In that moment, Jade pulled her knife and slit the back of the tent. By the time they'd turned around, she was already loping out of camp.

Their trail showed itself easily enough by the half-moon overhead, and Jade shut off her flashlight. At times the track consisted of a print against surrounding frost or a drag mark where at least one person had resisted or where Biscuit had to be tugged along. At other times she detected a small circular impression where a hiking stick had pushed into the scree. They'd skirted the glacier on their way up, towards the rim. The old Chagga storyteller had claimed Menelik was buried in the cone, so presumably, Julian intended to search it. Had Bebe promised to help in return for getting her role back?

The frozen ground made for decent footing. After an hour, climbing became harder, but tracking easier as her prey left first one item, then another behind to lessen their burden. She found a chocolate bar wrapper first, then a pair of field glasses that must have weighed too heavily around someone's neck, and for a moment, Jade wondered if someone was intentionally marking this trail.

She had to admire their stamina as she stopped often to catch her breath. The route threw several obstacles in her way: sharp chunks of lava that bit at her knees when she stumbled, and loose scree that sent her sliding back half a foot for every one forward. It would have helped if she'd had a stout stick for support, but she'd left too quickly to pick one up from the stacked supplies. The rarefied air attacked from the inside, leaving her light-headed. It wreaked havoc with her ability to concentrate. She stopped again, fearful that she'd missed something.

The sun hadn't risen yet, but on the eastern horizon, the stars were diminishing. The ephemeral dawn of this latitude teased her. Her pupils tried to adjust to the faint moon glow and this new, pale light. When she blinked a few times to moisten her dry eyes, she saw something against a lava slab that didn't match the rock's angular contours.

Jade knelt on the ground and turned on her flashlight. There, snagged on the sharp rock, was a frayed strip of leather. When she examined the ground nearby, she spotted two circular depressions and a skid line. She touched a dark spot on the rock. It felt sticky.

Blood. If she read this correctly, someone had fallen to their knees here and cut their hand or leg on the sharp rock. Whoever it was had probably held Biscuit by a leather lead, and the cat broke free. Possibly Biscuit's tugging caused the person to trip and fall to begin with. Or the clever animal just took the opportunity given to him. Once the lead snapped against the lava's razor edge, he'd escaped.

Where? Did they run after him?

She played her beam across the rocks just as the sun rose. The glacial fields shone a rosy gold with deep blue shadows in the sheer cuts. Far below, the saddle steamed in fog as rising mist met sinking chill air. And above? Above rose the snow-clad peak of the shining mountain, Kilima-Njaro. Normally, the view would have taken Jade's breath away, but in this case, the altitude had beaten it to the punch. Already the wind had picked up, dashing grit against Jade's face, and several snow-laden clouds formed overhead. She was grateful for the clouds. If they covered the sun soon enough, it would slow down the frost's melting, which would preserve the tracks and make walking easier. Once the ice holding the scree melted, she'd slip even more.

Jade turned off her light and shoved it in a coat pocket. Next she adjusted her woolen head scarf to cover her mouth. As her gaze swept the area for signs of recent disturbance, she found two. One set continued upwards towards the rim. The other took off to the right. Until someone stepped into the ice field itself, she couldn't tell who'd made which track, but she was willing to bet that Biscuit hadn't continued the climb. Hopefully by now he'd doubled back into camp and followed the others as they went down the mountain.

She looked beyond a lava ridge back to the now distant camp. It was dismantled, the porters and the remaining actors drifting away. She didn't see Biscuit, but then, she was having trouble seeing at all. Jade closed her eyes again to clear her vision. All she saw were little stabbing white spots flashing like fireflies on her eyelids.

And which way are you going?

Jade snapped an icicle from an overhanging rock and sucked on it. There really wasn't any question about it. She needed to go up and retrieve the others.

Suddenly, her legs felt slightly rubbery and unsteady, as though someone had tried unsuccessfully to pull a carpet out from under her. *Another earthquake?* A few of the smaller, gravel-sized rocks tumbled past her. *God must be walking on His mountain.*

She finished the icicle and pulled out a small chunk of jerked meat, wishing she had a chocolate bar instead, but she'd been thinking of food for Biscuit more than for herself. As she shouldered her bag, she heard booted feet scraping against loose gravel. Jade slipped her rifle off her shoulder and held it ready.

"Don't shoot. It's only me."

"Harry?" Jade asked.

He stepped into view from behind one of the larger outcrops on the trail. His broad-shouldered, muscular form was swaddled in a woolen coat and muffler, increasing his overall size until he nearly resembled the cape buffalo for which he was nicknamed. "Didn't think I was going to let you do this alone, did you?" he asked, panting from exertion. He handed a chocolate bar to Jade. "Here. Eat this."

"I'm awfully glad to see you, but what about McAvy and Murdock?" asked Jade as she unwrapped the bar and bit off a large chunk.

"Nosebleed from the altitude. Murdock faints at the sight of his own blood," he scoffed. "Shoved hot Bovril down the lot of them and sent them off with Nakuru. They'll wait for us for a while at Peter's hut. McAvy's actually taking charge of the actors. Looks like his role went to his head." He gestured to the ground. "What have you found?"

Jade swallowed, savoring the bittersweet taste of chocolate, and slid the remainder of the bar into her coat pocket for later. "The trail divides here." She pointed to the blood on the rock and showed him the leather strip. "Someone fell or was knocked down. Biscuit broke loose and escaped. It looks like he headed right. I haven't followed it far enough to see where he went."

Harry squatted and studied the ground markings. "I think he went alone, Jade. But it's harder to see than the trail going up. Why the hell Julian wanted him is beyond me." He followed the other set of tracks up the slope for a brief spell. "Unless someone repeatedly climbed, slid down and reclimbed, there's more than one set of tracks here." He looked up at the slope. "I never thought any of them could have made it this far."

He'd brought two stout staffs with him and handed one to Jade. Then he started to climb up the slope.

"Wait." When he turned back towards her she explained. "You need to know what I found out last night. I was looking back through those magazines you gave me on the train. Trying to find some insight into these people."

"Your Abyssinian isn't in any of the magazines, Jade. We . . . *you* caught her red-handed loosening the supply boxes."

"Right. But not bartering for a boomslang or replacing blanks with live rounds or arranging for someone to kill Wheeler."

"And your point?" he said, impatience edging his voice. He stamped about and slapped his arms to stay warm.

"Abeba's actions were those of someone trying to keep us off the upper mountain, away from a grave. But they weren't earmarked to harm anyone. The other actions were all intended to be deadly. I could understand if the more harmless activities came first and then it escalated out of desperation, but not the other way around."

"But the sock snake?"

"The first one was made by Budendorfer. He'd torn a hole in one of his and, being the practical joker that he is, he probably decided to use the other to scare an actress. But the second one on Pearl's cot? It was a woman's stocking. That snake might have been made by Bebe and planted there to get Pearl into trouble with Julian. Jelani found an odd stocking in what he thought was Abeba's bag, but he had the wrong bag. And Bebe said someone had been in hers."

"So you think someone else was behind all the other events?"

Jade nodded, trying to catch her breath.

"Julian," said Harry before she could continue. "He wanted that damned snake scene at any cost and something dramatic in his picture, so he had Zakayo shot." He stamped his foot against the rock. "And all to get some mythical treasure."

"No, Harry! Not Julian." She sighed at Harry's obtuseness

when it came to women. "Well, at least, not alone. Yes, he believes in Menelik's treasure, but he hasn't the brains to think of these schemes on his own. He'd likely try to bully or bribe you into taking him up higher."

Harry's brows furrowed in a deep scowl. "You certainly don't suspect Bebe of—"

"I certainly do. Remember how she got to play in that last scene? She'd lost that role to Pearl, so she may have promised Julian help in finding the treasure if he'd let her have it back."

"Jade, she's—"

"A *very* skilled actress." She lowered her voice, wondering if these outbursts had already been overheard. "She said she never knew that Wheeler was married, much less to Cynthia. Maybe she didn't when she began her affair, but she found out. Cynthia's photo is in the background of that article on Wheeler's trip to Abyssinia. It's hard to make her out, but not impossible. And it seems from Cynthia's interview that she'd traveled to a lot of exotic places. They all matched trips with Wheeler. He took his wife along, Harry. In secret, probably, but he did. And I think Bebe saw that photo and put two and two together."

"How do you know she saw the photo?"

"On the other side of it is an advertisement for Pond's beauty cream. I found that very page from the same magazine folded with the ad on the outside in Bebe's things. She'd dropped it when a mouse scared her. I just assumed she kept it for information about the cosmetics, but she doesn't use that brand. She uses the brand that I found in Rehema's bag, Pompeian."

She took a step forward and put a gloved hand on Harry's arm. "She thought she was pregnant. Wheeler wasn't going to leave his wife for her, and even if he did, either scandal would ruin her career. It already seemed to be taking a downturn with Julian favoring Pearl. But if Wheeler was killed, then she might escape any notice of her affair and his wife would take over the picture. She could plant ideas in Julian's head. *Everyone* could, for that matter. She slept with you so that if she was pregnant, she could name you the father. It would've been passed off as one of those casual romantic entanglements we seem to have so many of in Kenya."

"And the real snake?" asked Harry, his voice still skeptical. Jade thought she detected a note of hurt there as well.

"Probably meant for Pearl. Killing her would get Bebe's part back. I imagine she suggested switching scenes to Julian. And remember, it was her idea to have Cynthia fire at Zakayo. I'm sure she told Julian to put Zakayo in that scene. She's a schemer." Seeing Harry's confused look, she explained further. "Bebe saw Rehema curse the other girl. Probably promised her a way to guarantee the curse would work by trading her those datura seeds for a snake. The crazed native at the Muthaiga had ingested some as well, but in a different dosage. Just enough to make him attack Wheeler."

"But he also attacked Bebe."

"We don't know that. No one saw anything. She hired some poor man, telling him to simply rob or scare Wheeler. She met him out front and gave him something to drink for Dutch courage. But it gave him hallucinations and made him deadly. Then she came running in and went into her act."

Harry sighed. "You have no proof, Jade. Hell, how would she even know about datura?"

"Wheeler gave everyone detailed written information about Abyssinian customs. Maybe there's something in there. We'll have to find a copy to be sure, but you're right, I have no proof." She sighed, her chest tight. "Zakayo must have known about her and Rehema, maybe even helped with the translation, so Zakayo was conveniently shot. But I tell you, Harry, I can usually catch a person's tell, their sign when they lie. But her? I never knew she was lying all the time until I finally saw her tell the truth. When she said that she didn't need you anymore."

"You know for a fact she thought she was pregnant and isn't?"

Jade nodded. "I handle the women's personal supplies, remember?" Then after a pause she added, "I'm sorry she used you, Harry. I think she used Wells, too."

He stiffened. "You're a smart woman, Jade. But you don't know everything about other women. I won't believe it until I get proof. Julian may be forcing her along. Or maybe Abeba has forced Bebe to help her stop Julian."

Jade sighed, her headache growing worse. A bit of doubt about Abeba crept into her own mind. *I've misjudged people before.* "Just be careful and watch them all closely, Harry. Or you may not live to get your proof."

"What can any of them do, Jade? They're probably half-frozen by now. Come on. Let's get them and bring them down."

Jelani had heard the soft rip and knew Simba Jike had gone. In that moment, he'd made a decision. He wouldn't alert Bwana Nyati. Not yet. When later he'd innocently remarked that she'd cut her way out of the tent, the bwana's face had worn an amusing mixture of anger, shock, and admiration. Ah, yes, Jelani had seen how this man looked at Simba Jike. But Jelani knew that she was not meant for him and so did not need to answer to him.

Nakuru and his men had dismantled the camp faster than

a ravening pack of wild dogs could dismantle a dead antelope and just as neatly, leaving nothing behind.

Almost nothing. After helping, Jelani had slipped away, unnoticed by anyone but Muturi, his kinsman. Jelani had hidden in the cave that he and the other porters had slept in and watched until the safari lumbered down the path, a long, slow centipede of boxes and canvas borne over pairs of legs. As he expected, Bwana Nyati hadn't gone with them. He went up the mountain to find the ones who had run off. And to find Simba Jike.

You cannot help by following in body. Jelani knew that. Heard the voice of his mentor tell him. She faced too many dangers, too many enemies. Jelani did not doubt her ability to find and overcome the three runaways. But he felt Rehema's curse follow them up the mountain. And as before, it followed with savage claws and stealthy silence. The mountain, too, fought against her as it did against all who came uninvited to Ngai's throne, by sucking away their breath.

You are not alone, Simba Jike. I will pray to my ancestors and to your ancestor saints to aid you. Jelani opened his pouch and took out the sacred branch that he'd brought up from below. Then, after sprinkling it with water carried from the last stream, he settled himself in the cave and began to chant.

CHAPTER 25

Consequently, he left us no description of the top or the view from it.

—The Traveler

"Mr. Julian! Miss Malta! Abeba!" Jade shouted, and instantly regretted it. It took more wind out of her than she had to give. There was no answering call.

Harry repeated her call more loudly. When no one replied, Jade followed him up the mountain and into the wind. Once, the loose scree gave way and Harry slid back, colliding with Jade. After that, he made her follow several feet behind him. Soon the glacial ice and snow covered any other passage to the rim and they trudged and hauled themselves onto the hard-packed snow. Walls of ice layered like rock beds rose on one side, nearly terraced in spots and bordered with fringed ice draperies. Jade and Harry strained to see the faint, telltale boot prints.

"Julian! Bebe!" shouted Harry. "Can you hear me?"

His voice echoed off the mountain and reverberated into the distance.

"Help!" It was a man's voice, but weak.

Harry called again as they struggled towards the rim, trying to pinpoint Julian's location. It came from the other side of a ridge of ice. They hurried towards his voice and found him huddled in a ball. His labored breathing came in gasps, and a rancid puddle nearby indicated where he'd heaved up his last meal. A rent in his right trouser knee revealed blood.

Harry threw down his own pack and took out a spirit lamp. He lit it and melted chunks of ice in a tin cup. When it was hot, he poured in some Bovril beef powder. In the meantime, Jade massaged Julian's hands and rubbed arnica salve on his chest under his shirt.

"See if you can get him to drink this," said Harry. He braced Julian up against his arm while Jade plied the liquid.

"Come on, Mr. Julian," said Jade. "You can't cash in yet. You have to finish the picture."

Julian's eyelids fluttered and he looked at Jade uncomprehendingly. "Drink up," Jade said, and put the cup to his lips again. Like a baby bird's, his mouth opened automatically and he swallowed a little of the broth. Jade doled it out sparingly, giving his stomach an opportunity to accept it. Gradually, the man came around and his eyes lost their dim, glazed look.

"Meh . . . Menelik," he muttered.

"Don't worry about old Menelik," said Jade. "He's fine."

"Grave. Must find it."

"Not until you drink your Bovril," said Jade. She looked at Harry. "Well, he's alive. But he needs to get down now."

"It's a sure bet we can't leave him here while we look for the others," replied Harry. He turned to Julian. "Rex, where's Bebe? Where's the other woman?"

Julian blinked stupidly at Harry.

"Well, he's no good," said Jade. "You know what has to be done, Harry. I don't have the strength to help him down alone.

You're going to have to take him to Peter's hut to join the others while I continue looking for the women."

Harry didn't answer for a moment, his lips working as he struggled for an alternative. "Damn!" he muttered. "Jade, you can't go haring off on your own."

"We can't wait to take him down together and then return, Harry. By then, neither of us will be in any condition to get them and they could both be dead."

Harry frowned, then nodded. "Right." He let go of Julian for a moment and pulled off his pack. "Take the spirit lamp, the Bovril, and one of the mugs," he said. "In case."

"Thanks, Harry," Jade said as she crammed them into her own bag.

Harry stood, staring at her while she repacked.

"What?" she asked, glancing up.

"Ah, hell," he muttered, and grabbed her in a tight embrace, kissing her hard.

Jade felt the pressure of his lips and arms and pushed herself away. "Harry! What in blazes?"

He gritted his teeth and turned aside towards the director. "Julian. I need you to stand now. We have to get you to safety."

"No!" Julian's eyes widened. "The tomb. The treasure."

"Yes," said Jade, helping him to his feet. "That's where we're going. Harry knows where it is now. He'll lead you straight to it."

Julian blinked at Harry. "You know? Where?" He looked at the summit.

"It's not there," said Harry, following Jade's lead. "That's the secret. The story of the cone is just a lie to mislead everyone." He took hold of the director's arm to steady him. "Come along. One foot at a time." Together, they helped support Julian until he was capable of walking. "And, Jade," Harry added when she turned to leave, "be careful. I'm only letting you go because I trust you. I'm coming back up for you after I send Julian down with the others. And if I find you got yourself in trouble, I'll . . ." He let the threat hang.

"Right. But you may have to wait in line. I think Sam has first call there," she replied.

Sam sat on a board bench outside Serengeti station, staring east towards Voi, feeling like some old hound dog waiting for his master's return. Only he watched for the Nairobi train, which would carry replacement rails and solid-steel cross ties. It was nearing noon on Wednesday, and his patience had reached its end. With no car or horse to hire, and no runner willing to run the distance to Moshi, he had no choice but to wait.

Finally he heard a whistle blast. As he stood and peered into the shimmering heat waves rippling off the track, he saw the class G, forty-two-ton locomotive. Black smoke belched from its stack, sweeping over the two cars behind its tender. One held rails, fish bolts, cross ties, and tools. The other held the African men employed as manual laborers. Sam's own train had pulled off onto the crescent siding to wait its turn, the engineer snoozing in one of the passenger berths.

Sam waited until the car with the men pulled alongside him and grabbed hold. Several strong black arms pulled him aboard. Sam waved to them and greeted them in what little Swahili he knew. *"Hamjambo, wanaume,"* he said.

"*Jambo*, bwana," they replied, watching him.

He didn't know how to tell them he intended to work, *needed* to work to dispel the feeling of helplessness that plagued him. So he pointed to the tools, then to himself, and mimed swinging a hammer down. The workmen grinned and nodded and one clapped him on the back. Sam settled in and watched the station diminish as the repair train slowly made its way along the track. He closed his eyes and listened to the pistons' rhythmic pulse, heard the *clack-clack* as the steel wheels tumbled over the rails. He loved those sounds almost as much as he loved the sound of the wind and the silence high in the air.

You'll be there soon, he told himself. *Not long now. Some good honest labor to speed the job and you'll be on your way.* He coughed once when the train turned and the black smoke wafted over him. *And what are you going to do when you get there?*

That was the question of the hour, it seemed, and one for which he had no answer. If Jade wasn't in Moshi, he'd ask everyone he met until he learned where the safari had gone, and then he'd find some way to get to her even if it meant walking. He needed to see her safe, hear her husky voice, touch her hair.

And then? He didn't want to think about it. He'd been afraid for her in the past, but this time the anxiety had been too intense, overwhelming him. And as much as he loved her, she didn't seem to return it. He didn't think he could stand worrying about her another time, especially if he didn't have the right to. Maybe not even if he did. Before the hunt, she'd said she wanted to make sure that Biscuit was free to leave if he wanted to. Perhaps it was time for him to let go and give her that same freedom.

Jade trudged back to the spot where they'd found Julian, studying the ground for another set of tracks along the way. Between Harry's feet and her own, everything else was obscured. It was possible that the director had made it that far alone, but it was more likely he'd been left there when he couldn't proceed. *Why didn't they stay with him?*

She found what she wanted to see a few yards from where Julian had collapsed. At least one person had continued up towards the rim. But which one? Or both? Suddenly Jade wondered if the two women hadn't been in cahoots the entire time. Maybe Abeba's tale of hiding the tomb *was* all a lie. Jade paused and listened. At first she heard only the howling wind, which struck her with tiny icy fragments no matter which way she faced. She waited, trying to listen beyond it.

Then she heard it, rocks scraping and a soft, "Oof." It came from the other side of the Ratzel glacier, from inside the cone. She followed the narrow fracture in the rising ice tower towards the sounds. When she emerged, she stood at the rim. To her left loomed Kaiser Wilhelm's Peak and its sheer drop into the hardened lava wall. Below her, however, was a terraced ridge of ice, a shelf of glassy white that arced around the inner cone. At its widest, it measured nearly ten feet. And that was where two people were grappling with each other, Bebe and Abeba, their bodies locked together.

Jade was about to fire once into the air, but one look at the surrounding blue-and-white ice sheets made her stop. Too much chance of an avalanche, especially if the recent earth tremors had created fresh fractures. Instead, she broke off an ice chunk, took aim, and hurled it.

It struck the sides of their faces and they immediately flew apart. Abeba slipped and fell backwards with a piercing cry of pain, striking her head on the ice. Jade clambered over the side as Bebe struggled to clear her right eye of icy debris.

"Jade," Bebe said, still blinking and sputtering. "Is it really you? Thank my lucky stars! She was going to kill me."

Jade motioned for Bebe to move aside and sit down where

she could see her. "Is that so?" She knelt beside the other woman and tried to rouse her.

"Yes," answered Bebe. "Be careful. She's a killer." Her voice caught, whether from emotion, exertion, or the cold, Jade wasn't sure. "When I think what she did to poor Graham, what she intended to do to us . . ."

Abeba, though breathing, was unconscious. After a quick examination for blood and finding none, Jade looked up at Bebe. "How did she get both of you away from camp? How was she going to kill you?"

"It was horrid," said Bebe. She closed her eyes. "Rex was determined to find that grave. He thought that woman would help him. I heard them last night. He sneaked into your tent and freed her. She told him that the cheetah would show us the way. Just like the emperor's cheetah long ago. She tied a cloth around his mouth to muzzle him." When Bebe opened her eyes, they were moist with tears. She tilted her head back and spoke towards the sky. "I tried to make Rex change his mind, but he wouldn't listen, so I went with them. You know, to help protect him."

"Why didn't you wake Harry?" asked Jade.

"Oh, I just couldn't think," Bebe replied, shaking her head. "It's the altitude. It fogged my mind. And maybe . . . maybe I actually wanted to believe in the treasure, too." She turned her face to Jade, pleading with a look for her to believe her. "Didn't Harry come?"

"He came. He found Mr. Julian."

"Is he . . . is he alive?" she asked, her voice very small.

"He's alive. Harry took him back to camp."

"Oh?" Bebe squeaked, then closed her eyes and let one tear fall. "He left without me."

Suddenly you need him again. "I'm here. What happened next?" asked Jade.

"The cheetah broke loose farther down and ran off. That woman told Rex not to worry. She didn't need him anymore. Then she led us to the ice patch. She made us walk so fast just to keep up with her." Bebe tilted her head and looked at Jade. "Poor Rex. He was getting worse. Having difficulty breathing. It sounded all wet. When he collapsed, I begged her to help him, but she just laughed and said she would make sure that he *never* came back looking for the treasure, and neither would I. Then she pulled a gun out of her coat to make me keep moving."

"A gun?"

"She must have gotten it from the supply boxes. She's been in them before, you know." She looked straight at Jade. "You know how Morris is."

"Then how did you manage to get here and come to grips with her?"

Jade watched Bebe's face. Her expressive eyes were capable of meeting the camera lens or an actor's eyes and boring straight into them to deliver any line effectively. Eyes that made it nearly impossible to tell when she was lying or when she was telling the truth. But Jade didn't watch her eyes. She watched for her tell. Only this tell showed when Bebe told the truth, an event so rare as to be remarkable. So far in this tale, Jade hadn't seen it.

"We couldn't move Rex. He was too big for me and she wouldn't help. She planned to let him die there. But she made me come down here. I think she wanted to shoot me and hoped no one could hear the shot from inside the crater. Or maybe she meant to hit me and leave me to freeze. I don't know. But once we got down here, there was one of those tremors again. It caught her by surprise, and I was able to knock the gun out of her hand. If you don't believe me, you can see for yourself."

Bebe pointed farther down into the crater. "The gun's down there. You can see it." She rubbed her right eye with her fingertip before brushing the finger across her nose.

Bebe was right. There *was* a gun in the ash cone. The sun's rays glinted off a bit of silvery metal from a revolver. But so far, that was the only bit of truth out of Bebe's mouth. The fact that her left knee began to throb told Jade that the danger was greater than she presently imagined. Death stalked her again. And as she didn't have any backup, it might easily catch her this time.

Blast Harry and his trusting me. Sam would have insisted on coming along. Jade's head pounded and her breath came as gasps. *As long as they need you to get to safety, you're okay.*

"Are you all right, Jade?" asked Bebe. Her voice held more than an interested concern. She sounded worried. "Is it your head?" She broke off an icicle and sucked on it.

"Yes. But I'll be fine," said Jade.

"It must be from where she hit you," Bebe said.

How does she know anyone hit me?

Jade didn't speak the words, but in an unguarded moment, she expressed them with a frown. And in that second, Jade knew she'd made a mistake. *She knows that I know.*

Jade reached around for her rifle, prepared to defend herself and Abeba, but her movements were slower than usual. In the time it took to slip the weapon off her shoulder, Bebe gripped her icicle like a knife and charged at Jade, screaming with rage. It was echoed by another, more shrill cry at the rim.

CHAPTER 26

The snow and ice hide many secrets.
What will they reveal as they drift back?

—The Traveler

The repeated scream was clearly not any ordinary echo. This held a raspier note.

Leopard? The idea was ludicrous. Leopards had no business up on the peak. Jade's fogged brain couldn't reconcile the facts, but her reflexes kicked in, and she darted to the side, pivoting just as Bebe attacked. The ice dagger sliced through empty air where Jade's throat had been. Bebe crashed onto the glacial shelf, her icy knife shattering. That was when they both saw the leopard. It stared at them from atop the rim. Bebe screamed again, this time in terror.

"Get behind me," Jade ordered, wondering why she was trying to save someone who had just tried to kill her.

Bebe scooted backwards on her rear, crablike. When she was abreast of Jade, she kicked out and knocked the rifle out of Jade's hands. The Winchester landed a few feet away and slid to the edge of the terrace. Jade tried diving for it, but Bebe kicked again, this time hitting Jade just below the ribs. Jade fell to the side and, instead of grabbing the rifle, her arm knocked it over the edge. She heard it clatter a few feet farther down and come to rest. The blow knocked the wind out of her, and her stomach lurched from the impact. She tasted the acids rising in her throat, felt her lungs strain to suck in air. For a moment Jade knew absolute helplessness.

"I'll just leave you and Lwiza with the kitty cat," shouted Bebe. "You should have left well enough alone. I'll tell them that you died fighting to save me and that Abeba killed Graham to stop us. No one will question my part then, not even Julian unless he wants me to accuse him of helping me." Bebe scrambled to her feet. She hauled herself up off the terrace and onto the rim trail, which disappeared into a break in the thick glacial ice.

Jade swore, mentally consigning Bebe's name amongst every butt-sniffing dog that ever bore a litter. She gasped for air and knew she needed to get Abeba and herself away from the leopard before he decided to attack. *But where?*

The terrace spread around to the northeast for nearly a hundred yards. She and Abeba lay in the widest point. Farther on, it shrank to a two-foot shelf. Jade peered over the edge and saw her rifle on the rocks. She could get it if she climbed down for it, but it would take her too long and she didn't think the leopard would wait. Jade scrambled behind Abeba and gripped her shoulders. So far the leopard was busy with a search for the easiest way down to them. Jade wanted to be hiding somewhere defensible when he found it. Struggling for a purchase with her feet, Jade dragged Abeba backwards with her. She turned her head for a moment, making certain she still had the shelf behind her. That was when she saw the cheetah.

"Biscuit?"

Her eyes seemed to play tricks on her, making her pet larger than his size. His spots made rosette patterns instead of the little spots common to cheetah. For a moment, she thought the leopard had doubled back behind her, but when she looked to the rim, her stalker was still there, although he'd made some headway. Jade wasn't sure what good Biscuit could do, but somehow his presence gave her a sense of relief, the conviction that she wasn't entirely abandoned. She called to him, making both the chirping greeting and the churring distress call. He didn't answer, only turned his head and walked into the wall of snow. As he moved, Jade could have sworn she saw a set of dark, tabbylike stripes running along his spine.

You're hallucinating, old girl.

She started to drag Abeba back again and saw her walking stick lying near the woman's feet. *A weapon!* That and her knife were better than nothing if she could gain a defensible position. Jade reached forward, grabbed the thick staff, and strained to move herself and Abeba to safety. She reached the point where the cheetah had been and laughed.

An ice cave! And a deep one to boot.

"Hallelujah!" she said, and angled her way inside. The opening was wide enough for two people side by side but less than four feet high. Jade ducked low and pulled. The hard-packed snow was smoother here, making it easier to drag Abeba. Once inside, she pushed her into a corner crevice and prepared to make a stand.

Where's Biscuit? Jade had no doubt that she'd seen her own pet, and her fogged mind had distorted his appearance. As white spots danced in front of her eyes, she was glad to see at all. She turned on her flashlight and quickly scanned the cave. It was more than an ice cavern. The floor farther back turned to rock, and a few loose stones littered the ground. The breaks looked fresh, too, as though the recent tremors, mild though they'd been, had shimmied them loose. Behind them was a lava tube that led into an eroded and long-defunct side, or parasitic, cone that had grown when the main cone was sealed by debris. She could scoot in there if she had to, but it wouldn't be easy to get Abeba inside.

She pushed the larger stones to the entrance, narrowing the opening to a fourth of its previous size. The smaller ones she kept beside her as potential projectiles. Jade looked at her sorry weapons: one four-foot cedar staff, some rocks, and her knife. The last was good only for close fighting, and she didn't want to be that close to a leopard's arsenal. A spear would help.

Make one.

The voice in her head wasn't her own this time. It was Jelani's. *Blast! You are in a bad way.* But the advice was good. First she slashed the hem of her woolen coat into a long, spiraling strip of cloth. Then she lashed her knife to one end of her staff. A low growl on the other side of the rocks warned her to hurry. Outside, she heard the sound of claws scrabbling on snow and ice.

What the hell is that thing doing up here anyway? She remembered hearing a leopard's chuff at Bismark's hut. Had the leopard from the forest actually followed them all the way up here? The cat growled again, the sound echoing in the narrow tunnel. It pawed at the rocks.

"I need more rocks," she muttered to herself. "Got to plug up the opening."

She turned to pull out another of the larger stones from the back hole and noticed for the first time that the rocks appeared to have been purposefully placed there. As she reached for one, her arm muscles twitched with fatigue; she felt the darkness around her swirl as though she were a slowly spinning wheel. Then the bone-chilling cold crept up her body. It began at her feet and ankles, swallowed her legs, and slid up her midsection towards her chest. She heard a woman wail in grief, and, behind that cry, the combined voices of men chanting a dirge. The voices rose and fell with the quavering notes, and a vision of soldiers and splendor passed before her eyes.

Jade released the rock and the vision vanished. She fell back, panting. "Biscuit!" she called weakly into the black gloom. Her voice echoed back at her. Clattering rocks and a rumbling growl came from the front. She turned her head and again faced a pair of glowing yellow eyes.

He's through. But this time, she saw hunger more than hatred. For the first time, she realized that this creature was also weakened. Small consolation. A weak, hungry leopard meant a desperate one, and it would take only one good charge to kill her.

You must attack, just as you charged the lion on the plains. Jade heard the order as clearly as if Jelani stood beside her. Suddenly, her arms and legs felt suffused with warmth and strength. It might be only a strength born of fear, but it would serve.

She grabbed a stone and hurled it at the cat, hitting it on the nose. The leopard snapped its head back, snarling and spitting. When it dove back towards the opening, pain fueled its attack. She hurled a second, smaller but sharper rock. It struck near the cat's eye.

Jade didn't wait for the cat to regain its balance. She gathered herself together into a crouching stance, her makeshift spear gripped in two hands.

"Hyaaahhh!" she shouted, and lunged for the opening. Her knife point contacted hard muscle and rib, fur and fury. The leopard screamed but the cry died in a gurgle. Jade had missed the heart, but she'd nicked an artery and punctured a lung.

"Go!" she shouted as she wrenched her spear free. She

aimed another rock at the cat's head. The cat turned in time and the rock struck it in the ribs instead. The wounded animal skittered off.

Jade pushed her way outside and found sight of her Winchester. She'd have to track the cat and put it down. *Pay the insurance.* Otherwise, it would lie in wait and catch her off guard as she helped Abeba to the rim. She used the staff to brace herself and slipped off the terrace. Jade half crawled, half slid down the four feet to the rifle. The return climb was harder, as fatigue threatened to overwhelm her, but she finally hauled herself back onto the ice terrace.

The cat's blood trail was easy to spot, red rosettes on the snow. Jade followed it to the rim and counterclockwise towards the north. Her efforts weren't needed. The great cat lay dead in the snow, its golden eyes dimmed as by a fog. Its death caused a pang in Jade's heart. She had no idea why this cat had tracked her, but she felt the animal was just a pawn in some larger game, and she felt more like a murderer than a victor in a life-or-death battle. The least she could do for the leopard was give it a decent burial against scavengers. She shouldered her rifle and set to work covering the cat's body with snow.

"Rest in peace, *chui.* Forgive me." When she stood, she saw the golden-hued cheetah in the distance by the cleft in the glacier. She blinked and it was gone.

Jelani inhaled deeply. Keeping watch had exhausted him. He'd heard Bwana Nyati return with Bwana Julian and known that his friend had faced her greatest danger without the big man's aid. The woman called Bebe caught up to them and said that Jade and Abeba were dead, that Jade had killed

Abeba, then was attacked by a leopard. Bwana Nyati cried out and would have gone back up, but the woman said she could not take Julian down the mountain without Bwana Nyati's help. The director could barely walk and his mind was cloudy. And so Bwana Nyati led them down, pain riddling his face. Jelani knew the woman Bebe was lying. He also knew Bwana Nyati wouldn't believe him. The proof was for Simba Jike to give.

But now it is over. Simba Jike has won. Or will once she locks that woman away.

Beside Jelani, Biscuit stirred, sensing the young *mondo-mogo*'s movement. Jelani laid a hand on the cat's head and stroked him, grateful for the warmth the cheetah had brought when he'd found Jelani alone. Doubly grateful that Biscuit had stayed beside him even when his former master had passed through the abandoned campsite.

"It was *your* ancestral spirit that helped show Simba Jike the cave and saved her," Jelani said. Biscuit responded to his soothing voice with a deep, rasping purr. Jelani shifted and reached for the caches of jerked meat that he'd hidden away, wrapped in a cloth. He offered a large piece to Biscuit, who took it daintily between his teeth.

"Protecting Simba Jike is hungry work. Eat. We need our strength for when she returns."

By the time Jade got back down to the cave in the crater, Abeba had opened her eyes and Jade reassured her that she was safe. The initial fear in the woman's eyes turned to awe, but Jade didn't believe she'd inspired it. The fact that Abeba studiously avoided looking to the cave's rear told Jade all she needed to know. Her mind still searched for a rational explanation of the visions: altitude, shock, hunger. But her heart, her soul admitted the truth. They were next to the burial cave. *It really exists!* kept playing in her head. Part of her longed to rush into the tomb to see it. Another part was terrified of the vision's power. She forced herself to think about Abeba.

"Can you walk? Are you injured?" Jade asked.

"My leg, above the foot. It hurts."

"Let me look." Jade unlaced Abeba's boot and gently probed the ankle and shin, all the while pondering the wonders hidden beyond the rocks. Only once did Abeba wince, when Jade touched the bony rounded protrusion of the lower fibula. "Can you move your foot?"

Abeba gingerly flexed it. Jade decided from the growing bruise that she'd been kicked or had struck a stone when she fell. There was little swelling. Jade gathered some of the available ice, which she wrapped in her handkerchief and placed on Abeba's foot. "Hold that."

"I can walk," Abeba said. "You won't leave me, will you?"

"I won't leave you," said Jade. She took the remains of the chocolate bar from her pocket and handed it to Abeba. "Eat this." Jade took a long look at the rear of the cave. When Jade had dropped the rock, the dirge and wailing had ceased along with the horrid death pall, but she didn't want to experience them again. She had felt power here, a power she didn't want to confront directly. "Do you want to look or shall I replace the stones?"

"You would respect the grave and keep it secret?" asked Abeba. Now, perhaps, some of that awe was meant for Jade.

"Yes."

Abeba closed her eyes, as though meditating. After a moment she said, "We are safe. You may go in and look. It is well that you do, that someone else carry the secret. Bring to me the first two burial items that you see, but *only* two. Disturb no more."

"The first two," Jade repeated. "One of them had better not be a body," she muttered. She pulled out her flashlight and tentatively touched a stone. This time, the sensation of cold and death did not enter her. She heard no voices, saw no warriors. She carefully removed three more stones. When the opening was wide enough to admit her safely, she scuttled over the lower barrier and into the inner chamber. As her dimming light swept the chamber, she saw destruction. Volcanic stone, broken from the ceiling, had rained down on the burial. But glimpses of glory still existed, and she felt overwhelmed by a sense of antiquity and majesty so long forgotten.

A tangle of rusting blades stuck out at odd angles from under the debris. Jade counted seventeen. While far fewer than the hundreds of slain servants in Sina's tale, they did indicate the importance of this burial site. Jade tried to pull out one blade, but it wouldn't budge, not without dislodging more stones. A possible sword hilt turned out to be an arm bone. She shuddered when it crumbled at her touch.

She stepped over the remains of an offering table and spied a small golden object shaped like a cheetah. It was no bigger than a hen's egg, but the detail was exquisite. Jade picked it up and was surprised by how light it was. Then she saw from a worn spot that it was carved of ivory with an overlay of gold leaf.

That's one. She pocketed it and took another step towards the rear. Stones stacked as though into an altar or bier protruded from under a wall of rock that had fallen when part of this extinct side vent had collapsed in ages past. The exposed bier was covered by swaths of glittering purple cloth. It crumbled at Jade's touch, revealing a skeletal hand protruding from under the debris, rings on each bony finger. The hand clutched the end of a golden scepter, and one large ruby at its base winked at her. "Menelik!" she whispered, and felt her knees buckle at the sight.

She could no more retrieve the scepter than she could one of the swords, but as she reverently pondered the ancient hand, its little finger shifted and dangled from the rest of the hand. The ring it wore slipped off and fell to the floor, as though the king had given it to her. Jade picked it up with trembling fingers. It bore a lapis lazuli Star of David inlaid into the golden bezel. *That's two.* Jade crossed herself again, then slipped back outside. As she did, the ceiling rock shifted with a groan and hid the body from view. Jade handed the two items to Abeba and told her what she'd seen.

A tiny tear spilled from Abeba's right eye and caressed her cheek. "It is well," she said. "That is God's will. The glory of Solomon must rest forever."

"Not forever," said Jade. "Just until it is time. Isn't that what your prophecy says? After all, the scepter is still there as well. He is well hidden from prying eyes now."

Abeba looked gratefully up at her and smiled. "You are indeed wise and descended from royal blood." She handed the carved cheetah to Jade. "This is for you."

"Thank you. Now, let's block this back up and get off this mountain."

They met Jelani and Biscuit standing outside of God's parlor room. Jelani hailed her with all the dignity of a serene elder. It seemed to Jade as though the youth had grown another inch or two since she last saw him. Then she realized it was due to his erect carriage and the set of his shoulders. But it was his eyes that stopped Jade in her tracks. From them seemed to pour all the wisdom of generations.

"Jelani?"

He raised his right hand high in a silent salute. Biscuit was less formal. He butted her thighs four times, then wound himself around her, his rumbling, rasping purr sending vibrations down her legs. When Jade tried to relate everything that had happened, Jelani stopped her.

"I know, Simba Jike. Save your air. You have been through much."

They met Harry an hour later as he trudged back up the trail from Peter's hut. When he spied Jade, he ran to her and grabbed her in a tight embrace, squeezing her so hard that she couldn't breathe for several seconds. This time she didn't push him away. She frankly didn't have the energy left and she was glad to see him safe.

"Bebe said you were dead." His voice was choked with emotion. "I didn't want . . . I couldn't believe it." He noticed Abeba and Jelani for the first time, looked at the young Kikuyu with surprise, then at the Abyssinian woman with malice. "She said this woman attacked you—"

"Bebe's lies are lower than a snake's belly in a wagon rut, Harry." Jade gently slipped out of his embrace and stepped back, putting distance between them. "I've no doubt she thought we were dead. It was what she intended. As long as Abeba was suspect, no one would ever look twice at her. But when you announced that I still suspected someone else of Wheeler's death, then Abeba needed to die, and me too, so that no one would be left to question her story. She left Julian for dead as well."

"She said something about you two grappling for a knife and then something about a leopard. It made no sense, but . . ." He trailed off. "What really happened?"

Jade explained everything that had occurred from the moment she'd left Harry and Julian, omitting only the part about seeing the cheetah and the inner cave.

"I don't understand why that leopard followed us. Do you think it was the same one you saw earlier?"

Jade shrugged. "How's Mr. Julian?" she asked, changing the subject.

They resumed walking, Harry giving an arm to assist Abeba over the rockier parts.

"Julian regained some of his senses along the way, but he doesn't know anything that happened once he collapsed and not a lot before that. Once I made Peter's hut, I had Nakuru and the men make a litter for him. Hall, Talmadge, McAvy, and Murdock carried him. They'll rest at Bismark's hut tonight and continue down tomorrow. Do you think you can make it that far today? It's almost three o'clock now. It'll be dark before we get there."

"I can if Abeba can. I don't want to let Bebe get back to base before us. She may convince Julian to leave right away and then escape on the first train out of Moshi. Or she may kill him. It wouldn't take much and we'd assume he died of the altitude sickness."

Abeba declared that she was fine, and together they made good time across the saddle, down the heath, and into the forest, using their flashlights to find their way. When they arrived at the hut, Nakuru clapped his hands and shouted his welcome, rousing the others. Bebe came out last, her face ashen.

And then she turned and bolted down the mountain trail.

"Where's she going?" asked Talmadge.

Jade touched her pet's shoulder. "Biscuit, take her down."

The cheetah bounded after the woman, leaping over boulders. Within seconds he'd reached the panting murderess and launched himself at her back. When Jade, Harry, and the others caught up to Bebe, she was sprawled on the ground, Biscuit sitting atop her.

Harry hauled Bebe to her feet. "I've never hit a woman before, but—"

"Don't worry, Harry," said Jade. "I'll do it for you." She launched her right fist and punched Bebe in the jaw, knocking her flat on her backside. "Someone tie that thing up."

The next morning, a very subdued crew rose after dawn and trudged the final distance to their base camp. Jade insisted on making a side trip to the Chagga village, allowing only Biscuit and Jelani to accompany her. As soon as she entered the village, she strode directly to the banana grove with its eerie carpeting of ancestral skulls, the villagers following at a discreet distance. Jade handed her rifle to Jelani and stood in the grove with her fists on her hips.

"I am Simba Jike," she called out, speaking in Swahili. "I have faced your leopard and won. Not once. Twice. Now I am tired of your curses and your games. I will run no more. If you want me, here I am. Face me yourselves."

She waited, turning slowly until she'd made a complete circle. The villagers, including Sina, watched her, some with awe, some with fear. No one had challenged the ancestral spirits before. No one had dared come without a goat to sacrifice. After two minutes passed, broken only by the soft call of warblers and the clucking of a few hens, Jade lowered her arms. "It's over," she said to Jelani as she took back her Winchester. Then without so much as a farewell wave, she strode out of the garden and back to camp.

. . .

By late afternoon on Thursday, Sam felt as if he'd asked everyone in Moshi where the safari had gone, but no one seemed to know what he was talking about, even though he showed everyone Jade's photograph. It didn't help that his Swahili was limited to "please," "thank you," and a few other words. Finally a Greek man recognized her and spoke enough English to pass on what he knew. He drew a map for Sam, but it didn't appear that there were any vehicles for hire.

Sam was busy arranging for someone to guide him on foot when he heard the sound of motors. He hurried closer, as fast as his wooden leg allowed, and watched as first Harry's truck, then one driven by McAvy rumbled and bounced into view. Sam saw Harry pull a woman from the back of his truck. Her hands were tied, but to Sam's surprise it wasn't Lwiza, but Miss Malta.

As his anxiety mounted at not seeing Jade, another vehicle pulled up. Relief flooded his arms and legs as he saw her at the wheel. *She's all right!* Pride and passion warred for supremacy as he hurried to her side. *She's alive! She's all right!*

"Jade!"

"Sam?" Jade leaped out of the box-bodied car and ran to him. "Oh, Sam, it's so good to see you!" She threw her arms around him and hugged him close. Sam allowed himself the pleasure of embracing her in return, of scenting the outdoors on her skin, of enjoying how the sun reflected in a blue sheen off her black hair. But he couldn't allow himself to kiss her.

"I'm so surprised to see you here," she said, a bright smile on her dusty face. "But so glad! I missed you. I really did. And . . . ?"

Her eyes searched his. He could almost feel their cool green light penetrating through the darkness of his own eyes, searching out his soul.

"Sam, what's wrong?" She took a step back, leaving her hands resting on his shoulders.

"Nothing's wrong. You're safe. We . . . I discovered that Lwiza was not who she said she was and . . . Well, we tried to wire Moshi to warn you, but the lines went down and . . ." He let it drop, feeling very tired.

"And you came yourself to warn me." She cocked her head a little and her lips softened in a trace of a smile. "I'm . . . I'm touched, Sam. And honored. That was—"

"Probably an overbearing, untrusting thing to do," he concluded for her. "And from the looks of things, I was wrong."

"No, Sam! You were right. Wheeler *was* murdered. Lwiza wasn't Swahili. She's Abyssinian and came to protect the tomb. But it was Bebe all along. She had Wheeler killed because he wouldn't leave his wife to marry her, and he was going to drop Bebe entirely out of the picture. She knew she could control Julian better and salvage something of her career. She's been scheming all along and . . ." She stopped and ran her fingers through his hair. "And I don't want to talk about that. I've been doing some thinking. I really missed you and—"

He put a fingertip to her lips to silence her. "We'll talk about it on the way home."

CHAPTER 27

Moses came down from Mount Sinai, his hair and skin blindingly white. And so it is to a lesser extent after climbing Mount Kilimanjaro. Once cannot approach so close to God's throne without experiencing some life-altering revelation.

—The Traveler

Jade and Sam had limited their conversation on the train ride home to the safari and the crimes, refusing to discuss anything personal within earshot of Harry, but Jade knew something was brewing inside Sam's mind. Then there were all the reports to make: giving statements to Inspector Finch, handing over rifles and ammunition boxes and bags while the police sorted through fingerprints. In the end, Bebe's prints were all over Rehema's compact, Cynthia's box of supposed blanks, and the leather flask of drug-laced alcohol, as well as the old wallet found in Bahdoon's room.

There was no doubt that Bebe had used many people: Bahdoon to kill Wheeler, Rehema to get a venomous snake, and Homerman's incompetence to slip live rounds in to kill Zakayo. Finally she used Julian's lust for treasure to try to kill Abeba on the summit and blame it all on her. Bebe was kept in the Nairobi jail while various officials worked out jurisdiction for crimes committed by an American in both Kenya colony and

Tanganyika territory. But Jade didn't care what they did with her. All she could think about was Sam.

There was little private time for them to talk, and Jade felt as if she were about to snap, waiting until they were free to meet alone at his hangar. She wore the sapphire ring that Sam had given her on her left hand. He tugged an expansive sheet of oilcloth over his Jenny to protect it from the upcoming rains.

"It's so good to be back, Sam," Jade began as she straightened a corner over a wing. "I missed you so much."

Sam kept moving, tying down the heavy fabric on the other side of the plane. "I missed you, too, Jade. I'm . . . I'm going to miss you."

"Then you're leaving soon?" she asked. She slipped around the plane's tail to get closer to him. "For how long?"

"I don't know," he said, avoiding her eyes. "Certainly as long as it takes to sell my picture. Maybe longer." He bent over and tugged at one of the tie lines. "If I don't return, I'll sell the Jenny to Avery."

The words cut deep. After the wartime death of her pilot beau, David Worthy, Jade had thought that she was inured to such pain. She was wrong, and she felt as if old wounds had been sliced open afresh until she was numb.

"If you *don't* return?" Jade's eyes dampened with tears that wouldn't fall. Her throat felt tight, her soul, her being knotted in it. "I'll come with you then."

Sam straightened and held her gently by the shoulders. "No," he said softly. "I don't know how to explain it. I'm not even sure I understand myself, but I know we need time apart from each other."

"We've had time apart—"

"Listen to me, please. I worry about you too much. You're the smartest, the bravest woman I've ever met, but I can't handle the fear that rips through me every time you go off trying to set the world right. While you were gone, I had nightmares every night in which you were either poisoned, shot, gored, or mauled. I don't think I can live with that constant fear for you."

"I can change," Jade blurted out.

"I don't *want* you to change!" Sam's voice boomed. "You wouldn't be Jade anymore. You're Simba Jike. The lioness doesn't become a tame little pussycat. It would be cruel to expect her to try."

"Then . . . you don't love me?"

Sam grabbed her in a tight embrace, crushing her to his chest. He kissed her neck and hair again and again. "God help me I do. Passionately."

She felt his chest expand and shudder as he sighed deeply.

"Do you remember why you trained Biscuit to hunt?" he asked. "You wanted him to have a chance to be free. Well, I love you enough to give you that same chance. Hell," he added as he stroked her hair, "maybe I'm not the right man for you. Maybe you belong with someone like that damned idiot Hascombe."

Jade wrenched free of Sam's embrace. "Now, you wait just a blasted minute, Sam Featherstone! Don't you tell me who's right for me and who isn't. And if you'll remember, Biscuit's not going to make it free any more than I will. I had to step in when that lion stole his food. And if you think I'm going to go off with Harry, then—"

"Then maybe you'll find someone else or maybe no one," Sam finished. "You said all along that you felt hobbled by the idea of marriage. We both need time apart to think."

"But I *have* thought, blast it. I have. And I . . ." This time Sam didn't need to shush her. The words had choked in her hot throat. She pulled the sapphire ring off her left hand and held it out to him. "Here," she managed to say.

Sam put his hand over hers, closing her fingers around the ring. "Keep it. Whatever we decide in the end, there's a bit of sky locked in that stone. I did promise you that."

Jade's lips tightened as she swallowed and struggled to master her voice. "You're coming back, Sam," she said. "You'd better come back to me. If you think for one instant that I'm going to forget about you, then you're crazy. I'm going to see you in every sky and hear your voice in every lion's roar."

She pulled the silver Berber amulet out of her shirtfront and tugged the chain over her head. "And if I have to keep your ring without you," she said, slipping the amulet over Sam's head, "then you have to wear this."

Sam fingered the silver box for a moment, studying the filigree work. "Blasted thing's probably haunted," he said, attempting a smile.

"One can only hope," Jade replied.

TWO DAYS LATER, Jade stood on the station platform and watched as Sam handed up his valise. She still couldn't believe he was going back to America without her. She fingered the sapphire ring on her right hand. It didn't belong on her left. It didn't feel good on her right.

Another man. Another ring. And this time you're letting this man leave.

A mass of brooding clouds covered the late-September sky, cutting the burning afternoon sun's glare into a hazy twilight. The rains were making their way into Kenya earlier than last year. Most of Nairobi had retreated indoors into clubs, hotels, shops, or taxis in anticipation of the coming downpour. The first storm never lasted more than an hour, but its icy rain was no less brutal when it pelted the skin, forcing its way through shirts and dresses.

She watched him hand his ticket to the conductor. In a moment he'd be on the train and gone. And with his departure he'd leave a gaping void in her soul, an ache that already felt like a ravening lion devouring her from within.

The sky flashed white for a moment, just as it did when her magnesium flash went off.

Is God taking a picture of this? A booming rumble answered her.

Sam turned to wave good-bye. Jade bit her lip and forced her hand up. She saw his face tighten, and in the next instant she was in his arms and felt his burning kisses on her lips, her cheeks, her eyes. For one moment she thought he'd changed his mind.

"Take care of yourself, Simba Jike," he whispered as he turned to go.

"I love you, Sam," she called after him as he climbed the steps. "You'd better haul your horse's patoot back here to me! I'm giving you just four months. Four months! Do you hear?"

He was gone, swallowed up by the car. She looked in vain to see him at one of the windows, but he'd moved to the other side.

He's already distancing himself from me.

The whistle blew and the engine chuffed, its steam driving the pistons. The connecting rod pushed once and the wheels spun on the track, searching for some traction. Another chuff and the locomotive inched forward, jerking the cars along.

Jade followed the train out away from the station as the rains broke, washing her in a cold embrace. She felt the chill cut through her, a chill of emptiness.

"I'll get him back if it's the last thing I do!"

Her tears fell and mingled with the icy rain, carrying her vow into Africa's fertile soil.

AUTHOR'S NOTES

THOSE OF YOU who are familiar with Kilimanjaro might wonder about Menelik's cave. Taking a cue from geologists who write of eroded parasitic cones and lava tubes, I used the idea for the burial cave. It is not on the map because Jade promised to keep it a secret.

The legend of the first Emperor Menelik's campaign through East Africa springs from native stories. The Maasai claim it is why they no longer have any gold; it was all lost to Menelik. Mentions of it pop up in guidebooks, and, true or not, it made a fun premise for a tale of adventure and intrigue.

Although most histories don't mention her, mountaineer Emily Benham was the first woman to climb to the top of Kibo Peak on Kilimanjaro in 1909. Her biographer, Raymond John Howgego, has placed a brief account of her ascent with an extensive list of articles written by Ms. Benham at http://www.howgego.co.uk/explorers/Gertrude_emily_Benham.htm.

Another woman's ascent to the top of Kilimanjaro is recorded in Africa's *Dome of Mystery* (1930) by Eva Stuart-Watt. This young missionary lived with her mother and sister on Kilimanjaro from 1924 to 1927. She recounts many of the Wachagga stories, including their tale of humankind's fall from God's grace. Eva ascended the slope in September 1926. There's a great photograph of her kneeling next to the frozen leopard, first publicly reported by Dr. Donald Latham, who dug it out of the snows, and later made famous in Hemingway's *Snows of Kilimanjaro*. Ms. Stuart-Watt wrote of the leopard, "No one can tell what induced it to venture into a land so cold and desolate; but possibly the smell of meat carried by some safari had led it to follow their trail." I give a possible inducement and reason for its burial under the snows.

For a treatise on Kikuyu spirituality, there can be no better source than Jomo Kenyatta's work *Facing Mount Kenya: The Tribal Life of the Gikuyu*. In works I'd read previously, I'd always seen the tribal healer's title spelled as *mundu-mugo*, hence the use of that spelling in my first books. But Mr. Kenyatta spells it as *mondo-mogo*, and I bow to his knowledge and use his spelling in this book.

Some readers might recognize the reference to Mr. Clutterbuck, the father of Beryl Markham (née Clutterbuck). At this time, Beryl was wed to Jock Purves. It wouldn't last long.

I have been asked where people might find copies of *The Traveler*. This magazine is a figment of my imagination, and I write Jade's slightly irreverent copy just as I write Maddy's purple prose novel excerpts. *The Traveler* is loosely based on a magazine from that time period called *Travel*. Sometimes I sit on the basement floor of the university library's stacks and browse it. It may be possible to find it on microfilm through an interlibrary loan.

And if readers are interested in more tidbits of historical interest, I invite them to visit my weekly blog, "Through Jade's Eyes," at http://suzannearruda.blogspot.com/. A new one shows up each Monday, barring unforeseen circumstances.

Photo by Joe Arruda

Suzanne Arruda, a zookeeper turned science teacher and freelance writer, is the author of several biographies for young adults. She has published science and nature articles for adults and children. An avid hiker and outdoorswoman, she lives in Kansas with her husband. You can reach her at www.suzannearruda.com and read more about Jade's era at http://suzannearruda.blogspot.com.

KENYA COLONY, *February 1921*

Hunters speak of the dangers of the "Big Five," the deadliest animals they encounter in Africa. Lions, buffalo, rhino, elephant, and leopard top off the list. I would add the crocodile and, of course, the human.

—The Traveler

FROM HIS HIDDEN VANTAGE POINT, the man watched the young American woman called Simba Jike. The name fit not only because she moved with the unconscious fluidity and grace of a lioness but because she held herself with a lion's assurance as well. Only once had he ever seen her truly vulnerable: the day she stood in the deluge of rain at the train depot, watching the American leave her behind. He'd watched, too, recognizing that his opportunity had come.

A slight sound escaped his lips, half sigh, half groan, born of both desire and sorrow.

He'd heard about her and her exploits before he'd ever met her. All the colony talked about her unconventional behavior and attire, and she might have been shunned by Nairobi society but for the approval she'd received from old Lord Colridge and Lord and Lady Dunbury.

Her dusty tan trousers, boots, khaki shirt, and that old, worn-out, broad-brimmed rancher's hat seemed to embody Africa more than the Paris frocks and flowered straw hats of the British women. He'd also heard of her from his lover, who told a different tale. No grudging admiration there, and that was the source of his sorrow.

He could almost feel the strength radiating out of this American, see the pent-up passion. It smoldered inside her, flaring and flashing like green fire from eyes that could be as hard as emeralds or as soft as spring moss. Eyes that inspired desire like his lover's did once.

He recalled that passion in his lover, but they'd been apart for so long that his memory of her was as remote as a real person was from a photograph. And now his lover's passion had flared into anger and hatred. Other men might have freed themselves, moved on, perhaps towards someone like this human lioness, but he was bound to his mistress, tied by want and need and the remnants of love as well as by their past deeds.

When he'd first met this Jade del Cameron, he'd expected most of the stories to be exaggerations, embellished tales told by needy people longing to draw everyone's attention. Instead, he found the tales fell short of the reality, and he'd come to admire her.

That made his job all the more difficult.

He'd been ordered to break her.

The antler hilt felt cool in her hand, the well-polished knobs and curves as familiar to her fingers as a sweetheart's face. The hilt nicely balanced the length and heft of the blade. In short, the knife promised no surprises, provided the body did its part. It would. She'd practiced often enough and once, years ago, had pinned a rattler that had been menacing her sheepdog.

Her gaze locked on the target, gauging the distance, calculating the number of rotations before the blade struck. She stepped back a half pace and raised her right forearm even with her ear, willing a connection between her vision and her hand. The hand, like her eyes, was well-trained. She took a deep breath and dropped her arm on the exhale at the same time that she shifted her weight to her left foot. Her arm shot straight out in front of her, wrist taut, making one perfect line and freezing in position as abruptly as it had moved. As her fingers splayed, the blade spun twice in a graceful summersault, like a diver teasing the air before piercing the water.

Jade del Cameron heard the satisfying *thunk* as the blade bit into the wood and stuck, quivering slightly. A smattering of applause followed.

"Bravo, Jade," called Beverly Dunbury. "Spot on the bull's-eye." The speaker was British, classically lovely with shimmering corn silk hair, watercolor blue eyes, and the fair complexion generally associated with English ladies. She presented an interesting contrast to Jade, whose olive complexion, short, wavy black hair, and green eyes spoke of her exotic bloodlines.

Beverly nodded towards the target board. "Did you all observe how Lieutenant Jade kept her focus on the target? That's what *you* are supposed to do with your sling."

Lady Dunbury addressed a small herd of eleven girls, ranging in age and deportment from three gangly, restless ten-year-olds to a pretty, well-mannered brunette of thirteen. All were dressed in khaki blouses and dark blue serge skirts that came more or less to their knees.

"Will you teach us how to throw like that, Lieutenant Jade?" asked Helen Butterfield, the oldest girl. The daughter of a recently arrived settler, she boarded at the English school and showed the most interest in outdoor lore.

Jade winced at the title. "Please, Helen, you do not have to address me as lieutenant. I'm only assisting your, er, captain," she said, casting a sidewise look at Beverly. Her friend wore a simple walking dress of blue cotton serge and a campaign hat similar to the girls', only Beverly's hat sported a cock's feather plume and no chin strap.

Jade had proudly worn a similar skirt and trouser uniform as an ambulance driver for the Hackett-Lowther unit during the Great War, but she refused to truss herself up like a soldier now. She'd only agreed to help Beverly with the newly founded troop if she could still wear her usual trousers, white shirt and boots. It was the knife scabbard on her boot that had started this knife-throwing demonstration.

"I'm certain Miss del Cameron will be happy to teach the older girls in due time," said Beverly, "but for now you had better concentrate on using the sling. Besides being handy for chasing vermin out of your garden, it can be very useful in bringing down small game if you're lost and in need of food. And it will help you develop hand-to-eye coordination."

Jade retrieved her knife and slid it into her boot sheath as the girls each selected a small stone and pushed it into the pocket of her leather sling.

"Miss Jade, have you ever killed someone with your knife?" asked Elspeth.

"Elspeth Archibald!" scolded Beverly. "Is that how a Girl Guide talks?"

"I'm sorry," Elspeth said, although her expression suggested she was sorrier that she was being reprimanded. The downcast look vanished as quickly as a dewdrop under the hot Nairobi sun. "It's only that I've heard all sorts of exciting stories about Miss Jade. How she's captured criminals, and roped wild animals, and how she's flown a plane and—"

"Is it true you've been traveling the globe these past months, looking for your lost love?" asked Mary. The other girls' heads all snapped round in unison to stare wide-eyed at Jade.

"Where in the name of St. Peter's goldfish did you hear that load of . . . ?" asked Jade.

Undaunted, Mary persisted. "My mother heard from Nancy, the telephone girl, that your sweetheart died in the war. But Uncle Steven said that your sweetheart left you and went away." She put a finger to her lips and crinkled her brow as she tried to reconcile the conflicting accounts.

"Oh," replied Jade in a flat tone. And if the telephone operator was spreading stories, everyone in the blooming colony would know by now that Sam had left her at the train station.

Jade pulled her own sling out of her trouser pocket and picked up a small stone. "Shall we get back to your practice? Perhaps Mary would like to emulate William Tell's son, put a tin can on her head, and let us try to knock it off."

Mary hung her head. "I apologize, Miss del Cameron." Her head popped back up as though it was on a spring. "It's just that both you and madam here," she added, addressing Beverly in the approved Girl Guide manner, "have led such exciting lives driving ambulances and traveling, and we'd dearly love to hear about some of it."

"No!" Jade's voice was low but firm. "Now, if you are ready, we'll continue with your sling practice."

She put an empty canned meat tin on top of a fence post and lined the girls up, from youngest to oldest. "Remember what I taught you. Keep one strap wrapped around your hand, hold the other end loosely. Swing around several times to get the proper speed but keep your eye on the target, not on your sling. Release at the top of your downswing and let the stone fly."

Each girl took a turn. A few stones smacked straight down into the dirt by the girls' feet. Others made great sweeping arcs up and down, falling short or long depending on the girl's strength. One stone went straight up before plunking down on the thrower's hat. Jade explained to each girl what had gone awry: releasing too late or too soon or without enough speed and force. The last girl, Helen, stepped up and flung the stone with enough accuracy to graze the tin and make it jiggle.

"Very good, Helen," said Beverly. "It really is just a matter of practice."

"This is harder than archery," said Gwendolyn Walker, a plump little blonde. "I can't see where I'm throwing with the sling."

"That's part of practice," said Jade. "Teaching your hand to obey your eyes. It's not much different from throwing a ball." She told the girls to continue practicing, and let her mind drift while keeping half an eye on them. Beverly joined her.

"It's no good, Jade," Beverly said softly. "I'm not going to let you stand alone over here and brood. And," she added when Jade arched one eyebrow as though to express her disagreement, "I know you too well, love. You keep stealing off to be alone, and when I find you, you're in a dismal mood. I knew I shouldn't have let you wander off to France for the Armistice Remembrance. It simply was not healthy."

"I couldn't stay here, Bev. You know that."

"You could have gone to your home in the States and voted in that election. And you know you always have a home here with Avery and me."

Jade didn't argue. It wouldn't make any difference anyway. Beverly had always been protective of her friends, and now that she was the mother of a little girl, her maternal instincts had kicked into high gear. Jade had known she had to come back to Nairobi when Beverly had written to her in France, pleading for her help in getting the Girl Guide troop into operation. The four months which Jade had given Sam Featherstone to return to her had been nearly over and she wanted to be here when he came back. The desire had grown into a need, as vital as that for water or air.

If he comes back.

She shook her head to chase out the dark thought, which had clung to her like a parasite. Since Sam had left in September to sell his motion picture in the States, Jade hadn't heard a word from him. He'd intimated that he wasn't the right man for her, that she should forget him, but that was as impossible as forgetting how to breathe.

After the first two weeks of trying to keep busy, she'd turned her pet cheetah, Biscuit, over to Madeline and Neville Thompson on their coffee farm and taken a boat to Europe. She'd wandered through France, visiting the battlefields and searching out some old friends from the countryside. Then, at her mother's insistence, she'd spent Christmas with a distant cousin in Andalusia. Over the holidays, she'd sent a telegram to Sam, care of his parents in Battleground, Indiana. It read simply, *"I love you. Haul your horse's patoot back here. Jade."* She had no idea if he'd ever received it.

"Your house is crowded, Bev," Jade said. "Between baby Alice, her nanny, and now your sister, Emily, I wonder you don't kick me out for the space. It's time for me to find a place to stay somewhere in town."

"Nonsense. Emily's doing her level best to snag a husband in the colony. I should have her out of the house in no time."

Jade laughed. "I think you're actually more fond of her than you let on, Bev."

Beverly chuckled, a musical laugh like a gently rippling stream. "I suppose she has improved of late. For as long as I can remember, she's been my bossy, bullying, proper older sister. But she's had her own rough times, taking care of Father after Mumsy passed. Or perhaps all it took to temper her was knowing that I'm all the family she has left." She paused and watched as one of the younger girls, Clarice, accidentally clunked herself in the head with her sling as she spun it round. "Or maybe it took that same knowledge to temper *me*."

"Don't look at the sling, Clarice," Jade called. "Look at the target."

Bev laughed and turned back to Jade. "You never did tell Avery and me about your time in France. I'm happy to listen if—"

"There's nothing to tell, Bev. But since you won't let the matter drop until I do, this is the short of it. I went back to each of our corps shelters to do a story for the *Traveler* about the changes in the countryside since the war."

"A terrible choice of articles," muttered Beverly.

"Do you want to hear this or not?" Without waiting for a reply, Jade pressed on, eager to get it over with, much like removing a splinter. It wasn't any easier for going slowly. "I thought writing the article would help me think."

"You mean help to *forget*," said Beverly. "You thought that seeing places where you hadn't known Sam would get him out of your mind. And all it did was confuse you more, didn't it? You thought about David instead. You probably went back to the place where his plane crashed, didn't you?"

She had lowered her voice when several of the girls turned to watch and listen. Now she raised it to tell them. "If you are finished with your sling practice, then you may go inside and practice sitting quietly."

As one, the girls returned to their throwing, but Jade heard snatches of whispered phrases. "So tragic," and "How romantic," drifted back to her.

"Wonderful," said Jade. "I'm sure that will make the gossip rounds now. Don't the Kenyans have anyone else to talk about besides me and my dead or absent loves?" She walked back towards the girls.

"Perhaps it is time to put away the slings, pick up the stones and tins, and get ready for your mothers," said Beverly.

As if to illustrate her statement, a black Fiat driven by an Indian chauffer pulled into the Dunbury's drive. He opened a rear door and an elegantly dressed lady stepped out. More motorcars, a taxi, and a rickshaw arrived soon after. The women in the latter two were neatly but more plainly dressed than those arriving in the motorcars, but every woman wore a hat and white gloves. Beverly advanced to meet them.

"Ladies," she said, "you are just in time. The girls were about to go inside and organize the afternoon tea."

Jade stayed where she was. The daughters were an affable group by and large, if a little giddy at times, but Jade didn't wish to spend any longer with the mothers than was absolutely necessary.

"Aren't you coming, Jade?" whispered Beverly.

"If it's all the same to you, I'm going to wait by the lane for Emily to return with the mail."

Beverly laid a hand gently on her friend's shoulder. "Jade, dearest. I do hate to see you waiting for word from Sam. It breaks my heart to think that he might never come back, but it saddens me even more to see you so expectant, and then so disappointed." When Jade didn't reply, Bevery persisted. "Going to France was a mistake, Jade. All you did was mix yourself up even more. Now you have your feelings for Sam and whatever guilt or loss you still carry for David battling it out in your heart."

Jade fingered the sapphire ring she wore on her right hand. Every time she gazed into it, she saw herself aloft in the blue with Sam in his plane. It was impossible to look at the sky without searching for him, without listening to the familiar purring drone of the engine. Sam's engagement ring didn't belong on her left hand since he had broken off their engagement right after Jade had finally accepted him.

"I will always mourn David," said Jade, "but as I mourn for any good friend and for all those brave young men who died in that horrid war. But Sam *has* to come back. Because if he doesn't, Bev, then I have no home. Africa will be dead to me, and every time I return to the States, I'll be trying to find him there." She hugged herself against a gnawing emptiness and looked past the rose garden and the stables as if she might see the grasslands far beyond, where the great herds and the prides still roamed. "He's coming back, Bev. I'm not giving up hope."

"It's still early," said Beverly. "Your four-month edict was hardly enough time."

"One month to travel, two to sell his motion picture, and one month to return. More than enough," said Jade.

She called to Biscuit to join her and walked down the drive. She chose a shady bench under an arched arbor of bougainvillea and sat to wait for Emily. Bev's sister had driven off earlier in the day when the local newspapers had announced that the mail boat had docked in Mombassa two days ago. If one assumed a speedy unloading and sorting, the mail could have arrived on yesterday's afternoon train. Jade doubted that the mail would actually appear in the post office for pickup until tomorrow, but Emily had seized the excuse to do some shopping.

And perhaps accidentally run into one of the gentlemen she has her eye on.

Biscuit butted up against Jade, turning his head for an ear scratch. Her left hand did the job without her thinking or looking as she kept her gaze on the lane.

Maybe Bev was right. Maybe going to France had been a bad idea. But staying here would have been worse. Still, things had happened on that trip that she hadn't told Bev. Beverly had been afraid that Jade's nightmares would begin again. They hadn't. In fact, sleep had been her one respite. But awake? Awake she'd been pursued by living nightmares. Twice she'd had unnerving experiences, too insubstantial to be real, too corporal to be dreams. Once, she swore she heard the cries of the wounded drifting up from an old battlefield site.

She hadn't been in France for more than a week when she'd had her first vsion. She'd encountered several veterans of the war making their own pilgrimage and many wore their uniforms, or parts of them. So when Jade first spied the RFC pilot sixty feet in front of her, she didn't think much of it, except to wonder if he might have also been a friend of David Worthy's.

Then he turned. . . .

Jade's arms tingled anew at the memory.

David!

His face was a mask of tragedy and perhaps shame. And when she'd blinked, he was gone. She couldn't explain that to herself. There was no sense in trying to explain it to Beverly.

But that wasn't the oddest vision. The evening before she'd left France for Andalusia, she'd gone for a walk in a quiet little garden. The air was chill and damp, a fog hanging low on the ground so that everyone else in town had opted to stay indoors. Jade had sensed the presence rather than heard it. She felt no danger, no pains in her injured knee, which thanks to a shrapnel wound could be counted on to warn her of imminent danger. She only glanced over her shoulder out of curiosity. There in the shadows stood the old native she'd met on Mount Marsabit, the native who seemed to be the embodiment of spirit rather than flesh.

"Boguli?" she'd called, and her voice echoed the question now, startling her into awareness. The image had still worn his frayed gray blanket and stood rocking on his feet from side to side. He'd nodded to her, giving a greeting; then he pointed from his head to his heart as though trying to tell her something. She tried to reply that she didn't understand, but he vanished into the fog much as he'd slipped away into the mist-shrouded forests of Mount Marsabit.

The chug of a motorcar brought Jade's mind back to the present. She stood and looked down the lane. *Good, Emily's back.* She drove the Hupmobile over to the garage built beside the stables and parked beside Avery's Dodge truck. Jade went to meet her. As Emily walked to the house, she cradled several parcels in her arms and gripped a cluster of envelopes in her left hand.

"It seems most of the mail is still being sorted," said Emily, "but I have some good news, Jade. There's an envelope for you."

Jade hurried to join her. "From America?"

"Actually, I believe the postmark is Paris." Emily thrust a letter into Jade's hands. "I must get these inside. I suppose my darling sister is still entertaining."

Jade nodded but didn't reply further. She was too engrossed in the envelope before her. The handwriting was elegant and somehow familiar, but it wasn't Sam's tight hand. She pulled her knife and neatly sliced open the flap. Jade took out the paper inside and shoved the envelope in her pocket after replacing her knife in its sheath. But when she unfolded the single sheet of white paper, she felt her legs turn to rubber. Shaking, she found a bench and plopped onto it.

Tacked to the paper was a clipped newspaper obituary for David Worthy. And on the paper were written the words:

Why did you let me die?

It was signed, David Worthy. Even more unsettling, it was written in his hand.